When it's over,

and you see it with your eyes,

Would you rather have the truth

or a lie?[1]

Embracing

The

Truth

By Susan McGeown
www.susanmcgeown.com

Published by Faith Inspired Books
3 Kathleen Place, Bridgewater, New Jersey 08807
www.FaithInspiredBooks.com

Please notice, however, that I'm winking at my
Wednesday Night Girls ☺

AND

Also please note that I must go on record as saying that I am
eternally grateful to the wonderfully skilled and incredibly dedicated
therapists (yes, more than one!) that have enriched my life as well as
my family's. You are, beyond a shadow of a doubt, God's gift to me.
Fictional Aileen was created long before you came on the scene - but
God made her into a reality. *Thank you.*

Bibliographic credit appears at the end of this work.

To

Pam Frueh:

None of my books would be as polished if it wasn't for you
and your editing skills.
It's time I dedicated a book to you
although it's not the first time you've shown up in my stories:
You were specifically acknowledged
for all your hard work in editing and proofreading in
A Garden Walled Around and
A Well Behaved Woman's Life,
You were the physical model for the female minister in
Rules for Survival,
You were a banking magnate in *The Butler Did It,*
I killed you off in childbirth in *No Darkness So Great,* and
You were a nosy old woman sitting on the front porch in this one!!

Table of Contents

Therapy: The Hard Truth

Setting: Psychologist Aileen Burkart's office. It's March, 10, 2008, my very first visit to *this* therapist's office. I've dragged myself here out of desperation and as a last resort. Aileen reminds me a little bit of Jabba The Hutt sitting in her big throne-like chair, oozing power and superiority. I feel like Princess Leia must have felt in the wire mesh bikini with a slave collar chained around her neck. Yes, I'm here of my own volition, but only just. Kind of like if you felt yourself sliding off a cliff, and in desperation and panic you grab the vicious looking cactus to save yourself; it hurts like hell but it's better than the alternative.

Aileen: Here's the deal, Olivia. Therapists can only help you if you're willing to let them help you. You have to decide if you have a connection or not with that person. You have to be willing to have a dialogue with the therapist and feel that you would trust her observations, motives, and opinions. After a few sessions, you're going to have to ask yourself, "Is Aileen someone I can work with to make myself better?" Now, if I do something in particular that bothers you, let's talk about it. Maybe I can make accommodations that would work for both of us. But there may be some things that I just can't change. And if it's a big enough issue then I would encourage you to try another therapist.

Me: Like what?

Aileen: Well, say, for instance, you'd prefer to deal with a male therapist. (Chuckles.) I can't help you there, nor can I make any accommodations to satisfy that need.

Me: (Bitter chuckle.) Don't worry. I'd never seek out a male therapist. Hmmm, I can see your therapist antennae twitching already. Better get your pad and pen out and start making lists of all the areas we'll have to "address."

Aileen: Sounds to me like you've been in therapy before.

Me: Yeah, in my teens. Out of sheer desperation, my mother and stepfather, Paul, thought that maybe talking to a *professional* might help me. Paul, being a therapist himself might have influenced that thought process a bit.

Aileen: Did it help?

Me: No.

Aileen: Really? That's too bad. So, if it didn't work then, why are you here now?

Me: It shows how desperate I am and how out of control my life has become that I've once again listened to Paul over fifteen years later. (I sigh.) *Really desperate.* Voodoo and crystals haven't worked. Why not try psychotherapy again?

Aileen: (Getting out yellow legal pad and pen.) Okay, so let's get started. Why don't we make a list of things that you'd like to address during our time together?

Me: (Reaching into my purse and pulling out a crumpled piece of paper.) Here. There's a million issues to deal with but we can just start with this.

Aileen: (Takes paper, adjusts glasses, and begins to read.)

Me: In particular I'd like to discuss the line that says "Dean Kelly is excluded from being the biological father of Olivia Kelly." Actually, I've known this truth since I was sixteen, but now that I've got actual proof, I need to figure out what I should do. I'm tired of being lied to and determined to know the truth. No matter how badly my mother wants to keep it from me.

You can bend it and twist it ... You can misuse and abuse it ...
But even God cannot change the Truth.[2]

1: Honesty Is The Best Policy, But ...

Friday, March 19, 2010

"Richard? What was your answer to problem six?" I called on Richard not because he had his hand up or because I thought he knew the answer, but more so because he was once again distracted by Marylynn's outstanding cleavage.

"Huh?" Richard mumbled as if coming out of a deep coma.

His buddy William, required to sit on the other side of the classroom (to provide one less distraction for poor Richard), sniggered and called. "Yo, earth to Richie-boy. Get your head out of Marylynn's rack, man." The whole class laughed as Marylynn made an outraged gasp while still managing to appear delighted at being the center of attention.

Now I'd be the first to admit that Marylynn's cleavage was impressive, but having seen it regularly ... perfumed, tattooed (a daisy skewed toward the left), encased in both spandex and cashmere ... sigh ... you get the picture. It's reached the status of "same old, same old" for me. But then I'm not a fifteen year old male, so today's display (yellow polyester camisole overlaid with black stretch lace) was just too impressive to be ignored. "I asked you to tell us the answer to problem six," I said with skilled teacher-patience.

"Oh," Richard shuffled through the papers piled randomly on his desk and spilling out of his notebook. "Yeah, I did that ... wait ... oh, here it is," he spoke over William's continued hoots and cat calls and Marylynn's giggles, "... ah ... negative eleven?" He looked so hopeful.

3

"Good for you!" I exclaimed delightedly. Richard had come to extra help the last two Tuesday mornings (probably more for the donuts I always bring, but hey, whatever works) and I was happy for his success. He slumped back exhausted, as if he'd just run a marathon.

"William? Number seven's answer?" I said to Richard's friend who was still doubled over with laughter.

I watched William's enjoyment of sixth period's Algebra I class disappear as he struggled to get with the program. "Ah, Ms. Kelly, I didn't get that one. I tried and tried but that one was tough. I even asked my dad for help but he couldn't figure it out either." His sincerity was almost as big as his size thirteen sneakers.

But now it was Richard's turn to snigger and shout, "Hey! Get your head out of your ass, man! There *is no* number seven!"

As the class erupted in laughter, I wrote the night's homework on the board and stood back to avoid the stampede as the dismissal bell rang. Richard and I exchanged a high-five as he rushed past and William shook his head as he passed me smiling sheepishly. "Good one, Ms. Kelly."

"Do your homework tonight, William. *I mean it.*"

He sighed like I'd just asked him to come up with a solution to global warming. "I'll try, Ms. Kelly. Honest I will."

For some unexplainable reason, period six's Algebra I was the most enjoyable of all my classes. It's probably something I should take up with my therapist, Aileen, as to why I most enjoy the class with the worst test scores, the poorest homework completion rate, and the highest number of problem students. Maybe it's a reflection of my own poor performance throughout academic life? Or possibly I recognize others of like-minded self-destructive behavior? Of course there's always been my perpetual negative attitude towards authority figures ...

Aileen says, "Asking the proper questions is the central action of transformation. Questions are the key that causes the secret doors of the psyche to swing open.[3]" This is why I would never in a million years really ask Aileen to help me analyze this. She's always throwing crap like that out at me in our sessions and then giving me a smug, superior look over the dark rims of her glasses. I suspect I spend more time trying to throw wrenches in her theories then I do trying to figure out the meaning of her quotes … which is probably the reason I've been in therapy for over two years.

"You going to O'Reillys?" Clotilde, one of my teaching partners and my closest girl friend asked as she walked into my classroom. The boys absolutely love her with her white blonde hair, model thin body, and blue eyes the size of Delft platters. I'd tried to hate her when we first met but it's rather impossible. She's one of the sweetest people I know.

"What's on your face?"

Clotilde reached up and touched her cheek. "Here?" When I nodded she smiled, "We're dying eggs as part of my cultural immersion project. I was showing them how my Oma used to do it in Germany and I must have smeared the dye. One of the kids mentioned something but I was too involved to look in a mirror."

I shuddered in revulsion at the mention of her project. "You didn't … do what you did last year, did you?" Last year, Clotilde had brought in a dozen eggs, wax, pins, dye, bowls, etcetera and proceeded to demonstrate how to get the raw egg out while preserving the shell. You could either blow it out into a bowl or you could … suck it into your mouth and swallow it. Which, before a horrified class, was exactly what Clotilde did. The entire group of students had been heard screaming in disgust and one girl – Nancy something or other – made it as far as the girl's bathroom door before hurling her lunch all over the floor.

Clotilde rolled her eyes and sighed. 'No, I blew the raw egg into a bowl this time." Glancing up at the clock and calculating that there was still a few moments to talk, she came in and sat down on the edge of my desk. "I apparently am somewhat famous, however, over last year's demonstration. A number of kids tried to get me to repeat the show. I still don't get what the big deal was all about." I shook my head and laughed. If I hadn't been able to get her to understand last year, I sure wasn't going to be successful today. Clotilde looked at the clock, stood up, straightened her skirt, and walked slowly backwards while saying, "Come tonight. You'll have fun. I know you will." She waggled her white-blond eyebrows suggestively.

I gave her a pointed look. I don't always have fun. And she knew it. But I sighed and asked anyway, "Are you going right after work?"

The bell rang and Clotilde walked rapidly to her classroom across the hall. "No, we're meeting at like eight o'clock. I'll expect you!" she shouted and shut her door before I could answer. We both knew she could expect me all she wanted. That didn't mean I was going. In fact, based on her firm push, the likelihood was that I wouldn't show. I never did what anyone wanted me to do. It had been a persistent theme throughout my life.

Just ask anyone.

I began to pack up for home. I had the dream schedule this year. By sixth period I was done teaching for the day. Seventh period was my lunch, eighth period was prep (time to prepare my lessons) and ninth period was hallway monitor duty. Of course that meant I'd been going straight through from 7:20 a.m. with nothing but six minutes in between classes, but I was content.

That thought brought me up short and I stood there frozen in surprise, period three's quizzes clutched in my hand. *I'm content.* Aileen would go nuts if she heard me admit that. Yet, stunningly, I found it to be true. Over the course of my thirty-three years, there had been very few times when I could honestly say such a thing regarding my personal *or* professional life. Why, I'd been screaming, fighting, demanding, and ... assuming forever. Much to my detriment.

Just ask my family.

But take it from me. It's best to avoid my family. My perfect sister, Erin, would make you feel lacking in everything from chocolate-chip cookie baking to ideal child rearing to personal goals accomplished. My insane mother would tell you so many wild and crazy *true* stories regarding her and our family that your ears would probably start bleeding. My ... father's ... sobriety was always inconsistent at best so who knew what you'd hear if you could find him. And my grandmother, should she deign to speak with you, would probably give you nightmares (and that was if she smiled).

I know. You think I'm kidding. Or exaggerating. Perhaps you think like others have that I might have been trying to earn your sympathy or gain your undivided attention. Or perhaps you're under the mistaken impression that I subscribed to negative attention being better than no attention at all? Even as a child, I knew that no one could ever comprehend the truth about my family; unless they lived it. The trials, tribulations, emotions, and unspoken secrets made it impossible for anyone to put into words. Frustration created me: a seething caldron of angst and rebellion.

As a result, truth and honesty became of utmost importance to me. And while I can't trace the exact point of origin of that attitude, there wasn't really a moment in my life that it wasn't a focal point.

Unfortunately, that wasn't necessarily a good thing.

As a child, I used honesty as an opportunity for attention and was quite delighted with its results. I vividly remember my first grade teacher Mrs. Biuso saying, "Olivia, wasn't it nice to have Principal Munzenmaier visit with us today?" To which I responded, "No, her perfume makes me want to throw up." The shocked silence from both adults and children that resulted from my pronouncement … did little to discourage me. My teachers rapidly learned that asking Olivia Kelly her opinion about something never resulted in the expected response, and that suited me just fine.

With the discovery of the power of stating the truth, I had honed my skill to a high art form by adolescence. I could antagonize my sister, brutalize my mother, and avenge most slights sustained (real and imagined) simply by voicing the clear, unvarnished truth to everyone within hearing range. Honesty may have been the best policy, but a little tact and consideration certainly would have helped a bit, too. As I'm only just recently able to acknowledge that fact you can imagine what it was like dealing with me: personally or professionally.

Because of my fierce desire for the truth or in spite of this (who knows really), discovering my mother's blatant deception regarding things specifically concerning *me* launched me onto a lifelong path of anger. The firm belief that "I must be honest" validated many of my choices and justified the deep seated fury that was literally the fuel that kept me moving.

In the past two years of my life I still embraced that mantra that honesty was the best policy but now I tried my best to follow it *only with good motives.* In the past, even if the truth made you gasp in horror, made you blink like noxious gases are burning your eyes, if … Okay, I'll stop. You see, shockingly, *I've* been accused of not accepting the truth about certain things in my life, and much to my discomfort I've had to acknowledge that *perhaps* this was somewhat accurate. It honestly had never occurred to me – until very recently – that it was possible that there could be two versions of the same truth. Two years is a long time to be in therapy but not a very long time to completely reinvent yourself. I'm working as fast as I can.

Therapy: The Truth About My Mother – Part I

Setting: Therapist Aileen Burkart's office. It's August 11, 2008, five
months into this experience with psychotherapy, and I *think* I've
covered much of the horrible detritus that one needs to reveal
about oneself in therapy. I've been mentally poked, prodded,
unraveled and examined until I feel like a tangled mass of cold
spaghetti. And I know we're nowhere near done because … I'm as
nasty and as angry as ever. Aileen's wearing a purple scarf today …
and purple socks. What compels someone to color code her socks
with her neck scarf? Which begs another question: do therapists
go to therapy? And, if they do, is there a whole different style of
treatment? I mean, come on, how can anything truly be
"discussed" when both parties *have to have* some serious deep
seated, mumbo-jumbo styled agenda going on. As I attempt to get
myself comfortable on the nondescript brown couch in Aileen's
office, I notice with cringing horror that my socks … don't match.

Aileen: (Pen and pad poised and ready.) How was your week, Olivia?

Me: So I took Paul's advice and contacted you. Then I took your advice
and asked Paul to talk with my mother. Tried to get him to get her
to spill who my real father was.

Aileen: And?

Me: Well, if you were hoping for a gold star, a pat on the back, or even a
deeply appreciative thank you, don't hold your breath. (Mumble
under my breath) That goes ditto for Paul, too.

Aileen: Do you want to be more specific?

Me: Has Paul told you that we had a very, *very* poor relationship when he
was married to my mother?

Aileen: I told you, Olivia, I never discuss patients with anyone. Not even
with other colleagues.

Me: Oh, come on. Not even in a vague sense like, "Oh, Paul. I have this
severely angry and damaged woman I'm seeing who feels an
incredible level of rage towards her mother. I'm afraid she may do

something irrational. Could you give me any insight, from your *vast life of experiences* regarding similar relationships you may have had to deal with?"

Aileen: (Makes a note on her notepad.) You view yourself as 'damaged'?

Me: (Grinning like a Cheshire cat.) I *knew* you'd pick up on that. (At Aileen's continued silence...) Sure I'm damaged. Hell, and that's why I'm so angry at my mother. She owns it all.

Aileen: How so?

Me: Well, where would you like me to start? The fact that she has been married multiple times, and every single one of her husbands were Grade A, First Class Losers? The fact that the man I'd always thought was my father has *never* – and I am not exaggerating – *ever* been sober for more than six months? The fact that for a period of time when I was thirteen my mother, my sister and I *lived in her car*? Or, how about the time that she went completely nuts – I mean certifiable – so that they had to take her away and lock her up in a mental hospital when I was in college? As the story goes, a neighbor called the cops because she was outside in her pajamas *painting the family car* with an old bucket of paint. There were literally whole years of my life when I've been on my own – caring for my sister and myself because my mother was too tired, or too busy, or too crazy, or too *something* to care for us. I resent the fact that she considers herself a mother. And I've resented for as long as I can remember that I have to acknowledge her as my mother.

Aileen: You're very angry.

Me: (Rolls eyes.) That's an understatement. I've been angry for twenty years and it's always been directed at my mother. (I think for a minute.) Maybe even longer. Why my earliest memory is being angry ...

All truths are easy to understand once they are discovered;
the point is to discover them. [4]

2: Avoid Dark Corners At All Costs

Friday, March 19, 2010

Sometimes a student will come into my classroom now - a mass of seething fury - and I'll *just know*. Pictures of me in middle school and high school show a sullen young woman with a wild mass of black hair and huge, sad, violet eyes. I may have gained significant negative attention because I rebelled and refused and reacted inappropriately to just about everything, but as far as I was concerned you could tell I was troubled … *just by looking at me*. I've never needed to talk with Aileen about why I'm particularly drawn to the troubled students as opposed to the perfect ones, because the reason is obvious. *I remember* what it was like which, I suppose, is a significant part of my problem.

I've been journaling since the moment I could read and write. It started, surprise surprise, as a running list of things that made me mad when I was like seven or eight. It had been a particularly bad week and I was hiding upstairs in the closet of the bedroom that my little sister Erin and I shared at my Grandmother Miriam and Grampie Taylor's house where we lived with my mother and father. Something had happened to get me angry on Monday, and then something else had happened on Tuesday, and then something else on Wednesday, and by Friday I had such a list in my head that I grabbed my new Ghostbusters notebook that my mother had let me get at Kmart and wrote it all down. It made me feel better, so I took the time to add to the list all the stuff my mother had done wrong recently, what my Grandmother Miriam had said that upset me (she was always saying something), and what I was worried about regarding my father (always a substantial list). Somehow, seeing it all in black and white made me feel that I could somehow control things. A pseudo writer was born.

Now, don't worry, I'm not still doing the same thing at thirty-two. But I keep a daily journal and, well, I suppose since I'm trying to be honest and forthright here, a bit of that theme ... still exists. It didn't escape me that sometimes, on reading back what big matters had upset or angered me, suddenly seemed rather trivial and hot issues didn't always stay ... so hot. Aileen's been working for these past two years to help me change not only how I view the world, but also how I *remember* the world. I'm not exactly sure which has been the bigger job. Probably Aileen isn't either.

Clotilde was relentless about O'Reillys, eight o'clock, and my being there. I got one, two, *seven* texts and finally caved. Not so much because of her persistence, but more because I'm thirty-three, single, it's a Friday night, and Sophie was never very good company even in the best of times.

Sophie's my cat. Cat lovers such as myself took her superior, contrary, stand-offish behavior in stride while cat haters had a picture of Sophie Marie pinned to their dart board. There were many rules to remember regarding Sophie and, if you did, everything would be just fine. Rule number one: Sophie *never* does what you want her to do. Rule number two: you must *always do* what Sophie needs you to do. Rule number three: Sophie loves no one, but perhaps, if you're lucky, she may tolerate you. She's a calico with four perfect white paws and big, gold eyes.

"Hey Soph! I'm home!" Sophie has never greeted me. Instead she always chooses to wait until I came to her. That afternoon's sleep location was on top of the bookcase in my condo's very sunny living room. "Hey Miss," I crooned to her and reached up and gave her a scratch behind her ears, "How was your day?" Rule number four: pet only her head area, never her body area. (Painful consequences result should this rule not be observed.) Turning her head, Sophie gazed out the window completely ignoring me, and no doubt counting the hours until she'd be blessedly on her own again. "Don't worry, I'm going out tonight. It's sooner than you think," I murmured already dreading the evening ahead.

According to family legend, I asked for a penis for my fifth birthday. My best friend Benjamin Harayda must have been my influence. While I don't remember the specific request, I do remember getting in trouble for giving Benjamin a spectacular black eye and declaring, "*Girls* can have babies and *boys can't,*" which was apparently what my mother had explained to me in an effort to deflect my inevitable disappointment.

Welcome to the major quandary of my life: while I'm okay with the fact that I'm a woman there's not one aspect of my womanhood that brings me any particular joy. I hate my looks (Marylynn's cleavage has *nothing* on mine, let me tell you). I distrust every single male I've ever met, which has factored negatively in all of my romantic relationships (surprise, surprise). And while the idea of babies mollified me at five, at thirty-three it strikes a terror in my heart that leaves me seriously breathless.

All good reasons as to why I'm still in therapy.

Now, please, don't get me wrong. I do like men. Rather a lot, truth be told. Which was another thing that terrified me given that my mother is currently on her fourth - *yes fourth* - husband. What sane person wanted to follow in those shoes, huh? Having tried and failed with common laborers (husband number one), white collar professionals (husband number two), and malleable pencil-pushers (husband number three), my mother is currently hot and heavy with ... her meter reader. Oh, how I wish I was kidding. You have no idea. Having lived through the parade of husbands growing up *and* the in-between boyfriends (one was a Chippendale dancer) I was teeth-grittingly determined to be Different Than My Mother before the age of fourteen.

Hence my caution, which *was not* extreme despite what Aileen would have me believe. I've dated but have never had any serious, long-term relationships. I just can't find the desire or enthusiasm for all the effort involved. Growing up with so much drama, having a solid, predictable, uneventful life always seemed the epitome of maturity and adulthood for me. And I'm *very* mature.

Getting dressed to leave for O'Reilly's (while Sophie takes an extensive bath while sitting on my newly pressed blouse) I think about what womanhood has to offer me, and none of it is good: one week out of the month of agony and/or inconvenience, an outstanding size D distraction for any man no matter how I dress or how intelligent I am, an immediate classification of "bitch" whenever tough behavior is necessary in the workplace, and the negative perception of personal failure should the route of 'childless, single' be the preferred choice.

Is there any wonder why anger is my favorite emotion? *Is there?!*

For years I avoided alcohol of any kind given my … father's

history. As a little girl, that pungent "old alcohol" smell was more familiar to me than any male aftershave. Even still, drunk or sober, Daddy was always a sweet, affectionate, tender guy. In fact, after he had a six-pack or two I often basked in glorious, loving attention. I became His Favorite Girl Above All Else and His Number One Buddy. When he drank he was always happy to sit and watch television with me, was always willing to let me win at any game I chose for us to play, and on a number of occasions gave me permission to put my mother's make-up on him before he fell asleep on the couch. He'd say tender things to me like, "There's my lovely girl," and "No one loves me like you do, Livvie," and "Promise you'll always be my darlin'."

I was, without a doubt, Daddy's Best Girl.

Of course I didn't deal with all the fallouts, nor was I aware of them: lost jobs, unpaid bills, drunk and disorderly charges, and personal disasters like the time he tried to get into Mrs. Dodeman's bed with her when he confused our house with hers. Mother dealt with all that and much, much more.

My earliest memory – I was probably around four - is of sitting on the front porch of my Grandmother Miriam and Grampie Taylor's house excited because I could hear sirens coming. Even over the terrible shouting, I could hear those sirens and I couldn't wait for them to arrive. I was hoping that Johnny Gage and Roy DeSoto would be driving just like they did on my favorite television show, *Emergency!* But when a police car pulled up, I was just furious! What were they doing here?! Didn't they know that Daddy had cut his hand all up trying to get the front door open and that he was bleeding on Grandmother Miriam's front hall carpet? (You always had to take your shoes off when you came in to keep that carpet clean.) Didn't they know that my mother had a bloody lip and a big bruise on her head because Daddy had bumped her with the door when he finally got it open? We needed an ambulance, not a police car.

And maybe a fixer man to fix the front door. Its window was all broken.

The policemen took Daddy away that day in handcuffs and almost everyone cried. Grandmother Miriam was crying and shouting at everyone (I remember lots of neighbors watching) that, *"My son didn't do anything wrong!!!"* She kept screaming that over and over and even tried to get the policeman to stop from taking Daddy away which made the policeman angry and he shouted that she had to Step Back Now. Daddy cried as the policeman put handcuffs on him and kept shouting, "Don't let them take my truck, E!! Whatever you do, *don't let them take the truck!*" Even once he was in the police car I could see his mouth moving as he cried and banged his head against the window. I cried, at first because, besides being angry about the ambulance, I was of course worried about Daddy. I remember shouting, "I'll take care of your truck, Daddy, don't cry!" Sometimes he let me help him wash it. But then I heard Grandmother Miriam shout at my mother, "This is *your fault,* Elaine. *All your fault.* It's *always* your fault." I remember looking at my mother, and she was just standing there watching the police car drive away with Daddy as her bloody lip dripped down on her tee shirt.

My mother didn't cry that day. She wasn't upset or sad. She barely even blinked. It was then that I realized that she didn't really care at all. About Daddy. About me. When baby Erin's cries started to get even louder than they'd been she walked inside without saying a word.

"We'll get your Daddy back, Livvie, don't you worry." Grandmother Miriam said once all the neighbors went back inside and she wasn't shouting anymore. "Your mother can't keep him out of this house. This is *his home*, not hers. He's *my son* and *I* love him even if she doesn't."

My mother didn't love Daddy? Suddenly it made sense, and knowing that made me even madder. How could she not love Daddy? *I* loved Daddy.

And when the big tow truck came the very next day and took Daddy's truck away, *and Mommy let them*, I cried again because I knew how sad Daddy would be. Grandmother Miriam was right. It was all Mommy's fault. Every bit of it.

O'Reilly's was hopping when I arrived fashionably late at nine-fifteen. Everyone yelled various greetings. I heard, "You made it!" from Clotilde loaded with relief and - always surprising to me - delight. She was sitting in a big communal booth snuggling with Max, her beloved husband. They are a fascinating couple: she all glamorous and gorgeous and he all bookish and nerdy. He was just barely as tall as she, didn't wear glasses (Clotilde convinced him to get contacts) and regularly wore the same sweater (granted it was a Ralph Lauren but even Ralph wouldn't subscribe to wearing it every time he went out on the town).

"Olivia, it's good to see you!" Max said with sincerity. I blew him an air kiss which made him blush.

I noticed at least eight familiar faces around the bar including Phil, our assistant principal, who was also sitting in the big booth. Phil's tall, built, and very handsome; literally everything that appeals to me in a man and, unfortunately, he knew it. A very tempting package. He gave me a smoldering look across the table crowded with drinks and appetizers, briefly all the noise and crush of the place faded away as I met his gaze. I felt my pulse kick into overdrive and my body shifted into high alert. I had absolutely no idea how long we stared at each other.

Clotilde was suddenly by my side. "You look *great*," she murmured, and then grabbed my arm. "Come with me to the loo." Clotilde, having done her student teaching in England, had hung onto a number of kvetchy British phrases like "loo", slang for toilet and "ta" which meant thanks. If I

16

did it, I'd just look dumb, but when Clotilde did it you think, *Gosh, she's so sophisticated.*

We made our way through the still manageable crowd (real partiers start arriving at eleven, when I, hopefully, will be crawling into bed) toward the back and the restrooms. But we didn't go in. You only visit the bathrooms at O'Reilly's when you're desperate. "Max's friend Jay is coming in a little bit," Clotilde said hopefully. "Remember him from our New Year's Eve Party?"

Ahhh, so that's why my attendance was so critical. Clotilde was on the fix-up train again. Sigh.

She meant well, she really did. I took a deep breath and tried once more to explain things. "I told you. I'm taking some time off from men." I'd actually told her, "Clotilde, I'm not in a healthy space right now and my relationship history has never improved that situation." But I believe that did more harm than good. Having honestly (there's that word) explained what my difficulties in the dating field tend to be (more about that later) and my current solution, Clotilde had eagerly decided to assist in my recovery. "Clo, I've explained to you as best I can why I'm doing it this way." I looked at her pointedly willing her to remember some very specific, very private, and very horrible details she knew about me. "It's ... for the good of mankind."

"You're a beautiful, vital, healthy woman, Olivia! In the almost two years we've known each other I know for a fact you haven't gone out on a date *once* - and not for lack of trying on my part! I think it's time you got back on the horse! Jay was *very interested* in you when he met you at our New Year's party. He's asked about you a bunch of times. He's nice. He's good-looking. He's a *lawyer* for goodness sake so he makes scads more than we do. Didn't you think he was nice? *What* was there not to like about him? I told you I met him at church, right?"

Jay *was* good-looking, sincere, sweet, attentive, and clever in a cute, lawyery kind of way. He was nice all right which had Clotilde really listened to anything I've told her about me and men should have told her that quality alone was the absolute kiss of death when it came to my being interested. *I don't do nice guys.* "He just wasn't my type, Clo. I told you that on New Year's. In fact, I *begged you* not to try to fix me up with him."

I really had. It was when I had gone in to vivid, horrifying detail. She searched my eyes. "I was just *so certain* that once you got to know him you'd change your mind." I just stared at her and she sighed. "Okay, I'll give up on Jay."

Her meaning wasn't lost on me. She'd conceded this battle but was still fighting the war. Which was why I'd come to recognize her as a Good Friend – another thing I haven't had too much experience with in my life. Just as I've never gravitated toward nice men, I've never really acquired good friends either. Good friends don't quit on the people they care about, want only the best for the people they care about, and stay committed to people they care about.

Clotilde gave me a hug. I'm close to ten years older than she but she regularly tried to take care of me. Another good friend quality I suspect. "You don't think something crazy like with your curves, your violet eyes, and your gorgeous dark hair that a man wouldn't be interested in you. Do you?"

I rolled my eyes. "I've had enough men drool over me to know that I appeal to some," was all I'd allow.

Clotilde sighed. "I just don't get you." It's hard to understand life on the dark side when you've only heard about it from others. No matter how brutally honest they've been in telling the story.

"Clo, you're young – only twenty-four. I'm an ancient thirty-three. I've done all of my dewy-eyed mooning over guys already. Now I'm content to just slowly drift along down the river of life seeing where I end up. Maybe, just maybe, I'm meant to be single. Remember: for the good of mankind?" Now my good friend looks near tears and I lean over and give her a kiss on the cheek. "I'm working on things. I'm determined to be a better person. But I've got to do it my way, okay? Otherwise it won't be mine to own."

Clotilde studied me for a moment and then looked out across the bar, although we were too far away to see our group. She sighed again. "I just want you to find someone who loves you like Max loves me. It's so … *wonderful*."

"I'm happy enough. Don't I seem happy?" I grinned wide enough to make sure the dimple in my right cheek did its thing. "You got me to come out tonight instead of staying home with Sophie. I'm not the Crazy Cat Lady yet so that's a positive thing."

Clotilde looked at me again and smiled, but it wasn't one of her brilliant ones. "I understand why you're avoiding having a relationship. I even can applaud your rationale as well as your determination. And I understand that you don't miss love, Olivia. You've worked very hard to explain to me your theory on that subject. But that doesn't mean that I can't want it for you. I guess you can't really miss something you've never honestly experienced."

Suddenly, this young woman, ten years my junior, seemed so much more mature and adult than I, despite my drama-less, solid, predictable, uneventful existence.

"Phil's here," Clotilde said with disgust. Ahhh, Clotilde's other agenda was now out on the table for all to see.

"I know. I saw him."

"I glared at him but he just ignored me. I wish Max appeared more threatening. *He better stay away from you*." The last sentence was hissed through gritted teeth.

That made me laugh and hug her. "I'm a big girl, Clo. I can take care of myself. I got myself into this mess and I have been working to get myself out of it. Don't worry, I don't need you or Max watching out for me." I gave her one of my wicked grins.

Clotilde looked me in the eye and said, "Of course you do! And you can't stop us, either." She reminded me of one of those yipping Chihuahua dogs.

Late in the evening, when O'Reilly's was at the peak of Friday frenzy, and after Clotilde and Max had said their goodbyes and just as I was getting ready to say mine, Phil made his move. I'd been waiting for it, growing tenser by the hour.

"Liv," Phil said to me as I was making my way back from a bathroom run, "I'm missing you big time." He had waited in a dark, unoccupied corner which he skillfully guided me into. He's tall so that crammed into the corner like I was, the only thing I could see was him. "You missing me?" he murmured as he stepped in and tenderly kissed my neck. He managed to get almost every surface of the front of our bodies to touch.

Enveloped by his delicious scent and his seductive warmth I still managed to mumble, "Absolutely not," as I turned my face to avoid a full on kiss.

Undeterred, he nibbled at my earlobe and rubbed his hands up and down my sides. "I think you're lying, Liv. I've made some inquiries. You're still not seeing anyone. You've got to be terribly lonely."

"I can't help it if I'm holding out for quality," I said, but I felt a delicious shiver travel up my spine and remembered with blinding clarity how much I do enjoy men. And as Phil's not a nice guy he is AKA Just My Type.

Phil chuckled. "Come on … you aren't in any position to judge! You never gave me a real chance to prove myself. All that flirting and teasing, and I'll point out that when I can get you to make eye contact with me you're still giving me *that look* that sends me right out into space."

It has always been that way with me and bad guys. They had radar that sensed out my keen, almost unavoidable, interest in them as soon as they walked into a room. I'm embarrassed to admit that I gave myself a moment or two to enjoy the delicious attention and the intoxicating roll of desire that swept through me with Phil's attention. But I've got this honesty challenge with Aileen and I *knew* she'd ask me. She's got sensors that can be terrifyingly accurate when they're directed at me.

I pushed against Phil's chest and he took a step back and looked at me. Hopefully. Expectantly. Confidently. "I'm in a perfect position to judge, Phil. I'm different from the person I was when I first … approached you. At least … at least, I'm trying to be. The little I know about you is enough for me to be certain that whatever I may be missing *it definitely is not you.* " As I brushed past him I said loudly and clearly, *"Go home to your wife,* Phil. You can always hope that *she's* missing you."

Therapy: The Truth About My Mother – Part II

Setting: Aileen Burkhart's office. August 18, 2008, and my life suddenly
feels like I'm sitting on the top of Mount Vesuvius just before it
blows. I have an uncommon urge to go through Aileen's files and
find mine. What has she written about me? Does she save the
handwritten notes she writes or does she transcribe them? I've
seen various codes on the insurance bills that have started to come
in, but *what exactly does she think of me?* Am I worse than most?
Better? Boringly average? Am I fixable or am I simply someone
she's got to help to merely "keep alive and functioning?" I know
she's going to zone right in again on the topic of my mother. God
help us all.

Aileen: Do you think your mother loves you?

Me: (Pointed look. Implying indignant shock. Had she been spying on me
this past weekend?! A lengthy silence ensues. Finally …) My
mother told me she did just this past Sunday. Then she asked me if
I believed her.

Aileen: *Really.* What did you say?

Me: I said, "As much as you are capable of."

Aileen: (Aileen actually winces.) How did she respond to that?

Me: (I turn away and look out Aileen's African violet laden window, lost in
bitter memories of this past Sunday's dinner debacle at my sister
Erin's house. I never got to dinner because I stormed out in a
blaze of righteous indignation.) She didn't defend herself or
anything. She just asked me if *I* loved *her.*

Aileen: How did that make you feel?

Me: It really pissed me off.

Aileen: (Silence. She does that a lot. Just sits and waits for me to
eventually fill in the awkward silence. Rarely do I let her down.
Hey, she gets paid whether she does anything or not so one of us
needs to talk.)

22

Me: I mean, how can she ask me such a question? I've stuck around, haven't I? I've endured regular contact with her, haven't I? Up until now, I've never asked her for anything. I've tolerated her favoritism toward Erin! I've put up with her skewed memories of our life! I've endured her ever-changing loyalties that depend on her marriage and her mood! I've never asked her for one damned thing in my whole miserable life except for the *name of my real father!* (I take a deep breath and clam up. We can stay silent for the rest of the session for all I care. I'm done sharing.)

Aileen: So, let me make sure I have this right. Your mother is supposed to just *know you love her,* not because of what you say but because of what you do. (She looks down at her pad and reads off what she's written.) 'Tolerate.' 'Put up with.' 'Endure.' Is she aware of how you feel?

Me: (I'm sure as hell that she knows what I think. I spelled it out pretty loudly and clearly in almost those exact words. But I'm wise enough to keep my mouth shut and not tell Aileen that. I keep staring out the window.)

Aileen: Olivia, look at me. (Aileen waits me out and manages to make me feel like a petulant child, which is probably exactly what she was after anyway.) Here's a question you should consider. It's important, Olivia. If your *behavior* is supposed to show your mother that you love her – and please understand me, *I don't doubt that you do* - then you better consider seriously what her behavior *should show you.* I think the two of you are very similar, Olivia. And you need to understand that it's your similarities that are pushing you apart, not so much your differences.

Me: (I've never been so insulted in all my life.) You know, Aileen, I liked you better when you didn't talk so much.

The truth is rarely pure and never simple.[5]

3: Not All Grandmothers Are Sweet
Friday, March 19, 2010

There was a message blinking on my answering machine when I got home at about eleven-thirty from O'Reilly's. My ears had that overload whine from listening to too-loud music and I felt sticky and sweaty from dancing a little too much. It was a *different* evening (I really can't call it fun but it wasn't horrible either). But I don't think I was going to rush out to O'Reilly's tomorrow night or any time soon for that matter. If I were to grade myself on my behavior this evening it would look something like this: Effort: A, Making Healthy Choices: B+, Maintaining New Principles: C, and Improving Personal Preferences: D. If Clotilde was filling out the grades she would add the comment: *Needs to make a greater effort towards trying new and healthy things.*

I had a brief wave of concern that it was Phil who had left a message and it was, *I'm out in the parking lot, Liv. Please let me come in and talk. Please, please don't let it be Phil,* I wished as I punched the play button.

"Miss Kelly?" A strange woman's voice filled my living room as Sophie sauntered in and affectionately wound around my legs. Which let me know her food bowl must be empty, not that she missed me or anything. "This is Reverend Linda Harmer. I work at Integrated Health Center. At Doctor Aultz's suggestion, I'm calling in regard to a patient we've had here for a number of weeks: Ms. Vera Lynn Cummings. As you are listed as her closest living relative I thought perhaps you'd like to come and see her? Please feel free to call me here at the center. My direct line is …"

24

Vera Lynn Cummings. My mother's mother. AKA my grandmother. The woman I briefly referred to at the beginning as the one who would give you nightmares … and that's merely if she just smiled at you. I stood there in the quiet of my living room and thought with stomach-clenching horror that the last thing in the world I wanted to do – and I really meant *the very last thing* – was to ever see my grandmother again. She was the person who finally, after all my whining and screaming and demanding, told all The Truth that was necessary to know.

And just about destroyed me.

She told the truth about me: *You were an unwanted mistake from the moment of conception.* She told the truth about my mother: *Never knew a good man when she was looking him in the eye, and never knew a bad man when he was between her legs. Not enough courage to end it all and start fresh. Had to go ahead and have the baby, let it steer her life in a direction that was anything but what she wanted or planned.* And finally – at long last - she told the truth about my father: *Your mother will tell you she was* raped, *something that never occurred to me to claim. But then you've got to admit that it certainly is a convenient way to deflect the blame, isn't it?*

Welcome to my own personal hell on earth. And why Vera Lynn Cummings was probably the only thing that my mother and I whole-heartedly agree on: the woman is toxic and should be avoided at all costs.

That my grandmother had enough information to list me as her closest living relative was my own fault, really. It was also a vivid example that not everything my mother taught me was completely wrong. A shocking fact that was so incredible I determined to examine it further … some other time.

I met my grandmother for the first time a little over two years ago. Supposedly I met her once as a baby but I have no memory of that. When I contacted her out of the blue she didn't seem at all surprised and suggested we meet at a local restaurant that was quiet and intimate and one of her particular favorites. Meeting her was a little like looking face to face at my mother's alternate ego; the family resemblance was almost eerie.

25

There was my mother's face … but it was wrapped up in a never-before-imagined package: hair artfully arranged, make-up perfect, dressed for success in a body-hugging grey power suit, standing on four inch heels, and impatiently tapping inch long red fingernails. She looked like my mother's slightly older sister. As she sat across from me probably making her own cutting observations about me, I struggled to calculate how old she was. Mom had me when she was barely seventeen … I was thirty two … she *had* to be at least sixty-five. *No way does someone look this good without help,* I concluded cynically. *No way.*

"Call me Vera," she said as I was air-kissed and enveloped in a cloud of Joy. "I'm sure you think you're way too old to call me Grandma," she smiled, "and I'm too young to hear it." She ordered two gin and tonics without asking me, and for a brief moment I wondered if they were both for her.

Studying me with great intensity, she squinted her eyes through the smoke of her cigarette, "Well, the Cummings genes sure aren't strong in you, are they? Your mother and I would have killed for cleavage like that. What about the other one?"

The other one? "Do you mean my sister Erin?"

She nodded and frowned in puzzlement. "Are there any more?"

"No …"

"Well, does Erin look like your mother and me?" She'd spoken this last question somewhat slowly as if I was learning impaired.

"Erin looks a lot more like my mother than I do."

She flashed the waiter a dazzling smile when he sat the drinks down on the table then took a much appreciated sip before saying, "I've got some old pictures of my mother somewhere up in the attic. You'd be able to spot her in a crowd of thousands." She sighed. "But I don't think that's why you have decided to contact me after all these years." She didn't ask me directly, just settled back into the booth waiting for me to take the stage.

I remember my feelings that day and they were extremely unpleasant. Sure, I had been nervous about that first meeting with my grandmother. There had to have been some cause behind my mother's complete avoidance of her for the past thirty plus years. And that particular fact was certainly a critical one to take note of. Mother had never been a good judge of character. Just ask one of her numerous ex-husbands.

Once I met my grandmother all my caution radar had gone off the scale. I felt as if I was teetering on a fence, suddenly uncertain which yard contained the man-eating Rottweilers. Anger and entitlement had driven me to contact … Vera. (It was surprising to discover that deep down I hadn't felt too old at all to call her Grandma.) I knew this meeting would upset my mother and, if possible, make our relationship even more strained. Not because of anything my mother had ever said, but because of how my mother had handled her nonexistent relationship with her mother for my entire lifetime.

Stubbing out her cigarette Vera waited for me to speak. She took a sip of her drink and a slow, knowing smile seemed to gradually bloom on her face as she waited for me to talk. *I'm in way over my head,* I had suddenly thought. It was an intense realization that set off all kinds of warning bells in my head. I, Olivia Kelly, hadn't felt this uncertain and insecure in *years*. Taking a deep breath I wimped out totally and said, "Well, I was just hoping to connect with a part of the family that we'd lost contact with. Since it's only the four of us it seems a shame that we live so near to each other and yet never see each other. Don't you ever feel that way?"

Vera took the time to finish her drink and then reached out to pick up the second one that I had never touched. She arched her eyebrows in question and I nodded slightly so she took a grateful sip. "Actually," my grandmother said, "I've never felt that way. Why, until you called me this past weekend, I'd completely forgotten that I had any family." She paused to light another cigarette, inhaling deeply. "I guess only time will tell if you'll wish you had done the same."

My grandmother Vera smoked Winston Super Slim Menthol 100's nonstop, her drink of choice was gin and tonic on the rocks but *only after four o'clock,* and she drove a 1966 Corvette Stingray like a crazy old bat out of hell. She put away three gins that first afternoon while I desperately fielded questions about everything from my sexual preferences ("You're not gay, are you?") to my bra size ("What's it take to harness those things?") to my present love life ("Are you getting any?") to what my salary was ("They saw you coming when they negotiated *that* contract."). Her questions came like heat seeking missiles and I was so addled I answered every one of them. Standing in the parking lot after little more than an hour and a half, I watched her roar away chirping her tires as she shifted through gears. I had answered every single one of her questions and yet hadn't learned a thing about what I'd wanted so desperately to know.

Realizing that we were going to have to get together again if I wanted answers had filled me with total dread.

Sesame Street used to have a song that went something like "one of these things is not like the other, one of these things is not the same ..." Vera was right. The Cummings genes were strong, but apparently not in me. I never really thought much about it until I was in high school biology class in ninth grade and learned about dominant and recessive genes. A homework assignment one night was to go home and diagram what characteristics we got from which parent: tongue roll ability or not, ear lobe connect or disconnect, thumb arch, hair color, eye color, dimples, widow's peak ...

At the time, Mom, Erin and I were in a tentative state of truce. Husband number two – Paul - was finally gone, leaving both me and my mother in need of therapy and antidepressants, but at least with a roof over our heads. (Things had gotten so bad towards the end of that marriage that the three of us had lived in my mother's car until it was determined who got to live where.) I'm not exaggerating when I say that Paul and I never had one polite conversation in the three years, two months, and sixteen days that he and my mother were married. As the dust of the catastrophic marital dissolution settled, I had begun to rediscover the joy of applying myself and learning things at school, as well as the tentative, hopeful healing of my relationship with my mother.

But sitting at the kitchen table one night, the mental engines of all my internal war machines roared to life. You could almost smell the burning of the flag of truce as it went up in roaring flames. As I went down that list of inherited characteristics, literally every item on the *entire list* didn't match either my mother or my father. Not. One. Thing. I trembled in horror with the overwhelming realization after what I had learned that day in class: *Dean Kelly and I could not be related.* He was never – nor would he ever again be – Daddy. He was Dean Kelly. My mother's first husband. The man whom I had been told was my father, but who in reality was nothing more than a drunken lush who took advantage of a little girl's loneliness and desperate need to be loved. No wonder he'd let my mother take me away. No wonder he'd refused to speak ill of my mother and, even worse, regularly took her side in things. No wonder when I had begun to refuse to go with Erin for our visitations he hadn't made any effort to change my mind. No wonder Grandmother Miriam and Grampie Taylor seemed so absolutely relieved to see the back of me. I thought of all the things I said to my mother in support of my father and all the times I'd railed about the injustice that I was stuck with my mother when I so desperately wanted to be with my father. How she must have laughed at me. How he must have cringed at the possibility.

When you're fifteen and faced with a horrifying, life-altering discovery, you don't always behave with maturity and wisdom. I chose to negate the vivid, precious memories of Dean that I'd held onto so fiercely. I didn't think about the financial support that Dean consistently provided for both Erin and me through endless job losses and other financial crises. I didn't hear the messages that my sister brought home from *her father* about how he sent his love to me, how he wished I'd come visit next time, how he was waiting out in the truck to say hello to me … as usual. Instead, I looked at my mother that night and remembered with mind-numbing clarity all of the things she had done wrong so far (an impressive list). With dawning understanding I realized that I was well and truly on my own with *no one* to rely on or trust but myself. And I knew with absolute certainty that once again, *This was your fault, Elaine. All your fault. It was always your fault.*

Therapy: The Truth About Dean Kelly

Setting: Aileen Burkhart's office. It's January 12, 2009, a little less than
one year since this round of psychotherapy began. I've just
crawled out of the deep end which I went off of four months ago.
I've managed to drag myself to Aileen's which she will like
significantly better than my hysteria filled, late night phone calls.
Mount Vesuvius erupted and I was thrown into a stratosphere of
turmoil the likes of which I never want to experience again in this
lifetime. I've lost thirty pounds on the "Discover You're A Child
Of Rape" diet. I have spent endless days and nights crying and
raging. Maybe nobody can see it but I am wearing a black tee shirt
that says – written in blood red letters – I AM A CHILD OF
RAPE. Oh, yeah. And during this time my mother marries for the
fourth time - her meter reader.

Aileen: I'm glad you're back, Olivia.

Me: Oh, cut the crap. No you're not.

Aileen: Sure I am. I've got medical loans I'm still paying.

Me: (Offering a reluctant smile. She's got a sense of humor does our
Aileen.) Yeah, I guess this is better than my random, hysterical
phone calls.

Aileen: (All too familiar silence.)

Me: Thanks. For the phone calls. You didn't have to do that.

Aileen: Don't spread it around. I don't want the word to get out that I'm
offering free therapy by phone if you're hysterical enough.

Me: And drunk enough.

Aileen: (Rolling her eyes.) That too. (Looks at me analytically, trying to
determine just how fragile my mental stability really is I suppose.)
What are we going to talk about today?

Me: You're asking me?

Aileen: You're paying the fee. (At my silence ...) Okay then, let's talk
about Dean Kelly.

Me: He knew, you know. Not about … the rape … but he always knew that I wasn't his child.

Aileen: You're surprised about that.

Me: Hell yeah I'm surprised.

Aileen: You figured it out when you were fifteen. You're not giving him much credit.

Me: (Said with sarcasm.) Neither did my mother, apparently. She had no idea he knew. (Sigh.) I figured it out when I was fifteen and was mad as hell. I *hated* my mother for her deception, her lies, her secrets … As a result, it made me distrust every single thing about her.

Aileen: And yet for all that time Dean knew, too …

Me: (Aileen's looking at me. I'm supposed to realize something, I think. Something important.)

Aileen: (Aileen doesn't roll her eyes, but I'm pretty sure she wants to.) Why did you and your mother think he didn't know, Olivia? *Come on.* You really don't need me to ask the question. And you certainly don't need me to help you with the answer.

Me: (It's suddenly hard to talk because my throat is all choked with tears.) I guess because he never acted like he knew.

Aileen: And what's so important about that, Olivia? What do you need to understand about Dean Kelly based on *this truth* you've learned and *the facts* that go with it?

Me: (I shrug and try to look causally unaffected.) He didn't act any different because I guess he didn't care whether I was his biological daughter or not.

Aileen: Because …

Me: (It's a blinding, throat closing admission.) Because I was always his daughter, no matter what.

Aileen: (Handing me a tissue, and nodding.) See? That wasn't so hard, was it? Make sure you write that fact down in your journal on the plus side of things.

You never find yourself until you face the truth.[6]

4: The Past Is A Different Country
Saturday, March 20, 2010

Saturday morning I looked up Integrated Health Center on the Internet and read: *"Comprehensive range of medical equipment … State of the art medical care … Full range of hospice services … Dedicated and proficient staff … Reverence, compassion and hope in the sojourn ahead …"*

Hospice services. As in dying. Ah, crap.

I had intense moments of panic as I thought, "I want my mommy." Don't be surprised, I've thought that all my life, because I've never felt I had a "mommy". I had a "mother" and occasionally a "mom", but never a "mommy". Mommies were cuddly and loving. They brought brownies to school on your birthday, said stuff like, "How was your day, sweetie?", and didn't ever set fire to your father's favorite collection of *Playboy* magazines on the front lawn for all the neighbors to gawk at.

Once when I said something about my lousy past, Aileen shouted at me, "The past is a foreign country! We live differently here!"" I didn't admit how much I liked that quote, but I did. I'm proud to say that I've been working very hard to have completely relocated my country which was probably the most impressive thing I've tried to do in … well, I guess my entire life. Which meant that I *could* sit here, now, and list "positive" changes that have come about as a result of the nuclear detonation that occurred with Vera's brutal reveal of The Truth.

It took three painful meetings with Vera before I had the courage to ask, and then she was only too happy to tell me the horrible truth no one else had wanted me to know. Since that … time … I'd made a conscious decision to make wise choices. I was determined to avoid people who provided me no positive benefit. Which was why I never planned to see my grandmother again. (And which was one of the primary reasons I'd not been dating, either.) I was determined to look ahead towards a positive future. I was happier in my job and, consequently, a nicer person in general (although I was forced to admit that probably not everyone would agree). I now had a civil relationship with my mother, which was light-years better than what we had had for decades. (Hell, I even showed up at my mother's recent Wedding Number Four, although I took the cowardly route and watched it from a distance.) I now believe that even in his most inebriated state Dean Kelly never regretted being my surrogate father, which causes me … joy … every time I think about it. There was more, okay? But this happily-ever-after list wasn't my point.

My point was, even though I was "better" (such a relative term, you know?) that didn't mean I'd reached a point of tender forgiveness and tolerant understanding for my psychopathic grandmother. Nor, unfortunately, was I ready to seek out the company and advice of my perpetually hopeful mother. I'm better but I'm not *that* much better.

Which left me in a serious quandary. How had Vera put it on our first visit? *"I'd completely forgotten that I had any family. I guess only time will tell if you'll wish you'd done the same thing."* I could risk the continuation of bad/evil/hateful/toxic behavior by simply erasing the good Reverend Harmer's message and going on my way. *Phone call? What phone call? A message from a few weeks ago? No, I didn't know anything about that. What a shame… If I'd only known.*

I cannot communicate how much I wanted to do exactly that. But the dishonesty would eat at me. And sooner or later it would come out in a session with Aileen and it would only add more time to my already endless therapy sessions.

So, with gut wrenching anxiety, I decided I should go see Vera. It was a measure of how truly desperate I was that I once again thought *I wanted my mommy.* I stared at the phone and actually considered calling my mother. (That would delight Aileen to no end were I to tell her. Which I

33

won't.) But then I came to my senses. My mother and I had only just recently been able to resume the weekly Sunday dinners at my sister Erin's and my brother-in-law Dan's house. And we'd managed a number of casual, nonviolent phone conversations, too. It would have been foolish to risk our tenuous relationship by picking up the phone and initiating a conversation regarding a person who ranked #1 on both our lists of "People To Avoid At All Costs."

I could have called Clotilde. She'd go and would be delighted that I asked her. But sometimes her ... goodness ... made me feel so glaringly in the wrong. I mean how could she possibly be, at only twenty-four, so together and wise and smart and first-class? There's so little wrong with her and still so much not right with me that sometimes I ... just can't take her. And the whole God agenda weighed pretty heavily with Clotilde. Another can of worms I just couldn't deal with. I'd just add that to topics that needed to be covered with Aileen at some point in my endless future therapy, I suppose. Briefly I thought of Erin, too, but she was in the same "goodness" category as Clotilde, with the added complication that *we were blood related.* The good and the bad seed so to speak.

So I had to go. And I'd have to go alone.

Okay, so *this* was where a man would come in handy. Forget the sex or the conversation or even the companionship. All that crap was so overrated. No, I'd just like a man who would say, "I'll go with you, Honey." He'd tag along and stand by my side while I visited Vera. A silent, stoic presence that would provide moral support if I was unable to step out of the car once I got to the ... place. He'd provide a few erudite quips or comments when there was a lull in the conversation. Perhaps he might even be able to deflect some of Vera's ... aura. *Maybe* Vera might even prefer him over me and say, "Don't bother coming to visit next time, Olivia, just send your man."

I took the world's longest shower, spent almost an hour getting dressed and doing my makeup, and tried unsuccessfully to have some quality bonding time with Sophie (who was up in the top shelf of my closet and would only show me the tip of her tail). I printed out the directions to

Integrated Health Center and had a momentary spark of hope that perhaps there were no visiting hours on Saturday. A phone call dashed that hope when a cheerful receptionist said, "Oh come right over! Visiting hours are anytime."

Great. Just great.

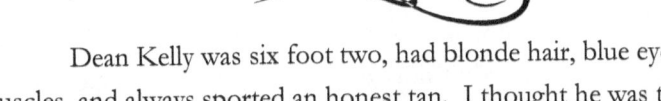

Dean Kelly was six foot two, had blonde hair, blue eyes, bulging muscles, and always sported an honest tan. I thought he was the most handsome man in the world when I was a little girl, and even today on the wrong side of fifty when he's out and about he can still turn women's heads.

He'd been a construction worker since he dropped out of high school to support my mother and me. When I was little, I knew he loved me, his tools, and his truck – in that order. Even when I was a toddler I knew the difference between a Phillips and a slotted screwdriver and could distinguish between his standard and metric wrenches. One time I completely disassembled Erin's crib while he and my mother were fighting. I learned my fractions playing with his ratchet set and the concept of measuring. Area and perimeter were something I *just always knew*. We built a step stool together (although I have only vague memories of the yellow paint), a mailbox, a see-saw, and I think if we went to Grandmother Miriam and Grampie Taylor's house you'd still see a partially completed tree house in the back maple tree. (I fell out of the tree and broke my arm when we were working one day and my mother would never let either of us go up there again.)

Daddy couldn't work on rainy days which made them my favorite. And a rainy day was absolutely perfect if Daddy drove me to school and picked me up in his truck. He always had new shiny and big trucks in a rainbow of colors. I didn't realize until years later that they changed regularly because they were repossessed for missed payments. Every night he hauled all of his tools out of his truck and locked them in the garage. I used to think he did that because he cared so much for his tools, but it was to make sure they didn't go if the truck did.

He called my mother "E", me "Livvie", and Erin "Reenie." I don't
ever remember him calling us any other names. I was seven years old and
in second grade when my mother left him, and for years and years it ranked
as one of the darkest days of my life. I remember that the only person who
didn't cry that day was my mother. She moved us to this ratty old
apartment in a bad part of town and I had to change schools and go to Mrs.
Kellers's every day after school, who watched me and Erin until my mother
got home from work. I missed Daddy so much I ached. And I missed my
old bedroom and my old backyard, the taste of Grandmother Miriam's
oatmeal cookies, the smell of Grampie Taylor's Brut aftershave, and my
best friend Benjamin Harayda and his brother's secret stash of candy that
he regularly stole from the local minimart.

From then on I only saw Daddy on Wednesday nights and every
other weekend. But even at seven I was well aware that Daddy often had
difficulties with transportation, which meant his truck was gone again or
someone had taken his keys. And the general concept of schedules and
time were never something that was important to Daddy – one of the
reasons why he was always so fun.

My relationship with Daddy changed, but not because of the
divorce or the new living arrangements. It was more so because he didn't
buy into my continual anger towards my mother no matter how hard I tried
to accomplish that feat. And I tried *for years*. I wanted him to be as mad at
my mother as I was. Just as vocally indignant. Didn't he miss me? Wasn't
he angry that we weren't living with him anymore? Didn't he want things
to go back the way they were? Couldn't he make my mother move back?
Every time he would come to pick up me and Erin, I'd go at him with the
same questions, the same demands. Over and over and over ...

He'd say things like, "You're mother is trying to give you a better
home life." "I need to work on some things before you can come back and
live with me." "I miss you, too, but I'm not such a good influence when
I'm drinking." "Don't you realize how hard your mother is trying?"

Eventually my anger grew big enough to include him, too. Every
time we got together, inevitably we ended up having the same old

discussion. Finally, one night when I was almost fourteen, Daddy pulled up in front of our home (my mother already divorced from husband number two had managed to keep the house this time) and said, "You know, Livvie. E says that most times after you've spent time with me you're even angrier than before you left. You spend a lot of time yelling at me and telling me what you need or want me to do and none of them are things I can do. *None of them.* I *can't* get your mother to come back to me. I *can't* have you come live with me because … it wouldn't be a good idea. Things *are never* going to be the way they were. You need to start looking *ahead* at things, Livvie, and stop crying about things that are done and gone. I know you're still young and that's hard to hear, but that's the way it's got to be." I didn't have anything to say to that. I remember slamming out of the car and stomping into the house.

The next time Daddy called to make plans to pick up me and Erin, I refused to go. And the next time. And the next, too. The very next year I would find out in Biology class that Daddy was really just Dean Kelly, not my father.

Integrated Health Center was a pretty place if you could forget that every single patient inside was dying, which sucked a little of the charm away. The one story facility was set back from the road and surrounded by rolling green lawns intersected with tree-lined paths. As I drove slowly up the entrance road, I could see wooden benches set randomly along the pathways. I parked in the first available space and sat in my car doing my best to stall, and perhaps wait for some cataclysmic event that would allow me to avoid completing this mission. I took in the early spring flowers blooming in the garden and the man sitting on the front bench. He was resting his arms on his knees, his head was bent, and his turquoise tie was blowing in the breeze. I couldn't see his face, but he had brown hair. I decided to wait – to give the guy privacy. I sat for almost thirty minutes before he stood and brushed both hands down his face. *Oh crap. He'd been sitting outside all this time crying.*

I decided then and there to leave. I couldn't do this. I needed to escape. Get the hell out of this nightmare. I put my hand on the ignition key ... and sighed. Crap. I'm living in a different country now. I couldn't help but remember that. I had to go in.

Walking inside, I took in the clean, shiny hallways, bright, well-lit spaces, and the profusion of potted plants. I gave the receptionist my name and she typed it into the computer.

"Vera Cummings," she read, "is in our Palliative Treatment Wing. Room six-twelve."

"Palliative treatment?" Hope sprung to life as I thought maybe Vera's having some new fangled medical procedure and I'm really *not* going to see the World's Nastiest Living Person on her deathbed.

"Palliative treatment means simply that we are no longer actively treating the patient's illness, but are working instead to ensure that the patient's comfort is optimal as directed by the patient's physician," the receptionist explained.

Note to self: Palliative treatment was *not* a hopeful, new-fangled medical procedure. "I see. Can you tell me which way to go?"

"First-time visitors are required to see one of our on-site counselors and review all pertinent information regarding the patient. In your case," she glanced at the screen, "Miss Kelly, you've got power of attorney and are listed as the executrix of Ms. Cummings estate, which gives you full HIPPAA access, as well. That means that besides meeting with today's on-site counselor Janet Weigner, you really should speak with both Dr. Aultz and Ms. Cummings' primary care nurse, Ms. Sehn."

My face must have shown my shock and ... *absolute horror.*

The receptionist smiled reassuringly. She'd obviously dealt with reactions like mine before. "Don't worry, Ms. Kelly. Each of our patients has a very detailed living will in place to help family members make even the most difficult decisions."

Oh, that helps.

Therapy: The Brutal, Awful Truth

Setting: Aileen Burkhart's Office. It's February 9, 2009 and I'm feeling out of sorts. If I were part of the cast of West Side Story I'd be "ready for a rumble." Don't know why exactly. But Aileen seems to sense it, which is dangerous.

Aileen: So, let's talk about the elephant you've been carrying around for months.

Me: (Said with all the terror and defensiveness I can muster.) I don't know what you're talking about.

Aileen: I'm talking about the discovery that you're a child of rape. (At my silent but direct, "drop dead" stare ...) Let's start with the basics. Do you believe your mother's claim?

Me: My mother hasn't claimed anything to me verbally. (I'm being evasive and Aileen knows it. In classic, bizarre fashion my mother had *written* close to three hundred pages of narrative letters detailing almost every personal issue she's ever dealt with from my ignominious conception all the way to what she finds sexually attractive with her newest man. I chose not to mention that. But don't worry. Aileen already knows about the letters. I even offered to let her read them but she declined.)

Aileen: So you haven't discussed this with her. (It's an affirmation, not a question.)

Me: It's been difficult to find the right time to say, "Mom, tell me about the time that I was conceived during your rape."

Aileen: Has either of you made the effort?

Me: No. (I think a bit and am forced to acknowledge ...) She's waiting for me to bring up the subject.

Aileen: So she would discuss this with you.

Me: (I shrug.) How would I know? (Aileen waits.) Yeah, I'm sure she'd talk about it. Like I said, she's just waiting for me. (I sigh.) But I believe it. That my mother was ... raped. It makes so much sense. (I roll my eyes.) Clarifies a lot.

Aileen: You're grandmother didn't believe it.

Me: Which is one of the primary reasons why I believe my mother. I don't
think Vera's opinion really matters about anything.

Aileen: You're opinion of your grandmother doesn't sound particularly
favorable.

Me: (I snort.) It is probably the one clear topic that my mother and I agree
on: Vera Cummings is the devil incarnate. Although it's another
topic we've never formally discussed.

Aileen: (Aileen stares at me. For a long time. I stare back at her. Still
ready to rumble. Finally, she nods, satisfied with … something.)
Rape is force. Rape gives no choice. Rape is a violent act of hate.
For a woman, it can be the single most destructive force of her life.

Me: Why are you telling me all this?

Aileen: Why do you think?

Me: Aileen, could you do me a favor just this once? Could you just spit it
out? I'm paying your salary and I'd really appreciate if you'd just
say it, loud and clear.

Aileen: Sometimes the smartest thing a person can do is admit that she
was wrong. It's particularly hard when it involves a lifetime of
assumptions rooted in childhood innocence.

Me: So, you're saying I'm wrong. And I need to admit it.

Aileen: No Olivia. I'm saying, you need to stop focusing on all the wrong
things you perceive your mother's done, and begin to focus on the
things she's done that were *right*. (She leans forward in her
intensity and I arch my eyebrows.) You have no problem listing all
your mother's mistakes and, it seems to me, that your mother has
no problem acknowledging them. But you need to start listing
what you're mother's done right. It might not be a long list, Olivia,
but it's an *important one*.

Me: You a big Pro Life fan, huh, Aileen? You want to give my mother a
big "hurrah" because she chose not to have an abortion?

Aileen: (She's annoyed, but she's working to keep herself under control.)
You're not going to be able to move forward in your life, Olivia,

until you acknowledge the *whole truth* between you and your mother. It's all up to you, Olivia. You can keep stomping and shouting and screaming and whining or you can make a conscious decision to accept what you can change and change what you can.

Me: Hmmm, that sounds profound.

Aileen: (Just as skilled at sarcasm as I.) How *wise* you are to recognize that, Olivia.

A lie gets halfway around the world before the truth has a chance to get its pants on.[8]

5: There Is Such A Thing As Hate
Saturday, March 20, 2010

The doctor, the nurse, and the onsite counselor said things to me that made absolutely no sense whatsoever because even before they opened their mouths my brain was in complete overload. Words like "hepatocellular carcinoma", "primary liver cancer", "stage four", "metastatic", "jaundice", "edema", "ascites" ... it went on and on and on. I sat there totally numb and gradually they began to realize that nothing was getting absorbed in my overloaded mind.

We sat and stared at each other for significant moments until the counselor (Jenn? Janet? Jill?) cleared her throat and said, "Ms. Kelly, forgive us. It would seem that we are going a bit too fast because you seem completely overwhelmed. Do *you* have any questions for *us?*"

I shook my head furiously, at a loss for words. An overwhelming urge to *get out* consumed me and I pushed my chair back, fumbled for my purse and hurdled out the door. Crashing directly into someone.

"Whoa!" My addled head registered that it was a man because I smelled aftershave and I was looking at a turquoise tie and white dress shirt. *The crying man*, I realized, *from the outside bench*. "I'm sorry," I mumbled.

I took a step back out of the embrace that he'd caught me in. "No. It's my fault. Forgive me." I tried to step around him because the *get out* urge had not diminished in the slightest.

"Hey. Are you okay?"

I looked up. *He was tall.* I gazed into kindly green eyes and a lock of dark brown hair drooped into his right eye. "No," I said loudly, clearly,

42

and forcefully, unwilling to lie and also unwilling to waste time on polite conversation, "I need to get out of here. Excuse me."

As I pushed past the man I heard, "Miss Kelly? Please ... don't leave. We were so relieved to finally have someone come visit Ms. Cummings, and *you* in particular, we just -,"

"You're here for Vera Cummings?" the man interrupted.

I looked from the counselor's sincere face to the man's. What did he know about Vera? "I'm her granddaughter, Olivia Kelly."

"Olivia Kelly!" he repeated my name with an exclamation like I was some world famous actress he'd been dying to meet.

"Come back inside with us, Ms. Kelly. Let's start again," the counselor said beseechingly as she reached out to gently take my arm. I felt like I was being dragged to my death.

I refused to take a seat as the door was shut firmly behind me. I heard myself say to the Center's collection of concerned employees, "I have spoken with Vera Cummings a total of three times in my *entire life*. I've come because of Reverend Harmer's phone call. I am completely unaware of any legal responsibilities I supposedly bear towards ... Vera."

The doctor looked at the nurse, who looked at the counselor. The counselor eventually looked at me and sighed. "I see," She bit her lip and looked at the nurse. "We had hoped ..."

Suddenly, I got it. "You'd hoped that there was someone that Vera cared about or cared about her," I said in dawning realization. "because she's not been any more tolerable than when I last encountered her and now, to make matters worse, she's dying."

My harsh words hung in the air for a moment and then the nurse burst out, "Exactly," almost as if she were trying to speak before professional etiquette once again regained control.

"Ah well," I sighed, "let's get this visit over with then. Don't worry. She couldn't possibly say anything more hurtful than I've already heard." As we made our way down the hallway to her room, I hoped with all my heart that I was right.

When you peel a hardboiled egg, the egg's appearance doesn't change. Not so with Vera Cummings. She'd been in the hospice facility for almost four weeks, and prior to that had been under treatment for liver cancer for over a year. Gone was the power professional; in fact, she was unrecognizable to me. She lay asleep in her bed: tiny, frail, and horribly jaundiced.

"Normally, our patients have family members that come and decorate their rooms to give them a personal touch," I heard spoken quietly behind me as I stood and stared at the person they'd told me was Vera Cummings. "Occasionally, we have a situation where the person is … alone … and the staff tries to pick up the slack. Sometimes other families in the facility also make contributions." There was a live plant on the window sill, a red stuffed bear holding a plastic balloon that said 'Smile!', and a handmade blue and yellow crocheted afghan folded at the foot of the bed.

"Vera, can you open your eyes?" the nurse said as she entered the room and efficiently checked all the things nurses check. "Come on, Vera! Look, you have a visitor," she said cajolingly.

I didn't know that jaundice not only affected one's skin but also the whites of one's eyes. Vera stared at me and I gave her time to focus on who exactly I was. As she'd made me her Absolute Authority On Earth I guessed that I didn't need to remind her. We stared at each other long enough that I was almost certain that every other professional in the room became completely uncomfortable and in various stages of high alert. Twice she went to open her mouth to say something but failed. Finally, with supreme effort, she said, "Well, I'll be damned," and *I think* she chuckled.

Left alone, much to my discomfort and everyone else's relief, what could Vera and I possibly say to each other? *Absolutely nothing.* And that's exactly what we did. For almost thirty minutes.

Grandmothers were almost as mythical to me as mommies. Except I had had much more experience with grandmothers thanks to my best friend as a child, Benjamin Harayda. He had a really cool grandmother who used to live with him. She used to play kickball with us in the street and loved baseball and if I was at the Harayda house when the ice cream man came would always buy me a treat along with Ben and his big brother, Arthur (my favorite was Chocolate Éclair.) Ben's grandmother was sort of like all the good kind of parent ideas all rolled into one. "Benjamin, if you want some of my strawberry shortcake for desert you will eat every single one of those eight green beans you were served, including the four that are in your pant's pocket." (I ate four and he ate four in the end.) "Olivia Kelly, just because you don't call this address home doesn't for one minute mean I can't demand that you wear a proper hat and gloves when you come over in this weather. You'll either march right back home to get those things or you'll wear something of Benjamin's. (I wore Benjamin's.) And she was the world's best hide and seek player. She had a secret place she used to hide in that we could never, *ever* find her. She didn't always use it (to be fair) but when she did we always gave up. We'd trudge out to the front porch, sit on the swing and yell, "We give up!" at the top of our lungs. Within minutes she'd come sauntering out with a twinkle in her eye and a smug smile on her face. "You just need to open your one good eye," she'd tell us.

I let my mind fill with memories of Ben's grandmother rather than my memories of my own. I'm not exactly sure being told I was the product of a rape could have ever been delivered in a positive manner, but I was absolutely certain it could have been done with more tenderness than Vera chose to tell me. Finally, Vera's eyes began to drift shut although she fought to stay awake. "Do you need anything, Vera?" I finally asked in the silence of the room. It was the least that I could do. She blinked slowly and then nodded ever so slightly. "What?" She said something but it was too faint for me to hear. "I'm sorry, I didn't hear." I leaned in closer. "Tell me again."

In a dry whispery voice she said distinctly, "A carton of Winston Super Slim Menthol 100's."

"Will you be back?" The counselor asked me. She was hovering by the main door as I was leaving. I honestly didn't know, and I told her. She nodded. "I understand. It's a difficult thing ... death."

That made me sigh, and I looked out the front door. "It's not her death that's hard." I paused. "I'm sorry, I can't remember your name." She told me, 'Janet.' I repeated it in the hopes that I'd remember it. I was lousy with names. A relatively successful technique I'd adapted lately has been to apply students I'd taught to names of people I was newly introduced to. But I'd never taught a Janet in my limited teaching career which severely limited her chance of remaining for any length of time in my short term memory. "I feel like an imposter coming here. I'm not a caring granddaughter. Nor am I a grieving visitor. I'm not someone who cares whether Vera Cummings lives or dies. I feel very awkward coming here, just not for the reasons that I suspect most people do."

"It was good of you to come, Ms. Kelly," she said to my back as I walked out the front door. "Thank you."

As I drove down the winding road to leave, something in the rear view mirror caught my eye. It was the crying man, his turquoise tie blowing in the stiff spring breeze like a flag. He was standing there, obviously watching me leave.

With his hand raised in what appeared to be a salute.

I went to college to become a big, dazzling, awe-inspiring white collar professional. I was going to make big money and be well thought of - the exact opposite of what my mother had done. I had a head for numbers which became apparent during a high-school career which eschewed homework and studying of any kind. Math, consistently, was the only subject I did well in and actually enjoyed. I went to a county college for the first two undergraduate years because it was the only institution of higher learning that would take me. *Then* I transferred my exceptional GPA (okay, I'll brag: 3.96) to a prestigious four year college where I eventually finished with degrees in mathematics *and* engineering.

For over a decade, I lived the life I had determined I would live. I was well paid, sought after, and steadily advanced through the large corporation that had hired me right out of college.

And I was miserable.

But I never attributed my unhappiness to the wrong career choice. I was still heavily into the blame game with my mother right up until about six months ago, if you want the awful truth. Almost everything I did could be traced back to my mother in one way or another. (Unhealthy and immature, but still, nonetheless, the glue that held me together.) My failure in love (regularly a flaming disaster) I shrugged off to the pitiable example I'd grown up observing. I worked – almost manically – to be strong and confident with everyone I met. (I was never going to be hauled away in my pajamas like my mother had been when I was in college to spend four weeks on the sixth floor psychiatric ward of the local hospital.) I linked dissatisfaction with my job directly to the lack of discipline I'd grown up with – it wasn't an easy transition to go from my mother's lackadaisical techniques to sixty-five hour minimum power weeks. (But I was tough. I could do it.)

I hadn't really been discontented with my friends. Honestly I hadn't. They were all yuppie professionals like me. Few were married; none had kids. We air kissed each other when we were together and gossiped relentlessly about each other when we were apart. I'm not bragging but we were that glamorous group of people you see at a club who walked in like they were royalty and were all so beautiful and so stylish and *so together.*

The day that Vera told me The Truth, I had met with her for the third time (at another "favorite place" where she was on first name basis with the bartender). She arrived later than I and I could tell as she walked toward me that she a.) was already feeling no pain and b.) was mad as hell. As she walked toward me she was a smoking fuse ready to ignite.

I'd finally gotten up enough courage to ask her for information about my *biological* father. No more games. No more beating around the bush. Frankly, I didn't think I could tolerate another meeting with her so it had to be now or never. But I needed to be tactful and clever. Having already had another unsuccessfully brutal argument with my mother on the same topic only a few days prior, I knew that Vera was my last hope.

Vera never gave me a chance to say a word that day. She just walked up to me and detonated. I've thought back on that last visit with my grandmother many times. In my memory now, it's stored in two categories. There is the actual conversation – the horrible things she threw out like an endless stream of putrid vomit that I couldn't escape from. And then there was the underlying emotions that provided the force of it all: fury, hate, revenge, and disgust. I had never felt such intense emotion directed specifically at me.

Not once have I discussed with my mother the topic of Vera – before or since. And in spite of this, Vera absolutely clarified something beyond a shadow of a doubt for me that day: I may doubt the reality of love but I am certain of the existence of hate.

I … learned something that day as Vera left me broken and reeling in that bar: the truth doesn't always set you free – sometimes it almost kills. I actually spent quite a few weeks trying to determine if this particular truth was worth living with. Aileen was pretty fierce with me when we talked by phone. Her predominant theme was, "Let this be a starting point, Olivia, not an ending note." I decided to follow her advice, albeit reluctantly.

Months later, I *was* capable of acknowledging that at our first encounter Vera had given me the perfect advice that I had failed to take: *I'd completely forgotten that I had any family. I guess only time will tell if you'll wish you had done the same thing.*

Therapy: The Truth About Plans

Setting: Aileen Burkhart's office. It's March 16, 2009, and I've been doing
this for a whole year with no end in sight. I see she's got fresh
flowers on her desk. Tulips. I hear Vera's voice firing questions at
me regarding my sexual preferences and my love life and am
embarrassed to be wondering about Aileen's. Was Vera brave and
bold or obnoxious and nosy to want to know such things about
me? And ... why did she even care? And then I think: *no one's ever
sent me flowers ...*

Me: What do you mean what are my plans? (I know what she really
means, I just don't want to head in this direction. Aileen's tried a
few times. Unsuccessfully, I'm proud to say.) You mean, what am
I going to do for my summer break? I'm hoping to teach summer
school. You get paid for that you know.

Aileen: (We *both* know I'm not fooling anyone.) What are your future
goals, Olivia? Where would you like to be in five years?

Me: (I shrug and decide to make Aileen work a little harder for this one. I
look closely at Aileen and she's got a rosy glow going on. I think,
as Vera would put it, that Aileen's definitely getting some.)

Aileen: We can talk about your professional life, although we both know
that's not what needs to be addressed, Olivia. I'd like to know your
five-year plan for your personal life: romance, family relationships,
and personal growth expectations you have. What about love? Do
you have it? If not, do you miss it? Are you interested in acquiring
it?

Me: I don't believe in love. Never experienced it, never felt it. And stop
looking so excited. I have no interest in debating this with you
today.

Aileen: All right, then let's go back to my original question about personal
or professional five-year plans?

Me: (Neither of these options, besides the professional one, seem even
vaguely appealing. But something tells me Aileen's going to be like

49

a starving dog with a bone with this topic: she's not going to drop it like the love one.) Well, for personal growth, I'd certainly like to be truly finished with *psychotherapy*. God, (I do a pretend shudder) I can't *imagine* still sitting here with you in five years.

Aileen: (Aileen smirks. She does that now and then.) No one's making you come here, Olivia. Tell me *honestly*, are you better than you were when you first sought me out a year ago?

Me: (I sigh. She's pulled the Honesty Card. No fair.) Yes, I'm better. We both know it.

Aileen: I'm not the one that counts here.

Me: I know.

Aileen: How are you better?

Me: (Sarcasm rears its ugly head.) You want a list? (Aileen stares at me. *She wants a list.* Crap. I think for a minute.) Okay, my game players have shifted. (I've got her attention now, because I'm talking metaphorically and she likes that stuff.) They're all the same players, but each one now has more accurate roles. Accuracy is important. Critical even. My mother is not the complete bad guy and my ... Dean Kelly ... is not the complete good guy. My biological father will never be in the game, and his absence is not as destructive as I thought it would be. In fact, I've discovered that *never knowing* someone can be a rare privilege. Which brings me to my grandmother. Vera. Too bad I didn't have the "never knowing" privilege with her ... (I give Aileen a smart ass look.) Now there's a noble goal – for my personal family relationships. I don't plan on having anything to do with Vera for the rest of my life. That's a definite. Which would even work regarding my relationship with my mother. Why, it's a perfect plan!

Aileen: You know what they say: "Life is what happens to you while you're busy making other plans.?"

Never assume the obvious is true. [10]

6: Sometimes You Just Have To Ask

Sunday, March 21, 2010

"Aunt Livvie," my six year old nephew Liam said to me when I arrived for Sunday dinner at Erin and Dan's house, "Janine is your *niece*, right?" I was not even inside the house yet, but knew from experience that the question was not as simple as it seemed. Standing directly behind Liam was his almost two year old sister, my *niece*, Janine. She's naked but for her diaper and a long, trailing, purple feather boa. (Potty training wasn't going well. Neither was clothes selection.)

I stepped inside, shut the door, and squatted down in the hall to face the two of them. Liam was for many years the Reigning Child Of Terror but now, frighteningly, he had become the Voice Of Sanity And Reason, and Janine has stepped up to the terror plate. "Hey, how are my favorite kids on the planet?" I asked completely avoiding the question.

"Do you know that a 'kid' is really a baby goat?"

"Are you sure you two aren't goats?"

"No, I a *switter*," Janine said with force. For a horrifying moment I was afraid she was trying to say she was a stripper.

"A 'switter'?"

"Sister," I heard clarified from inside the living room. I turned to see my mother's husband (Number Four), Alec. "Janine will only admit to being a *sister*. Liam seems determined to get her to acknowledge that she's also a daughter, a niece, a little girl …. He's not been very successful, so now he's enlisting the rest of us in the cause. Hey, Olivia. Good to see you." I got an enthusiastic hug.

51

Alec is a good guy, actually. Best of the bunch (well, so far) and all that. He's been … good … for my mother. In more ways than one. "Hi Alec. How's meter-reading/pastry-baking/guitar-playing going?" A jack of all trades, Alec seemed to do a little bit of everything.

"Fine, just fine. I meant to call you earlier this week. You should come by Agape Shop this Thursday. We're doing a benefit show for one of the band member's favorite charities. The music will be *excellent* of course," he gave me a wink, "the pastries will be *exquisito*, and you can't argue with the cause."

"What time Thursday?" I had no intention of going, but I knew how to be polite.

"Doors open at seven-thirty, we start rocking at eight. We plan to play until ten." He turned and put his hand out even before my mother made an appearance.

"Is that Olivia?" I heard and then my mother walked into the living room looking young and fit and casual in low-rise blue jeans, sneakers, and a black tee shirt with a Batman logo. The specter of Vera loomed for a moment and I forced myself to smile at my mother and make my mind blank. "Hi Sweetie. It's good to see you." She said. I got a hug, a kiss on the cheek, and a big whiff of her favorite almond - scented perfume.

"Hey Mom. Nice tee shirt."

My mother looked down at herself almost as if she can't remember what she's wearing and then laughed softly. Glancing quickly at Alec, she turned to me and said, "Batman's my hero." I'm not sure, but I think she blushed a little bit. "Alec got me this on our honeymoon."

"Actually," Alec clarified, "I bought it before we left for Bermuda. I didn't want to run the risk of not being able to find a Batman tee shirt once we were on the island." Then they both cracked up laughing.

This behavior was typical with my mother and Alec. Ninety percent of the time they seemed to be in their own little newlywed world. I wandered into the kitchen to see my sister, Erin, AKA Domestic Goddess Of The World. "Hey, Sis, what's for dinner?"

Erin gave me a hug and a kiss and launched into a detailed listing of tonight's menu, and while I looked at my sister I was staggered by the strength of the Cummings genes. *Oh My Goodness.* I knew exactly what Erin would look like in twenty years (and turned and looked at my mother giggling just as Alec bit her neck). And I knew exactly what my mother would look like when she's … days away from dying. From liver cancer. Her skin and eyes will be yellow, and her stomach will be horribly distended, and there will be a stale, old smell that will be hard to forget …

Oh God … oh dear … oh no … I never should have gone to see Vera. I thought I was doing the right thing, I really did, but I realized with horrifying insight that it was a very wrong thing to do. I stood there frozen in recent memories and the dawning realization of future nightmares.

It was a measure of my power and control that I was certain that both my mother and my sister noticed my crisis … and did nothing about it. Experience had taught them that acknowledging an upset with me had the same effect as pouring gasoline on a fire. But Alec wasn't so experienced. Or maybe he just liked to live dangerously. "Olivia? Is everything okay?" He put a reassuring hand on my shoulder. Which was another big no-no; trying to hug or comfort me in times of distress.

The world seemed to stop rotating for long moments as my sister and mother held terrified breaths and Alec looked politely expectant. I realized I was at a fork in the road. I could do my usual, which I must admit hadn't won me many fans, or I could live in this new country I'd moved to. "Actually," I heard myself say to Alec, "I'd appreciate a moment of your time. Could we go out on the porch and talk?"

"Sure," Alec said with easy-going calm. As I followed him out to the porch, I heard Liam say, "Hey Mommy, why are you and Minnie staring at each other with your mouths wide open?"

Of course, I immediately regretted my impulsive request the second we both sat down and I was at a complete loss for words. Talk about backing yourself into a corner. But finally, Alec began to chuckle, breaking the tense silence. "What I wouldn't have given to have a snapshot

53

of your sister's and your mother's faces just a minute ago." He shook his head in wonder. "It would have been a priceless picture."

I imagined the picture framed and hanging up on Erin's wall of precious family photos and that made me laugh, too. "I don't know where to begin," I said at last.

"Can I tell you the very first thing that intrigued me about your mother?"

"I'm afraid," I said in all seriousness and that made him chuckle again. We both know my mother very, very well.

"It was her flat out honesty. By the time I'd met Elaine, she'd reached a point in her life where she no longer put on airs or tried to impress. She embraced that 'here I am, take me or leave me' attitude. I found it completely refreshing and told her so. *That* pissed her off." He snorted with laughter and shook his head. Alec was quiet for a bit then, lost in fond, bizarre memories, I'm sure. "What I'm trying to say, Olivia, is that you can't go wrong with honesty. Ever. I'm willing to listen if you're interested in talking."

So I told him about the phone call from Reverend Harmer and Vera and what 'palliative' meant. I described with vivid detail what I saw and learned yesterday trying my best to be as clear as I could. "I think you can appreciate the destructive power of my grandmother and yet this isn't something I feel I have the right to keep from my mother. And I don't even want to consider what kind of nuclear detonation me, my mother and my grandmother, *combined in one conversation* could create. So, I'll do the cowardly thing and dump it all on you. You can decide whether my mother should be told. Or not." I waved my hand in casual dismissal. "Do whatever's best."

"It took a hell of a lot of courage to go and see Vera."

"Save it. I can pat myself on the back anytime."

Alec gave me a pointed look. "I'm allowed to tell a person when they impress me. And, you should know, that doesn't happen often. I'm a cynical whatsit and it's always a daily struggle just trying to assume the best in people. I know most of your mother's secrets and Vera has ... a lot to answer for. And while I'm annoying you by being polite and complimentary," he grinned and gave me a quick wink, "I'll also thank you for being kind enough for wanting to do 'whatever's best' regarding all this. I appreciate what a big step out of the box it was for you to talk with me."

"I didn't plan it," I said with impatience, "it's just because you're not smart enough to keep your distance from me."

He leaned towards me and had the audacity to bump my shoulder. "I have a weakness for obnoxious, take-charge women, didn't you know that?"

I looked at Alec and he looked back at me. *He really seems to care*, I thought. "What are you going to do?"

Alec shook his head and sighed. "Not my choice. Your mother – *and your sister* – are grown women. We'll tell them the deal and let them decide for themselves." He glanced towards the front door, "Besides, there's no way in heck the two of us can go back in there and pretend nothing was said out here. Elaine and Erin would hold us down and then they'd sic Liam and Janine on us. We'd break inside of two minutes."

That made me actually giggle.

And I don't giggle.

When I was nine years old and Erin was almost eight, my sister gave me a present. She'd wrapped the gift up in some left-over paper and a reused bow that had seen better days (my mother was a champion saver so we never got to tear open gifts we always had to *unwrap carefully* so that the paper could be reused). It's one of my most vivid memories of just my sister and me. She was always the quiet, cooperative, serious one and I was always the loud, obnoxious, difficult one. *And always would be.* Close in age we experienced a lot together, and yet we always seemed to view the world from two completely different angles. That day she was dancing around me unable to contain her excitement. It was contagious and, throwing caution to the wind, I tore through the paper in my enthusiasm.

It was an old carved wooden box that she'd always kept her treasures in. But she'd transformed it. Erin had obviously worked and worked using scraps of old material (my mother was also a champion sewer) and had carefully decorated the inside of the box making it beautiful from all angles. I remember touching the outside of the box with its carvings and the inside of the box with its profusion of textures. The box was just as pretty inside as outside, even with my eyes closed. Other than the material, the box was empty.

Even at nine, I knew it was more than just a pretty box. Maybe it was Erin's expression when I finally looked at her; all serious and seven-year-old tense. "It's to put happy things in, Livvie. You know how you're always writing things down in that notebook of yours? Here, I'll show you." Taking the box from me Erin looked inside and said, "I think you must be writing down all the things that make you sad and mad and ... worried. Like," she looked at me and suddenly I felt like she was the older sister, "when you get missing Daddy or when you get angry at Mommy or when you just start to feel ... sad ... Now you can write all that down in your notebook, and maybe the box will help you have some happy things to write about, too. Then you can put that notebook in this box, even if you have more sad things than happy things. Cause when you close it, no matter how bad things are," she shut the box and smoothed the top, "you can just look at how pretty things could be."

What my sister had tried to do meant a lot to me. But even at nine I knew things couldn't be that simple.

No matter how much I wanted them to be.

Therapy: The Truth About Me – Part I

Setting: Aileen Burkhart's Office, April 20, 2009, one year and counting.
I've begun to perceive psychotherapy kind of like a spider web.
Initially, out on the far edges, you're calm and collected. You can
see where you've been and you know to be cautious where you
step. But suddenly, you discover you've gone too far towards the
center. All of a sudden it's incredibly complicated, and heart-
poundingly frightening. There's a strong possibility that you may
never escape. I feel like a bug in the center of Aileen Burkhart's
web. Not surprising, today she's dressed in black.

Me: You know, I thought a lot about what you said last week. And you're
wrong.

Aileen: Oh?

Me: Yeah, I don't dislike relationships. Even men have their uses.

Aileen: (Getting out her pad and paper – which she knows I hate.) This
should be good. Go ahead, I'm ready.

Me: I mean, okay, I have issues with all the father figures my mother
brought home. But that doesn't mean men can't be good fathers.
So Dean was ... weak. I see that now, but there are a lot of
memories I have where he *tried* to be a good dad. He meant well.
Paul liked to pretend he was strong – with my mother and with us,
but he was weak, too. And my mother's third husband – Richard –
jeeze he was weak *and* delusional. Thought he could waltz into our
lives and we'd all join hands and go skipping off to fairy-tale la-la
land. But fatherhood's something that only men *can* do. That's
one good use.

Aileen: I'll write that down: Men *can* be good fathers. Keep going.

Me: And, I mean having someone to take you places and buy you things is
never a bad thing.

Aileen: So, men are good for ... attention?

Me: You make it sound dirty. Everyone likes to have someone fuss over
them now and then. That's what I'm talking about.

Aileen: How about for love?

Me: (I shrug.) I knew you'd get back to that topic. I've told you I don't believe that there's such a thing as love. It's all in your head. Of course, if you have that 'chip' in you that you *want* that kind of stuff, then you go out and *look* for that kind of stuff. Eventually you find someone who wants the same thing and you get together. (I shrug again.) Or you settle for something less. It's a lot like looking for the pot of gold at the end of the rainbow. It doesn't really exist, and eventually you have to come to terms with that and just grab what you can.

Aileen: Are you saying everything between a man and a woman in love is just an illusion? A figment of imagination?

Me: No, that's not what I'm saying. (For some reason, I'm really, really mad all of a sudden.) There's hormones and sex and pheromones and reproduction. That's real. I've experienced passion with men. It's appropriate … and even enjoyable now and then. It's just I don't have the romance/love 'chip!' In fact, I don't want it! I think believing in love makes you weak and vulnerable. I don't *need* a man to make me feel complete. I don't *need* a man to make me feel appreciated. I don't *need* a man to make me feel vital. I don't want to be part of a couple. I'm happy on my own. (Get me a soap box and a microphone. I'm on a roll, here.)

Aileen: (Aileen scribbles something industriously for a few moments and then looks up from her pad.) Are you?

Me: *Am I what?*

Aileen: Are you … (looks down at her pad) … complete? Appreciated? Vital? Happy? I may not agree with you on your opinions of love but I certainly agree with you on the importance of those personal qualities. Which one shall we discuss first?

The truth is not for all ..., but only for those who seek it.[11]

7: I Knew A Perfect Man Once

Monday, March 22, 2010

After a day that included an unscheduled fire drill, a young woman being sent to the office for lack of underwear (noticeable, apparently, due to the shortness of her skirt), an endless faculty meeting (on the district's new online website), and a session with Aileen, I had no hopes that the flashing message light on my answering machine heralded good news.

"Ms. Kelly, this is Reverend Harmer from Integrated Health Center. I'm calling to inform you that your ... that Vera Cummings passed away at about eleven o'clock this morning. She has made very detailed arrangements regarding her final wishes and I'm just calling to keep you informed. At your convenience, you'll need to come and pick up her personal effects. Please feel free to call ..."

Ah, great. Just great. The end to a perfect day.

Life had taught me that postponing the inevitable didn't make things any easier and usually just made things worse so I made the decision to do what I needed to do immediately. Sophie and I had a dinner of tuna (me: with mayo, sweet relish, swiss cheese and a hard roll, Sophie: drained tuna water in a bowl, can with remnants on the side). I took a shower and decided to dress in optimal-comfort clothes which meant jeans, sneakers, and a long sleeved tee shirt. My hair, contained all day while I taught, was allowed free reign and dried gradually into an unruly, curly mass. I opted for minimal make-up (just in case I shed a tear or two), fortified myself with three Oreo cookies, brushed my teeth, and off I went.

I had moments of immense guilt because driving up the winding road to Integrated Health Center was nowhere near as terrifying as it was last time, because I knew Vera was dead. How awful was it that I felt *relief* over the death of someone? I decided, however, after some deep self examination (Aileen would be nodding approvingly) that my reaction to Vera's death was a testament to *Vera's* life choices and not my own. So far my score card of exemplary behavior was looking good. This week, anyway.

Janet Weigner and Reverend Harmer met with me and we worked efficiently through all the paperwork I was required to sign. Vera's possessions (at least what was at IHC) fit into one small black carry-on suitcase. It was obvious they hadn't given me the afghan. We shook hands, I thanked them for all their help, and walked with purpose towards escape. I was only ten steps away from freedom when I heard shouted breathlessly behind me, "Olivia Kelly!!" I stopped and turned and saw the crying man rushing towards me down the hall.

He had on another smart looking suit, with a crisp white shirt and a vivid red tie that was once again flapping like a flag as he walked briskly towards me. I stood and waited, Vera's life packed neatly in the case in my hand.

Once he reached me, he suddenly seemed at a loss as to what to say. "I ... I heard about ... Vera ... I'm sorry for your loss."

I shrugged. "Thanks, but we weren't close. I hardly knew her."

"Oh."

I smiled politely and took a step backwards. "Well, if you'll excuse me. It's been a long day."

"Do you remember me?" he asked with sudden desperation and a step closer.

I had a flash of him sitting out in the sunshine on the bench just the other day; of his bright turquoise tie and the way he wiped his face of tears. "Well ... Friday I -"

He immediately started shaking his head. "No, not Friday. Before that." He smiled. "We've both grown up a lot, that's for sure. But I never

60

forgot those eyes of yours," his gaze swept my hair, "and that wild hair. And, just a moment ago, when you smiled, I remembered that dimple."

He was unbalanced. Perhaps in actuality he was a patient from the psychiatric wing. It was the obvious answer. It was really not at all surprising that this man had sought me out given my proclivity for always attracting the wrong kind of men. "I'm sorry. I don't know what you're talking about." I was firm and decisive and, clutching Vera's suitcase, I turned to leave.

"The last time I saw you," he raised his voice a bit, "was the summer between eighth and ninth grade. 1990. You were visiting your Grandmother Kelly's house with your sister Erin."

That stopped me in my tracks. Because the guy obviously *did* know me. Somehow. With my hand on the exit door, I turned and looked at him. He walked towards me and stopped just close enough that I could smell his aftershave and see his clear, green eyes. He let me study him and waited patiently while I searched my memory. Slowly, he began to smile and his eyes crinkled and before my eyes this professional adult male morphed into a skinny fourteen-year-old with a black eye and a mouth full of braces. Same smile and crinkly green eyes though. Softly he said, "I called you Jerry after my Aunt Amy brought us matching Ben and Jerry tee shirts from Vermont."

It was my turn to step in closer, filled with delighted surprise. *"Benjamin?!"* I said. *"Benjamin Harayda?!?"*

"The one and only," he nodded with a grin. "It's great to finally see you again after all these years, Olivia Kelly."

Whenever I could, I've escaped the realities of my life and I've used a variety of effective methods. As an adult, I used work. As a college student I used my studies. In high school I brought rebellion to a high art form. As a child, I used the Haraydas.

When my mother divorced Dean Kelly, I not only lost my father and my best friend, Ben, I also lost my childhood escape – The Harayda

House. They lived two doors down in a house that was identical to all the other neighborhood houses in structure, but light years different from mine in atmosphere. Don't get me wrong, there was nothing traditional about it. Grandma Harayda, who lived in the tiny back bedroom, was a New York sports fanatic who watched every televised sports event possible. I remember dinners with the television wheeled into the dining room so that the final quarter wouldn't be missed and I still can't hear the Wide World of Sports intro music without flying back in time to Sunday afternoons watching the Haraydas black and white Motorola. Mr. Harayda was a Merchant Marine, gone for two months at a time and then home for two months. He'd be gone long enough that you'd forget he existed and then suddenly he'd be home all booming laughter and wild stories. Mrs. Harayda was capable, efficient, organized and precise. She could bake a cake, change a tire, and repair the washing machine, all the while helping me and Benjamin with our homework. Ben's big brother, Arthur (of stolen candy fame and nine years our senior), used to call me "Little Bit" and would regularly pick me up and sit me on the refrigerator … and leave me there. "ARTHUR!" Mrs. Harayda would yell, "GET LIVVIE OFF THE FRIDGE! I need to get dinner started and can't get to the hot dogs!"

As I child, I couldn't put into precise words what was different about my house and Benjamin's; I just liked to be at his more than mine. Both were loud, both had shouting matches, and both were nothing like the television families I saw on TV. One time Benjamin said, "In your house, we always have to tip-toe." And he was right. Not so much because we needed to keep quiet, but because calm was always so tenuous that even a pin dropping could set off an explosion of epic proportions. The Harayda House was a place where every smell and every sound communicated loudly and clearly that, "A Happy Family Lived Here." It was my most favorite place on earth.

Benjamin was my best friend, my partner in crime and (here's a laugh) the man I had every intention of marrying by the time I was seven years old. It wasn't so much because I loved him, but I'd decided it was the best way to become part of his family. I don't remember ever formally asking him (nor do I remember him declining). I just started to say things like, "When we get married, we should get bunk beds but I want to be on the top." Or, "Once we're married, we're never going to have stew. I hate stew." Or, "When we get married, I think we should paint our house pink." He never argued with me, never disappointed me, did everything I told him, and always stuck up for me.

In essence, he was the perfect man.

"Ben! It's so good to see you!" I said to him with true enthusiasm, and as I went to give him a hug I was brought up short by Vera's suitcase. And remembered where we were. "Oh ..." I deflated like a balloon, "what ... who ... why are you here?"

"My Grandmother. Remember Grannie Blue?" Immediately I had a picture in my mind of a tiny, wiry old lady with a Jets tee shirt, a Yankees baseball hat, and a wild shock of blue tinted hair (hence her name) playing kickball with us in the middle of the street and screaming, "Throw me the ball, Bennie! QUICK!"

"Oh, no. Grannie Blue?"

Ben nodded. "Yeah. Final stages of ovarian cancer. We've been taking turns keeping her company." He gave me a small smile. "The craziest patient this place has ever seen that's for sure."

I looked down at my suitcase and then back up at Ben. "At least she's not the nastiest patient this place has ever seen. My grandmother won that award."

Ben doesn't deny my assertion. Reaching up he puts a warm hand on my shoulder and squeezes. "I heard about Vera. I'm sorry for your loss. Are you okay?"

I shrugged. "We weren't close at all." I gestured with the suitcase. "But I won the prize to be in charge of final arrangements anyway."

"If you need anything ... help, advice ... I've got experience -" I cut off further words with a firm shake of my head. "Hey, would you like to come and say hello to Grannie Blue? I made the mistake the other day of telling her I'd discovered Vera's granddaughter and she's been bugging me ever since about wanting to see you."

I had this horrible flashback of Vera just days ago and was unsure if I could take another deathbed visit. "Are you sure it would be all right?" My face must somehow have communicated my reluctance.

"It's okay. I understand. You've just had to deal with some very difficult stuff. Don't worry about it." He was taking his leave, I could tell even though he'd not moved an inch, and suddenly I didn't want him to walk away.

"No. No, honest, Ben. I'd love to come and see Grannie Blue if you think she's up for it."

Grannie Blue still had blue hair, but it was a wig now. *Electric* blue. As in the Smurfs. "Someone got her the wig as a gag gift after she lost all her hair during chemo. Only Grannie has refused to consider it a gag and has been wearing it ever since," Ben murmured as we stood in the doorway. Perched on top of her blue hair was a blue Yankees baseball cap; a horrifying clash of blues if ever I saw one.

"She's asleep," I whispered, "maybe I should come back."

"She does sleep a lot," Ben acknowledged, "the pain meds do cause that. But she also has been using it as a ploy to get information." He looked pointedly at me, "*Never assume anything* with her." Then he grinned and rolled his eyes.

"Now Bennie," came a dry, papery voice, "don't go spillin' all my secrets. How's a girl going to find out anything if you do that?" Grannie Blue opened her surprisingly bright blue eyes and then squinted at me. "Who's this looker?"

"Grannie, it's Olivia Kelly. Vera's granddaughter. Remember? I told you about her on Friday? She's come to say hello."

"Of course I remember. I'm dying. Not senile. Come over here, dear. My hearing's perfect but my eyesight's not what it used to be and I need to get a good look at you. Bennie will tell you I don't bite. Not anymore, anyway, since they took my teeth."

64

I laughed because there was nothing else I could do, and that made Grannie smile. She really didn't have any teeth. Ah, she liked an audience. "Hey, Grannie Blue. It's good to see you although I wish it was under different circumstances." I pulled one of the room chairs closer to her bedside and sat down. Ben leaned his shoulder against the wall and crossed his arms.

"Little Olivia Kelly. You had a younger sister, didn't you?"

I filled in all the blanks about Erin: career, marriage, children, and the happily ever after domestic goddess title she owned.

"What about that mother of yours? Such a sad little thing when I knew her."

"She's happier now. On husband number four and so far so good."

"Four is it? Well, well, that's a total if ever I heard one. Any of them rich?"

"Grannie!" Ben exclaimed.

"Ah, I'm just having some fun. Nothing much I can do except say outrageous stuff these days."

"Unfortunately, none of her husbands were rich, but at least all of them were gainfully employed."

"Well that's a blessing. My husband, God rest his soul, had a bit of 'lazy, good for nothing' in him that I regularly had to discourage. Got me and the kids in some dire straits a time or two, I'll tell you. Hey, that father of yours still drinking?"

"Grannie!" Ben said again.

I laughed again and smiled at Ben. "It's okay." To Grannie Blue I said, "He's struggled with it all his life, Grannie. It's been quite a battle. Currently he's got a little over two years of sobriety under his belt, and that's the longest he's ever been sober in my lifetime."

"Praise the Lord," Grannie said with sincere reverence. "Demon alcohol is a terrible cross to bear. I battled mightily with tobacco. Haven't smoked since 1973 but I still dream about it." She closed her eyes in fond remembrance and smacked her lips. "Loved everything about that horrible

65

habit. But the Lord helped me to overcome it and, as a result, gave me a length and quality of life I never would have enjoyed. Isn't that right, Bennie?"

Ben nodded. "That's right, Grannie." A rattling was heard in the hallway and he pushed off from the wall. "It sounds like the tea and cookies are here. Let's get things set up." With practiced ease, Ben cleared her bedside tray and elevated the head of the bed a bit. "That good?"

"Perfect," Grannie said. "Now you two get lost. I'm going to sip my tea, watch Wheel of Fortune, hopefully stay alive long enough to watch Jeopardy, too, and then go to sleep. I don't want any interruptions. It's one of my favorite hours of the day." Turning to me, she said, "You come see me again if I live a few more days, okay? I'm headin' home any day now but I'd enjoy seeing you again. You know, you're right, Bennie," she said with a definite twinkle in her eye, "she's *hot.*"

Walking down the hall together, Ben finally said with a sigh, "I never said you were hot."

I had an unexplainable urge to tease him. "Oh, *great.* Thanks for nothing."

"No! I mean, I told her you were pretty and we talked about what we remembered you looking like when you were thirteen and ..." He heard me laughing, stopped talking and walking, and blushed furiously. "Oh. I fell right into that one."

I grinned at him. "I remember that you were gullible when you were thirteen, too. I could trick you into doing anything I wanted you to do."

"I don't remember being gullible. I remember being ..." he paused and took a deep breath, "... cooperative and easy going."

I laughed and nodded. "Yeah. That, too."

Narrowing his eyes, he said with a smile, "I remember you being bossy, demanding, and incredibly opinionated. You even gave me a black eye once!"

Shrugging I said, "I've been accused of much worse things which are just as true."

He gazed at me with a look I've seen ... before. Intense interest. Hunger. Desire. (Hey, don't forget the cleavage ... it's the cross I have to bear.) He was practically smacking his lips. "All these years, Livvie. I've never forgotten you. I've always wondered what you were up to ..., what you became ..., where you ended up." He shook his head in amazement. *"Olivia Kelly."* He said my name again, like he did once before like I was some mythical goddess he'd always dreamed of meeting live and in the flesh. He actually lifted his hand like he was going to touch me and see if I was real, but he caught himself, fisted his hand, and took a deep breath.

And then he said exactly what I expected him to say, "Are you interested in stopping somewhere for a late dinner or cup coffee or something?"

Therapy: The Truth About My Mother – Part III

Setting: Here I am again: Aileen Burkhart's office. It's May 18, 2009 and
I've brought along with me a Starbucks Grande Biscotti Chocolate
Cream Frapuccino (they grind up a biscotti and add it to my frozen
coffee … *yum*) and have decided to do this every time I come.
Kind of like a reward for good behavior.

Aileen: Tell me about your mother's new husband and her new marriage.

Me: His name is Alec. He was her meter reader. Still is, I think. I wonder
if she gets a rate reduction? They're all hot and heavy, lovey-dovey
right now, which is already beginning to get old. They'll be married
a year this November. The fact that she's still happy is already a
world record for my mother. She and Paul and even she and
Richard were already miserable by this time.

Aileen: What's different?

Me: (Roll my eyes.) With every man, my mother adopts a new cause.
With Dean it was *Alcoholics Anonymous*, with Paul it was *Therapy And
You: Perfect Together*, with Richard it was *Depression: Nobody's Perfect*.
With Alec it's *Jesus Is My Savior*.

Aileen: (She's intrigued.) She's found God?

Me: Oh yeah. Big time. Goes to church. Has her own Bible. Attends
Bible Study. Doesn't say stuff like, "Praise The Lord" or anything
but she's told me a number of times that she's praying for me. (I
snort.)

Aileen: Do you believe that she's sincere?

Me: (I think for a minute.) Yeah, she's sincere. In all fairness, she was
sincere about all the other causes, too. It's like once she gets
involved with a man she suddenly seems to have the tremendous
burst of personal growth. It's for the better in the end, but usually
the casualty list is phenomenal.

Aileen: Are you on the casualty list?

Me: *Hello.* Erin and I were the initial first two.

Aileen: You're contradicting yourself you know.

Me: (Thinking: *Oh crap.*) I don't know what you mean …

Aileen: Well, you've said you believe that your mother is sincere. You've also mentioned a (she looks down at her pad) 'tremendous burst of personal growth'. Both of those things have a positive connotation. But not so the word 'casualty'. How can those positive things bring about something negative?

Me: (Trying to look puzzled.) You lost me on that one.

Aileen: No I didn't.

Me: (Thinking again: *Oh crap* and then also thinking *That didn't work.*) You're trying to get me to reevaluate my thinking again. About my mother. And my past.

Aileen: That's right. Come on, Olivia. You're a smart woman. Let's just get this over with and then move on to something else.

Me: (I get up and walk over to Aileen's African violet window. They're all in bloom: pinks, purples, whites, blues …) We've already talked about how I seem to make the same mistake over and over in a relationship. You want me to realize that my mother may make mistakes, but she learns and moves on.

Aileen: Which is an exemplary thing. Not necessarily a casualty.

Me: You know, Aileen, you're starting to sound like my mother's number one fan.

Aileen: (Aileen shrugs.) Making mistakes isn't a crime, Olivia. Failing to learn from those mistakes and repeating the same error over and over again is. The only information I have about your mother is what you have told me. I'm just making observations. Feel free to correct me at any time.

Olivia: Is that the point then?

Aileen: (She sighs.) I'm not going to say it, Olivia.

Olivia: You want me to acknowledge that my mother has done a better job at fixing up her screwed up life than I have because at least she continues to progress forward. I've been stuck on this square in the game of life for years.

Aileen: Make that decades.

In seeking truth you have to get both sides of a story.[12]

8: Nice Men Never Interested Me
Monday, March 22, 2010

Of course I didn't go for a late dinner or coffee with Benjamin. Thanks to Aileen ... and time ... I'm better, but nowhere near perfect. I did what I always do when a nice man showed interest in me – especially friendly, kind, nonthreatening type – and froze him out. I've never gravitated towards nice men and Ben was certainly a nice man. And maybe, I suppose, especially because he was Ben ...

But although Ben accepted my "no" for late dinner or coffee, it didn't stop him from following me out to my car. Standing in the glow of the parking lot lights we ended up leaning against my car laughing and talking and reminiscing for over an hour.

"Remember the time you convinced me to put mud in Arthur's boots?"

"Remember the time your father fell asleep in his truck – right in the middle of the street - and we got Arthur to help us get the truck in the driveway because we were afraid we'd get arrested for driving without a license?"

"What was the name of that old lady on the corner of the street that used to scream curses at anyone who stepped on her lawn?"

"Did you know that Georgie from up the street ended up robbing a liquor store and is still in prison? We always knew he'd end up in trouble, didn't we."

"Remember the time the cops caught us climbing on that old train car and you started crying because you were afraid he was going to put us in handcuffs?"

"Remember the time we tried to sell holy water instead of lemonade and Mrs. Corliss saw us filling the jug with the garden hose and told us what we were doing was a sin?"

Driving home I realized how strange it had felt for me to just relax and laugh and be casually at ease. I caught myself smiling once or twice in the dark all by myself over the memory of little Olivia Kelly and her perfect man Ben Harayda. Eventually I got thinking of grown-up Olivia Kelly and her adult version of the perfect man which was not such a nice picture at all.

My last long-term relationship was with Rick, a man I had met at a corporate function and lasted for approximately two years. He was exactly what I wanted in a man. The very epitome of what I looked for, gravitated to, and was always determined to end up with.

Wealthy, confident, capable, and take charge, Rick was also handsome and clever. We began a provocative banter at the bar that first night and kept it up through dinner, the cab ride to the hotel, an explosive night under the sheets, and over room service the next morning. Our relationship was an arrangement that suited both our needs. I didn't want false declarations of love and wishes for eventual fairy-tale endings. Rick didn't want the white picket fence, two point three children, and a domestic goddess waiting for him when he got home each night.

He had that already.

Married men doted on you. Married men were predictable. Married men tried harder to make you happy. Married men didn't have the capacity to disappoint, because you knew exactly what you were getting. Married men didn't want to talk about sticky topics such as bills and too-long work days and who finished the last of the milk. Married men bought you presents and took you out to shows and treated you to expensive meals at classy restaurants. Married men sent better emails and said sweeter things to you on the phone. Married men smelled nicer and dressed more stylishly.

You could laugh all you want (or maybe frown in disgust), but even today I still believe that all those statements are true. Even at a point in my life when I should understand all the negative things about being involved with a married man, I still had some very fond memories ...

Which was why I was still not dating.

When I finally ended it with Rick it wasn't because I wanted something that he couldn't give me (I wasn't one of those pitiful women sobbing for him to leave his wife!) It was because I had fallen off the deep end emotionally in discovering that I was the product of a rape and couldn't abide contact with anyone; let alone a man. Learning that fact about yourself stripped you down below the skin level and the rebuilding project (still currently in affect) was a lengthy, time-consuming process.

At this point in my reconstruction, I no longer desired the (let's see if I can remember some of the lengthy list that Aileen and I came up with) emotionally-silted, future-destroying, deviant-based title of mistress, but that didn't mean that dating a man who was ... normal? ... available? ... compatible? ... appealed to me.

Having a healthy relationship (as defined by Aileen) still absolutely terrified me. When I admitted that to Aileen she said I had to figure out why - which I didn't really need to do because we both knew that I already knew why. Healthy relationships can't be controlled. Healthy relationships left me open to hurt and disappointment and those feelings of abandonment and loneliness I'd been running from for decades. After all this time and all this therapy, I still really didn't think that the upsides of a "healthy" relationship could in anyway outweigh the inevitable downsides. I might have been better enough to understand how detrimental my choices for relationships had been thus far but that didn't mean I was eager to try something different.

Unfortunately, I came to all these conclusions and decisions while heavily flirting with Phil, my assistant principal. I'd been hired as a high school math teacher midyear (January of 2009) to fill an opening from a retirement. From the very first day that I waltzed into the school, briefcase and #2 pencils in hand, I'd recognized Phil's interest and he'd recognized my potential. Now maybe you don't know, but part of the thrill of an illicit relationship is the chase and the expectation. It's that forbidden candy allure that you remember from childhood in modified form. Phil and I did the looks and the harmless yet provocative conversation. This progressed to tentative touching and hugging which created an enjoyable (yet platonic) relationship in which coffee after work and casual visits to my classroom were appropriate yet highly anticipated. Until finally the first few stolen yet incredibly passionate kisses occurred whereby the final line was crossed and the chosen path made abundantly clear. At which time, I was at a point in my therapy with Aileen and my own personal self-examination that I decided I needed to reevaluate things. As I knew I wouldn't be able to do that with Phil in the picture – in any way, shape or form – I made the celibacy decision. Poor Phil had no vote in the matter much to his frustration. In fact, almost a year later, he was still ever hopeful.

I fell asleep Monday night with memories of Ben crowding my mind. A dream or a nightmare woke me up and my alarm clock told me it was … well, I couldn't see what time it was because Sophie was fast asleep on it. How could that be comfortable? I picked up my cell phone and it said 3:02 a.m. I tried to remember the dream, and although the details were fuzzy I knew with certainty that it was about Ben. Slowly, like distinguishing landmarks in a heavy mist, pieces of the dream drifted back to me. We had been playing in Ben's back yard, trying to construct a club house more wonderful and more magical than Dean and I had ever managed to even plan. And we were succeeding. In the dream I felt the thrill and the excitement of it all coming together and our unparalleled delight. I was holding up a critical wall and Ben was hammering it in place when I was called away. Maybe it was my mother's voice … I can't remember, but I immediately began to cry. And Ben began to cry, too, because he knew that the club house would never be completed if I went home and I had no choice but to go. *This is our one and only chance and we will*

not succeed was the awful, horrible, gut-wrenching reality. In the dream, suddenly I'm driving down the winding road away from Integrated Health Center and there in my rear view mirror was young fourteen-year-old Benjamin Harayda sobbing and raising his hand in a permanent farewell salute.

I should have gone for coffee! I thought desperately there in my bed. *Oh God. I should have gone.* The feeling was so intense, it was almost heartbreaking, and I worked to steady my breathing which had become irregular. My heart was pounding now, not from the dream/nightmare, but from the distinct knowledge of the unparalleled mistake I'd made in real life that could not be undone.

But it can be undone, my quiet voice of reason said calmly. *Just go see Grannie Blue after school and Ben will be there. You can talk with him, somehow manage to wrangle another invitation out of him or just flat out ask him out to coffee yourself.*

A horrible realization made me sit upright in bed. *What was I thinking?!* I've *never* asked a man out, ever. (Married or not.) Nice men have *never* interested me. Furthermore, I've *never* second guessed my reaction to nice men. And I *definitely* don't flirt with nice men or encourage nice men or *lay in bed at night thinking about nice men.*

Crap. Clear as a bell I realized the horrible truth: Aileen had completely ruined me. Already I'd become one of those giddy, clinging, eyelash batting imbeciles I have always disparaged.

Despite that realization, the intense desire to repair my wrong with Ben disturbed me through an endless day at school. I decided to drive directly to Integrated Health Center, not even going home to bask momentarily in Sophie's disinterest. Consequently, I arrived before Ben and was greeted by Grannie Blue alone, reclining in her bed.

"Little Livvie! What a pleasant surprise. Here I've been sleeping the day away, and now that the pain is getting ready to come sit here in bed with me, I'll have you to distract me."

"Shall I go call a nurse?"

Grannie shook her blue head. "Nah." Glancing at the clock she said, "I should be able to make it another hour or so until we have to call them."

Get a nurse at 4:10. Come hell or high water, that's what I'd be doing in sixty minutes, running out of the room like a cartoon character in my haste.

"Looking for my Bennie?" Grannie said slyly and gave me a knowing wink. Was I already that obvious? "He's quite a catch you know. Girls have been chasing him forever, but he's just too dang picky. 'What are you waiting for?!' I keep yelling at him. 'Why can't you make me a great-grannie? I ain't got all day you know!' Guess what he always said to me?" I nodded my head, horrified to already be on this specific topic and it had only been … (I glance at my watch) … thirty seconds. "He says to me, 'Grannie, you know you can't rush God's timing or God's plan, and that's what I want. She's out there. I'm sure of it. But I've got to be patient. And so do you.'" Grannie Blue snorted and rolled her eyes. "My clock's ticking here. Why can't God speed things up just a bit?"

Now what do you say to something like that? I stared at Grannie, at a complete loss for words, certain I looked like a terrified deer in the headlights.

"You have a young man?" Grannie asked me, and she took a breath and closed her eyes. *It was 3:16.*

"No, not at the moment. I'm too busy dealing with my own life. I don't dare complicate it by getting involved with someone else's."

"Ever been married?"

"No."

"Engaged?"

"No."

"Gone steady?" But by then she was grinning at me and I grinned back and chuckled. "No need to rush that walk up to the altar. You only want to do it once so you might as well take the time to do it right. Or you'll spend a lifetime dealing with your impatience and making regret your best friend."

"Did you do it right?" What a personal question it was to ask, but visiting with Grannie Blue tended to create a sort of alternate universe: standard rules seemed to not necessarily apply.

"Well … no one gets it *all* right, you know. I didn't understand about true love when I got married so how could I get it right? But back in my day, once you discovered the error of your ways you didn't just rush right off to a lawyer and get a divorce. You stuck it out. Through the good, the bad, and the ugly."

"So … you've got a regret tattoo, huh?"

Grannie Blue thought for a moment. "You know, I always wanted a tattoo. Didn't admit it to many but I wanted," her eyes twinkled, "Yosemite Sam holding up his revolver and the words 'Back Off' on my upper arm." I was fairly certain she was serious. "But yea, my whole body's covered in regret tattoos. But life's not that cut and dried. At least as a Christian it isn't anyway. I've always stood on the promise that God would never leave me or forsake me, but that didn't mean I didn't regularly mess up or didn't regularly have to deal with hardships." She looked at me and I noted that her blue eyes and blue hair kind of played off of each other.

"Do you know that we're supposed to be thankful to God for all things? Some stupid minister told me that one time when I went to see him with all my troubles. When I first heard that I thought it was the biggest load of … garbage I'd ever been told. I was supposed to be glad that my Henry was happier playing the ponies then paying our rent? I was supposed to be happy that my Henry's greatest skill was avoiding any responsibility that had his name on it? I remember asking those questions … and a pile more …" She rested back on the bed again and I was suddenly vividly reminded that this little old lady is in a hospice … dying.

"Grannie, this is too much for you. Just sit and rest. Can I get the nurse yet? Turn on the TV? Read you something?" *Anything.*

"I'll rest when I'm dead, Olivia. I was just sitting here this morning talking to my Lord and I asked Him what He still needed me to do. Something tells me that watching *Wheel of Fortune* isn't too high on His list

76

of priorities right now. God's been loving and tolerant of me and mine, Olivia. He put up with my anger and my sarcasm in my early years. I remember saying things to God like, 'Thanks that Henry got fired again, God,' and 'Thanks that I have to get a second job now,' and 'Thanks that all of my kids are wearing patched hand-me-downs.'"

Grannie Blue and I sat there in companionable silence while I thought of odd things *I had* to be thankful to God for.

"But funny things started to happen. Things I couldn't ignore. Like at my second job cleaning office buildings I did such a thorough job that my employer got a compliment about it and I got a raise. It was nice to hear a positive thing, you know? Which made me work harder at my first job as a waitress, and my tips improved there, too. And one night the big boss at the office where I cleaned offered me a day job supervising his cleaning staff at a large hotel he owned in town. It was a big enough pay raise that I was able to stop waitressing. I laughed and joked, *Good thing Henry's such a good for nothing. I never would have gotten this job if it hadn't been for him!* Except suddenly I realized I was serious. Except suddenly I realized that it was true. I remember standing there and realizing that stupid minister had been … right. You *could* be thankful for all things if you trusted God enough to lead you where He needed you to go."

I poured Grannie a glass of water from her bedside pitcher and helped her take a generous sip. "My life was different after that, Olivia. When bad things happened or I screwed up and made a bad decision, I tried to always be thankful for the Lord's guidance and for *all* things in *all* circumstances. Gradually, I felt a peace in the midst of some of the worst storms because I *knew* – God regularly, faithfully proved it – that if I *just hung on and trusted,* God would get me to a safer spot as soon as possible." Grannie Blue looked at me. "So, I can be thankful for my Henry and the twenty-eight years of ups and downs that we had together because it brought me to a point where I'm a faithful, God-fearing woman. You can have regret tattoos but God can make them so beautiful – so different – that you forget what they were originally for. That's the magic of solid faith."

I suddenly wanted to sit there and talk to Grannie Blue all day. "You said that you married Henry before you knew about true love. What did you mean by that?"

She was quiet for a long time and I glanced at the clock again. Maybe I should get the nurse no matter what she originally said. *It was 3:36.*

"I came to *understand* Henry through God's tolerance and love. I cared for him until he drew his last breath and his last words to me were, 'You were always good to me, Edith. Thank you for that.' It was the kindest thing he ever could have said to me because it was sincere and it was true. I loved my babies; would have given up a million times if it hadn't been for them. I've outlived all three of them, you know. Now I love my grandbabies and great-grandbabies. I look at my life – what I was and what I am now, who I was and who I am now – and I can see God's true love and boundless caring for me in every second. I look forward to my next life so I can be reunited with those who went before me, and I delight in this life as I continue to watch God's grace and mercy unfold. Can I ask a favor of you?" she murmured before I could ask her if I should get the nurse again.

Uh-oh. "Sure."

"When I die, will you come to my memorial service?" She was looking at me seriously, breathing a little bit quickly. *It was 3:56.*

"Oh ... ah. Sure. Of course. If that's what you want."

Dipping her head once in a brief nod, she said, "Mmmm-hmmm. That's what I want."

"All right, then. I'll be there." In the silence I stared at Grannie Blue. Her wig was a bit skewed to the left. "Shall I go get the nurse?" I just couldn't sit there and watch her agony.

"Is it time?"

Yes. "Not 4:10 yet if that's what you mean."

"I'll wait a bit more than," she sighed. *It was 3:58.*

"When Bennie comes, he prays with me. That always helps. Do you pray?"

Oh God. "No. No I don't."

78

"You should. Everyone should have conversations with her Lord." She tried to take something off her table.

"Here, let me do that." I picked up a book. "Is this what you want?"

Grannie smiled. "My Bible. Read me something, will you?" I must have had that look on my face again that said I was completely and totally out of my element, and she winked at me. "Just open it up and start reading anywhere you want."

The book was well used, the black leather cover soft and supple like an expensive leather jacket. The pages were whisper thin and there were numerous bookmarks, ribbons, newspaper clippings, and other bits protruding out the edges. The book fell open in my lap and I begin to read. *"Oh God, You are my God. I earnestly search for You, my whole body longs for You in this parched and weary land where there is no water. I have seen You in Your sanctuary and gazed upon Your power and glory. Your unfailing love is better to me than life itself, how I praise You! I will honor You all the days of my life, lifting my hands to You in prayer. You satisfy me more than the richest of food, how I praise You. I lie awake mediating on You throughout the night. I think of all the ways You have helped me, and -"*

"And I dance with joy in the shadow of Your wings," Grannie Blue said on a sigh. *"I follow close behind You. Your strong right hand holds me securely."*

"All that trust Him, will praise Him," I heard clearly from behind me. "Psalm 63. I preached on that passage just this past Sunday."

The words have cast a spell of sorts on me and it took me a moment to turn, and then longer moments to process who had just spoken. "Preach?" I said to Benjamin. He was standing in the doorway. Today his tie was dark green and his suit was navy blue.

"God hasn't answered the prayer about Ben getting married and giving me grandchildren yet," Grannie Blue said between short gasps, "but He did answer my prayer about professions. My grandson the preacher!" she said with pride.

Preacher?! PREACHER?!? My mind reeled. I stood and said with incredible urgency, "It's 4:10! I have to get the nurse!!" and rushed past

Benjamin, down the shiny halls, and skidded to a stop in front of the nurse's station. "Grannie Blue needs her pain meds!"

"Grannie Blue?" the nurse said with a thoughtful frown and then smiled in recognition. "Edith Harayda. Got it." I stood in a daze watching nurses do things nurses do as people went in and out of Grannie's room.

Benjamin eventually came out and walked slowly down the hall towards me. His hands were in his pockets as he stood there looking at me, studying my face with great intensity. We stood in the hallway for long moments. "She's asleep," he finally told me. "I'm supposed to tell you that she's *very thankful* that you came and visited her today." When I looked at him silently he added, "I'll say thanks for coming to visit her, too. She loves company." At my continued silence he finally sighed deeply and said, "It's a big deal, huh?" and I thought, *Oh, you have no freaking idea.*

"I don't do nice guys." I swallowed, and then I shook my head at the impossibility of it all. "And preachers? Oh. No. *Never.*" He arched his eyebrows.

It was his turn to be silent. Finally he said, "I'm not proposing marriage, Olivia. I was just hoping to drink a cup of coffee with you."

I stepped into his personal space. "I thought it was a sin to lie," I murmured under my breath. I may have been off the playing field for a while, but I knew an interested male when I saw one. Preacher or no.

I watched his pupils dilate. He didn't step away but instead took a deep breath and then closed his eyes briefly. Finally, I was looking into his serious green eyes. "Just because I'm attracted to you doesn't mean I'm going to act on it. You're a beautiful woman, Olivia." He laughed. "But that's nothing new! I thought you were the most beautiful girl I'd ever laid eyes on when we were both *twelve!*" He reached out to touch the side of my face, still continuing to meet my steady gaze. "And right now I'm a man who'd *just like to have a cup of coffee with you.*"

Forget last's night's dream/nightmare. Forget my middle of the night panic about incorrect choices. Forget any of my forward progress with Aileen over what constituted an "appropriate relationship" and what constituted a "psychologically flawed association." Ben *was not* just a nice man who wanted to have a simple cup of coffee with me, *nor would he ever be.*

With dawning horror I realized he'd always been my point of reference of what "could be": that knight in shining armor that I'd given up all hope of finding a million years ago. Why, not only was he the only person I'd ever wanted to marry, he was *the only human being on the planet* who had never let me down. How powerful an attraction was that?! He was someone I'd never forgotten and standing there looking into his handsome, sincere face I was horrified to discover that he was also the epitome of everything I found attractive and sexually appealing in a man. My twisted subconscious had obviously used little Ben Harayda to design *that* blueprint, too.

Now maybe you're thinking *you only knew him for a few years between the ages of five and thirteen,* and I wouldn't disagree with you. Nor could I explain the attraction; *the pull* that I felt standing there looking at this man from my past. But they had been the happiest years of my life. Nothing since then, no matter how pitiful you want to judge me or my life, had ever come close. He was everything I'd missed, everything I'd ever wanted, and everything I'd ever hoped to retrieve. The potential of what he offered in addition to that cup of coffee … oh my. He was The Poster Child for why I avoided nice men and all wonderful possibilities they provided – as well as the disappointments.

I realized with heart pounding clarity that I had never been so terrified of another human being in all my life.

"I'm nothing but trouble and your guardian angel's already working overtime, Ben," I said glibly as I walked backwards away from him and his cologne and his intense expression. "Let's not push him over the edge, okay?" And I made tracks to my car as fast as my high-heeled feet could move me.

Therapy: The Hopeful Truth

Setting: Aileen Burkhart's Office. It's September 21, 2009 and we've taken the summer off. Why? Because I'm a teacher and teachers have a bizarre need to do totally different things during the months of July and August. This was a perfect excuse for me to avoid Aileen. I notice that Aileen's got a tan. And a new hairdo. And … well, well … I think I see a little tattoo peaking out of her low cut neckline.

Aileen: So? You were supposed to spend your summer coming up with some *healthy, mature, realistic* personal goals for the next year. How'd you do?

Me: Is that a tattoo I see, Aileen? Seems like one of us had a wild and crazy summer.

Aileen: (Smiling a smile that says my deflective tricks will continue to be ineffectual.) You were supposed to write them down. You *committed* to that.

Me: It's not fair how you take advantage of my newly found personal integrity. Just because I made the mistake of telling you that honest and truth were my personal mantra – in a weak moment I might add. When you use words like "honest", "promise", "commit", and "truth" it's like I'm hypnotized or something. I've got nowhere to hide when you do that.

Aileen: You have realized that your integrity is your greatest strength, haven't you? Many people refuse to acknowledge the reality of who they are or what they've done or where they're destined to end up. It's a good thing, Olivia.

Me: I wrote the list. But it's a good thing I had eight weeks to do it.

Aileen: It was hard.

Me: (A bit choked up in the throat, I nod. Aileen stays silent probably hoping I'll cry. She loves that. But I rally.) Here.

Aileen: (Shaking her head and crossing her arms.) Nope. I don't want to read it. *I want you to say it out loud to me.*

Me: Sometimes, I really hate you. Do you know that?

Aileen: Yes, I know.

Me: (We sit for a good few moments in silence. Both of us stubborn, determined women. Finally, I unfold the piece of paper I've had clutched in my hand all along.) You know, we started our relationship with me bringing you a piece of paper. (Aileen blinks at me but stays silent.) Okay, here goes. These are the things I most want out of life. Kind of like if I had three magic wishes or a sorcerer's wand.

Aileen: But these things have to be realistic. *Doable.*

Me: (Narrowing my eyes.) It's *my friggin' list.* I wrote what I wanted most. (Aileen sighs and picks up her pen and pad. Apparently she'll fight me on this later if necessary.)

#1: I'd like to die having spent a majority of the rest of my life happy. I'm acknowledging that I've got to pay my dues regarding my share of disappointment and unhappiness, but I'd like to not look back on my deathbed and think, *Damn, I should have done this or that …* So that means I'm going to work to consciously make good choices that will have positive results.

#2: I'd like to have a best friend again. I thought back over my life and the times that I had one were … better. Even when things were really bad, having a friend made things easier. But it's got to be a quality relationship. I don't want to have to pretend I'm someone I'm not, nor do I want to have to hide my … foibles. And I realize that in order to accomplish this I'll have to be a little bit more … open … and willing … and (oh brother) … nice. Clotilde's in the running. I've even considered Erin. But maybe I'm going to have to just pick a stranger off the street.

#3: I'd like to settle things with my mother. It's time, I guess. Clear the air so to speak. Clean out all the dark closets and dank rooms. Not that I need to have detailed explanations or gory details, but I'd like to sit down and talk with her and listen to whatever she wants and needs to tell me. She told me one time that I could ask her hard questions and she'd give me answers. Hell, when I was going through my big crisis right after I found out The Truth she practically wrote me a book, she sent me so many letters trying to explain things. It's time to put this dog to bed.

Aileen: That's it?

Me: (I think: *What, does she want blood?!*) This isn't enough?

Aileen: This is tremendous progress, Olivia. I'm very pleased with what you've come up with. These are all noble, necessary goals. But I don't need to tell you that; you're an exceptionally intelligent woman. I'd just hoped … (she looks at me pointedly but doesn't finish her sentence.)

Me: (Shaking my head in disappointment at Aileen's foolish expectations and hopes.) I told you Aileen, *I don't believe in love.*

All truth is simple ... is that not doubly a lie?[13]

9: Memory Is A Fickle Thing

Tuesday, March 23, 2010

You're probably thinking how horrible I am that I haven't mentioned Vera's death since Reverend Harmer called me and I went and collected her things at Integrated Health Center. Of course, if that thought never occurred to you then you might consider making an appointment to see Aileen, too.

Aileen says that emotions like sorrow and anger, but also joy and hope (and love – which I've discounted), are "viable emotions that shouldn't be suppressed." I laughed when she originally said that and reminded her about my favorite emotion – anger – and what complications it could cause should I "let it all out" and annihilate much of the eastern seaboard. But Aileen pointed out (and I was forced to concede the validity of her statement) that the only emotion I've ever really done well *was* anger. Perhaps my anger was working overtime ... Perhaps if my anger could be ratcheted down a bit and I *allowed* my other emotions the opportunity to surface, life might become a bit more ... balanced.

Leaving Grannie Blue that second visit (and cursing myself for committing to come to her eventual memorial service) I refused to think about Ben, and his sincere green eyes, and the seductive words he'd uttered ... *I'm a man who'd just like to have a cup of coffee with you.* You see, he didn't just *say* those words to me, he *gave them* to me. He stood there with his open and honest face, close enough that I could smell his very appealing aftershave and feel the warmth of him by his gentle touch on my face, and delivered that line with all the intensity of a ... desperately genuine, kind

85

man. With that phrase I knew that not only did he want to have coffee with me, but that he had wanted to have coffee with me for a very long time and would continue to want to have coffee with me probably for the rest of his life. Some invitation, huh? It was going to take quite a bit of work to forget about *that*.

So, I drove directly ... to my mother's house to talk about Vera. See? I got to the topic of Vera eventually.

I just needed something bigger and more terrifying to make me move in that direction.

Once my mother and Alec had recovered from the shock of my impromptu visit and realized there was no disaster, we sat like civilized adults on their front porch and discussed what had to be done. Vera had been very thorough in the ... advanced preparations ... of her death, and Integrated Health Center had handed me a typed out list of arrangements, conditions, and demands that she herself had put together. She had already paid for immediate cremation and wanted absolutely no memorial service. The list provided the name, address, phone number and email address of the lawyer in possession of her will, and I was the designated executor. It didn't appear that there was very much for me to do except sign things and oversee these final aspects of Vera's life that she literally couldn't do for herself once she was dead. I was, quite clearly, a necessary evil who, I realized, *hadn't even followed through on her last request* and brought her a carton of Winstons.

"She was quite brilliant," my mother murmured as she looked at Vera's precise list. "I'm sure you get your number sense from her, Olivia. Did you know that she was awarded a full, four-year scholarship to Princeton when she graduated from high school?" Alec was holding her hand, his thumb gently stroking. "I've always wondered if she would have been any happier had I never come along and she'd been able to get her degree like she'd always wanted ..."

"My life surely wouldn't have turned out as well," Alec said quietly.

My mother smiled at him, leaning over to clunk her head with his. "Mine either," she said ruefully.

"I'll help you go through the house," Alec said to me.

"So will I," my mother said with a little bit of force.

"You don't have to," Alec said turning to my mother. "Olivia and I can do it. And I'm sure Dan and Erin will help." The two of them are looking at each other doing that nonspoken communication thing couples sometimes do.

"It doesn't make a difference, Alec. I've been in the house as recently as a few years ago."

"Enjoyed it so much that you can't wait to get back, huh?"

"At least I know I won't have to worry about getting in any arguments with my mother."

"Yeah, all you have to deal with are the *fond memories*," Alec said pointedly.

Fond memories. They're talking in code but it's not to keep things from me. Rather, it's to put easier words on horrible things. *Fond memories* I know referred to the house where my mother lived with Vera until she moved out to get married to Dean. *Fond memories* as in the location where I know my conception took place. *Fond memories* as in the location where my mother was raped by my father.

In my time with Aileen, I've recovered some memories of my mother. Maybe that's not the right term, but they're memories that morphed and changed once I began to view my past with a more objective eye.

Some things I hadn't thought of for years just came to me at odd times. I'd wake up in the middle of the night and they would just vividly be there. Or I'd be out running errands and a smell or a feeling would trigger a flash of memory so abrupt that I'd stop and stand there as the world continued on. Other times, memories I'd held onto and thought of endlessly would all of a sudden shift and change. What I thought was true suddenly wasn't quite accurate anymore, and I'd realize that I'd not been honest with the way things really were.

They're not memories that my subconscious has suppressed because they're too horrible to face. Actually, quite the opposite. They're memories that are so soft and … quiet … that they just got smothered by the force of my feelings of anger and betrayal.

In one memory, I'm about eight I guess. I'm already on the Anger Train. We were living in the ratty little apartment we'd first moved into where Erin and I shared the only bedroom and my mother slept on the living room couch. I missed Dean so much I slept with one of his dirty construction tee shirts that smelled of sweat, cigarettes, and that familiar old alcohol smell. I had woken up to a sound that I'd come to associate with my mother, and had lain in bed listening to the whir of the sewing machine. She would make clothes for me and Erin and often sewed after we went to bed and/or before she left for work in the morning. Sometimes, I'd wake up in the middle of the night to pee and she'd even be sewing then. I wondered if she even slept some nights.

It's the one thing I could always admit that I liked about my mother. She could sew *anything* and I mean anything. All I had to do was point to something on television or in a store window or in a magazine and say, "This is the coat I want" and it would magically appear. She even made our pajamas because I didn't like the scratchy tags and sharp seams that store bought varieties always had.

I heard my mother walking down the hall to our bedroom and I closed my eyes and pretended to be asleep. In our room, I heard her open our small closet door and get out a hanger. Quietly, she tip-toed over to Erin and I heard her fix the covers because Erin always kicked them off. Then she came over to me and I felt the strength of her stare as she stood looking down at me. She didn't have to adjust any covers because I was always burrowed under sheets and blankets and a million stuffed animals and … one dirty construction tee shirt. My mother sighed and tucked Dean's tee shirt closer to my face. "I'm sorry, Olivia," I barely heard her whisper.

After she left, I opened my eyes and saw hanging on the open closet door what she'd left. It was a magnificent jean jacket. It looked like it was bought in a store, but I was with her when she bought the denim material on the clearance table for fifty cents a yard. It was exactly what I'd wanted and I jumped out of bed and walked over to examine it, absolutely delighted. It was a biker denim jacket, with a wild diagonal zipper that cut across the front of the coat and ended high up on the right shoulder. At the waist was a big, brass buckle that I knew cost almost as much as the material did. I touched the sleeves where she'd even managed to sew some truly excellent decorative patches that she must have gotten at a second hand shop or something. *"Oh wow!!"* I said in amazed wonder.

"Like it?" I jumped because I hadn't realized that my mother had been standing there all along watching me examine the coat. She gave me one of her rare smiles. "The zipper was a pain in the butt to do, but I think it looks just like the one Madonna was wearing in that picture you showed me."

Even at eight years old I couldn't do it. I just couldn't reward her. Looking at her standing there in that ugly, bare hallway with the awful tan paint and feeling the uneven, gritty floor beneath my bare feet I just couldn't forget that this was all her fault. "It's okay," I said in a purposely flat, toneless voice.

"Try it on," she said with forced enthusiasm, "let's see how it fits!"

"Nah, I have to take a shower," I told her and walked past her into the bathroom.

Although I wore that glorious coat constantly for almost two full years I never once told her thanks. And she never mentioned it again.

In another memory, Erin and I are sitting and waiting on the back steps for Dean to come get us. It was summer and we had a big plastic bag between us that had bathing suits and towels because Dean had promised to take us to a friend's house that had a big, built-in pool. With a diving board. And a slide. Erin and I sat and waited so long we finally had to move to a different spot because we were starting to get sunburned.

Erin wanted to go inside. She was thirsty. She was hot. Then she said the unpardonable thing, *"I don't think Daddy's coming again, Olivia."* I remembered going ballistic. My mother had been so unenthusiastic about us going. She'd acted annoyed when I had asked for a big bag and hadn't been eager for me to get the bathing suits and towels together. I knew she just didn't want us to have any fun with Dean. I turned to say something angry and mean to Erin and suddenly my mother was there.

"How's it going out here girls?" she said. When she sat down beside us on the steps, she had three tall glasses of iced tea and a package of Fig Newtons, our personal favorite cookie.

"I don't think Daddy's coming again," Erin said and gave me a nervous glance.

"Well, I just called Daddy," my mother said and she took a sip of iced tea. "He was having a little bit of trouble with his truck."

I knew what that really meant. Either he'd had an accident with it or the man with the tow truck had come and taken it again. Either way it meant that we wouldn't get to see Dean for weeks, or probably months, until he could get it all straightened out again.

My mother was eating a Fig Newton. "I offered to drive you girls over, but Daddy's having a pretty rough day today."

I knew what that really meant, too. It meant that probably, when my mother called, my father was still asleep. Having a rough day usually meant he wanted to just sit on the couch because he had a headache from being out late the night before. If we were still living there, he and I would have had a wonderful time just hanging out: Daddy and his best girl, Livvie.

"So I was wondering if you two would be willing to go swimming with *me* instead. What do you think?"

Erin started jumping up and down and saying, "Yes! Yes! Yes!" She even spilled her iced tea but my mother just shrugged.

"What about you, Olivia? We could go up to the beach at Round Valley and swim."

I knew what she was doing. She was trying to get us to forget about Daddy. *I'll never forget about Daddy.* I looked at my pink and blue Jelly sandals. "There's no diving board or slide at Round Valley," I said.

"Can we get ice cream?" Erin asked. "Daddy said he'd take us for ice cream, too."

"I'll see if I can swing that."

I knew what that meant, too. It meant 'no' because there wasn't enough money but she didn't want to say that right away.

"What do you say, Olivia?" my mother asked as she ate a second Fig Newton.

"Say yes, Livvie!!" Erin said. She was still hopping up and down and my mother picked up her iced tea glass.

"Okay," I finally said.

This memory was a different kind of memory because I'd never forgotten it. I'd just remembered it for years colored with anger. When I finally was able to think about it *without* anger, I saw that not once had my mother said an unkind thing about my father that day. Not once. She'd even tried to help him out by offering to drive us over. And when I finally thought about the whole day at Round Valley, about the hotdogs we'd eaten and the sodas we'd drank *and the ice cream we'd enjoyed*, I had absolutely no recollection of my mother eating one single thing that whole day but those two Fig Newtons she had eaten sitting on the steps.

Therapy: The Truth About My Mother – Part IV

Setting: Aileen's Burkhart's office and it's November 2, 2009. This month my mother and Alec will celebrate their one year anniversary as husband #4 and wife. Hooray. We've been picking apart My List for weeks and I have no hope at all that today will bring anything different. But Aileen surprises me.

Aileen: What are your plans for the upcoming holidays?

Me: You extending me an invitation?

Aileen: We've never talked about holidays. Do they constitute good or bad memories for you?

Me: (Thinking …) You know how people often get depressed around the holidays? Because the holidays never turn out to be as "nice" or as "wonderful" as they'd hoped or dreamed or remembered? (Aileen nods.) Well, holidays for me were always pretty good for that same reason. I never had that little girl perfect memory of holidays because I was always wrapped up in the misery of day to day. So when Christmas or Thanksgiving or a birthday or … hell … Fourth of July came around I never expected much. (Thinking again …) But they often turned out … pretty good.

Aileen: Can you give me some examples?

Me: Dean was usually on his best behavior because he knew he couldn't disappoint. Which meant he usually went down in a flaming ball of disastrous fire within a day or two, but still … I usually managed to take a break from the Anger Train because it was hard to stay mad at the world when the world was trying its best to make you smile: Dean, Erin, Grandmother Miriam and Grampie Taylor … Even once my mother and Dean divorced big efforts were always made on holidays. Usually we were together. My mother always made sure there was something special to have or get or do … even if it was some homemade crap or just a break from the usual routine … There were a number of Christmases where she made Erin and I each a shoebox full of doll clothes for our Barbies …

92

dresses, hats, coats, boots … It was like uncovering a box full of buried treasure.

Aileen: (Aileen perks up like she's just been electro-shocked.) Whoa-hoo! Is that a positive comment I'm hearing about your mother?!

Me: (Giving Aileen The Glare, a look honed to exquisite perfection by most seasoned teachers – I'm still working on mine …) If I haven't made any progress after over a year and a half of therapy with you Aileen, that's not saying much … *for you and your skills*.

Aileen: (Grinning delightedly.) So you are absolutely, unequivocally acknowledging some positive behavior on your mother's part. We've danced around such a thing, you've admitted that perhaps your past perceptions may have been incorrectly skewed, but you've never flat out acknowledged a constructive contribution in your past by your mother to me.

Me: Want me to take a bow? Look, I get your point, okay Aileen? It's time I stopped viewing the world from eight year old selfish eyes … or even fifteen year old angry eyes. I *was wrong* about a hell of a lot of stuff.

Aileen: (Sighing.) I want you to cut yourself a break, Olivia. Being wrong isn't a crime - refusing to change when you know you are wrong is. No one's keeping score here except yourself. (Aileen leans forward with intensity.) And that includes *your mother.*

Me: You sure about that?

Aileen: Why don't you ask *her?* What exactly are you waiting for? Tell me honestly, what have you got to lose, Olivia? Or, more importantly, *what have you got to gain?*

If you're going to tell people the truth, be funny or they'll kill you.[14]

10: Funerals Are Part of Life
Thursday, March 25, 2010

Dedicated professional that I was, I stumbled out of my front door clutching my travel mug filled to the brim with strong black coffee and my briefcase containing period five's graded tests. If it hadn't been six-thirty, I might have taken note of the beautiful spring morning, the birds singing, the crocuses and daffodils standing proudly in my garden ... but it *was* six-thirty so I could have cared less. At least two mornings a week I tried to get to school early to do some of the nine million things teachers need to do when they didn't have students. Except because I always brought a box of Dunkin' Donut Munchkins and was always willing to help if you showed up at my door I was rarely without students. It was a good thing, but it was also a bad thing. First period started at seven forty-five, so if traffic was good I might just accomplish what I hadn't managed to do yet this week – get some early morning work done on my own. Mentally I calculated *six more days until Spring Break* as I made my way to my car.

I liked my condo. It was a cute two bedroom, two floor place that tried hard to look like a small little cottage – if you blurred your eyes and didn't take note of the Sampson's place attached on the right. I had a corner unit which gave me more windows and more places to plant flowers when I felt inclined (which was rarely, I admit, but I liked the option). The condos were clustered around a large communal parking area, and as I made my way across my postage-stamp front lawn to my parking space I heard the unfamiliar roar of a motorcycle.

My nephew Liam loved motorcycles and fancied himself an expert on them. When he was little and you asked, "What kind of motorcycle is that, Liam?" he'd inform you with all seriousness, "It's a big … black one." Now he'd tell you the make, the model, and the engine size. I watched in growing surprise as A Blue One made its way directly toward me and stopped.

The driver was dressed in ratty old jeans torn at one knee and big sneakers that hadn't been laced properly. A leather jacket, gloves and a dark helmet obscured other details, so I did what I'd learned in self defense class and put my finger on the red panic button on my key chain and scanned my surroundings for potential neighborly support.

I racked my brain trying to fit a student – past or present – into the biker's form. I didn't broadcast my home address but I did live in a town very close to the one I taught in and occasionally ran into students and parents alike. Just when I made the decision to go back into my condo, the biker reached up, unhooked his helmet and took it off. My mouth dropped open in surprise.

Surprise because it's Ben. Surprise because the ripped denim/leather jacket clad/motorcycle persona was not one I would have attributed to him. And surprise because he looked like … hell (if you'll pardon the poor analogy). He was unshaven and his eyes were red-rimmed; there were dark shadows under both his eyes that looked like bruises.

Grannie Blue.

Immediately I sat my briefcase at my feet and coffee mug on the roof of my car and walked over to him as he sat on his bike. "When?" I asked quietly.

"Late yesterday afternoon," he said in a voice rough with sorrow. He went to say something else and then swallowed and squinted off into the distance.

Putting my hand on his arm I said, "I'm so sorry, Ben." It was a useless thing to say even if it was meant with all sincerity.

He turned and looked at me with sorrow filled eyes. "I've been riding aimlessly all night. Thinking about her and her life. Her influence."

He sighed and rubbed his face with his gloved hand. "I'm supposed to do her memorial service. Tomorrow."

Good grief, that had to be difficult. I'd never really thought of life from a minister's perspective. Didn't they have a book or something with all the words written in it for marriages and funerals and confirmations and ... stuff? All you had to do was just look up the category in the index, plug in the appropriate names in the applicable spots, and then read the words with a sincere expression on your face? *Dearly beloved ... With this ring ... Ashes to ashes ...* But doing such a thing for someone you loved or cared about ... that had to be almost impossible.

He seemed to shake himself. "She wanted me to give you this," he said as he reached into one of the saddle bags to pull out a tightly wrapped package. Managing a tiny smile he said, "I have no idea what's in this. Apparently she got one of the nurses to help her do this just the other day." Something heavy was wrapped inside a number of plastic shopping bags. Taped on the outside of the package was an envelope which said in neat handwriting, 'To be delivered to Olivia Kelly, Granddaughter of Vera Cummings'. "I'm pretty sure that the nurse wrote what she dictated ... I didn't know if I'd ever see you ... or when ... so I'd planned to leave it in your mailbox."

Frowning I said, "How'd did you know where I lived? I'm not listed ..."

He had the grace to look a little embarrassed. "I'm a part-time chaplain at IHC so I have access to records. Your address was listed as part of Vera's information." He searched my face. "I ... well, I ..." He cleared his throat. "That first day that I realized who you were, I looked in Vera's file to see ..."

Taking pity on him I murmured, "It's okay, Ben," and took the package.

Before I had time to think about it I stepped close and hugged him – leather jacket, helmet, and all. I could feel his start of surprise, a long moment of hesitation, and then I'm suddenly being held in a tight embrace.

Finally he pulled away and I gave him a moment as he looked off into the distance and sniffed.

Finally, I asked, "Are you going to be okay?"

He took a deep breath and then slowly nodded. He looked me directly in the eye. "I'm a believing man, Olivia. I know for a fact that even in the darkest, hardest times that good can be found. I also know that life has to have sorrow as well as joy, tears as well as laughter. Grannie Blue taught me that. Not necessarily because she *said* that, but because she *lived* that." As he kick started the bike and revved the engine I could see his green eyes crinkle, so he must have been smiling. "Have a good day, Olivia. Mine will be better now that I've had a chance to see you."

I stood watching him roar out of the parking lot and thought, *a motorcycle riding, black leather jacket wearing preacher man ... what an intriguing novelty.*

I didn't open Grannie Blue's package until I got home that night, dealt with a phone call from Vera's lawyer, ate dinner, attempted some bonding time with Sophie, and changed into my pajamas. In other words, I stalled for as long as possible. Clueless as to what she could have sent me it still seemed to have "Danger" written all over it. Finally, when all procrastination avenues had been exhausted (except cleaning the bathroom which I just didn't have the energy for) I sat down in my favorite comfy chair and tore open the envelope.

Immediately I realized that Ben had been wrong. Apparently, Grannie Blue had only enlisted a nurse's assistance to make sure the package was addressed and put together properly. It was immediately obvious that the nurse had taken no part in writing this letter because the handwriting was practically illegible and it took me long moments to sort through what I was meant to read. Then I sat for a long time staring at what was written on the paper, disbelieving what I saw:

ALWAYS REMEMBER:
Love is patient and kind.
Love never gives up, never loses faith, is always hopeful and endures forever.

97

Three things will last forever — faith, hope, and love.
But the greatest of these is love.

Be thankful for all things, Olivia.
Even dying, I got to spend some time talking with you, and that was something to be
thankful about.
Love, Grannie

Inside the package was Grannie Blue's Bible.

The Memorial Service for Edith Marie Harayda (AKA Grannie Blue) was held on Friday morning, March 26th, 2010, at eleven o'clock in the morning at Christ's Church, two towns over from where I lived. I took a personal day from work to attend my "grandmother's memorial service," and no one knew the truth that my *real* grandmother was in a cardboard container waiting for me to pick her up at Bethany Crematorium. Hey, I can only deal with adult difficulties gradually and you had to admit that it had been *quite a week* for me.

Christ's Church was bright, open and airy with blue as the predominant color scheme. I couldn't remember the last time I'd been in church although I did have childhood memories of attending church (always with Ben's family). While I'd never been pulled to attend as an adult, I realized as I sat in the far back row that I had fond memories of church just the same. I read through the program I'd been given celebrating the life of Edith Marie Harayda, AKA Grannie Blue. There was a picture of her with her 'real' blue hair; it's the Grannie Blue I remembered that played kickball with us in the middle of the street.

Snatches of quiet conversation floated around me, interspersed with soft chuckles and exclamations of, "I couldn't believe she did that either!!" on more than one occasion. I saw *a lot* of Yankees, Nets, and Jets sports attire on young and old alike, too. These were Grannie Blue's friends and family, and I was sure everyone had a story to tell.

"Pastor Ben!" I heard behind me and turned to see Benjamin in all his ministerial glory. Actually, he was just wearing another nice suit with a dark blue tie, and I wondered why I was so relieved that he wasn't wearing dark flowing robes and a pointy hat.

"What's up, Jen?" he asked a tremendously attractive young woman in a form-fitting dress and spike heels.

"Have you seen Phillip? We were supposed to rehearse one more time and he's disappeared!" Jen looked left and right into the growing crowd, her big gold earrings flashing underneath her shiny, dark hair.

"Upstairs in the sound room. I think he's changing mikes."

"Oh, thanks."

"Ben, so sorry to hear about your Grandmother," an elderly man said. "Church just won't be the same without her sitting in the front pew each Sunday stirring things up."

"You're so right, John. I'm going to have to leave it up to Amanda here to provide critiques now when I preach," Ben said to the diminutive older woman standing next to John. As Amanda stepped in to give Ben a hug his eyes scanned the crowd and came to rest directly on me. They widen in shock and surprise. I gave him a small smile and a slight nod hello.

"Would you excuse me?" Ben said to the couple as he shook both their hands and then walked toward me.

Since I was in the last pew he walked over and squatted down behind me so that we were eye level. "Thank you for coming," he said in a quiet voice. "I never expected to see you here."

"I promised Grannie Blue that I'd come to her memorial service that day we talked. I told her I always keep my promises."

He stared at me solemnly and then cocked his head in thought. "Always?"

I grimaced. "It's a curse." I looked around and whispered, "I've done stuff in my life that will probably send me straight to hell – do not pass go, do not collect $200 - but my word has always been my bond. If I said I'd do something, I do it. You can always count on that."

Ben looked at me intently taking in my carefully arranged (and serious) hairdo, my specifically chosen (and maturely subtle) jewelry and my appropriately subdued (and plain black) dress. "A good quality to have and not one many people aspire to anymore."

"That's me," I said with skilled sarcasm, "always someone you can count on…" I purposely left the ending of the sentence open hoping he was wise enough to understand that the statement wasn't necessarily a positive one. I had a flash of his red-rimmed eyes in my parking lot yesterday. He may have cleaned up well but the sadness was still right there beneath the surface. I have an incredibly strong urge to reach out and touch him and consequently I fist both my hands in my lap. "How are you holding up? Is there anything I can do?"

He took a deep breath and when he spoke he was so quiet that I had to lean towards him to catch everything. "The whole family is hanging in there. We all had time to say our good-byes to Grannie. Now it's just going to take some time to adjust to life without her. She's always been a force." Ben leaned in and said, "Olivia, can I ask a favor?" I eyed him suspiciously as it was highly apparent I was being railroaded into something. Holding up one hand to deflect my obviously less than kind thoughts, he murmured, "I was just going to ask you one more time if you'd go and have that cup of coffee with me." His voice dropped even lower making me lean in even closer. "You know how you're here because you promised Grannie Blue?" I nodded hesitantly. "Well … she made me promise that I'd ask you out to coffee once more *the very next time I saw you*." He gave me a sweet smile but couldn't disguise the twinkle in his eye. "Of course she didn't let me know that she'd gotten a promise from you that you'd attend her Memorial Service."

He couldn't possibly be hitting on me here in a church – his church – at his grandmother's funeral. Could he? "You're asking me out? Now?"

I grinned delightedly as he blushed and muttered, "I've spent a lot of time at the hospital with Grannie, Olivia. It's kind of like an alternate universe and you often walk out stunned at what's been said and what

100

you've promised. I recognize that this isn't the optimal time or place but I try very hard to keep my word too and …"

I remembered sitting with Grannie Blue that afternoon and sighed. "If you only promised to ask me out to coffee 'once more' it seems like all I have to do is turn you down one more time and we've both met all our obligations." At his silent stare and continual blush I knew that there were definitely more promises made regarding me and coffee. That Grannie Blue was one sneaky woman. Determined, too. "Just coffee?"

"Just coffee," he nodded with wide-eyed, innocence. "I'd just like to have an opportunity to catch up with you. It's important to me, Olivia. I've never forgotten you … Grannie always … well … she knew how much I … well …" He sighed in frustration and looked out the window.

I know what he was talking about. I had never really forgotten him either. *It's just coffee,* I thought to myself. Maybe my own subconscious was reading more into this than there really was. After all, it *was* a pretty incredible coincidence that we'd run into each other like this after all these years. And that we still remembered each other so fondly. "Okay."

His relief was palpable. Standing, he touched my hand briefly, "Thanks."

I heard someone calling, "Pastor Ben!" and he looked down at me. It seemed as if he wanted to say something else but he was called again, and this time the tone was more urgent. "Pastor Ben!!"

"Go on," I urged him with a tiny wave, too.

Not five seconds ticked by before a teenager in the pew in front of me turned and gave me a brilliant smile. "Hi!" she said, "I'm Kate! So you're dating Pastor Ben?"

I actually turned and looked behind me, thinking she was talking to someone else. "Huh?" I finally managed.

"I heard you two talking and him asking you out for coffee," Kate said.

I could have pointed out to her that this was *a funeral,* and that in a few moments Ben would be giving a *eulogy for his grandmother,* but I deal with

101

teenagers all the time and knew the pointlessness of common sense. So I just stared at her.

"My friend Mandy knows you," Kate said holding up her phone, alive with flashing texts. "She's in your second period math class. She's sitting over there." Kate pointed and I turned horrified eyes in the direction she'd indicated.

There was Mandy Ennis, waving frantically at me, cell phone clutched in her hand and mouthing dramatically, "HELLOOOO!!"

Oh no. Oh God ... "We're not dating!" I tried to explain to Kate desperate to stop the texting tide that had probably already begun. "We're just friends!!"

Kate gave me a knowing look. "We've been trying to fix up Pastor Ben *forever!* This is so cool! He *never, ever* brings a date to *anything.*"

Is she implying that Ben has brought me as his date to his grandmother's funeral?!

"- and now he's going to bring you to the coffee social afterwards where *everyone* can meet you."

"Coffee social?!" I gasped before I could stop myself.

Kate nodded, took a moment to text with furious intensity, and then said, "After the memorial service. There's always coffee and cake and sandwiches for everyone so people can visit and get to meet everyone."

My face must have shown my absolute horror.

"Oh, don't worry. I'll stick by you. I know everyone. I'll introduce you." She took a moment to send probably another fifteen simultaneous texts. "I just texted Mandy and told her to meet us after the service. She'll help introduce you, too."

Like the launching of an ocean liner (the *Titanic??*) I sat and watched with growing dismay as the texting frenzy did its work. The place was crawling with kids. Teenagers popped up all over the sanctuary to stare in my direction, and an entire row of youth leaned over from up in the balcony to get a look at me.

Once again I thought loudly and clearly, *I want my mommy.*

Therapy: The Truth About Love ...

Setting: Aileen Burkhart's Office. It's January 11, 2010, the start of a new
year, and I'm a little tired of being ... difficult. It's not a nice
discovery to realize that I'm not any easier to work with than a
significant number of my students. I have to admit that I am ...
better than when I first sat down on this boring, brown couch.
Suddenly, I understand why Aileen ... puts up with all this ... It's
the same reason I decided I wanted to teach. To make a
difference.

Me: It's my turn to ask some questions.

Aileen: O-kay. Shoot.

Me: What do you think is the biggest area that I still need to work on?

Aileen: (She sighs and closes her eyes. I bet she even counts to ten.) It
doesn't work that way, Olivia. You know that. I don't have a
check off list that I'm waiting to complete so that once it's done I
can say, 'Okay, Olivia! You're finished!"

Me: But you *do* have an expectation of what a healthy, whole human being
should be like. The fact that I'm *here* implies that I'm *not done*. I'm
just asking you to tell me what you *know* I still have to work on.

Aileen: (Taking a minute to really look closely at me.) You're different
today ...

Me: It's 2010, Aileen. I'm not getting any younger...

Aileen: Well, I'm not going to spell it out, Olivia. That won't do you any
good. *You* know the answer to your question. *My* job is to just
lead you to the point where you can acknowledge the answer. *Your*
job is to learn how to look at your life – at any day or any time –
and evaluate *on your own* what was good and what you still need to
work on. Anger might be your favorite emotion but arguing is still
one of your most favorite activities. You want to be finished with
therapy? It's *never* going to happen if I *tell* you things that you need
to learn. *That's* what people do who *don't go* to therapy.

103

Me: Mumbo-jumbo psychological B.S. (I sneer a tiny bit.) It's time for
you to earn your pay, Aileen. Come on. Let me hear it. Tell me
what you really think.

Aileen: (She sighs. She so put out, you know. But she's got a glint in her
eye and I know she's actually got me exactly where she wants me.)
Okay, Olivia. Watch. I'll give you an example about why giving
you a list of things you still need to work on won't work. I'll just
put one thing out there for us to discuss. In fact, there has been
one subject I've broached before with you, Olivia. But you don't
want to discuss it. Because you don't believe in it.

Me: (I roll my eyes.) You're talking about love. (She arches an eyebrow.)
I know you are. And you're right; I'm not going to discuss it!
What's the big, friggin' deal?! Why aren't I allowed to believe or
disbelieve in something?! It's a *free country*, isn't it? *Isn't it?!*
(Suddenly, I'm breathing heavily like I've just run a mile.)

Aileen: (Aileen's doing her silent thing; watching me like a rattler watches a
mouse. After long moments of silence, she breaks first.) Okay,
let's hear it again, Olivia. Tell me how there is absolutely no
possibility of love anywhere in the world. Here's your chance to
convince me once and for all and I'll never bring the subject up
again.

Me: (But I'm silent now. Big time silent, because suddenly I feel on the
verge of tears. *Crap.* I sniffle. I sigh.) I can't.

Aileen: You can't what?

Me: I can't tell you that there is absolutely no possibility of love anywhere
in the world! (I say it angrily, almost spitting out the words.)

Aileen: Oh? Why is that? Where in the world have you seen love, Olivia?
(She watches me stand up and walk to the door. It's obvious I'm
leaving.) That's something you need to check off your 'get better
list.' The ability to say your truth - *out loud.* Instead of keeping
them inside and burying them under mountains of indignant anger.
Come on now, don't run away, Olivia. This is important. Critical.
Maybe even number one on your list.

Me: (I stand there with my back to her and my hand on the doorknob. But I don't leave.)

Aileen: You've spent your whole life being angry: at your mother, at your nonexistent father, at Dean Kelly ... Why? Do you want me to tell you why, Olivia? It's all about this nonexistent emotion you refuse to discuss. I've got a different perspective and for once I will just tell you instead of making you spend heaven knows how many more weeks and months dancing around this topic you refuse to face. You *missed* love as a child. Big time. And rightly so. *You don't miss things that don't exist, Olivia.* You miss things that you need but you don't have enough of. Due to circumstances beyond your control you were raised within an atmosphere that was ... stingy ... with its love. And the hungrier you got for it, the more you recognized its scarcity. Somewhere along this road called life it became easier to believe that this thing you craved so desperately simply didn't exist. It was certainly easier to believe that than the idea that you in particular were simply unlovable. That *incorrect* perception has gotten you through life to this point but has also perpetuated your unhappiness. There are examples of love everywhere – even in your dysfunctional childhood, Olivia. I can't make you acknowledge them, though, any more than I can keep you coming back to see me. But I can continue to keep trying to point you in the right direction so that maybe, possibly, eventually, *finally* you will at least face in the right direction. You came in here today with a new and different attitude. Good for you! You want me to tell you what I really think so here it is in a nutshell: *Love exists and you, Olivia Kelly, are entitled to have it be an integral part of your life.*

There's a world of difference between truth and facts.[15]

11: Big Fish In Small Ponds

Friday, March 25, 2010

"I spent the first third of my life not thinking twice about how unique Grannie Blue was," Ben began. Behind him, projected on the wall were various candid shots of Grannie Blue in all stages of her life – from black and white photos of her as a young girl, to formal wedding poses, to glimpses of her as a wife, mother, friend, grandmother ... and crazy old lady. I *think* I see at least two pictures that even include me – all wild hair and skinny legs and sad, violet eyes. "She was just my Grannie who pitched a mean curve ball, made the world's best macaroni and cheese, and would always stick up for me when I wanted to stay up late to watch a game on television.

"Grannie taught me that life was what you made it, that love was a conscious choice, and faith was the only foundation worth building your life on." Ben grinned. "And that was before I turned thirteen.

"Adolescence makes you stupid." The people at Grannie Blue's memorial service chuckled at this. "If you're sitting out there disagreeing with me it's only because you're presently in adolescence and well ... I rest my case." More laughter. "As a teenager, I'm ashamed to say Grannie Blue embarrassed me. Who wanted a crazy old grandmother with blue hair, red high-top sneakers and a Jets jacket showing up at their games? And, anyone who heard her make comments during my sermons had a *vague idea* what she was like on the sidelines of any games I played. She had loud, opinionated comments for me, my coach, the ref ..." Ben shook his head, "it was not a good thing for anyone involved." More laughter.

106

"Strangely, my friends liked her. The guys thought she was cool because she could rattle off player and game stats with the best of them, and the girls got a kick out of her because of her unique ... fashion sense." Ben rolled his eyes and everyone cracked up. I thought, *I never knew a funeral could have so much laughter.*

"When the guys came over to hang out they always wanted to know where Grannie Blue was and if she'd made a batch of her brownies. My high school baseball coach asked her to be a chaperone at the senior prom and I worried for *weeks* that," Ben paused and I think he might have blushed a bit, "they were actually dating." He waved his hand as if to ward off the idea and everyone roared with laughter. "I spent a lot of my adolescence trying very hard to avoid Grannie Blue." He paused long enough for all of us to appreciate ... the mistake that was.

"The Lord began to call me to serve while I was in college, and I did my best to ignore the message. I didn't want to be a minister! I wanted to be a world famous baseball player! Didn't God understand that? Didn't He know? Grannie Blue came to every one of my college games and," Ben sighed in defeat, "of course made a name for herself there. She was there the day the scouts came to check me out ... and saw them leave without speaking a word to me. I'd played a lousy game and even my coach was too disappointed to come and talk to me at first. But Grannie Blue showed up immediately; walking right into the locker room to find me lacing up my sneakers fighting back tears.

"'Well, that was an answer to prayer!' she said as I sat there trying my best not to howl in misery. I remember looking at her like she'd finally gone off the deep end.

"'Don't give me that look, Benjamin Harayda!' she said to me. 'I've been praying for you and your future since the moment the doctor slapped your bare behind.'

"I reminded her that I'd *failed.* That the scouts couldn't get in their car and drive away fast enough. How I'd never play pro ball now. *Never.*"

"'Pro ball wasn't really what I had in mind for you,' Grannie told me that day, 'but then it's not up to me, is it?'"

Benjamin said quietly to the congregation, "You need to know that I'd not told *anyone* about God's call to be a minister. *No. One.* I sat there in the boy's locker room with my crazy grandmother and waited for her to say it. And she did."

"'I've always felt,' Grannie Blue said to me, 'that you'd be a great third baseman. But, I always *knew* you'd be an even better preacher.'"

Benjamin had been standing in the center of the altar, but now he walked over to one of the two podiums. "These last years I've had the privilege to recognize the treasure that Grannie Blue was.

"Grannie Blue's life was an example of what God wants each one of us to do. We are called to serve God faithfully, to be obedient to His commands, and to be diligent with our commitments. We're supposed to make God smile." Ben walked down the steps and stood closer to the audience. "And while it's not our place to judge," he said softly, "I think Grannie did a good job in all those areas.

"Besides being a champion prayer warrior, she was an outstanding Bible reader." Opening up his Bible he thumbed to a spot and then put his finger in to hold the place. "When it was clear she wasn't going to beat this illness," Ben said, his voice was rough with unshed tears, "she stunned me by saying how blessed she was." A picture appeared behind Ben of Grannie Blue at her most outrageous: bright electric blue wig, Yankees baseball cap, and (I squinted my eyes to be sure) a Go Jets! flannel nightgown, "I remember shaking my head in disbelief that she could say such a thing.

"'Now Bennie,' she said to me, 'I'm no hero and I could do without all the pain and discomfort, but you see God's given me *plenty of time* to finish up all I need to do here. How can I not be thankful for that?' She took the time to speak with each of us and tell us special things that I'm sure we'll treasure forever. 'And when you do my *big, fancy* memorial service,' she told me," and he rolled his eyes so that everyone burst out laughing again, "'I need you to give everyone there a going away Bible verse from me.'" Ben smiled. "The only thing more important than her sports teams was her Bible." I thought of the enormity of the gift she'd left me and had a wave of guilt over the knowledge that I'd never truly appreciate it like I knew she'd wanted me to. Let's face it: Bible reading and I are not perfect together.

Thumbing through his Bible, Ben said, "She had many favorite passages and an incredible memory, but there was one verse in particular that she wanted me to 'give' to you. It's from the book of Ephesians, chapter three, verse twenty. Grannie Blue said this verse was the sum total of her life. At the beginning of her life it was a promise she leaned on and at the end of her life it was the foundation she stood on." Behind him, words appeared transposed over Grannie Blue's picture and Ben said loudly and clearly, "*Glory be to God! By His mighty power at work within us, He is able to accomplish infinitely more than we would ever dare to ask or hope.*"

I think about my number one goal– to die having spent a majority of the rest of my life happy. When I wrote that I attributed my success or failure to my own free will, my own determination, and my own ability to distinguish between good and bad choices. But reading Grannie Blue's verse I understood that there are other people who look at life quite differently. '*His* mighty power at work within us' completely eliminated my skills or my will power or my personal ability to direct the future. Kind of like instead of driving the car, I just need to make sure I choose the right chauffer and then sit back and leave it up to Him.

Stunningly, that really appealed to me.

As for the second part of the verse about accomplishing 'infinitely more than we would ever dare hope or ask', well who wouldn't want to end up on that side of the equation?

The service lasted for a little over an hour with friends and family speaking, the singing (by the congregation and by Jen and Phillip), and Ben's eulogy. The crowd made its way into a large hall where coffee was being served along with cake and sandwiches. There were more photographs of Grannie Blue and I spent a bit of time looking at the pictures of her life.

Ben is a big fish in his little church pond, and it became rapidly apparent that due to my negligible association with him I was more fascinating than most church guests. Every teenager seemed determined to check me out: I was cell phone photographed at least three times, acknowledged by two more current math students, and no matter where I tried to stand there always seemed to be a heavy preponderance of youth. I even started to think that the adults were beginning to look at me with more purpose, but then decided that it was just my paranoia. Kate, Mandy, and a sub-collection of hanger-ons (Kris? Sue? Marilyn? I can't remember them all …) became my posse. At least three times I told them they could go off and do their own thing, that I'd be *perfectly fine on my own*, but they wouldn't hear of it. Lucky me.

Kate's mother was the church secretary, so she knew everything about everyone and offered a steady stream of tidbits that were alternately shocking, funny, and enlightening. I determined not to respond or react to anything they said, no matter what. I learned what college Pastor Ben went to, when he graduated, what his GPA was, and what fraternity he had joined. I'm told that Pastor Ben's mother was the lady in the black skirt and green blouse, Pastor Ben's Dad has been dead for a long time, Pastor Ben's sister-in-law was not here because she'd just had a baby less than one week ago (a boy, Bradley James, 8 lbs. 6 oz., 21 inches long), and that Pastor Ben's brother was nowhere near as hot as Pastor Ben.

"See that lady over there in the dark blue dress? Her name is Karen, and for a long time everyone thought that she was dating Pastor Ben in secret. But then we found out that she was just seeing him privately for some counseling sessions." Kate shrugged, apparently in frustration that neither of them knew the primary concern of the session, and then looked at Mandy. "Pastor Ben told us he wasn't dating anybody when we went on the winter youth retreat. Remember when Martin asked him if he was gay?" The two of them cracked up laughing. "The look on Pastor Ben's face was sooooo funny."

Mandy felt compelled to assure me, "Don't worry. He's not. I'm positive."

Yes, I bit my tongue to keep from asking how she was so sure. Don't forget, I'm in a crowd of teenage girls …

"How're you so sure, Mandy?" Kris (I think) asked, wide-eyed and curious.

"I asked him one time who he thought was the hottest actress. I listed a bunch of them and he had a reason why each one wasn't.

"Like what?" said another member of my posse.

"Well, he said that Keira Knightly was 'too skinny', Angelina Jolie was 'too controversial', Pamela Anderson was 'too fake', Lindsay Lohan was 'too much trouble'…"

"What's that prove?" Kate said dismissively.

"It proved," Mandy said with all the logic a fifteen-year-old can muster, "that he'd *thought about* each one of them. That makes him not gay."

I was forced to admit to myself that this was a strange thought process, but not altogether misguided. In a desperate effort to get us off the topic of Ben's sexual preferences and the kind of women he did consider "hot" I asked how long Ben had been the minister here. I'd gradually moved once again to a far corner, desperately trying to escape from all the curious teenagers scoping me out.

"He's not the senior pastor, you know," Mandy's explained, "he's the *youth* pastor. I sure hope he told you that. He preaches sometimes but deals with us kids *all* the time." I realized that bit of information would help explain the tremendous number of youth present. "He's been here since I was in fourth grade so that's five years now."

"All the girls think he's *so hot*," Kate said with a giggle, "and all the church ladies are always trying to fix him up with their daughters or nieces-"

"Or granddaughters or sisters or even young women that they think he might like that they meet on the street," came a deep male voice from behind me.

"Hey, Mr. Harayda," Mandy said.

I turned to see Ben's older brother, Arthur Harayda, towering over me. "Arthur!" I said in delight. "I recognize that expression! It's the exact same look of mischief you used to give me-"

"-before I set you up on the refrigerator," Arthur said with a grin. "Don't worry, Livvie, you're safe. Although Grannie Blue wouldn't mind such shenanigans at her memorial service, there's a bunch of others here that probably would. Lowering his voice he muttered, "And please, call me Art. No one calls me 'Arthur' except when I'm causing trouble."

"I bet you hear that name quite often then," I laughed. I sobered and touched his arm. "I'm so sorry about Grannie Blue."

"Thanks for your kind words, Olivia. I think Grannie would be quite tickled at this big turn out." It may have been close to twenty years since I'd last seen Art Harayda but the smile he gave me was identical to the one I remember from my childhood. "Ben's sent me to rescue you. He's occupied being a minister and he's worried about," he looked at Mandy and Kate and the rest of the group literally hanging on every word he was uttering, "the company you're keeping."

"Why the girls have been very welcoming and most enlightening," I informed Art with a broad grin.

Art sighed and took my arm. "That's *exactly* what Ben was afraid of."

Therapy: The Truth About Aileen

Setting: Same old. Same old. February 22, 2010. I've been doing this for almost two years. I'll let you know if something changes.

Aileen: Give me a rundown of your last four weekends.

Me: Food shopping, bill paying, apartment cleaning, endless paper grading and lesson planning, sleep … I think I shaved my legs at least once and had Sunday dinner at Erin and Dan's.

Aileen: You still go every Sunday for dinner?

Me: My mother says it's a good Sunday if my nephew Liam and the words "fire", "blood" or "vomit" are not mentioned in the same sentence with him. (That makes Aileen laugh like I knew it would.)

Aileen: Gone out at all?

Me: No, although Clotilde keeps bugging me about going out with them to O'Reillys. That has potential for all kinds of one night stand action. I've never really been interested in that but maybe I should. Or maybe I could hook up with that nice guy from the New Year's Eve party who left me stone cold but whom Clotilde thinks would be just perfect for me. Something's better than nothing, you know? (I pause for dramatic affect.) Or, I could always take up Assistant Principal Phil's offer - he continues to dog me and we did have some pretty hot action in the supply room that I still remember from over a year ago.

Aileen: Proud of *any* of that? (I look out the window. She knows I'm not.) Are you lonely, Olivia? I just asked you if you'd 'gone out at all' and you immediately equated that with male companionship. That's *very telling*. Do you miss having a man in your life? You've told me that there's no one with potential at work and you spend most of your evenings and weekends on your own. It was your decision to stop dating all together until you sorted some things out for yourself. (She gives me a serious look.) I was *trying* to find out where the opportunities are for you to meet new people in general, Olivia. Currently, you've put a hold on romance, you've disconnected from all your old friends, and you've isolated yourself from anything other than professional or familial responsibilities. Is this what you want? Are you happy? Do you think it's time to step out a bit? Venture into new and uncharted waters? Thinking about those personal goals of yours, I'm just wondering where you're going to find this best friend you're looking for. And let's not forget that desire for happiness with no regrets. Based on what you've just described to me the search area is extremely limited. Food store? Parking Lot? Gas Station? (Aileen shakes her head.) Not a lot of opportunities there.

Me: You could at least give me a bit of positive reinforcement regarding Phil.

Aileen: Hmmm, since when do want my positive affirmations? *You* know that was an exceptionally wise choice to not move ahead any further in that relationship. That's old business we don't need to rehash. Does he give you a hard time at work?

Me: (I think.) No. He really doesn't. And since I'm the one that flirted big time initially, it's not like he started it. I need to spell it out loudly and clearly to him to give up any hope of every hooking up with me. I need to stop playing the run and hide game with him. (I think some more.) Not getting involved with him ... that was the first good thing you helped me accomplish.

Aileen: (Clutching her heart like Redd Foxx used to do in the television show *Sandford and Son* – "I coming, Elizabeth! This is the Big One!!") Is that a positive comment about me and my counseling? Wait, let me get a tape recorder so that I can save this for posterity.

Me: Sarcasm *does not* become you.

Aileen: (Grinning at me) Right back at you.

Me: (Speaking of sarcasm) You know, maybe, you're right. I should start volunteering at a homeless shelter or the local hospital, or even start driving around elderly folks to help them do their errands. Think I would have any luck in a nursing home or an AA meeting? Where's a good location to scout out the perfect guy?

Aileen: (Her face lights up with a brilliant smile.) Anything is possible, Olivia. It's the *attitude* that matters, not necessarily the locale. I met my husband in the unemployment line.

Me: Are you serious?

Aileen: I'm as serious as a heart attack.

12: The Twilight Zone Does Exist

Saturday, March 26, 2010

I'd never seen my mother cry.

Not when Dean, Husband Number One, made her bleed. Not when living with Paul, Husband Number Two, was so miserable that she preferred to live with her two daughters in her 1981 Ford Pinto. Not when Richard, Husband Number Three, decided to take every pill in the house and curled up for an eternal rest in her bed before she got home from work one day. And not when I screamed at her over a year ago, 'Why can't you just, *for once in your miserable life,* do something just for me?' when I was trying to get her to tell me the name of my father, AKA her rapist. Each time things got rough my mother just got tougher.

So, it shocked me to find my mother with tears silently streaming down her face as she was cleaning Vera's oven Saturday afternoon. Alec and Dan were doing the heavy lifting, carting load after load of items out to the dumpster we'd rented. Erin and I were rifling through the remains of Vera Cummings' earthly existence finding very little we had an interest in claiming. (Liam and Janine were on a play date with friends.) Everyone was slightly tense - resigned to the task ahead of us and unwilling to let anyone suffer through it alone.

The process was surreal. Vera was certainly cognizant of her imminent demise, causing her to make detailed provisions for the disposition of herself and for her final earthly moments both in life and after her death. Not one single aspect of her final days had not been scrupulously detailed in legal documents that I had been given in my capacity as the agent in charge of carrying them out. Yet her house and all her earthly possessions, for all intents and purposes, were abandoned without thought. When we gained entry to her house (which was only allowed after her death and when all meticulous stipulations regarding her death and cremation were *legally acknowledged as met*) we found a house that showed no sign of preparation for anything. There were dirty dishes in the sink and a dishwasher partially filled with more dirty dishes. The refrigerator was loaded with molding food and there was even dirty laundry in the hamper and an unfinished load of wash in the washing machine. Her bed was unmade, a rank towel was in a heap on the bathroom floor, and the kitchen garbage pail was potent enough to smell it in the front yard. It would appear to be Vera's final slap at the Cummings women left behind, and none of us missed the message. Alec and Dan, grim with disgust and anger, silently did whatever tasks we asked of them. In addition, Alec had been uncharacteristically glum all day leading me to believe that he was significantly concerned about my mother and her being there.

It had not escaped me that my mother had avoided the tiny living room and opted to clean both bathrooms and now the kitchen. "Mom?" I said quietly and rather than answer me she made a concerted effort to crawl deeper into the oven. Sliding down with a box of eight hundred year old lotions and perfumes, I sat down quietly on the yellow linoleum and … waited.

"I don't think this oven has ever been cleaned," my mother's voice echoed.

"And it's enough to bring you to tears?"

That made her snort with what I hoped to be laughter. "Eww, not a good idea. Now I need a tissue." Pulling herself out of the oven, she sniffled and wiped her nose on the edge of her tee shirt that read, *"There are no stupid questions but there are a lot of inquisitive idiots."*

I reached up to grab a napkin from the remains of our takeout lunch and handed it to her.

Sighing, my mother said, "What a waste of a life," and blew her nose.

"Oh, that's why you were crying."

The Cummings genes are kind to its women, I thought as we sat there in surprisingly comfortable silence. My mom, on the wrong side of fifty, still looked pretty darn good for her age with clear hazel eyes and (granted) chemically assisted, non-grey hair. I realized that a lot of her good looks stemmed from her positive attitude about herself and life in general. Not that she's a Pollyanna or anything. Before she found the God Club she was definitely in the "Who Gives A Crap Anymore?" club. But today, sitting on the floor wearing yellow rubber gloves and with snot on her shoulder, she's got a peaceful attitude about her that can't be ignored.

"I feel guilty," she finally said.

"About Vera?" I couldn't keep the shock out of my voice.

My mother nodded. "Maybe I should have tried harder. I knew she couldn't live forever, even if the bad do die old." She smirked at me, and suddenly Billy Joel's tune *Only The Good Die Young* was jingling in my head.

"Are there *any* good memories of her?"

Closing her eyes, my mother let her head fall back against the wall. She was quiet for a long time, and I thought how I probably never should have sat down in the first place. "Do you have any good memories about me?" she finally asked as her throat worked convulsively.

Oh. So that's where this was headed. "I was just thinking the other day about those shoeboxes full of doll clothes you used to make us each Christmas."

"You always wanted troll clothes, not Barbie clothes. What a nightmare they were to sew." She didn't look at me.

"And remember that night when there was that horrible storm and the power went out and Erin and I were so terrified? You let us pick what we wanted for dinner."

"And Erin was a good girl and said she wanted a peanut butter sandwich and grapes but you took the ball and ran with it," my mother said.

I grinned at the memory. "I had chocolate chip cookies and a Hershey bar and strawberry ice cream with whipped cream on top."

"And Erin ended up in tears because she wanted what you had but also knew how important it was to eat nutritiously."

I snorted in disgust. "You convinced Erin that eating poorly every time there was a bad storm and a power failure was probably okay."

My mother finally picked her head up and looked at me. "To this day Liam and Janine have 'thunder storm Hershey bars'."

"I have good memories of you, Mom." It was not just a lie to make her feel better and thanks to Aileen I could say it with the utmost honesty and sincerity. For long moments we just looked at each other.

"You didn't always."

Shrugging, I murmured, "I had anger issues." So far, the understatement of the day.

"Which was my fault." It's said as a statement of fact she just threw into the game.

For the very first time in my life I wondered, *could my mother have done or said anything that would have extinguished the brilliance of my anger?*

What if she had stayed with Dean? I had a sudden flash of walking in on her and Dean in the front hallway. Dean was fast asleep, snoring loudly through a bloody mouth missing two front teeth. Stoically silent, she had a pail and a rag and she was wiping up vomit which was all over the floor … and the walls … and down in the heating vent grate.

Or she could have never married Paul … or Richard. And stayed alone. I have another flash of her laughing; her smile lighting up her face at something Richard said to her. It was in the early days of their marriage, when they were still in the unrealistic blush of infatuation. The memory had stuck with me because it had been such a shock to hear the sound of her laughter …

Or, I thought, *she could have been the same kind of mother that Vera had been to her.* What would my life had been like if she had let me know every single moment what a hardship I'd always been, what a disappointment I continued to be, and what a horrible reminder I would always be. *How was it* that I went until the age of thirty-two not knowing – or having any possible inkling – about the circumstances of my conception? How incredible a feat was that for my mother to have pulled off?

Or she could have … never had me … and spared us both incredible decades of angst. She could have chosen a completely different path all together. Taken the easy way out so to speak …

"You were nothing like Vera, you know," I felt compelled to tell her.

She smiled wryly. "I think that might be one of my greatest accomplishments."

"And you're wrong. About my anger being your fault. You could have done things differently but I don't know if I would have been any happier." Now it was my turn to close my eyes and clunk my head against the kitchen sink cupboard. "Anger's always been so easy for me. I don't know how or why it became my favorite emotion … but lately I've been working to change that. It's taken me a long time to realize that I'm a grown woman so I need to stop behaving like a spoiled, angry child."

"You're a magnificent young woman and I'm tremendously proud of you," my mother said with force.

"I'm a daughter whose been a handful since the day I was born." I threw back unwilling to bask for even a second in her false perceptions.

"You've always been wonderfully unique," she amended.

Looking her right in the eye I said, "I haven't fit in any mold, fulfilled any expectation, or ever taken the comfortable way out. Ever."

My mother opened her mouth to say something, then looked at me and cracked up laughing. "Oh man, is that ever true!"

I had to laugh, too. "Why Mom?" I finally asked when we'd both gotten a hold of ourselves. "Why are you sitting here in this hell hole, dealing with the nightmares of your past?"

My mother finally wiped her streaming eyes on her tee shirt. With surprising force she said, "Are you seriously asking me that?" I felt like I did sometimes when Aileen was getting intense and I knew I was heading for the wall. Still I nodded. "Olivia," my mother said with firm conviction, *"I love you.* We may not be 'normal' or 'typical', but *we're a family.* We stick together *no matter what.* We're there for each other *in all things.* Love doesn't turn on and off like a water faucet."

I got what she was trying to tell me. "Love is patient and kind," I murmured remembering vividly Grannie Blue's note, "and never gives up."

My mother suddenly said as if I'd flashed her, "You're quoting scripture to me?!"

Uh oh. As silly as it sounded, it never occurred to me that what Grannie had sent me was a Bible verse ... "Grannie Blue wrote it in a note to me just before she died."

"Grannie Blue?"

So still sitting on the kitchen floor, I told my mother about encountering Benjamin and visiting with Grannie Blue and about her memorial service and how it never occurred to me that she had left me scripture. My mother smiled. "That's from the book of first Corinthians, chapter thirteen, the love chapter. *Love never gives up ... Takes pleasure in the flowering of truth. Puts up with anything. Trusts God always. Always looks for the best. Never looks back. But keeps going to the end.*[17]" She blushed and mumbled, "Alec whispers it to me all the time ..."

Whoa. Here I was having a meaningful conversation with *my mother* which inspired me to quote a deceased woman's final words only to discover that I was voicing the Holy Scriptures which also appears to be Alec's favorite love poetry. I felt like suddenly I'm in some alternate universe. "It's been a weird week. I've been having some real Twilight Zone coincidences."

"You should ask Alec sometime about his theory on coincidences – Twilight Zone or otherwise," my mother said with a smile. "He says there's no such thing. That anything that looks like a coincidence is really God's Handiwork In Action." I watched her examine the outdated kitchen and saw her expression turn melancholy again. "This place has difficult memories for me, but not for the reason you think. I *lost* myself in this place when I was a little girl and that was my mother's fault. It took me years to finally put everything back together and get on the right track. You came along *way* before I was ready to care for myself, let alone nurture and raise a child. I *do own* a lot of your misery and I'm sorry for that. I did the best I could but we both know it was miserably lacking.

"But I'm a completely different woman now, Olivia! *Transformed.* I'd just like another chance to be a positive part of your life. Tell me honestly, am I asking for too much?"

Tell me honestly. She would put it that way. I felt like I'd been hypnotized and was incapable of bending the truth. So I looked at my mother and just let her have it with both barrels: the clear, unvarnished truth. "No, it's not too much for you to ask. I've been trying to figure out a way for us to begin again. I might as well stay here in the Twilight Zone. Maybe it's a better place after all. Coincidence or no."

Therapy: The Truth About Me – Part II

Setting: Aileen's office as usual. It's Monday, March 29, 2010, and for the
first time since I showed up with my paternity results almost two
full years ago, I want to be here because I'm ... once again ...
desperate.

Me: I've met a man.

Aileen: Oh? (I know she's thinking: *Whose husband is it this time?*)

Me: He's a nice guy. A *single*, nice guy. He asked me to go out for coffee
on Saturday but I couldn't because I was cleaning out Vera's house
with my mother, Alec, and Erin. But, I think I would have gone
otherwise.

Aileen: (I suspect she's trying not to laugh out loud.) Well, well. Let's
hear all about him!

Me: (I sigh. In voicing this aloud, I'm acknowledging to myself the reality
of what I've been trying to ignore.) I'm interested in him. (Aileen
and I stare at each other, stunned to be in this strange, new
territory.)

Aileen: Olivia, we spoke about this very subject just a few weeks ago. This
is a good thing. You are in the driver's seat. You are the one who
drives this boat. There is nothing to be so ... tense ... about.

Me: No, it's even worse than it seems. (I pause for the full affect.) He's a
minister.

Aileen: (For the first time in over two years of therapy, I've shocked
Aileen into speechlessness. She just sits there and looks at me. She
starts to laugh but then catches herself immediately.) Tell me
about him.

Me: (I give her the whole rundown about him being a childhood friend -
Ben's even been mentioned a time or two, I'm sure he's in Aileen's
notes somewhere. How we ran into each other - I have a flash of
me sarcastically asking if it's possible to meet the perfect man in a
nursing home and Aileen's apparent good luck in the
unemployment line. And how Ben got me to promise to go out

for coffee at Grannie Blue's memorial service. Then, I burst into tears.)

Aileen: (She lets me cry and then watches me help myself to her tissues and blow my nose.) Come on. Let's think this out. You can do it, Olivia. Why the tears?

Me: I hate that you've brought me to this place, Aileen!! *I hate it.* (Aileen just blinks at me.) This place can't be better than where I was. *It just can't be.*

Aileen: Why are you crying, Olivia? (I consider giving her the finger, but hold back.) We've talked about this. Big emotions mean big feelings. Understand the feelings and you can better understand the emotions. Are those tears of anger? Hurt? Fear?

Me: (I grit my teeth.) I'm afraid, okay? Absolutely TERRIFIED! But you already know that. You just want me to admit it. And now you'll want me to list everything that's terrifying me. So here goes. I'm afraid of getting disappointed and hurt. I'm afraid I'll make a fool of myself. I'm afraid that if I screw this up I'll lose any of the progress I've made here with you, and I want to get *away from you,* not add to my time! (I glare at her.) I'm afraid that I'll screw this up by being clingy or needy or weepy or crazy like my mother. You're going to tell me to just be myself, that's all I need to concern myself with, and that's no comfort *at all!!* I've never been a nice person, Aileen! *You* know that better than anyone!! Why would anyone nice want to have anything to do with me?! You're going to say I should continue to be honest about my feelings. But that's what I'm doing right now and why I'm in tears! (I'm shouting now.) The reality is if I'm *just myself,* Ben can't possibly be interested in me. Or all he needs to do is find out *my history* and he'll run screaming in terror in the opposite direction. (I'm not shouting anymore because I too busy blubbering again.) And – here's the worst of it – I'm afraid you'll say I'm better and I'm afraid that I'll know I'm better ... but I won't be any happier. And I'll *still be alone.*

Aileen: Well done, Olivia. *Well done.* Now listen to me! (She waits until I blow my nose and sort of pull myself together. Then she says slowly and clearly and precisely ...) *Wisdom is nothing but healed pain.*[18] (She's quoting sayings to me at a time like this?!) Acquiring wisdom hurts but *we can't move forward without it.* Now, I'm not saying that getting involved with a ... *nice* ... man is or isn't going to hurt! But what I *am* saying is that *life hurts.* Growth hurts. Change hurts. You can try to avoid the pain of living by refusing to grow and change, and that's just what you've done for all these years! You've packed yourself into a tight little angry package thinking it's the best way to protect yourself, but all you've done is stunt your growth. I'm not even going to get into the debate about love with you. I just want you to *start living. Go have coffee* with this man, Olivia. Who cares if he's a preacher or a garbage collector? *It's just a cup of coffee!!* When has a person's profession ever guaranteed anything about him? It's time you began to step out and give yourself *the opportunity* for happiness. Once you've made that first step, then stay alert, stay intelligent, stay honest, and decide if you're going to take another step. One step at a time, girl, just *one step at a time.* Nothing more and nothing less.

Me: I knew you were going to say all this.

Aileen: (Aileen shakes her head vigorously.) It's not my voice you're hearing, Olivia. *It's your own common sense* that's finally being heard. Once we ratchet down those angry screams, it's amazing what you're going to discover about yourself.

Truth is mighty and will prevail.
There is nothing wrong with this, except that it ain't so.[19]

13: Some Guys Just Won't Take A Hint
Monday, March 29, 2010

My first experience with a married man was when I was a college junior. And, before you start judging me too quickly, I had no clue he was married when we first met. He was incredibly good-looking, which was the first thing that caught my eye, with dark brown eyes and thick, wavy dark hair. He wasn't a polished professional – which was my personal goal – and for some reason that made him all that more appealing. He had a weather-roughened face and hands, cement-spattered work boots, soft faded jeans, and an old, plaid flannel shirt. Aileen has made me acknowledge the similarity in professions between him and Dean, and I couldn't argue that fact, although I did point out their complete difference in physical appearance. We caught each other's eye in a sandwich shop and when I walked out with my early morning cappuccino and corn muffin he was leaning against his pickup truck waiting for me.

"I'll risk the embarrassment of getting shot down just for a chance to hear your voice," he said as he sipped his coffee and made no effort to disguise his visual inspection of me.

By twenty I was already well experienced in shooting men down. Physically I'd developed early and I had already learned the hard way that letting boys … and young men … too close only added new items to my Why I Distrust Males list. His frank inspection and cheesy come-on also didn't earn him any points. Taking a sip of *my* coffee and checking *him* out, I rolled my eyes and kept on walking - not because I wanted him to go away, mind you, but because I wanted him to *work for it*. He didn't disappoint; he followed.

As I unlocked my car I threw over my shoulder, "*Please* don't ask me if I'm a student or what I'm studying. Because I'm not going to tell you."

"If I guess what your major is, can I have your phone number?"

Clever. Very clever. I turned and looked at him. "You've got one guess."

"Business, with a specific interest in finance and international banking." He took another sip of his coffee, looking exceptionally smug and pleased with himself. I found out later that he'd seen me walk in and had checked out my car whose back seat was loaded with textbooks. But at that moment he'd impressed me with his insight.

"You good with numbers?" I asked him and he shrugged. I rattled off my phone number, got in the car and drove away without looking back.

Of course he called, and that's when we exchanged names. His was Jeff and he was working on campus building the new fine arts theatre. We went out for dinner and then he took me dancing and I had an absolutely fabulous time. That first night he confessed that he was living with a girl, but that the relationship had soured and they were only together because of an unbreakable lease and financial issues.

Yes, I believed him, because at that point in my life I was still … an idiot.

We dated for almost three months and he was the most wonderful man I had ever encountered in my whole life. He called me faithfully every morning (usually from the pay phone at the sandwich shop where we'd met) and managed to see me briefly almost every day and for a formal date at least once a week. He made simple things like going for a drive or to the movies fun and different because we tried to never go to the same place twice. I'd come out to my car after classes and there'd be a flower or a love note stuck under my windshield wiper. There wasn't a shadow of doubt in my mind that when he wasn't with me he was thinking of me. He was the only man I'd ever met who caused me to rethink my firm theory about the nonexistence of love.

But I kept my head, having learned through the real life school of disastrous love of Elaine Cummings Kelly Richardson Brockman, that nothing was ever as good as it appeared. Even though dating Jeff was wonderful, I was determined to be wise and strong and mature. Up until that point I had managed to hang onto my virginity by the skin of my teeth which, according to Jeff, made me all that more special. He championed my "high ideals" and claimed to be delighted with both my determination to succeed professionally and my personal high standards.

Over those first three months I never questioned him about his living arrangements or the old girlfriend, believing firmly that trust was critical for any relationship to succeed. I convinced myself that not being bothered by not having his phone number showed how independent, secure and self-confident I was.

I finally slept with him at the Sun and Fun Motel in a special overnight away. At the time I saw the decision as My Personal Choice but in retrospect Jeff had spun a very subtle campaign to get me to finally give it all up. It was the very same night he had told me he loved me over a candlelight dinner at a cute little Italian restaurant at the Jersey shore and had given me a lovely 'promise' ring shaped like a heart. It was a perfect evening - everything I had always hoped and dreamed of.

The next day as we walked the beach hand-in-hand, he told me that he had a confession to make.

His wife didn't understand him. He definitely didn't love her. She had unresolved emotional issues that hadn't become apparent until after the marriage (which had happened only eleven months ago). He swore that it was absolutely true that they were only still living together because they couldn't afford a divorce and that they hadn't been together as a couple *in months*. He *really did love me*, he *really did want to be only with me*, and he was desperate to get a divorce *as soon as possible*. He promised to speak to his wife the moment he got home. He committed to do everything possible so that we could be together *for the rest of our lives*. I remember standing there watching a brave late fall surfer and thinking, *I knew there was no such thing as true love* and then, *I never would have wanted to marry this guy even if he'd been single.*

Perhaps his marital state had never occurred to me because I had never had any particular desire to be his wife. I didn't go around polling people to see if they had ever won the Miss America contest, did I? Listening to Jeff rationalize away his life, I realized with stunning clarity that it wasn't that he was someone else's husband that bothered me so much as the fact that he seemed to desperately now want to be *mine. Ewwwww, what an awful thought.*

Walking alongside Jeff on the beach that day I'd never felt so alone in all my life. More alone than when my mother had left Dean. Having experienced the wonder of companionship and belonging and all the other astonishing benefits of being part of a happy couple, the last thing in the world I wanted to do was go back to my previous state. In the end, I drove home with Jeff, silent as a stone, while he exhibited a range of emotions that began with earnest desperation and escalated to righteous indignation. When I got out of the car his, "You're the love of my life, Olivia!" had morphed into, "Have a nice life you self-righteous bitch!"

Now I know another woman may have taken away something totally different from this experience. But at that time in my life I chose to be positive. Hadn't Jeff and I had a wonderful three months together? Hadn't I managed for a while to be the happiest I'd ever been? In reality, the only two things that had caused a problem was that he'd lied to me and that he thought I wanted him to leave his wife for me. I'd never asked for professions of love nor had I hinted that I was looking for something permanent. My requirements for happiness were incredibly less complicated: I'd simply been delighted to experience the thrill of being uniquely special to someone.

From that moment on, consciously and unconsciously, I determined that dating married men was actually perfect for me. As long as we were both honest about what we wanted it was perfect for satisfaction on both sides. See? Honesty has always been … important to me.

There was a message from Ben on my answering machine when I got home from Aileen's on Monday, March 29, 2010. My head was full of snot because the session had been a tough one and I felt like I've been used as a punching bag. I listened to Ben's message; polite and to the point. He left his number (home and cell) and asked me to call him back so we could decide on a good day to go have that coffee together. Since I was trying to be honest, I'll admit that I listened to his message three times and smiled quite a lot as I made Sophie and me our dinner.

He'd patently refused to acknowledge that the coffee I drank after Grannie Blue's memorial service counted towards the favor I had committed to. The look of incredulous disbelief on his face would have been enough to make me laugh out loud had we not just exited a memorial service. "You think I asked you out to coffee *here? Now? And that we've already had it?!*"

"Well I'll warn you, a majority of the youth in the church sure think you did, and I suspect a majority of my high school students will have us married by the time I show up for school on Monday."

He sighed. "I tried to talk to you as quietly as possible."

"Kate apparently has ears like Superman."

"Kate Larsen?" He looked so horrified that I momentarily considered lying to him. But that's not my style, even if it would have allowed him to sleep soundly that evening.

I nodded. "Kate Larsen and her friend Mandy Ennis and a significant number of hangers on with names like Kris and Sue and Marilyn …"

"That's who you were talking with when Art came and rescued you?!"

I grinned like a Cheshire Cat. "I know about your college GPA, that your sexual preference *is not* towards men, and that you think Keira Knightly is too skinny, Angelina Jolie is too controversial," I paused for a moment in thought, "and there was another famous woman you critiqued but I can't remember who it was..."

"Oh dear Lord," he said and put both hands over his face in absolute mortification.

I couldn't help it and chuckled. "Ben, relax. *I teach high school.* I deal with this kind of thing every day. I can't remember how many times I've been asked what my bra size is ... or if they're real. There's a persistent rumor that I'm having a torrid affair with the assistant principal, and twice I've been told by students that their fathers want my phone number." I tugged on his arm to pull his hands away from his face. "There's not much a teenager can do that can shock me anymore, and I've been teaching for less than two years."

"So, I've got tomorrow afternoon free," Ben finally said and then looked at me and watched my reaction.

I don't play games. I'm on the honesty train. "Tomorrow's not good as I have to help clean out Vera's house. Just a big day of fun and laughter it will be, too."

"So, I'll just call and we can talk and pick a day that works?"

There was a subtle implication that once I got in the car and drove away he wondered if he'd ever see me again. "You know where I live, Benjamin Harayda. I'd bet, since you looked at the IHC files," and he blushed beet red, "that you also have my phone number, email address and other personal information. I don't think I can stop you from trying to contact me."

"I only wrote down your address and phone number," he confessed, "*before* you turned me down when I asked you out for coffee. And I wouldn't have contacted you except that I had Grannie Blue's package for you and ... then ... she made me promise a few things about you and coffee ..."

A few things. Hmm, that sounded interesting. It was my turn to give him the stare. Aileen, I realized, had taught me well.

We were standing in the parking lot directly behind the church. He surprised me by crossing his arms and glaring at me. "Wanting and doing are two different things, Olivia Kelly. I *want* lots of things," and he had the audacity to give me a smoldering look that would rival any I've ever received, "but maybe it's time you realized that I'm different from the other men you've known."

"How's that?" I challenged, realizing that provocative banter and outrageous flirting could be just as much fun with nice guys.

Leaning in he kissed me gently on the cheek and whispered, "I'm not telling. You'll just have to figure that out for yourself."

Suddenly, much to my amazement, for the first time ever I wanted to do exactly that with a nice man.

"What do you think, Sophie? Should I call the guy back?" Sophie was sitting on the kitchen counter waiting to drink the milk dregs from my cereal bowl. (What? It's Special K. I love having Special K for dinner.) If I forgot and tipped the bowl up to drink, she would walk over and sit right between the bowl and my mouth. She does this with dignity and hauteur, communicating clearly how gauche I am to forget to share with her.

But he's a minister, my head said. What if he said something incredibly creepy like, "Praise the Lord! This is Pastor Ben!" when he answered the phone? This nice guy was so incredibly out of my league that I sat for long moments while Sophie drank my milk imagining one disastrous scenario after another. The mental nightmare slide show went on and on until the message blinking on my answer machine no longer brought a smile to my face, but instead a grimace at what I'd gotten myself into with one innocent promise.

I decided I'd never call him. Spare us both. Maybe he'd get the hint and realize that I was just too much trouble to bother with.

Therapy: The Truth About What Really Matters

Setting: Aileen's office. Monday, April 5, 2010. Here I am again. I am in that difficult place where I've told Aileen about something (Ben) and now I know she's going to ask me questions, and I know she's not going to be happy with my behavior (I've not answered any of his calls or returned any of his messages) and I'm absolutely certain that I don't want to pick this apart with her. Consequently, I will have to keep her away from this topic.

Me: Define for me your idea of the perfect relationship.

Aileen: (I get The Look. She knows I'm … scheming … but goes along with it.) I know you've had little experience with healthy, strong relationships between men and women, Olivia. But tell *me*, what do *you* think are the qualities of a good relationship?

Me: You're asking me?

Aileen: Of course I'm asking you. Come on. Tell me something you've always imagined about the perfect relationship.

Me: My mother tried "the exact opposite" solution a number of times. That didn't work.

Aileen: Then tell me about a family on television that you like … like *The Cosby Show*.

Me: How about *Roseanne* or *Married With Children?* (Aileen just looks at me. I know where she's going with this though and the reality is … I know I need to know this stuff. Recently, I've found that I *want* to be better, stronger, healthier, wiser … not so much because I want to get away from Aileen - always a noble goal, but more so because I want to *finally*, be screwed together properly. Oh, I want it *now*.) Honesty. And trust. They go hand in hand really. (Aileen nods.) Good communication – really talking about things. I guess I would call it 'honest communication.'

Aileen: Come on. Pretend you've got a magic wand here. Create the perfect relationship.

Me: He'd be wickedly handsome and just ooze sexuality. He'd be smart and confident. Have his own teeth and be gainfully employed.

Aileen: The *perfect relationship*, Olivia, not the perfect man. I'll also point out that as you yourself are not 'perfect," matching up with the perfect man wouldn't be the best choice. In fact, that's a hint ...

Me: Okay. I guess, given that I'm *less than perfect*, flexibility might be good.

Aileen: Should there be any fights or disagreements?

Me: (I go to say something but then catch myself and think for a moment.) I was going to say no, but I don't think that's correct. Disagreements aren't always bad if you're both better off for it in the end. You know, like correcting wrong assumptions or having new insights. I've seen that happen with my mother and me. There have been bad arguments ... where we both just walk away bruised and bloody, and then there have been good *discussions* where there may have been tears, but in the end we both understand each other a little better. So fights or disagreements are okay; just fight fair I guess.

Aileen: How do you "fight fair"?

Me: Being respectful to each other, I guess, even when you're angry.

Aileen: (She looks down at her pad.) Okay, so you've got honesty, trust, good communication, flexibility, being respectful of each other ... (She looks up at me.) Is that it?

Me: Sexual attraction is important. (I throw that out very defensively.)

Aileen: (Aileen laughs out loud.) Do you think I'm going to disagree?

Me: (Thus ensues a long period of silence: me because I'm thinking, Aileen because she's letting me.) I had sexual attraction in all my other relationships. (Aileen smirks at me but stays quiet.) Commitment is good, I suppose. You know, having a common goal or purpose for the future.

Aileen: You mean like a couple committed to meeting regularly but secretly for some honest, flexible, respectful, sexy interaction between the sheets? (Aileen waits a beat and then says quietly.) Is that still all you want, Olivia? (When I turn and look away she

134

leans forward and says even more quietly.) You had enough
courage to tell me about Ben the last time you were here. Even if
you'd not told me *anything else* I would have known what a big deal
that was. There's no one here but you and me right now, Olivia.
Tell me *honestly*, is this the highest expectation you have for
yourself?

Me: (I shake my head because I can't get myself to say anything.)

Aileen: The Olivia I met two years ago and the Olivia I'm talking with now
are two different women. You've moved to a different country,
remember. At some point, this time in your life will be a distant
point on the horizon that you will remember as perhaps one of the
hardest times in your life but also, hopefully, one of the greatest
times of growth. I'm asking you, Olivia, is that the highest
expectation you have for yourself?

Me: No.

Aileen: So, what else do you want then? (But I sit there. *Here we go again,* I
think angrily. The Love Conversation yet again. I am determined
to remain as mute as a stone like I always do when she drags me to
this topic. She sighs.) *To change is difficult. To not change is fatal.*[20]
And just because you haven't actually *seen* something or actually
experienced something doesn't mean it doesn't exist. It doesn't mean
you can't hope for it or want it.

Me: (Angry sarcasm comes and sits with me on the couch.) You mean like
the pot of gold at the end of the rainbow?

Aileen: (Sharp right to the end.) No, I mean like the Himalaya Mountains.
Or love. It's time to decide what really matters, Olivia.

Me: What do you mean 'what really matters?'

Aileen: (She shrugs.) If you don't want to talk about love and
relationships any more you can generalize this … apply it to life in
general. But I think it's a pretty plain question. In other words:
What is important to you? *What matters to you?* What is worth
fighting for?

Me: Are you talking about God and stuff? (Aileen shrugs again. She's thrown out her discussion lure and now she's waiting to see if I'll grab the hook. I glare at her.)

Aileen: What do you value, Olivia? What – or who – is at the top of your list of priorities? The government? (I snort at the ridiculousness of such a thing.) Your employer? (I raise my eyebrows. Is she insane?!) Your mother? Alec? (Eye roll.) Your wonderful therapist? (I laugh out loud.) *Everyone* has *something or someone* they care about and value. How about yourself? Maybe you care only about yourself? (That makes me think for a moment but … no, I don't really care much about me on the whole, so I shake my head.) Okay. Forget people. We both know you don't care about love. (I resist sticking my tongue out.) Maybe you care most about anger … or revenge … or - here's a unique one – sarcasm. (Now I'm silently glaring at her.) I suppose it's possible that you don't care about one single thing. Hmmm, (she pretends to think, tapping her pen on her pointy little chin) that might mean I'd have to come up with a new diagnosis: *the condition of perpetual uncaring*. (I realize she's actually trying to piss me off. Like poking a tiger with a big, sore thorn in its paw with a hot, sharp stick.)

Me: (At my furious silence, Aileen picks up her accursed pad and begins to make notes.) What are you writing? For once, I demand that you tell me!

Aileen: My grocery list. I'm going food shopping after you leave. (As I go to challenge her on this she turns her pad around and I read: *onions, toothpaste, chocolate chips, eggs*)

Me: I don't know what I care about. There, are you happy?

Aileen: No. That's the whole point. Are you?

I never give them hell. I just tell the truth and they think it's hell.[21]

14: Rolos Are Still My Favorite Candy
Thursday, April 8, 2010

Just once I'd like to walk out of Aileen's office head held high, back ramrod straight, off into the sunset a whole, complete, capable, confident woman. But the closest I got to that delusion was the hope that a lifetime of twisted logic and poor choices wouldn't take another lifetime to repair. Hey, one has to dream. By Thursday, I was still wallowing in Ben avoidance, convincing myself that this was the wisest choice.

I came up with creative excuses to not even check the ever-growing list of messages on my answering machine and make the most of my spring break week. If anyone really wanted me they'd call my cell phone, right? Ignoring the steady blinking of the voicemail indicator on my machine I … took Sophie to the vet for her shots and babysat Liam and Janine for three long days and two endless nights so that Erin and Dan could have a romantic getaway date. I went outlet shopping with Clotilde, wrote lesson plans for the next month, resumed my evening exercise regime, and finally decided to … clean my oven.

Which was the night Ben showed up at my front door. I knew as soon as the doorbell rang that it was him. Not because I never got any visitors, but just because deep down *in my bones* I knew I had pushed him as far as he would go.

When I opened my door Ben stood there, hands on his hips, giving me the accusatory eye. "You said you always kept your promises." He looked good in jeans, which he wore along with a Yankees tee shirt, and enormous, sloppy sneakers. A motorcycle helmet dangled from his hand.

137

I tried to look tough. "It's only been a few days Ben. I didn't know there was a time limit."

"Tomorrow will be two weeks," he pointed out.

No way could I beat him in this honestly. So I leaned against my doorjamb, crossed my arms (don't forget my most spectacular assets) and said, "So you wanna come in for your cup of coffee?" How far would I have to go to convince this goody-goody minister that keeping his distance from me was the wisest choice to make?

I learned things about Ben as I watched him study my posture and the glint in my eye. He seemed to never speak with haste and each answer was always careful and precise. "Don't want to *intrude*," he said. "I'm just riding around enjoying the evening and I thought maybe I'd better come and make sure you're not dead in your condo. I suddenly thought," he had the audacity to grin, "maybe that's the reason you haven't answered my *five* phone messages. I had to come by. It was the polite thing to do."

"Got an extra helmet?" The idea of riding on the back of his motorcycle suddenly seemed rather appealing.

"No. But I'll bring one tomorrow night when I pick you up."

"Aren't you confident."

He sighed. "Hopeful."

Looking at this persistent man standing in my doorway, I suddenly wanted desperately to spend an evening with him drinking coffee. "I don't want to go anywhere close by. I've spent the last two weeks dealing with endless questions about you, our impending wedding, and whether or not I'm already pregnant with twins. If anyone saw us out and about together there's no telling what they'd do."

"Has it really been that bad?"

It was a great question; if only he knew. Surprisingly, I hadn't minded all the wild gossip. Suddenly there was a tremendous howling from inside. "What's that?!" Ben blurted out.

"My roommate, Sophie. I suspect she wants me back inside." He was going to be polite, I could tell, and just accept my answer. "Don't take everything I say at face value, okay?"

"I thought you were all about honesty."

"Oh, I am." Sophie gave another howl, louder than the last. I suspected she was walking around the condo with a Dixie cup in her mouth. I'm not sure why she does it but … she does. "Maybe you'd like to be introduced to Sophie."

Wise man. He looked incredibly suspicious.

Suddenly Sophie rounded the corner and was standing behind me. I knew this not because she howled again or because I looked, but because I heard the paper cup drop on the tile floor. Ben leaned slightly to the left to look past me and then chuckled. "Sophie?" he asked and I nodded. "Hey pretty lady," he murmured as he squatted down and held his hand out. The little hussy sauntered right up to him to check him out.

"She doesn't quickly accept strangers," I warned, "especially men. You have to work hard to get to know her." Sophie, true to form, proved me wrong by rubbing passionately against Ben's outstretched hand and purring with all she had.

"Sounds like someone else I know …" Ben said without looking up.

Now it was my turn to sigh. I owed him an apology and an explanation. "Come on in and I'll make you a cup of coffee."

He looked up at me as he rubbed Sophie. "I don't trust you. You'll probably claim between the memorial service and this time that you've fulfilled your obligation." He waited a bit and then said pointedly, "And I want more than that."

Reaching down, I grabbed his arm and tugged. "Come on in. You can relax. We can plan what we're going to do tomorrow night. Even if we do drink a cup of coffee now I'll still drink one again with you tomorrow."

Ben and I met for the first time when we were both hiding out in the woods behind our homes. And before you make any assumptions, he was the one involved in criminal activities; I was just escaping the everyday horrors of my life.

Grandmother Miriam had a way of seeing life, exactly as she chose to view it. Her son Dean was a hard-working laborer, a dedicated father, an unappreciated husband, a perfect son, and a man with more trials and responsibilities than was fair. Being her granddaughter, I basked in a similar rose-colored aura ("Elaine, stop being so hard on the girl," "Elaine, there's nothing wrong with her expressing what she wants to eat/wear/do/have," "Elaine, have you ever taken a moment to look at things from the child's perspective?!"). But even at an early age I knew that Grandmother Miriam was nuts. Grampie Taylor knew it too which was why he spent a majority of his married life trying to remain out of sight.

My mother had me when she was barely seventeen, and Erin came along less than two years later. She got her GED, worked full time as a receptionist at a local doctor's office, and went to school at night in an effort to get her teaching degree. Noble aspirations to be sure, but as a result I rarely saw her, and Grandmother Miriam was my Primary Care Giver.

Grandmother Miriam was a fanatic house cleaner. Even now when I think of her she's vacuuming, mopping, dusting, scrubbing ... I was never allowed in the house with my shoes on and was restricted from doing anything that she deemed "messy." I could go outside but I couldn't get dirty, and while I was always allowed to "go find a friend to play with" I wasn't ever encouraged to bring one to the house. Grandmother Miriam's greatest accomplishment (she used to tell this story all the time) was when a woman from the neighborhood told another woman that 'Miriam's kitchen floor was so spotless you could eat off it.' Grandmother Miriam heard about this through the neighborhood grapevine and I'm sure it's still one of the Best Days Of Her Life.

About once every two weeks, Grandmother Miriam went on a "cleaning spree" which involved the washing of walls, windows, drapes, rugs, upholstery, bedspreads ... On those days I was required to "make myself scarce." When I was little (two? three?) I wasn't allowed to step off the front porch, but by five I was allowed to wander around the neighborhood for the better part of the day.

Just as I knew Grandmother Miriam was nuts, I also knew I was an oddball. The neighborhood couldn't help but be aware of my father's … problem, the family's endless fights, and the financial disasters we endlessly suffered as with Daddy's trucks which were regularly towed away. The difference between "us" and "them" was only clarified with the start of kindergarten and my introduction into the world of peer pressure. Normal childhood relationships weren't in the cards for me and (said with an angry glint in my eye), *I couldn't have cared less.*

I killed endless time lost in my imagination with no one but myself for company. Erin, only a year younger, was regularly called 'the baby' and was rarely allowed to do the things I was. Daddy and I had favorite television shows (*The A Team, Knight Rider,* and *The Fall Guy)* and I'd regularly wander around pretending I was 'Bad Attitude' Baracas (a personal favorite) or Colt Seavers or Michael Knight. Which was what I must have been doing that first time I had a conversation with Benjamin Harayda.

"What are you playing?" I remembered hearing from high above me as I wandered around in the tiny back woods that bordered our development. It took me a while to put a face with the voice. A boy sat high up in a cedar tree. I knew who he was of course. He was that nerdy kid with the sports crazy grandmother who lived two houses away. Although we weren't in the same classroom at school we were in the same grade, walked the same route to school, and played on the same playground every day at lunch. His name was Ben.

"Nothing."

"Wanna come up?"

Yeah, I did. But I'd broken my arm that previous spring trying to build a tree house with Dean and my mother had forbidden both of us from climbing trees ever again. While that prohibition wasn't enough to stop me, the truth was I'd developed a slight fear about heights and was quite content to keep my feet on solid ground. "I'm not allowed."

"Oh yeah." Ben landed in a skillful crouch in front of me. "You broke your arm, didn't you?" Even at the tender age of five I already was well aware that my family was the highlight of neighborhood gossip.

I nodded. "Building a tree fort with my dad."

"Where?"

We spent the rest of the day wandering around the woods, critiquing the fort Dean and I had never finished and then, with growing excitement, planning another one we thought we could build. It was a glorious, magical day filled with laughter and companionship. Grandmother Miriam's cleaning spree had never flown by so quickly or been spent so enjoyably. Ben seemed genuinely happy to be in my company even though I spent a lot of time saying obnoxious stuff like, "My dad is a builder and he can bring home wood for us to use," and "My dad taught me how to use real tools and I'm sure he'll let me borrow them." Ben, whose dad was away for one of his two month deployments as a merchant seaman, was suitably envious that my dad was home every night. I vividly remember how good it felt to be the object of envy!

Towards the end of that first day Ben produced a rather smashed package of creamy, chocolaty candy from the back pocket of his pants. "Want a Rolo? My brother, Artie, steals candy all the time from the corner store over by the high school. I know where he hides it all so I snitch some sometimes."

"So you stole this candy from your brother who stole it before that?" I teased and Ben grinned and nodded.

Even now I remember the delicious taste of that candy as the caramel slowly melted in my mouth. "Wanna meet out here tomorrow after school to work on the fort?" Ben asked me as we sat side by side on a massive tree trunk.

"Yeah," I said. "I'll bring a canteen and you bring some more candy."

"Deal," Ben had said, and he'd stuck his hand out for me to shake. "Let's be best friends, okay Olivia?"

That night, sitting on the couch watching television with Grampie Taylor and Daddy, there was an advertisement for Rolos. *"Do you love someone enough to give them your last Rolo?"* the announcer asked and there was only one person in the whole wide world that I thought of.

I think that first night Ben and I sat in my living room with Sophie flirting outrageously with him was a test for both of us.

Ben had no idea that I had never been interested in such a nice man before, nor did he realize that I had never had a sustained conversation with one for any length of time. What did nice men like to talk about? I knew about flirting and sexual innuendoes and double entendres. I knew about crossing my legs just so and working my most stellar attributes to maximum advantage. I was amply skilled at the power of the tease and the significance of certain kinds of looks. Why, had I been forced to confess, I'd never brought a man home to my place without the express goal to end up in bed with him. These realities kept exploding in my mind as Ben and I laughed and talked causing numerous, internal alarms.

I kept hearing Aileen saying things like, *Just be yourself* and *It's just a cup of coffee sitting in your living room* and *You live in a different country now* and *See, I told you nice guys could be hot and fun.* We kept things light trading funny stories about dealing with teens and with updates about our families. We reminisced for a long time about when we were little, scrapes we had suffered through, and crimes we had gotten away with. The conversation was free and easy, and after almost two hours, I had forgotten about my initial awkwardness about the situation. It was all vanilla ice cream but I think we passed each other's tests. Ben apparently hadn't changed his mind. Carefully lifting a sleeping Sophie off his lap, he laid her on the couch and stood up. "I better get going. I'll pick you up tomorrow at five o'clock. If the weather's good we'll take the bike so be prepared. Okay?"

"Aren't you supposed to ask me?"

Ben kept right on making his way towards the front door. "You forget. I did ask you. And you already accepted. In fact, you promised." On the front step he turned and looked at me. "I'm not as gullible as I was when I was eight."

"How about when you were twelve?" Ben just stood there in the glow of the porch light. I smirked at him through the screen door. "Well, that still remains to be seen I guess. You have no idea what you're dealing with here."

Stepping up to the door he looked me right in the eye with those big green eyes of his and said, "I could say, Olivia, 'right back at you'." We stood there for a moment or two looking at each other. In a low voice Ben said, "But instead I'll say what I'm really thinking: I'm looking forward to finding out." Up until that moment, it had never occurred to me that ministers could flirt and use sexual innuendoes and double entendres.

Journal: The Truth About Happiness – Part I
Thursday, April 8, 2010

I had a man in my apartment tonight and I didn't sleep with him. Oh, I
wanted to but … I'm trying the Good Girl Path and that seems to
include sexual frustration and an extensive list of 'no-nos'. That's a
list I should work on sometime. I'd need a new journal, though.
I feel like I am at a fork in the road or, better yet, a crack in the sidewalk.
While neither side looks particularly appealing to me, everyone
seems to be pointing towards one side over the other.

Why am I doing all this? Why am I working so hard to reinvent myself? Why
am I persisting in rejecting what makes me comfortable and being
drawn to things that not only terrify but don't even appeal to me?
Why? If I can't answer that question, how can I possibly make
decisions about anything? I keep hearing Aileen say, "What really
matters to you?"

So I've been sitting here for a long time. I told myself that I cannot close
this book and go to bed until I come up with some answers about
why I am going through all this therapy and self examination. I'm
being Aileen … to myself. All I've managed to do is come up with
a list of reasons *I'm not* doing this:

1. I'm not doing any of this because I want to please anyone. I've
    never been interested in pleasing anyone, and that hasn't changed.
2. I'm not doing this because I'm trying to impress anyone. I still
    fully embrace the mantra 'accept me or get out of my way'.
3. I'm not doing this because I want a better life, because since I've
    started on this path the quality of my life has decidedly diminished.
    As a result, I'm poorer, lonelier, and more unsure of myself and my
    future than I've ever been in my life.

Come on, Olivia.

This entry has taken me over two hours to write. And I'm finally at the point of tears. I am overwhelmed with how … messed up … I really am. But, suddenly I think I realize *why* I'm doing all this and *what* matters to me. It is so simple, so basic, that I've ignored it because I thought the answer needed to be much more complicated. Kind of like The Holy Grail of reasons.

For once in my life I want to be truly happy.
And I'm willing to go to any length to achieve that.
That's why.
That's what matters.

Truth alone wounds.[22]

15: Everyone Has A Confession To Make
Friday, April 9, 2010

It poured the next day when Ben and I were supposed to go out for coffee so I wasn't surprised when he showed up in a nondescript four-door blue sedan. "Light years away from the bike," I teased as he held the door open and I slipped in. It was early, about four o'clock in the afternoon, and the TGIF mantra had never been sung so loudly by me. Ben had texted me asking if I could leave an hour early as the rain had caused a change in his plans.

"Goes with the minister suits I have to wear during the week. The bike only comes out on my days off."

"Which are?" I prompted realizing that Sunday surely couldn't be the day.

"Fridays and Saturdays, usually," he said, sliding in behind the wheel and starting up the car. "Sometimes church functions intrude and then I just switch, and there are often evening meetings so sometimes I have mornings off ... or long lunches. It's casual."

I shifted so that I could stare at him. Why not? He wasn't hard on the eyes. He was wearing a casual pair of tan slacks, a black polo shirt and boat shoes. Without socks. "Where are we going for coffee?"

"You said you didn't want to go anywhere close."

"That leaves a rather large area to choose from ..."

"Could it be a surprise?" He glanced over at me and I shrugged. "And stop staring at me. You're making me nervous."

I shook my head. "Sorry, you don't seem like the type who gets nervous easily."

"Why do you think that?"

"Well, mainly because you're a minister! You stand up in front of hundreds of people and preach. You regularly deal with the most difficult of situations - hospital visits and funerals, and I can't imagine what else! I'd guess you rarely get rattled."

Ben laughed and rolled his eyes. "How is that any different than what you do every day with your students? I at least have an expectation of respect and cooperation from my … students. And don't even talk about me being rattled! You should have seen me when I first learned who you were at IHC. I practically hyperventilated."

"Why?" I suddenly remembered his reaction to me in the hall that day and his exclamation, *Olivia Kelly!* like someone had just said I was Marilyn Monroe or something.

He made a big show of studying the traffic and signaling and merging onto the highway and didn't answer. Then I caught him glancing at me out of the corner of his eye. "You're still staring."

"I know." I crossed my arms and kept looking at him which eventually, just as I'd hoped, made him blush.

"I never forgot you, Olivia. Never. I've thought about you a lot … and our friendship. Do you remember the day you found out that your parents were getting a divorce?" I searched in my memory and … finally shook my head no. "You came to me … sobbing. Said you didn't want to go. I remember it like it was just yesterday. Said you *knew* things would never be the same. Said you knew that you'd lose your father and me," Ben swallowed, "the only two people that you loved in the *whole world*. I know we were both barely eight years old but we had been best friends for almost three years. As an adult, I can trivialize the whole thing. Rationalize it away as nothing as dramatic as it seemed back then." Ben was quiet as we drove. "But I couldn't forget you, Olivia. That look on your face. You begged me to run away with you. Do you remember asking me if I'd bring you food and stuff if you decided to hide in the woods and live in our fort?"

Suddenly, I did. It's another one of those memories that came to me with a flash, like an explosion. I remember the panic and fear and hysteria and desperation. "Yeah, I remember," I finally said quietly. "I was dead serious, too."

"You were always dead serious."

I sighed. "Yeah, I suppose I was."

"We made promises to each other," he said quietly in the dark of the car. Suddenly, I clearly remembered that, too. Promises never to forget each other. Promises always to be best friends. *No matter what.* "I can only imagine how hard it was for you … I remember crying after you left; being beside myself with helplessness. Grannie Blue helped me in the end."

I turned back to Ben because for the last few moments I'd been staring blindly out the window. "How?"

Ben smiled. "She smacked me on the back of the head and reminded me about prayer. 'Bennie, do you realize how powerful it is? Don't you remember it's your strongest weapon? You better get on your knees and start talking to God about that friend of yours. *Now.*'" Ben looked at me pointedly and then focused back on the highway ahead of us. "She promised to pray for you. And I've prayed for you every single night since then." He swallowed and I think he blushed a bit. "To this day."

He gave me something incredible at that moment. Whether I embraced the concept of prayer or God … to know that for literally my whole life there had been two people wanting only good for me. Sitting next to Ben, driving to an unknown destination, I was suddenly overwhelmed with the enormity of it all. "I never forgot you, either, Ben. In fact you were the last best friend I ever had." I meant this to be flip but it came out sounding rather pitiful.

He glanced at me and then went back to watching the road. "At least I was able to look forward to your visits after that. I crossed my fingers every Wednesday and every other weekend that Mr. Kelly would get in his truck and drive away and come back with you." I snorted because we both knew how irregular that turned out to be. "Grannie Blue was good about that, too. She tried to explain that sometimes it was best that Mr. Kelly *didn't* drive – that it was safer for everyone involved."

We drive in silence for a while both of us lost in thought. Finally Ben asks, "I used to think stupid things like if I ate all my lima beans in one minute you'd show up on the weekend or if I could avoid fighting with Arthur for the whole week you'd show up on Wednesday night."

"Oh Ben ..."

"I missed you like crazy when you stopped coming to visit your dad. At least we'd been able to see each other occasionally ... sporadically. And we wrote ... although neither of us was very faithful with that and by the time you stopped coming to see your father we were barely writing at all. I even risked going to speak with Grandmother Miriam about you when I finally realized you weren't going to come anymore."

That made me groan. "That couldn't have been good."

Ben made a face, confirming my assumption. Grandmother Miriam's rose-colored perception of me only lasted as long as I treated her son with the respect and dignity she felt he deserved. I'm sure she knew about the arguments Dean and I had after my mother and he divorced, because half of them were at her house during visitations. So when I started refusing to go to see Dean my status as daughter of her beloved son no longer held substance. Grandmother Miriam had contacted me just once after that when I was about thirteen. In a carefully worded letter she let me know that while Elaine still bore blame for everything that had ever gone wrong for Dean Kelly in particular and the Kelly's in general, she wanted to make sure I understood that it was *my existence* that had caused Dean the greatest stress and trouble. Elaine might have been the storm, but I was definitely the deadly lightning bolts. I always suspected she thought I had gone over to the dark side, taking my mother's side in the he said/she said messiness of a shattered marriage. She had no idea that I had simply cut off my nose to spite my face.

"Your grandmother was ... pretty upset ... with you," was all that Ben would politely allow.

"Is there a ministerial course on how to reword horrible situations into palatable phrases?" I asked which made him laugh. "She never forgave me when I refused to go to see Dean. Even after I resumed my relationship with Dean, she always had a chip on her shoulder for the years that I 'put Dean through all that hell.' Whenever I saw her she had this look on her face like she'd just bitten into a really nasty piece of fruit."

"Why do you call your father 'Dean'?"

Crap. Most people don't think twice when I simply say, 'Because he's not my biological father,' but Ben would notice the difference between that statement and my endless years of hero worship of Dean. I stopped looking at Ben and began intently looking out the front windshield.

"Uh-oh. Is that too personal a question? No big deal, Olivia. Forget I asked it." He reached over and gave my hand a squeeze.

I took hold of his hand with both of mine. "Dean's not my biological father, Ben. I didn't find that out until very recently. It still … is upsetting." His hand tightened in mine. "I'm really screwed up. You should know that. It's pretty much impossible for you to have any kind of conversation with me and not encounter some serious mine fields."

"So, you've got two options when that happens," he said in an unperturbed tone. "You can either answer me honestly when that happens and let me deal with the facts or you can tell me to mind my own business, and I will."

"There's a third option. You could just drive me home right now and retreat to safety."

But Ben shook his head vehemently. "No, that's not an option at all. *That option* wasn't even on the table before you bumped into me at IHC." He blushed again. "I've been dreaming of being with big violet eyes, wild curly hair, and a lone dimple for over twenty years."

He took me to New York City for coffee.

To the Waldorf Astoria.

Once we went through the Holland Tunnel I started firing questions at him like bullets, but Ben just laughed and said, "You've come this far, you might as well relax and go with the flow." As he carefully and precisely drove through the crazy evening traffic, it suddenly made sense to me why he'd wanted to leave as early as possible.

"You had this in mind all along," I said to him as the valet drove away in his car and we walked into the glorious entrance.

He surprised me by shaking his head. "No. Had the weather cooperated I would have picked you up on the bike and we would have gone somewhere else." He guided me purposefully through the lobby and gave me a dazzling smile. "I can't really see a valet parking the bike, can you?"

I had a sudden flash of what I must look like, walking through the incredible opulence of the Waldorf Astoria hand-in-hand with this confident, handsome man grinning from ear to ear like a fool and I suddenly stopped in my tracks. Ben turned, smiled, and said, "What?"

"This is fun ..." was all I could manage.

Ben took a step closer to me and looked down at me as people bustled around us. Reaching up, he cupped the side of my face, leaned down and lightly kissed me on the mouth. "I agree." Suddenly I was a little girl again looking into the eyes of a little boy as he offered me a Rolo and we made plans to be best friends.

I had a fancy cappuccino served in a beautiful bone china cup while Ben had a pot of tea. Our dinner consisted of funny little tea sandwiches because technically we were in the Park Avenue lobby where formal High Tea service was regularly served. We talked about safe, general topics like politics and sports.

"So it was Grannie Blue who convinced you to be a minister, huh?" I asked eventually.

"Are you prepared for God talk?" When I looked questioningly at him he explained, "God and I are not separate, Olivia. I don't want to scare you off."

"Maybe that's one of the reasons you're still single," I quipped, "Nothings a bigger turn off in a guy than him thinking he ranks right up there with God."

"I'm sure the fact that I'm a minister is the major reason I *am* still single," Ben acknowledged. "What's your excuse?"

He was quick. I kept forgetting that. I played with my empty cappuccino cup for a moment and suddenly heard Alec's voice in my head saying, *'Can I tell you the very first thing that intrigued me about your mother? … It was her flat-out honesty.'* Next, I heard Aileen's annoying voice harping endlessly about honesty and truth. So I looked Ben in the eye and said, "I have severe issues with healthy relationships."

"Such as?" he responded conversationally like I'd just said I really enjoyed certain kinds of Chinese food.

The urge to dump on my mother reared its ugly head for a moment, but I fought it back. "It's taken me a long time to appreciate quality when I see it … in myself and in others. I've not had many examples of healthy relationships so I've kind of been stumbling along just picking up anything that appeals for the moment without taking the time to weigh all the pros and cons."

"Are you purposely speaking in ambiguities?" He poured himself the last of the tea from his pot and doctored it up with cream and sugar.

"You're the first 'nice' guy I've dated in … probably my whole life."

He laughed. "Just because I'm a minister?"

I blinked at him. "Just because you're single."

"Oh."

He gave me a look with his big, puzzled, green eyes. His question and my response floated between us like a big, nasty fart. I sat there watching him process everything. Finally he sighed and asked quietly, "Are you dating any … 'not nice' guys right now?"

Great, his perception of me was so bad he had me doing things even I had never considered: dating two men at once. "I haven't dated *anyone* in almost two years. I've been trying to get my head straight. I'm still a work in progress, but the fact that I'm having the best night in years certainly says a lot." At his continued silence it was my turn to sigh. "Look, it's okay Ben. We're just two adults who knew each other as children, getting together to have a casual chat. No big deal. We'll drive home, you'll drop me off, and we'll wish each other all the best, all right? No harm. No foul." I felt the old anger start to percolate and recognized it as a welcome, old friend.

"I've stumbled into another mine field, I see," he finally observed. I'd picked up my purse and for some unknown reason was actively looking through it like the key to the fate of the entire free world was somewhere inside. "You've answered me honestly, Olivia, and I thank you for that, but you're apparently unhappy with how I've dealt with it. Maybe next time you'd be better off just telling me to mind my own business." At my continued silence (I was sitting across from him with my purse on my lap, ready to go, giving him a killer glare) he had the audacity to smile and quietly ask, "What did I do wrong, Jerry?" He used the endearing nickname from long ago.

What *did* he do wrong? I scrolled through the conversation and felt my anger deflate with the obvious conclusion. I closed my eyes and said, "Nothing. You didn't do anything wrong, Ben. Anger's my favorite emotion so I always revert to it but the appropriate feeling right now is actually shame. Please don't think I'm proud of my dating history. It's just a lousy fact I have to carry around just like -," I caught myself just in time. I was going to say, "... just like I'm a child of rape." Wouldn't that have put a quick end to the evening?

But Ben stepped up to the confession plate and threw out a big one, "... just like the fact that due to a high school indiscretion I have a seventeen year old son somewhere out there that I may never get to know."

"I told my sister about you today," I said to Ben on the phone the next day. It was Saturday evening and I was curled up on my couch chatting with a nice man. How abnormally normal was that picture?! He'd called just to "say hello" and tell me how much fun he'd had last evening. At this point no second date had been mentioned and I was very okay with that. "She remembered you." I sniggered.

He sighed a world-weary sigh. "What did she remember?"

"She remembered the time Arthur locked you in the backyard shed and your mother called the police when she couldn't find you. And when the police found you how your mother completely freaked out at both of you and kept screaming to the cops that they could 'have you both.' It was especially significant for us Kelly's because for once the cops weren't showing up in the neighborhood because of us."

"He still claims he forgot about me, you know."

"He used to claim he forgot about putting me up on the refrigerator, too."

"He's probably still using that same line with his wife, Carol."

"Do you know what else Erin remembered? She told me how you used to come over and sit on the front porch with my mother."

Ben hesitated. "Yeah, I used to go over and sit with her sometimes. She wasn't home too much, but when she was she usually sat on that front porch. Summer and winter." He sighed. "She was always so sad."

That surprised me. "Really? That's what you remember about her?"

"Oh yeah. She was the saddest person I knew. I don't think I ever saw her smile. Not once. And I used to try – I'd tell her funny stories or jokes and she'd just look at me and say, 'You're cute, Smiley.' You know, I just realized something: she was close to ten years younger than we are now …" We were both silent, lost in thought. Finally Ben asked, "How do you remember your mother?"

Actually, it was a good question. I realized that memories of my mother involved mostly *me* reacting to her, and so I took a moment to think. The sad woman Ben remembered wasn't a stranger but back then misery loved company and we were for sure one, huge miserable family. I had a flash of her grinning and blushing wearing her "Batman Is My Hero" tee shirt, just the other day at Erin and Dan's and realized that she was certainly happy now. "My biggest memory is of her not being there. And then not doing what I wanted her to do when she was there." This was said in a flat, unemotional tone. That was better than the roaring fury that used to be there, right?

"I probably noticed how sad she seemed because she used to call me Smiley. 'Come over and sit and smile at me, Smiley,' she used to say if she saw me skulking around the neighborhood."

"How come I didn't know about this? Why does Erin remember it, but I don't?"

"I think," Ben said thoughtfully, "you were still asleep. I've always been a dawn riser – still am – and Mom would tell me to 'get myself outside' to start running off some energy and not wake Arthur who could sleep until noon. I'd wander all over the neighborhood and knew all kinds of secrets like Mr. Kiloski always read the Walters' morning newspaper before they did, and lots of times Joey Enyingi came home by crawling into his bedroom window at six a.m."

"Really?!"

"Oh sure."

"So you knew that Dean often didn't make it inside to sleep."

Ben surprised me by chuckling. "Yeah, I knew about that, but honestly didn't think much of it. There were mornings when Mr. Kelly was sleeping in his truck or on the porch but usually when my dad was home he often slept on the couch, too. So couch, truck, porch ... what difference did it make where a dad slept? I figured it was pretty normal."

"Oh." For some reason the fact that Ben didn't think much of my dysfunctional upbringing was a huge relief.

"You know, I felt the same way about my dad; about how he was never there when I needed him and, once he was home, always too busy doing things that Mom needed him to do before he left again. I developed a lot of anger about it."

Geesh, maybe it was in the neighborhood water or something.

Ben didn't give me a chance to say something profound or insightful, though. "And then he went and died suddenly in Porto Alegre, Brazil and came home in a box."

Oh. "How old were you?"

"Fourteen." He paused. "It was right after you stopped visiting with … Dean. I went off the deep end for a while. A girl named Marisa calmed me down for a while when I was fifteen … but that only got me out of the frying pan and into the fire."

He'd been quite open at the Waldorf. When the pregnancy had been confirmed when he was sixteen, Ben had wanted to marry the girl and she'd wanted to … go off to college. He'd been positively vitriolic when she'd brought up abortion, and at first was determined to take the child and raise it himself. It was Grannie Blue who'd been the strength and support Ben needed, not telling him what to do but simply encouraging him to think it all through. Then make a decision that *would be best for the child.* In the end he and Marisa had agreed to put the baby up for adoption. Somewhere in some sealed adoption file was all of Ben's contact information and a private note that he'd written to the son he never knew but one day hoped to meet.

Therapy: The Truth About Happiness – Part II

Setting: Aileen's office, Monday April 12, 2010. I got here early and have calculated the following (much to my disgust): 2 years @ 50 weekly visits = 100 sessions. Aileen's hourly rate (don't get me started that we only really meet for 45-50 minutes …) = $120 x 100 = $12,000 in Aileen's pocket all thanks to me. My copay = $25 x 100 = $2,500 out of my pocket. That's a hell of a lot of shoes. Or purses. Or even just Grande Biscotti Chocolate Cream Frapuccinos. And wait a minute, I forgot about my deductible each year … !

Aileen: (Thanks to Ben there is an entirely new source of information to examine and pick apart.) So Ben refers to your mother as 'the saddest woman he knew'?

Me: Don't look so smug. We've already established whose side you're on.

Aileen: (Aileen rolls her eyes but refuses to rise to the bait.) What did you think when you heard him call her that?

Me: Well, I didn't disagree with him. It would seem that sadness was in ample supply for many of us Kelly's.

Aileen: Do you still think your mother would be called the "saddest woman" Ben knew if he met her today?

Me: No, you know that. And you're going to ask why, so I'll just keep talking. It's because she's a completely different person now.

Aileen: Keep going. Why is she a completely different person?

Me: She's rid of Dean. And me. (Aileen just sits and looks at me, so I sigh and forge on.) She's doing a job she loves. Her two children are relatively happy and healthy and stable and productive. Oh, and she's got herself a new man.

Aileen: Is having a man the magic formula for happiness then?

Me: I think happiness comes in all shapes and sizes. It's kind of like a pyramid, but you never know when you've hit the top so you keep climbing. For a while you can be happy on one level, but then something changes and you want to climb up another step.

Aileen: (This has got her intrigued ...) What about those people close to you? How does your happiness affect them?

Me: Well, for my mother it made her *happier* to be away from Dean so she took that step up, but it sure didn't please me. I wonder about Erin. I'll have to ask her ... Anyway, then she tried the 'support herself step', 'the Paul step', 'the be on her own again step', 'the Richard step' ... (I get silent, suddenly, lost in thought.)

Aileen: Richard didn't give her a chance to decide about the next step, did he?

Me: No. She stayed on the 'forced to be on her own again' step for a long time. For a while it was pretty obvious that that was as far as she was going to get with the happiness pyramid. She found happiness with Erin and Dan and Liam - Janine wasn't around yet - and her job. I think she was pretty content.

Aileen: She didn't find happiness with you?

Me: No way. I'm sure I sucked whatever happiness she was trying to hold on to completely away whenever I was around.

Aileen: And then Alec showed up.

Me: (I have a flash of him, the first time I met him at a Sunday dinner at Dan and Erin's. And I burst out laughing.)

Aileen: What's so funny?

Me: Do you know that the first time I met Alec he was wearing a plastic Batman mask? He'd been playing trains with Liam, and Liam let him wear his precious mask. Alec just stood up, walked over, and shook my hand Batman mask and all. I liked him instantly, even if he was with my mother. (I have a flash.) Do you know, my mother wears a tee shirt all the time that says, "Batman Is My Hero" ... suddenly I get it.

Aileen: (Aileen lets me digest all this for a few moments.) We were talking about happiness ...

Me: Yeah, well. So I think, to some extent, you can control your own happiness – but only to a point. There's life, and other people you're involved with who can help or … interfere with your progress.

Aileen: What should you do with those interfering people?

Me: Stay away from them!

Aileen: Just like your mother did with Dean? (I give her The Look which has no apparent affect because she then says,) And, if she did that with Dean, why didn't she do that with you?

Me: Because I'm *her daughter*. It's a law. Mother's have to suffer the trials of their children.

Aileen: Okay, so then why did she bother with Alec? Why risk the nightmare of another failed relationship? Why didn't she just stay on the happiness step she was on with her job and being independent and Erin, Dan and Liam and just avoid you once you were no longer a child and just a … nasty, happiness-sucking adult? Why did she keep seeking you out even though you – let me make sure I get this correct - (she looks down at her damn pad) "sucked whatever happiness she was trying to hold on to completely away"?

Me: (I give up the fight.) Because she believed in love. Because she *loved me*. Okay, Aileen?! Happy?! And, it's a good thing you're sitting down because I guess the only reason I kept coming back to her was because deep down I guess I knew that. And … Alec … she worked pretty hard to scare him away. And he just kept coming back for more. Which is exactly what my mother needed, I guess. Someone to love her enough to fight for her. Someone to pull her *up to* the next happiness step whether she wanted to go or not. God, how corny do I sound?! (I shake my head in disgust.)

Aileen: So … let me make sure I have this correct: you are at this precise moment in time acknowledging that love *exists*, and in the case of – at least your mother – it has influenced her happiness.

Me: (We stare at each other and I think, *you never quit, do you?*) Yeah. (I shrug.) Okay. *Maybe*. (At Aileen's satisfied expression I shout,) *I said, 'MAYBE'!!!*

Truth is not only stranger than fiction, it is more interesting.[23]

16: Nobody's Perfect

Wednesday, April 14, 2010

"Aunt Livvie, would you like my spinach?"

Liam, my favorite and only nephew needed my help, and far be it for me to disappoint. "Could I, Liam? I just love cold spinach and I've eaten all mine."

"*Olivia …*" Erin gave me a tolerant glare, 'you love my child, don't you?', as she watched me scoop up and eat a forkful of cold spinach.

"Me?" Janine said, offering me a piece of mangled dinner roll which I also ate obligingly. This time Erin rolled her eyes and laughed.

At least once a month aside from our weekly Sunday meal, I have dinner on my own with Erin and Dan. (Tonight it's just Erin, the kids and me. Dan, big time business executive, is at an overnight conference and I'm here to provide comic entertainment.) I'd like to say that I've been doing this forever but that would be a lie. Only recently I have started accepting some of the numerous invitations that have always been extended and which I used to avoid.

For years I didn't like my sister much. Does that shock you? I'm into honesty now, so it seemed only right to admit. And I'd guess, if you searched inside your own darkest corners, you'd have similar shocking admissions. But remember that different country I live in now?

Erin's a tough act to follow. Always has been and, I suspect, always will be. As a child she was perfect, as an adolescent she was ideal, and as an adult she is faultless. Of course I consistently worked to make her look that much better by contrast.

But as things had recently started to improve with my mother, so, too, had they begun to look up with my sister as well. And I was happy for it.

"I called you Friday. Alec was doing another concert at Agape Shop and wanted us all to come." My sister gave me a knowing look. "You really should go at least once, you know, Liv. The music is great, the food is great ... and they don't," Erin hesitated, "choke you with a bunch of God stuff."

You might be surprised to know that Erin's encouragement delighted me. A very short time ago, Erin making suggestions about my free time would have seriously annoyed me. I would have taken it as a correction or a criticism or an attempt to push her superior attitude on me ... But no more. "He's invited me a bunch of times." I sighed in resignation. "I suppose you're right."

That made Erin laugh and then grin at me. "You're different. Lately." It was a statement loaded with emotion, primarily praise. "I remember lots of things, Liv, and you telling me I was right *about anything* wasn't one of them."

"Do you remember me ever apologizing?"

Erin looked at me across the dinner table and smiled, but spoke to her son. "Liam, one more bite of the spinach and you're good to go. Don't forget, there are those brownies we made for desert."

"And ice cream?" I asked.

Janine shook her head. "Whip ceam."

"Ooo, I loooove whip ceam," I said, and winked at my niece.

With practiced ease, Erin got Janine cleaned up and out of her high chair, Liam to finish his meal, and efficiently began to clear the table. "You're a tough act to follow," I said as I searched for plastic containers for the leftovers.

Erin snorted. "Because I cooked dinner and got my kids to eat it? Oh yeah. I'm incredible."

"You do everything well, Erin. That's what I mean."

"You really think that, don't you." Erin stood in the middle of the kitchen, staring at me, a can of whipped cream in her hand.

I stood up and faced her. "Well, yeah."

"I'm pretty perfect," my sister said to me in a flat, emotionless voice.

I wasn't sure where we were going with this but I knew it was important. I hadn't apologized for decades of my irrational, spoiled behavior. Here was my golden opportunity. With complete sincerity I said, "Erin, I never measured up to you. Ever. You've always done everything well." I looked around the house. "You have a wonderful home, a great marriage and two terrific kids. You work hard and seem to know instinctively what choice is always wisest. I knew that when I was ten, and I still know it. I don't think you've spent most of your life angry at everyone. I don't think you've ever said hurtful, hateful things just to make someone feel smaller than you. I don't think you've been so wrapped up in yourself that you've completely missed having a normal life."

"No wonder you hated me," Erin finally whispered quietly.

"I never …" but I stopped and just stood and stared, because I would not lie to her. She deserved the truth. Finally, I looked away. "It wasn't you, Reenie, it was always, *always* me."

"So what? Through all your super therapy, you've reached a point now where you can tolerate my magnificence? Even maybe understand the need to learn from my wonderful example? Perhaps you've even reached the point where you're spending time with me just to absorb my incredible aura."

This had gone horribly wrong because I was certain that my sister was ballistic with anger. I stood there, and was suddenly terrified to say one more word.

Erin watched as I stood paralyzed with … unease. Finally she sighed, crossed her arms and leaned against the sink. "Have you ever had *one* glass of wine, Olivia?"

Huh? I swallowed. "Uh, sure."

Erin shook her head. "I never have. Even the very first time I tried alcohol, I drank a whole bottle. How about this, Livvie: have you ever drunk a fifth of vodka in one sitting and had to have your stomach pumped?" I shook my head and suddenly found myself fighting back tears. *Oh no ...*

"Well that's good. It's not a pleasant experience, let me tell you. Have you ever woken up in a place where you not only didn't know the people with you but couldn't remember how you got there in the first place?" I shook my head again. In my head I had now begun to say over and over again, *oh no, oh no, oh no ...*

Erin got the brownies and began cutting them, her movements sharp and quick. "How about this? When you go out for the evening do you ever drink two or three drinks before you leave?" I didn't need to respond because she wasn't looking at me anymore. "Sometimes I'd drink a whole six pack before I left the dorm, but I always denied it if anyone asked." She began to fill the coffee carafe with water and then measured out the grounds. "I was really good at hiding things," she laughed briefly, "or so I thought. I had places to stash my empties and excuses for why certain mornings I couldn't make it to class." She turned and smiled at me but there were tears streaming down her face. "Some months I had my period two or three times."

Completely clueless about what to say or do, I simply walked over and hugged her. We stood like that for a long, long time. Against my shoulder she murmured, "I've been an acknowledged alcoholic for over eight years, Olivia. Dan got me going to AA meetings in college." She made a sound that sounded like a laugh. "Actually, our fourth date was to an AA meeting. Twice I've slipped up. I've been sober for over four years now." I hugged her tighter. "Mom knows. So does Alec. Even Dad knows, because occasionally I've gone to meetings with him." She pulled back and looked at me. "I didn't purposely keep it from you. Actually I tried to tell you a few times but it just never ... worked." The tears started again. "I guess I should have made more of an effort. Maybe if you'd realized that I wasn't so perfect things would have been better between us sooner."

I shook my head with disgust. "Even now, I'm not confident that I'd recognize a good decision if it bit me on the … nose."

"Maybe," my little sister said to me, "we could help each other make good decisions *together*. Since now we both know that neither one of us is perfect."

Aileen was right. I'd lived my whole life wrapped up in this tight little angry ball not seeing much around me. I'd lost *decades* shouting and screaming about what I didn't have … shouting and screaming so loud that I couldn't hear or see what I did have. Wednesday night, once I got home from Erin's, I wandered around my condo looking at its cool, modern décor and realized there wasn't one family - connected picture or knick-knack anywhere to be seen. This place I called home was as purposely devoid of warmth and emotion as I was.

I lay on my expensive butter-soft leather couch going over and over memories of me and my sister. Like every one of my screwed-up relationships, every interaction with Erin was always colored by what I believed to be true. Always on the defensive, always anticipating a problem, always knowing the fault lay with others. I closed my eyes and still the tears leaked out. How could I have gone all this time without knowing the truth about Erin? So distant, so unfeeling that not only didn't I notice, but she never felt comfortable sharing with me. How could I have been so blind? How self absorbed am I? The enormity of what kind of person I … was …

I sat up. I'd used the past tense. The enormity of what kind of person I *was*. I lived in a different country now. I was determined to be different.

And I was determined to be happy.

I dragged out my journal and my favorite blue pen and wrote *Love* unable to escape Aileen's constant harping and the emotion I'd felt at Erin's tonight. I took the time to make up my own definition: *unconditional affection that cannot be prevented or deflected or stopped.* <u>*No matter what.*</u>

Evidence of love I wrote underneath that. And then I started making a list.

1. My mother with me. (The most difficult and most unlovable child in the world).

2. Dean with me. (His unswerving loyalty and constant support in the midst of his drunkenness and my rejection still causes me awe.) <u>He stayed true to me.</u>

3. Erin and Dan with their kids. And each other.

4. Grannie Blue … in many directions.

5. Clotilde and Max with each other – exemplary couple.

6. Liam and Janine towards me. (Blind adoration … is a better word.)

7. My mother and Alec with each other.

I looked at the list and could *almost* write *Ben with me.* Spending time with him is creating the same kind of feeling that I get with my mother and Dean and Liam and Janine … that I couldn't escape its power even if I tried with all my might. But the skeptical, tough-assed side of me smirked at such a thought. And the terrified, wounded little girl in me whimpered.

I pressed on, alone in my condo with Sophie sitting regally on the table, waiting for the chance to curl up on my journal (another favorite sleep location): *People I Love.* And then I smiled to myself and added: *Easy Ones*

1. Liam

2. Janine

I sighed. Not a big list, but a truthful one. I thought of my mother, Dean, Erin, even Alec and Grannie Blue and the reality was, the qualifier in my definition – *no matter what* – had prevented me from writing down their names. Haven't I repeatedly spoken of my hatred for my mother and Dean, my dislike of Erin, my scorn of husband # 4, Alec? And I wouldn't have thought twice about Grannie Blue but for the past weeks. Yet, I doggedly wrote down *Hard Ones* and listed four names. Why? The real truth of the matter was after everything I'd said and done and felt those people are still in my life. I'd weeded a lot of people out of my life over the last few years but there was no denying that there were some that I couldn't seem to get rid of … *no matter how hard I've tried.* Which in a bizarre, indirect way qualified them …

Hard Ones

1. My mother
2. Dean
3. Erin
4. Alec (still tentative though)

And last but far from least, I write one more name.

5. Ben

This last name was easier to write than each of the others. My childhood love for Ben (yes, I was going to write 'affection' but … it just didn't fit) was a consistent thread that had never broken. Plus, I got the distinct impression that now that he had reconnected with me, I might be unable to get rid of him *no matter what.* So why didn't I put Ben on the easy list then? The answer was obvious. Because of every name on this list, only Ben had the potential to break my heart.

Therapy: The Truth About Hope

Setting: Aileen's office, April 19, 2010. I've done a lot of thinking about what Benjamin has told me about himself and his history – not all of which is happy and rainbow filled. I feel like my perception of life and the world has shifted completely. Again, you may think I'm foolish or stupid or possibly both, but I've been so wrapped up in *my own* issues and *my own* complaints and *my own* daunting list of personal failures, disasters, and errors that it's never really occurred to me to think about *others*. I just assumed that if you were walking and talking and functioning and occasionally smiling and laughing that you *had to be* not only okay but relatively crisis and tragedy free. And good, nice, kind people, *normal people* would not only have charmed lives but be unable to relate to a damaged piece of goods like myself.

Aileen: Would you describe yourself as a hopeful person?

Me: (Is this a trick question? I rapidly ponder the pros and cons of answering this question either with a 'yes' or a 'no'. In the end, I take the middle road, which in reality is the truth.) I don't know. I certainly have never thought of myself as hopeful.

Aileen: I was thinking about you this weekend and I think you *are* a hopeful person.

Me: Okay …

Aileen: Why do you think I've come to that conclusion?

Me: (Wouldn't this whole thing be *so much easier* if she just spelled it out for me? But no …) Because I keep showing up here? Even though we both know how much I hate it?

Aileen: (She writes something down.) Actually, that could be indicative of autophobia – extreme hatred of oneself. You do things that will make yourself unhappy.

Me: Oh. Well. How about the fact that I've been working on reestablishing a relationship with my mother? And that recently we've actually had some rather … pleasant times together?

Aileen: (More writing.) After over thirty years of issues with your mother, you've managed to reconcile much of your animosity and try to reconnect with her. Does that sound like you've made progress … or simply abandoned your principles?

Me: Are you serious?! (Aileen just blinks at me.) All right, how about the fact that anger, my previously *most favorite emotion*, has taken a back seat in my life and that happiness and sorrow and excitement and satisfaction … have been much more prevalent lately?

Aileen: (She shrugs and makes a note.) As long as you're certain that your emotions are *balanced* and you're not simply replacing one over-used emotion with another.

Me: (I sit there for a few moments. When anger comes and sits next to me, I discourage it and try to think. Where is she heading with this? Is she *trying* to get me to storm out of here in anger so she can leave early??) All right. Then what about the fact that I've chosen to be *celibate for over two years* rather than choosing to continue to date men with whom there was *no possibility* of love or happiness?

Aileen: (More damn notes.) Where's hope in celibacy? I foresee a number of things, but not a future.

Me: (Hello sarcasm.) How about I'm dating a minister?!!

Aileen: (Shrugs dismissively.) Big deal. I'm almost certain that's not addressing your celibacy issue. And who says there's any possibility of (she looks down to read) 'love or happiness' with *you* and *a minister?* Maybe you've just chosen a new, hopeless category of men to get involved with. (She actually laughs briefly.)

Me: What is this, Aileen?! Are you trying to get me annoyed? Are you trying to piss me off? What do you want from me?

Aileen: (She speaks very precisely to me.) I want you to answer my question. Would you describe yourself as a hopeful person?

Me: *Damn right I would!* Who but *me*, with *my history*, would be dumb enough to *believe in love* after all this time?! What person who knew me before would *ever* believe such a thing could be possible?

Aileen: (She's scribbling furiously now. When she finishes, she looks up and she's grinning delightedly at me.) Look what you just did. (She tears off the top sheet of her pad and holds it out for me to take.) This is what it says:

<u>Olivia Kelly's accomplishments over the past two years of therapy. (April 12, 2010)</u>

1. Continued to do things that were difficult because she knew they would be beneficial
2. Rearranged life-long misconceptions
3. Repaired damaged relationships
4. Acknowledged past mistakes and sought not to repeat them
5. Acknowledged past wrongs and sought to repair them
6. Listened and acted upon sound advice
7. No longer ruled by emotions but thoughtful introspection
8. Stuck up for self when questioned and challenged using logical rationale
9. Defended personal choices with sound reasoning
10. Believes that despite everything she's been through, everything she's experienced, everything she knows to be true, that love is real and possible.

Aileen: (She waits until she's sure I'd read her list not once, not twice, but three times, blown my nose, and gone and stood by her African violet window.) I'd say you're getting better, Olivia. What do you think about that?

How much truth can a spirit bear, how much truth can a spirit dare?[24]

17: Simple Questions
Saturday, April 24, 2010

Late Saturday afternoon, April 24, found me sitting on my front step enjoying a Top Ten Day waiting for a very handsome man to pick me up for a ride on his motorcycle. From the time I was little, the best, the most perfect days qualified as a ten under my theory that over the course of my life there would probably be only ten top days. Brilliant sunshine, perfect temperature, and a soft gentle breeze with the smell of new grass, rich earth and spring flowers certainly helped qualify this day for that distinction. I'd finally agreed to a second date with Ben because I enjoyed his company, but also because I wanted to see what Date Number One would have been had there been no rain. He'd certainly done an outstanding job with a day that didn't qualify as a Top Ten so I was pretty hopeful.

I've always had a secret fascination for guys on motorcycles: tight jeans, leather jacket, and a shaded face mask can make even the ugliest guy seem hot, don't you think? As Ben roared into my parking lot he was even more appealing because I knew he really was good looking underneath that helmet.

"Hey," he said with a grin as I walked toward him. "You look cute."

No one's told me I was cute since I wore pigtails. "Cute? What am I, six?"

He had the audacity to look at me pointedly from head to toe and muttered, "You are absolutely *not* six years old. But I like the jacket and

171

I've rarely seen you dressed down in jeans. You look younger ... softer," he shrugged, "I don't know. But I like it."

"You look pretty good, yourself." Unstrapping a second helmet, Ben held it out to me and I stood there like a six-year-old waiting for him to put it on me. But as he went to do just that I said, "Don't I get a kiss hello?"

He froze and I instantly wondered why. He'd kissed me a few times – all definitely G-rated but still delightful, so I was intrigued by his sudden hesitation. "All I do is think about kissing you," Ben muttered almost to himself. His tone was far from happy. Reaching out, he smoothed some of my uncooperative curls. Slowly and deliberately he tucked stray strands first behind my right ear and then my left. The anticipation that built about that kiss was astronomical and I probably could have stood there forever. All the while he studied my face and hair with an intensity that made me wonder if I'd done something wrong with my make-up.

"Is everything okay?" The emotion flowing around us was suddenly so thick my voice shook.

Our eyes met finally and Ben said, "Depends on which side you're on." *What the heck did that mean?* Then he laughed, leaned forward and gave me a quick peck on the mouth. "There, that'll have to hold you," he said firmly. I had the helmet strapped under my chin before I could find my voice again.

Have you ever ridden on a motorcycle behind a man? It's very erotic. Especially if it's only a second date. Things are still very reserved, and yet there's a whole lot of sexual attraction going on. I probably know very little about nice guys. I may not know much about single guys. I definitely know nothing about ministers. But I knew everything about what was going on between Ben and me. Call it chemistry or attraction or, in my case, rampant horniness, it was there like a six hundred pound gorilla riding along with us on that motorcycle. Ben was very attentive as we drove, asking me each time we stopped if I was comfortable and if everything was okay. But three times he reached down and touched the side of my thigh as we wove through the traffic and then along the quiet country lanes. It was very circumspect, just a polite acknowledgement of my presence since words were impossible but each time the world completely fell away and all I was aware of was that warm, open palm on my leg. I have never been so intrigued by so little. If this was what it was like with nice guys … oh what I'd been missing!

We rode for a good forty-five minutes and finally stopped at what I can only describe as a fairy-tale cottage in the middle of a tiny village. Ben parked the bike and we both worked to get our helmets off. I did not want to know what my hair looked like. "The Waldorf Astoria let me down last time," he said as we looked at what I read was Sally Mae's Traditional English Tea Shoppe. "My plan was to take you here where you wouldn't be served coffee and so, technically, you still wouldn't have fulfilled your promise. That way I was certain I'd get another date with you. But the Waldorf served you that darn cappuccino …"

"So it's a real place where you can go in and eat?"

"Oh yeah. Fantastic scones, real pots of tea, and you can even get cucumber sandwiches and authentic shepherd's pie. I found it a long time ago when I was out riding."

With less grace than I would have preferred I got off the bike and waited while Ben did whatever bikers do with their things. Then he took my hand and led me inside.

I wanted to order a Tiddy Oggie AKA a Cornish Pasty just because it was such a ridiculous name for something you're supposed to eat, but in the end I took the safe route and ordered a chicken pot pie. Ben had an *authentic* Shepherd's Pie (made with lamb *not beef!*) and we both ordered different kinds of tea so we could share and compare.

In a very short time the food arrived. The pot pie was fabulous and I said so after my first bite only to discover Ben just looking at me. "Is something wrong?"

"I, Well I … always say grace before I eat," he finally finished lamely.

"Shame on you then," I said as I put my fork down and wiped my mouth with my napkin. "You didn't pray at the Waldorf."

That made him blush. "Actually, I did, but it was a sneaky prayer. Remember I said I was 'thankful that I'd finally managed to get you to go out for coffee with me and that we'd had a safe drive into the city despite the rain'? That was my prayer."

It was my turn to blush because I remember vividly how I had responded to his 'prayer.' I said something along the lines of, 'And I'm thankful that Mr. Waldorf and Mr. Astoria had the foresight to construct this classy place so that I could be catered to in the luxury I so amply deserve.' "Just in case you're wondering, my response *wasn't* a prayer."

He grinned at me. "Do you mind?" He extended his hand to me palm up and I put my hand in his. I watched as he closed his eyes, bowed his head and said, "Hey Lord, thanks for the safe ride, the beautiful weather, the gorgeous company, and the delicious food. Keep us ever mindful of You. Amen."

"'Hey Lord'? Isn't that awfully casual? Even disrespectful? Shouldn't you be talking in fancy words like 'Thou' and 'Thee'?" Ben smiled but he couldn't answer because his mouth was already stuffed with Shepherd's Pie. "And did I get in trouble for not closing my eyes or bowing my head and ...," but I caught myself and instead took a big bite of my meal.

"And?" Ben prompted, but I shook my head. No way, while we were discussing prayer was I going to discuss where my mind wandered whenever he touched me – even when he holds my hand in prayer. "There's no special prayer language, if that's what you're asking. Prayer's personal, sincere, honest ... but it doesn't have to be formal. Did it make you uncomfortable when I did that?"

I shrugged, chewed and thought. "Honestly? Probably a little. Firsts often make me a little jumpy and overly observant though. But the two old ladies off to your left watched the whole thing and definitely approved."

"How do you know that?"

"They mouthed, "Lord Bless You" when they caught me looking at them. That's a first too."

"I'm a regular guy, Olivia, but for *this* regular guy, God plays a big part in my life."

I took a sip of my tea (Earl Grey, with cream and one sugar). "Well *this* woman is *far from* regular and even *farther* from God."

"The first thing – being far from regular - I couldn't care less about – in fact that's probably part of your tremendous appeal. As for the second one – your distance from God – I guess I have to ask if it's a conscious decision or simply the way life's taken you to this point?"

"Am I anti-God? Is that what you're asking?" Ben nodded and shoveled in more lamb. "No, I'm not anti-God. I don't think I'm even anti-church because I have fond memories from childhood attending church with you – remember Vacation Bible School?" to which Ben grinned and nodded again. "Aside from the whole sorrow cloud floating around at Grannie Blue's service, I have to admit that sitting there listening to you talk and hearing the music – boy, Jen and Phillip can really sing! – was quite … nice." When Ben went to open his mouth to say something, I added, "But I have no interest in attending church or anything on a regular basis," which made him shut his mouth and take another bite of food.

We ate in silence for a few moments and I had time to consider how this was the second time in as many dates that conversation had lead us to a place that had put us both in opposite corners. Last time it was because I had confessed to having a history with married men, and this time because I effectively shut and bolted the door against the possibility of my becoming the nice little girlfriend sitting regularly listening to Ben preach. Last time Ben helped get things on track. So tonight must be my turn.

"Why are you still single?" I asked. "Arthur implied that the whole church was on a campaign to set you up with every available female in a fifty-mile radius."

Ben shrugged and said, "I'm picky, I guess."

"Have you agreed to any of these fix ups?"

He looked surprised at my question. "I've agreed to every one of them, actually. I'm always willing to meet someone for a meal or a cup of coffee, although everyone has come to understand how particular I am I have had fewer candidates lately." He laughed. "Or maybe, now that I think of it, I've rejected almost every available female in a fifty-mile radius and they've just run out of options."

"You've agreed to *every one?*"

"Yeah. Why not? She's out there I've just got to find her. Who am I to try to dictate the way God is going to send her to me?"

"So you're waiting for God to send you the perfect woman." My head said, *Phew, that lets me out of the running.*

He nodded. "Perfect *for me*, not perfect meaning faultless. No way do I want a perfect woman."

"So, let's hear about Ben Harayda's Perfect Dream Woman. I want the list."

"No."

Very abrupt. Very definitive. *Very intriguing.* "No? How come?"

"Too personal? Too embarrassing? I'll make a deal with you. You write down what your perfect man is like and I'll write down what my perfect woman is like and then we'll trade."

"I don't know what the perfect man is for me. Until recently, I was so far off track it wasn't even funny." I gave him a pointed look and reminded him. "I shared my history with you."

"Growth involves positive change, and human beings should continue to grow for their whole lives." Ben made a face. "I sound like a therapist. Sorry."

"Trust me, I won't get confused. You're a lot cuter than my therapist." The moment it was out of my mouth I was horrified. Then I made it worse. "CRAP," I said loud enough that the two old ladies at the other table gasped in outrage. In a lowered voice I acknowledged, "Now you know just how screwed up I really am."

But Ben just pushed his plate away and leaned back in his chair, the picture of a satisfied male. "Good for you for going. I went for about three years in my mid-twenties. It was the best thing I ever did for myself … and for all the people that cared about me, too." I just sat there with my mouth hanging open, staring at him. Finally, he leaned forward and took my hand. "Olivia, there are two things that can change a person. One works on your head and one works on your heart."

I looked down at his big hand holding onto mine and then back up at him. "Okay. I'll bite. Tell me what the two things are."

"Serious, sound therapy can help us get our heads aligned correctly. And having Christ at the center of our lives gives us completely new hearts."

"What if a person's heart is just fine already?"

"Without Christ?" I nodded and that made him shake his head. "Sorry, not possible. It's a critical decision, Olivia, that everyone must address at some point. A 'yes' or a 'no' decision with absolutely no middle ground." When I went to say something he picked my hand up and kissed it, which shut me up fast. "Stop. Answer me this one question with an honest 'yes' or 'no'. *Just this one* and then we're going to change the subject and go for a walk in the moonlight, okay?" He waited until I had decided I would let him steer the conversation - and the rest of the evening - and nodded. He took the time to take my hand and hold it tightly in both of his. Then he leaned forward and whispered, "Tell me honestly, with a 'yes' or a 'no' - is *your* heart just fine, Jerry?" There was that nickname again.

We sat staring at each other for the longest time. I'm not even sure either one of us blinked. He called it a simple question, but we both knew it wasn't. In fact it was probably The Most Important Question In The Whole World. And, to top it off, he'd played the honesty card.

"No," I finally said but perhaps I just mouthed the words. I don't think any real sound actually came out.

"Check please," Ben said, but he was still looking only at me.

My mother rang my doorbell at ten o'clock Sunday morning. Later I would learn that in the huge Dunkin Donuts bag were chocolate frosted donuts (six) and two Grande Biscotti Chocolate Cream Frapuccinos (which I'd raved about to everyone I know). But it was her cat Harry, yowling at the top of his voice in his cat carrier, that demanded the most immediate attention. She looked completely frazzled and I was fairly certain she had slippers on her feet. My first thought when I saw her was – of course - *oh no, she and Alec have broken up.*

"Mom? Are you okay?" I had to raise my voice over Harry's pitiful cries. Before she could answer I held open the front and screen doors and we did the awkward dance of trying to maneuver in a space that was never designed for two women, takeout food, and a trembling cat carrier. "Come in! Come in!"

"Oh Olivia! I'm so sorry to show up like this unannounced! I've been waiting until a decent hour to ring the bell but Harry's going to have a heart attack if I don't do something soon." Rushing past me she sat Harry's carrier down on the hallway tiles and turned to face me. She looked near tears. There were dark circles under her eyes.

"Mom …," I stepped towards her with real concern, "whatever has happened between you and Alec I'm sure you will be able to work things out …"

My mother blinked and then shook her head. "No, there's no problem with me and Alec! It's the house! A water pipe burst in the upper bathroom while we were out last night, and when we got home … oh, Olivia, you should see the place. We've been up all night trying to deal with the mess. Alec's there now trying to salvage things but it's a disaster …" She bit her lip and looked down at Harry in his carrier. (Who was now completely silent.) Sophie approached Harry with all the animosity she could muster: back arched, tail five times its normal size, ears flat, and a steady stream of spitting. "I forgot you had a cat …"

"Sophie. As easy to live with as I probably was in my teens." My mother flashed me a worried look but I smiled and she seemed to relax a bit.

Wringing her hands, my mother began, "We can't go to Erin and Dan's because of all the cat allergies and we can't take Harry with us to a motel." Sophie was now crouched in front of the carrier door growling menacingly. For only the second time in my life I watched my mother begin to cry. "Alec and I have been up all night trying to deal with everything and Alec said for me to come here, but I didn't think it was a good idea because you and I have only just begun to really talk and enjoy each other's company, and it's just the best thing that's ever happened to me – us talking and laughing and enjoying each other's company - and I don't want to mess that up, but Alec said to stop being silly, that of course you'd let us stay here with Harry for a few nights - that you were one of the most forgiving people he knew - while we get the repairs done, but I don't want to risk causing any new riffs between us – we certainly could never live happily together before! - and this new - found relationship is too important to me to risk so I've been sitting out in the car since about five a.m. trying to figure out what to do, and Alec has called me twice on my cell and I lied and told him that I was already here, and now he just called and said he's on the way and he's going to be so upset that I lied to him because I've never done that ever – oh the truths I've told that man! - but what finally got me out of the car is the fact that I've been sitting there for over five hours, and if Harry doesn't get to a litter box soon I don't know what's going to be worse …"

I'm not sure, but I suspect that my mother would have kept on talking forever. Periodically she sniffed and wiped her nose on her tee shirt sleeve (which – in case you're interested – said in big, bold letters *Don't worry, I'm right behind you.* Then, in much smaller letters, *Using you as a shield.*) I also suspect that if I had tried to interrupt her and say something witty or funny or even serious or astute she wouldn't have even heard me. In between the crying and the rambling and Sophie's growls I heard her say some of the sweetest things she's ever said to me: *best thing that's ever happened to her? Too important to risk?* And, even more stunning, I was *one of the most forgiving people* Alec knew?! What, has this guy spent most of his life in a correctional facility or something?! In the end I did the only thing I knew would guarantee to shock my mother into silence.

I hugged her.

189

Harry easily outweighed Sophie by ten pounds but spent all of his time huddled in his cat carrier, only leaving for necessary trips to the litter box. Sophie, calm, serene, and In Charge settled herself in the middle of the floor about five feet from the carrier's opening. She took an extensive bath (including my favorite parts: her face and ears) and then settled down for a nice long nap ... with one eye open and both ears tuned.

On that first, bizarre Sunday morning my mother and I sipped on our Frapuccinos (which I had to microwave since they were about six hours old). I must say that even reheated they were still fabulous. We munched on donuts and I anticipated Alec's arrival and put coffee on and cooked up some eggs and bacon. Alec's a pastry chef, so we weren't concerned about saving him any donuts. In fact, we decided to eat the entire collection of donuts and hide the evidence before he showed up to avoid hearing the inevitable diatribe over superior and inferior pastries. When he arrived he was in not much better shape than my mother, although he never shed a tear. He'd already called some of his "buddies" and they planned to converge on the disaster later this afternoon after he got a bit of sleep. It seemed the upper bathroom and kitchen were ruined and even the dishwasher and stove needed to be replaced.

Alec, direct man that he was, got right to the point as he sipped coffee and shoveled in his breakfast. "Are you okay if we stay here for a few days, Olivia?" He glanced at my mother, who was curled up on the couch trying valiantly to stay awake. "Elaine's concerned that it will put too much stress on the two of you. She thinks I don't know, but I'm pretty sure she sat in her car for like three hours before she got up enough nerve to knock on your door."

"Six hours," my mother and I said simultaneously which made Alec laugh and roll his eyes.

He shook his head and said, "You two ...! It's *me* who should be worried about staying with the both of you for any length of time. I'll probably never be the same."

Alec was one smart man.

I looked at my mother and gave her a reassuring smile. The tears had stopped but I didn't know how far away they were. "It's fine, honest. Although I don't know how comfortable the fold out couch is."

Alec shrugged, "Don't worry; I've slept on a lot worse. In fact, I slept on a fold out couch close to a year right after -"

"Will Sophie be okay with Harry?" my mother asked from the couch. She looked tired and tense.

"As long as Harry follows her rules I think it will be fine," I said with a determination I didn't quite feel. "And besides," I said to Alec trying to make things lighter and funnier than they really were, "my mother said that you think I'm one of the 'most forgiving people you've ever met'. I'm sure people have thought a lot of things about me, Alec, but never that! It seems you've led a pretty restricted life. Where have you been for most of it?" I laughed out loud, "Prison?"

Alec literally spat his mouthful of coffee out across the breakfast table, Harry began to howl, Sophie began to growl, and my mother started to cry again.

Therapy: The Truth About Celibacy

Setting: Aileen's office. It's Monday as usual, April 26, 2010. If I think that, given our last session Aileen's going to pat me on the head and say we're done ... Well, of course I don't think that. If there's one thing I've learned (that wasn't on Aileen's very nice list last week) it's that Aileen is a pit bull. Once she sinks her teeth into you she never lets go. I'm better, but I've still got old stuff to deal with. Besides, today *I've* got something to talk about. Time for me to steer this boat.

Me: You made a crack last week about celibacy. And how there's no hope in it. Were you serious?

Aileen: Not getting any with the minister, huh?

Me: Answer the question.

Aileen: How about this: why have *you* chosen celibacy for these last two years? I'll answer your question after you answer mine. I didn't tell you to be celibate. You decided that.

Me: No fair.

Aileen: Deal with it.

Me: I think more rationally about a guy when things aren't physical. You can lose perspective too soon if you give in to the sexual attraction – which was the only thing I used to look for.

Aileen: But sexual attraction is important in a relationship ...

Me: Did I say it wasn't important? I'd say it's absolutely critical. But it used to be *the only thing* in my relationships that I bothered with. (I think for a few moments.) Sex is a little like a drug. Get enough of it and you can blot out a lot of undesirable stuff – also known as *reality*. (Aileen laughs.) Laugh all you want. Ever get the hubby to buy you a new dishwasher by making (I wink) promises? You often have fresh flowers in here. Does hubby get lucky every time he sends you a bunch? I'd give him a thumbs up if he has an easy technique that works for him. You married couples probably do it all the time. (Aileen's no longer laughing and is now listening

182

rather intently to my speech.) With me it was all I bothered with. Take the sex away and all the men I've been involved with in the past were … pretty uninteresting. So, I just decided I'd wait until a guy came along that was interesting … without the sex. Who knew it would take over two years?

Aileen: So … was celibacy necessary for you?

Me: Hell yeah.

Aileen: Okay, so you've answered your own question.

Me: But you said celibacy offered no hope of love, happiness or a future.

Aileen: (Aileen shook her head vigorously.) No I didn't. I *asked you* if you thought there was any hope of love, happiness and a future between you and a minister. (Aileen shrugs.) Granted, celibacy will probably play a bigger part in this relationship than any of your others. But ministers, to the best of my knowledge, don't object to sex. They just (she makes a show like she's thinking but I know she's just getting ready for a zinger so I brace myself) tend to embrace celibacy because their Boss forbids premarital sex. I'm pretty sure it's because their Boss realizes that … *sex is a little like a drug. Get enough of it and you can blot out a lot of undesirable stuff – also known as reality.* (She repeats my words exactly as I said them. Straight faced.)

Me: Ben and I have *a lot* of sexual chemistry.

Aileen: So. You bragging? (I glare at her.) Look, Olivia. The two of you are going to have to talk this out. It would be *really wise on your part* to determine *in advance* if you would be content to have a romantic relationship with a man *without sex*. Especially *this man*, as you seem to have finally found a guy who's 'interesting without the sex.' Have this concept thought out in your head before the conversation comes up. (She thinks for a minute.) You used to live completely in the past. That made you angry. You've done an excellent job learning to live in the present. You're happier now. But you've also got to begin to anticipate the future. You've got your wish list, but now you need to look at everything in your life and consider it in relationship to what you *want to happen in the future*. Your work. Your friends. Your daily decisions and long-term choices. And you should be doing this with Ben or any other man you consider getting involved with. What does Ben offer – now - that will impact your future? Determine the pros and cons. How do they measure up? Is it worth the time and effort?

Me: All I asked about was celibacy. I know I answered your question. Now you answer mine. Is there any hope in celibacy?

Aileen: (She sighs. Poor thing, she's just so put out.) In relation to you, right? Not in general, concerning worldwide implications? (I hate when she's sarcastic and I flip her the finger. She laughs and then leans forward.) In your case, Olivia, right now … celibacy in a relationship is the best thing. It will keep your (she smirks) 'focus on reality', and if this guy hangs around and actually convinces you that he likes you (she does a pretend gasp) or loves you (she does a pretend shiver) it's probably the only way you'd ever really believe him. Because another truth we haven't really discussed – now that you've acknowledged there *is* such a thing as love – is if you believe you're *lovable*. (She grinned a really evil grin.) But that discussion is for next week.

Integrity is telling myself the truth. And honesty is telling the truth to other people.[25]

18: The Future's Not Ours To See
Saturday, April 24, 2010

Ben and I kind of talked about celibacy that second date night. Sort of. We talked about the topic without ever using the word or addressing the subject directly. We did this walking hand in hand under the moonlight the night he took me to the tea shop.

"I ... like you a lot, Olivia," Ben said after we'd walked for a time, and then he snorted. The Tea Shoppe was on the edge of a small park that included a pond surrounded by a stone path. We stood for a while and admired a pair of swans swimming gracefully across the water. I channeled Aileen and stayed silent seeing what it would get me. "How adolescent does that sound? This whole thing is awkward ... no difficult ...," he sighed in apparent frustration, "I'm thirty-two and yet suddenly feel like I'm on a date for the first time in my life! In one sense I feel completely at ease and comfortable with you and in another sense you're a total stranger to me. One minute I'm talking to you like we're best friends again and the next minute I'm completely uncertain how I should respond to something you've said or asked. Part of me is *thrilled* to be with you ... you're like this mythical person that I'd never thought I'd speak to again." He snorted again, with what I recognized to be frustrated awkwardness. "And part of me is actually losing sleep over what exactly I should be doing with ... *us.*"

"'Doing with us'? What's *that* supposed to mean?" I was going to tease him about his 'simple cup of coffee' line, which was obviously an understatement of significant proportions, but suddenly he didn't seem in the mood for teasing.

185

Ben stopped walking, turned, and gave me a direct look. "I ...," he swallowed and looked off into the dark woods. Behind him the swans glided gracefully completely comfortable with *their* relationship. Didn't they mate for life? "I have spent all of my life," he stopped abruptly, "correction, a major part of my adult life working very hard to stay focused on the right things ..."

I stepped into his personal space suddenly ready to brawl. "Are you saying I'm wrecking your focus?"

Ben laughed and looked down at me in the moonlight. "No, you're not wrecking my focus, Olivia. I'm just trying to explain to you who I am and what type of man I'm trying to be ..."

"You're talking in riddles." I wasn't sure I shouldn't still be ready to fight and the fact that he'd laughed didn't make me feel better.

"Okay, I'll put it plainly. I've worked very hard to keep a tight rein on my emotions. They tend to ... get me into trouble. I try to be calm, cool, and rational. For the most part, lately, I've been tremendously content with my career and my life in general. I've learned to handle even the most difficult situations – like giving the eulogy at my grandmother's memorial service – with a confident assurance. It may sound stuck up but I try rarely to doubt myself, Olivia."

"So now you're saying I'm making you doubt yourself?! Gee, keep talking, Ben. You're making me feel *so good.*"

Ben laughed again, but this time he pulled me into his arms. "I'm sorry. I'm not saying this as clearly as I want to. You're making me feel things I haven't felt in a long time, Olivia. You're making me look at my life and acknowledge what I'm missing." He kissed the top of my head and then touched my face gently so I'd look up at him. "Suddenly I'm not calm, I'm not cool, and I'm not rational ... Everything that I thought was so set and orderly and in the right place now needs to be reexamined." When I went to say something else, he put his finger against my lips. "It's a good thing, Jerry, honest it is. It's just ... been a long time since I was so unsettled and up in the air with things. I want to keep doing the right thing. But I want you, too."

I heard loudly and clearly what he was saying. While he wanted my presence in his life, in doing so I was making him question things about himself. And he wasn't sure that was a good thing ... or a bad thing. There was a lot I wanted to say, but none of them were very positive or encouraging and I wanted to hear everything the man had to say. I worked hard to stay objective. Calm. Cool. I focused once again on the swans and tried hard to breathe slowly and easily.

"Look, I believe God works in mysterious ways, okay? Grannie Blue taught me that on more occasions than I can count. I don't believe in coincidences because to do so would take God out of the equation. That means I believe that everything that's happened to me ... and to ... us ... in these past few weeks is by Design. It's just a little wild for me, okay? Not the way God usually presents things to me, all right? It's making me feel ... different ... but that's not necessarily a negative thing. I just need to make ... good choices. Go slow and easy. And I'm not so sure I want to go slow and easy." He swallowed and took a calming breath. "I cannot dismiss the fact that Olivia Kelly, whom I've never forgotten and whom I always thought I still had unfinished business with is suddenly ...," I'm pretty sure he blushed although I wasn't positive in the moonlight and he looked away towards the pond and the swans, "... the woman I'm holding in my arms, having coffee with, and driving on the back of my motorcycle."

I hear him mumbling *'Depends on which side you're on'* and suddenly I get what he's trying to say but not say. He's thinking wild and crazy thoughts about me and him and us and ... I gave him an impatient look and reminded him, "You said it was *just* a cup of coffee, Ben ..."

"Yeah, I know what I said. I wasn't necessarily lying to you. Although I suspect I was lying a bit to myself."

"If I'm making you ... different ... then I take that as a bad thing, Ben, no matter what you say, because you're a *good guy* to start with. So as I see it the only way you have to go is down ... then simply let this all be *just a cup of coffee.*" I walked away to stand at the pond's edge. "If you remember, I was a pretty tough sell for that cup of coffee. It's no big deal. Just take me home, shake hands good-bye, and go off on your merry way.

No harm. No foul. No damage done." Suddenly I felt like the demon seed. See, right here. This is the absolutely perfect example why me and nice guys just don't mix: I will always be a bad influence.

"I bicycled all the way to your apartment once. Did your mother ever tell you?" I turned and stared at Ben in silent shock. "Guess not. I knew the address because we used to send letters, remember?" I nodded. Truth was I still had them somewhere. "I got a little desperate to see you when you suddenly stopped coming to Grandmother Miriam's to visit with your Dad. We were like thirteen … I … knew how you felt about him so I knew something had to be really wrong for you to miss those visits. You didn't come one time, then two, then three. Suddenly I was frantic! I watched for Erin to show up for the next visit and then went over and tried to see her to ask questions."

I let him talk. He walked over to me, took my hand, and we resumed our walk around the pond. Our footsteps crunched loudly on the gravel. "I never got to see Erin but I saw Grandmother Miriam." He swallowed audibly and squeezed my hand. "She told me you were dead."

"*What?!*"

We were half way around the pond by then and I suddenly couldn't stand anymore and sat down on a nearby bench. But Ben stayed standing, his back to me with his hands thrust into his pockets, looking out at the pond. "And I believed her. At first. It all made horrible sense why you'd suddenly stopped coming, you know? I came home hysterical but my mother knew a vague sense of the truth and talked with me until I calmed down."

"What did she tell you?"

Ben shrugged. "That when couples divorce, it's hard on everyone: mothers, fathers, children … and grandparents, too. No one knows everything that goes on in the privacy of a family anymore than we can understand another person's thoughts. She was certain that you hadn't died and encouraged me to write to you and even said she'd drive me over one day to see you. But instead, I decided to go see for myself. I got a road map from the car and took off on my bike." He walked over and finally sat by me, his big, long frame slouched next to me on the bench. The whole right side of my body stood at attention with the warmth of his nearness. "When I think on it now, it was quite a feat that I managed to get there at all, let alone in one piece. I crossed two major highways, a notorious traffic circle, and finding your apartment in the middle of a busy city took a lot longer than I had thought. But I got there eventually."

"But I wasn't there." It was odd to feel such a crushing disappointment about something I missed almost twenty years ago, but I did.

Shaking his head, he murmured, "No, you weren't. Your mom was though. I stood there in the doorway sweating and panting and very near tears. She brought me inside and got me a drink and sat me down on your couch. Then she called my mom and told her where I was and that she'd drive me home. When I told her what Grandmother Miriam had told me she sighed and said, 'Smiley, Olivia's alive. She's at her girlfriend's.'"

Probably Annette's place. A girl who lived a few apartment buildings over whose mother was never home and whose father didn't exist. We bonded on our mutual hatred of our parents - mothers in particular.

"I've always been a pretty astute person, Olivia. Even when I was thirteen. I picked up that your mother *hadn't* said you were fine or happy or even okay ... you were merely 'alive'. And while I'd gotten a surprising smile when she'd first opened the door, the woman who sat next to me at that moment was the Mrs. Kelly I was used to: serious and sad. 'She misses you terribly Ben,' your mother told me that day. 'Besides missing her father, I'm pretty sure there's no one Olivia misses more.' So I asked the obvious question: why had you stopped coming to visit?"

I was sitting by Ben but my thoughts were far away. There were the "old Olivia's" memories and newly formulated revised perceptions crashing around in my head so fast I couldn't seem to keep up. "I did miss you terribly," I finally conceded. "Aside from Dean you were the only person that I really, truly ... liked." I almost said loved, which was more accurate but too difficult to admit. My world of happiness and good times was tiny enough as a child and anyone who could make me experience gladness pretty much was showered with adoration. At least in those early years.

"Your mom said you were very unhappy and confused about a lot of things, and were having trouble sorting everything out. Whether it was the truth or not, I took it as a grown-up way of saying *and the actual specifics are none of your business.*" Shifting a bit, he put his arm around me and was quiet for a time. "I worried that maybe I'd done something to make you annoyed at me, too," he finally whispered.

I turned so fast to deny that our noses bumped. But he didn't give me a chance to speak. "I wouldn't have given up without a fight so easily," he said quietly, "but then Dad died and, well, everything got bad, fast."

"And my mother married Paul and we moved again." I added.

"Life kind of swept us both apart," Ben murmured. "But that doesn't mean I ever stopped thinking about you. Wondering about you. Missing you. I've always … wanted to reconnect with you." He sighed. "Always."

Twenty years. *Twenty years* had gone by. We were still close enough that all I could really see were his eyes, dark in the moonlight and staring at me intently. I reached up to touch his face and then the texture of his hair, which was long for a minister. Ben closed his eyes and sighed and let his head dip forward to touch mine.

"We were *just childhood friends,*" he whispered, "and yet the thing we had always felt bigger than I could understand. Important. Critical. *Worth it.*"

I kissed him then because I'd been wanting to for so long. My hand slipped down to the back of his neck and I let myself just melt into him. I'd read my share of romance novels and their descriptions of first kisses (because this kiss was a *real* kiss, nothing G rated about it) never came close to describing how I felt kissing Ben. I had a burst of feelings and emotions that built up and then just exploded inside me. I wanted to laugh and I wanted to sob. I wanted to keep kissing him until I died, and yet I wanted to run screaming in the other direction. I wanted to get naked on that public bench with him but I wanted to shout, *Hey! Are you supposed to be kissing me like this?!?!* I felt absolutely terrified to be in such a strange, foreign place, and yet I felt as though I'd finally come home.

Long moments later found us sitting quietly, as close as two people can be fully dressed sitting on a public bench. "What next?" Ben finally said.

Pulling out of his arms I sat up and looked at him. "I'm going to forego what immediately came to mind when you first asked that question.'"

Ben grinned knowing exactly what I was referring to. "That's a wise thing, I guess." When I kept staring at him he got serious. "I need to keep seeing you, Olivia."

I laughed. *"Need?"*

He nodded. "Yes. Need. I'm trying to go slow. I'm trying to be wise and careful. I'm trying to be sure that I'm thinking with my ... head." I couldn't really see but I'd bet real money that he was blushing. "But I want to be with you. Spend some time with you. Really, finally get to know you. See if we can ... mesh our two very different, very complete lives."

'Very different lives': the understatement of the evening as far as I was concerned. Were he probably any other person I'd have already invited him home to spend the night with me. Probably the whole weekend. And yes, I did consider just putting it out there to him. But once you've thought it through in any detail I could see the headlines: LOCAL IMMORAL HIGH SCHOOL MATH TEACHER DESTROYS WELL LOVED MINISTER'S LIFE IN STEAMY SEX SCANDAL.

I sighed and put my head on Ben's shoulder. "Do you want to come to my sister Erin's house for dinner Sunday? Be advised, you'd have to deal with my mother, her husband, and Erin and Dan's two *extremely precocious* kids Liam and Janine." I sat up and gave him a pointed look. "It *would not* be easy."

Ben looked at me and then, as if he couldn't help himself, leaned in and gave me another tremendous kiss. With the same pointed look I'd given him minutes before he said, "Do you want to come with me to a

Christian rock concert I've got to chaperone next Friday night? And, if you're not sure that "Christian rock" will appeal to you, you should also know that I'm taking twenty-three teenagers along with me, too."

"Well, certainly two ways to keep us on the straight and narrow," I teased.

"Exactly what I was thinking," he muttered.

The concert Ben had invited me to was the following Friday at a college auditorium about an hour's drive away. Ben and I had decided that I would meet everyone at the church at five. Two huge fifteen-passenger vans idled in the church parking lot and I immediately climbed up into the one with Ben at the wheel. Fifteen curious pairs of eyes bore into the back of my head. I was uncertain what I was dreading more: spending the evening with Ben in front of such a nosy audience (many of whom I knew) or staying home and discovering more disturbing information such as the fact that Alec spent four months of a one-year sentence at Butner Federal Correction Facility in Raleigh, North Carolina for insider trading. Apparently another career he'd tried (in addition to meter reading, pastry baking, and Christian rock musician) was as a licensed New York City stockbroker. By the end of the week, Alex, my mother and I had developed a polite yet not completely comfortable existence with each other and I had adopted the Doris Day motto of *que sera, sera.*

Sitting waiting for the last few stragglers, it was obvious that Ben had laid the law down with the kids. I could tell because they were sitting up straight and being so polite it was almost painful. That casual, shockingly open atmosphere teens adopt when they're relaxed and at ease was as nonexistent as Alec's good standing with the Securities and Exchange Commission.

"What did you tell them?" I asked Ben after ten minutes of agonizing silence.

No one said a thing until I asked the question again, louder, with my teacher voice. "If we behave inappropriately then we can't go on the summer mission trip," came a disembodied voice from the back. I watched Ben glance into the rearview mirror to try to catch the culprit.

"What's appropriate behavior?" I inquired. I finally punched Ben in the arm lightly. "Tell them that it's *appropriately polite* to answer my questions."

Ben looked at me and sighed and then looked up again into the rearview mirror. "I didn't say you couldn't speak."

"You said no teasing, no jokes, no crass innuendoes, no inappropriate questions, no personal questions, and no gossiping," someone volunteered.

"I don't even know what half of that stuff is, Pastor Ben, so I'm just going to keep my mouth shut the whole time," came a female voice.

I laughed. "Oh, Ben. I'm tough. I can take it."

But he shook his head vehemently. "I still can't believe what they told you at Grannie Blue's service, and that was only two of them for about twenty minutes. What are you going to hear spending *a whole evening* with *twenty-three of them?* I must have been out of my mind to invite you to come along, and *you* must have been as insane to agree to come!"

"Should I just go home?" I was serious, although I wasn't angry. If he was going to be a nervous wreck all night it would spoil everyone's evening.

"No," Ben murmured in a defeated tone.

"You sure?"

He looked at me then, *really looked at me* across the expanse of the front seat. It was the same wonderful look he gave me just before I got a *really great kiss* from him on our second date. "I want you to stay."

I turned to the sea of expectant faces behind me. "New rules. You will be polite. You will be cooperative. But you will enjoy yourseves, too. And, if Pastor Ben and I have a nice evening, on the way home I'll tell you a story about when we both got in trouble with the cops when we were seven years old."

"Did you say *seven years old?*"

I grinned at Ben as he winked at me and put the van in gear. "Yup, seven years old. Was that before or after we got in trouble for vandalizing the local Catholic Church?"

Ben laughed. "Before, I think."

I hadn't really expected much from the evening, but ended up enjoying myself thoroughly. Dealing with a group of teenagers is light-years easier when you're with another capable adult who you can laugh with, roll your eyes at, and count on for backup. Like a well-oiled machine, Ben and I dealt patiently with anything that couldn't be ignored.

It had been an odd week dealing with my mother and Alec snuggling on my couch watching *Dancing With The Stars* and eating peanuts (which he shelled for her) and I was stressing about this rather bizarre third date, so I'd not even thought twice about the fact that we were going to a *Christian rock concert*. I had only as much experience with Christian rock as Alec could squeeze in this past week practicing his guitar on my deck. Walking into the massive college auditorium, I was stunned to see speakers as big as cars, miles of wires and cables and flashing lights, and kids as far as your eyes could see in all shapes and sizes dancing and grooving to the tunes. The first few tunes I listened to politely with vague interest, but after a while I had to admit that I did finally think *this is going to be a looooong night*. The music was loud and wild and, well, typical music in that unless you had the words memorized you didn't have a clue what they were saying. Now I enjoy music as much as the next person and have quite a mean singing voice in the shower, but that's songs I *know*. Belt out a Bonnie Raitt ballad or a Sinead O'Connor song or even some Grateful Dead tunes and I'm right there, the queen of karaoke. But this stuff was just as unintelligible as any other rock and roll played loudly enough to make your ears ring.

Different bands and singers performed over the course of the evening. It was an upscale talent competition with contestants coming from all over the eastern seaboard and vying for national distinction. Kind of like the God version of *American Idol* I decided. The kids had debated endlessly in the car about who they thought would win, and apparently Jenn and Phillip from Grannie Blue's memorial service had made it as far as the semi-finals before being eliminated.

Suddenly the mood changed. The lights came down and all the rock band boys and girls left. A young woman came out by herself and the crowd got quiet. She carried a guitar slung around her neck and had long, flowing black hair. *Wish mine looked that good,* I remembered thinking. Our group sat down and leaned forward intently in their seats … waiting. Everyone's faces were illuminated by the glow from the stage, and I took the opportunity to look at Ben and smile. Even if the music wasn't to my taste, the company wasn't half bad. "This is one that you'll be able to understand all the words to," Ben whispered in my ear, giving me a delightful shiver.

And then the young woman started to sing. Her voice reached out across the hundreds of rows and thousands of people and whispered right to me.

> *Dress down your pretty faith. Give me something real.*
> *Leave out the thee and thou and speak to me now.*
> *Speak to my pain and confusion.*
> *Speak through my fears and my pride.*
> *Speak to the part of me that knows I'm something deep down inside…*
> *I've known now, for quite a while, that I am not whole.*
> *I've remembered the body and the mind,*
> *But dissected my soul.*
> *Now something inside is awakening,*
> *Like a dream I once had and forgot.*
> *And it's something I'm scared of*
> *And something I don't want to stop…*[26]

When she finished, I wanted to cry out, "No! Don't Stop!! Sing Another!!" The crowd exploded with clapping and whistles and hoots of enthusiasm, and for the very first time that evening I joined in *sincerely*. Thankfully, she began to sing another song and suddenly I wanted - no needed - to hear every word she said.

The heart is a lonely thing to lose in the dead of night
The heart is a sad thing to lose in the throws of a fight
The heart is the match to the fire
And the embers of desire, to keep it burning
I am a shell of the manner and the means
Mine is a story of nothing as it seems
But when we have come this far
And still don't know who we are, does it keep burning?
When it's over, and you see it with your eyes
Would you rather have the truth or a lie?[27]

The audience exploded in shouts and clapping with me once again part of the crowd. "Having a good time?" I suddenly heard whispered in my ear, and I realized that at some point we had all stood although I had done it completely unconsciously.

I grinned up at Ben in delight. "I liked those last two songs a lot," I said breathlessly. "Do you know what they were?"

"I've got them in my car, Jerry. I'll lend them to you, okay?"

I nodded and got drawn back to the stage. Another band had come out and launched into a haunting, rocking beat. "Grannie Blue's favorite hymn made into a rock anthem," Ben said to me over the intros to the music, *"It Is Well.* We sang the hymn at her memorial service but this version sounds a lot different." He put his arm around me and pulled me close and we bumped and rocked to the tune. He sang every chorus to my ear with a beautiful, deep voice. And that's how we spent the rest of the evening.

In the end it was one of the best dates of my life.

Therapy: The Truth About Me – Part III

Setting: It's May 3, 2010 and Aileen's practically on the edge of her seat when I walk into her office. She can't wait to discuss if I believe that I'm lovable. But I've broken out and done something novel this past week. I've *talked with people* I trust about this idea of being lovable … or not. Well, I actually talked with just Clotilde because we had an assembly (Annual High School Talent Show) on Friday that took up two periods and we were stuck in the back of the auditorium where the sound system was poor. We had a brief, disjointed conversation in between acts and dealing with problem students – which were many. But that's better than I usually do.

Me: I talked with my friend at school about being lovable.

Aileen: Clotilde?

Me: (How does she do that? Remember names and people so easily? What is it, like her job or something?) Yeah, Clotilde.

Aileen: Why listen to Clotilde? (She gets ready to write.)

Me: She's young, but she's got her head on straight. She's normal – in a broad sense of the word at least. Happily married. Well thought of by parents, students and administrators. She's nice to me but honest, too. Like she'll tell me when she doesn't agree with me and can give a valid reason why. She's intelligent and dependable, not flighty or vapid.

Aileen: Okay. Sounds like a relatively sane young woman. More importantly, you've listed viable reasons why you trust her. Good.

Me: Yeah, well, Clotilde said some interesting things about being lovable. (Aileen arches her eyebrows – not a good look – to urge me to continue.) Clotilde said that *no one* is particularly lovable. That deep down inside – the real heart of us – none of us is very nice. We can put on good faces for short periods of time, but in the end time will tell the truth.

Aileen: (She's practically vibrating with interest.) Really ... But you described her as happily married. Someone obviously thought she was lovable. How did she explain that?

Me: Yeah, I pointed that out, too, after I recovered from the shock of her answer. She said that Max was 'Her Special Gift'.

Aileen: From whom?

Me: Huh?

Aileen: A gift must be given from one person to another. It implies a source as well as a destination. Who gave Max to Clotilde?

Me: (Shrugging.) I don't know! Maybe she got lucky in the unemployment line like you did.

Aileen: (She's shaking her head.) Oh no, not good enough, Olivia. If you're going to embrace someone's philosophy - use it as evidence to support *your* philosophy - then you need to get to the bottom of it. You can't just skim bits off the top just because they sound good. That will only lead to trouble in the future: incorrect opinions, validations of wrong behavior, weak foundations to build on in the future. You need to go back and ask Clotilde more specifics. Take the time to understand where she's coming from and then decide if her theories really agree with yours ... or not.

Me: (I shrug and roll my eyes. *Whatever.* Here I thought I'd done a good thing.)

Aileen: Now, prior to your conversation with Clotilde, is seems to me that you already had a preconceived opinion about whether you were lovable. Am I right?

Me: (No sense denying it. I've already painted myself into this corner.) Yeah. You're going to make me say it so I will. I was going to say that I don't think I'm lovable, but I was also going to acknowledge that I haven't met too many people who are particularly lovable either, so I didn't think my opinion of myself was necessarily a bad one. That's why I was so surprised when Clotilde agreed with me. That doesn't usually happen.

Aileen: Except Clotilde has at least one exception to her rule: Max. Do
you?

Me: (Thinking…) Well, the lovable I'm talking about is different than the
lovable like parents might feel for their child or like an aunt would
feel for her niece and nephew. That's a law; you don't have a
choice with that. But I'm talking about *choice lovable*. The decision
to decide a person is lovable who would otherwise be a perfect
stranger, or because there's no rule about it.

Aileen: Okay … So you're talking about relationship lovable. What
happens between a man and a woman. Which, I'll remind you,
you've only just acknowledged as existing.

Me: Yeah, yeah. Stop gloating.

Aileen: So, cut to the chase. (She blinks at me.) *Are you* relationship
lovable?

Me: (I get silent. And, crap, I suddenly feel like crying. Double crap.)

Aileen: The question upsets you.

Me: You knew it would.

Aileen: I knew it would. (At my lengthy, continued silence…) Olivia, if
you don't *believe* that your 'relationship lovable' then what happens
when/if a man you're involved with reaches a point where he
confesses his love for you? How can you believe him? If you've
been intimate with him you'll probably think, 'Oh it's just the sex.'
If you haven't been intimate with him – which has never been an
issue with you until now – and he confesses his love maybe you
might think, 'Oh he's just *trying* to get me in bed for sex.' Do you
get what I'm driving at?

Me: Yeah. (And I don't admit it but I've thought those things – come on
who doesn't?)

Aileen: How about this. I want you to think about what qualities you
possess that make you lovable, Olivia. Or, if you must, the
qualities you think you posses that make you unlovable. And it was
good that you sought out Clotilde. Do that again. (She has the
audacity to wink at me.) When you're asking her where she got her

Max gift from, ask her also what qualities she and he share that make them lovable to each other. And ask your mother and Alec what their lovable qualities are. And Erin and Dan, too! This should be a lot of fun for you, don't you think? Why maybe you could even ask Ben …

Tell me the story, where old is made new,
the promise of ages, and all things that are true[28]

19: Living Together Is A Bad Idea
Wednesday, May 5, 2010

My mother and Alec ended up staying with me for a week and three days. No one was happier to leave than Harry, who had endured endless torture from Sophie, who refused to let him eat from his food dish and occasionally used his carrier box as an impromptu litter box. Alec (meter reader by day and pastry chef by night) took a week's vacation from his day job and worked nonstop to get the house livable again. I'm not sure he slept, truth be told, and neither did my mother.

And while there were no more shocking revelations regarding Alec's dark past, watching my mother with Alec in such an intimate setting was incredibly eye opening. Shocking even. My mother was a happy woman. She laughed and teased and even giggled. She was affectionate and tender and did thoughtful things like making one a cup of hot chocolate at night and even leaving a homemade breakfast sandwich warming in the oven when she left in the morning. She was at ease and casual, flirting and loving with Alec and open and eager with me.

I'd never met her before in my life.

It was an okay week, actually, considering the potential for disaster. We joked around with each other, told funny stories about the cats, and enjoyed late meals on the deck that we took turns preparing. Completely surreal. My mother and I avoided any serious conversation, which was probably the main reason the week went so smoothly. But Alec and I talked all week. He told me about the fun things my mother and he had done the few years they'd been together and the grand plans they had once they both retired. I heard all about his past including life as a high flying Wall Street stockbroker and as a prison inmate. He was full of excitement over a mission trip his church was sponsoring to Haiti that was planned for July and showed me a picture in his wallet of a World Vision Child he's been supporting for years. (Her name is Vanessa, she is eleven now and has lived with her mother and younger sister in El Salvador.) Each evening he broke out his guitar and played for about a half hour. He had a nice voice that was kind of like warm molasses —slow and smooth and heavy. I enjoyed listening to him (usually he was out on the deck while I was upstairs getting ready for bed but I could still hear him.) Tuesday night, with no energy to do anything but lay like a slug I was still on the deck when he started tuning up so I teased him that maybe after the endless week of work on the house he'd have been better off sleeping instead of playing.

"Can't," he said with an easy grin, "gotta feed my soul." I knew better than to ask, but he must have seen it in my face that I had no clue what he was talking about. "It's my evening devotions – the guitar playing. Sure it's practice, too, but a lot of the times the music speaks to me and I get a real blessing out of it. I talk to God and let Him talk to me through the music."

"I went to a Christian rock concert the other night. Not all of it was bad." That intrigued him, and I ended up getting invited once again to one of his concerts at his church. I should have kept my mouth shut, but I never seem to learn. "Do you only play Christian stuff?" I asked trying to steer the conversation away from the invitation I hadn't responded to.

"Well, I started off wanting to be the next Eric Clapton," and he broke into an excellent rendition of *Cocaine* with a wicked glint in his eye.

That made me laugh. "God must be covering His ears!"

"Probably. Here's a better one." Alec launched into a countryish, rockin' song and sang with gusto and abandon there in the twilight of my deck.

You say I've got trouble

I've got trouble all over me
I've got trouble since the day I was born
and it's not just a struggle
it's the blood running through my veins
it's all the clothes I've ever worn ...
and when I'm with You I feel so overdressed
the trouble is I'm not above or beyond anything
so I know You must be good for me
as far as You can and as bad as I am
I know You must be good for me
I'm a terrible lover
I never love You the way I should
and every single reason's wrong
oh my sister, my brothers
we've got history on our heels
and we're running like we broke the law
with friends like these tell me, who needs the police ...[29]

I laid there in the spring evening while Alec sang and realized that it was me he was singing about. That song could be my theme song. 'Trouble all over me' ... 'Trouble since the day I was born' ... 'The blood running through my veins' ... Oh. My. God. It took me a while to come back to reality and I realized that Alec was looking at me with a bemused expression, and that he'd stopped playing.

"I've had a lot of reactions to my playing but I don't think I've ever had anyone completely zone out and escape to another place because I was so bad," he said ruefully.

"Oh! It's not that Alec. It's an ... incredibly powerful song. It just hit a little too close to home for me." I looked out into the dark evening because I suddenly couldn't look him in the eye.

"Huh?" He frowned in puzzlement. "I was singing about myself!" he chuckled. "I could give you a list a mile long of people who'd back me up with that, too."

"You think so? Sorry, but you don't have *my heritage.*" I said that sharper than I intended. I'm *sure* he knew all my mother's secrets, which meant he knew most of mine, too.

Alec put his guitar down hurriedly and came over to kneel beside me. "Olivia," he said in an intense, low voice as he gripped my arm, "it's a song about redemption. Forgiveness. *'As far as You can and as bad as I am, I know You must be good for me',*" he recited to me, "it's about the undeniable fact that *no one* is too much trouble, *no one* has too dark a history that the power of Christ can't transform them." He was so freaked that he gave me a little shake. "Look at me, Olivia. This is too important." And he waited until I looked into his eyes. "You are as vital and important to God as you *let yourself* be. There's *nothing* stopping God; all the barriers come from our end."

I gave him a sad smile because he was so clueless about what it's like to be who and what I was, and there wasn't a thing I could do to help him understand.

Thank goodness for him.

To think that this is the man that Aileen had suggested I discuss my level of lovability with! And while having him kneel at my side in desperation and say specific things about my "too dark history" implied one thing, the power and might of the words he'd just sung struck a completely different chord for me. "Relax, Alec. It's not a big deal."

"It *is* a big deal!" he exploded.

"What's going on? Is everything okay?" Suddenly my mother was standing in the door.

Alec and I look at her like we've been caught sharing a crack pipe. This topic the two of us were dancing around, my notorious conception and subsequent life, was something neither of us had any desire to discuss with my mother. In fact, explaining a crack pipe would have been easier.

But Alec surprised me – not for the first time and I'm sure not for the last. "I screwed up, Elaine. I shared a song with Olivia and it was a mistake."

My mother looked at Alec and they communicated telepathically. Then she looked at me. "What song?"

"It's nothing," I said and tried to brush by both of them, but Alec stepped in front of the door.

"It's crucial," Alec said with conviction. "I played my theme song – *Trouble* – and Olivia said it's her song, too. But not in a good way."

My mother sighed, she obviously knew the song. The sigh came from deep inside her and she visibly worked to remain calm and together. "I don't know what it's like to carry around the stigma that you are a child of rape, Olivia." It's the first time I've heard my mother use the word in my entire life. "I imagine it makes you feel alone and isolated and I ache with that knowledge and the realization that I'm powerless to fix that. We've never talked about this and I've been afraid to push things. I wanted it to be in your own timeframe. But you need to know that I have never, ever, *ever*," she caught herself for a moment and took another deep breath, "thought of you that way. *Never*," she said with gritted teeth. "You were my precious baby. A miracle. A gift. A delight. Sunlight in the midst of the most awful storm. I have an endless list of regrets for mistakes and bad choices that I have made over the course of my life," this time she took a step forward so that I could see in her eyes all the way through to her heart and her soul, "but I never *once* regretted my decision to give birth to you." My mother stood there proud and defiant. "You were the reason I could never reconcile with Vera. She couldn't look at you without disparaging you, and I couldn't stand that. It was a good decision. You are the reason *to this day* that I'm thankful for drunken Dean Kelly who loved you like his own even though he knew all along that I'd lied to him. Dean was a desperate decision at first, but now I clearly see God's hand in it. You are the reason I was so delighted when I had a second daughter because what could be more wonderful than one daughter but two? For a long time in those early years you and then Erin were the only points of happiness in my life. You were the reason why I've never stopped trying no matter how many times I've fallen flat on my face, because I *needed* to show you that I wouldn't give up. I always hoped that you could maybe, *possibly*, one day be proud of me."

My mother looked at Alec and smiled and then looked back at me. The tears were there. "*Nothing matters* in the past, Olivia. It's all ashes. All that matters is that you stay focused on the future." She waved her hand dismissively. "*I don't look back anymore.* What good is it? Can I change it? Reinvent it? Make it disappear? That's the greatest gift God has given me. The understanding that it's all *gone*, and that I can have joy and hope and life and love simply by trusting and believing in Him." She took my hand, and I realized standing there that we've never really touched. "You above everyone else can understand how powerful that promise is, Olivia. You, above everyone else, knows what a different person I am as a result."

It was a really beautiful speech and I didn't have anything to say in reply. The three of us just stood there in the dim light and finally, awkwardly, I said, "I think I'll go to bed, I'm exhausted." As I turned to go up the stairs I saw Alec and my mother in a tight embrace.

On Friday, Ben and I went out for our fourth date. I realized as I prepared, that we were fast becoming a real, honest-to-goodness couple. We talked on the phone – I knew his general schedule and he knew mine, we occasionally texted silly things over the course of a day to each other and when this weekend rolled around I found myself naturally assuming that I would be seeing Ben. All this ended up making me extremely tense.

Aileen's been like a hungry dog with a bone regarding the concept of my lovability – whether I am or whether I am not. Her questions and fact points and sly innuendoes won't get out of my head and I felt like a nasty pimple almost ready to burst. How could anyone really love me? That question might sound ridiculous/immature/ignorant (feel free to pick one) but deep down in my heart of hearts I really did wonder. I mean I didn't have a stellar lineage. Nor had I accumulated an impressive list of supporting fans. Having to ask someone their opinion of whether I was lovable (or not) sounded downright pitiful. And if someone ever volunteered it spontaneously, well it would only have made me incredibly suspicious.

Which left me right back where I started with my insecure doubts and nowhere to go but down.

Was it any wonder why I have done everything humanly possible to avoid having the discussion with *anyone*? Clotilde was number one on Aileen's list (too bad I didn't have a list). I suppose I could have taken the opportunity to talk about the subject with my mother or Alec while they lived with me (but what a shame, that chance was now gone). Observing Alec and my mother up close and personal was more than enough thank you very much; I didn't need to hear anything more put into words.

Yet I found myself looking at couples – *good couples, solid couples* – and the reality was I didn't really need to have a formal discussion on why it was working for them. Every single one of them seemed to have an innate communication with each other, a tolerant respect, and an honest enjoyment of being with each other. Somehow, those things combined with some magic fairy dust or something seemed to cause them to be "in love". For however long they could make it last.

You might be inclined to remind me that I had already admitted that I had a love for Ben but nothing is ever that simple with me. Sigh. And I couldn't tell you why. I did know that none of my "nice/genuine/kind" behavior felt genuine. More and more I was feeling like a big, enormous imposter who was going to be unveiled or discovered ... soon. Very soon. Ben might like what I'd allowed him to see so far but all bets were off once he knew the whole, horrible truth.

Ben and I decided to do nothing big or fancy tonight: no crossing state borders, no big surprises. We were just going to go out to dinner. Simple. And I'd suggested economy as well which was why we ended up a few towns over at a little Italian joint that had plastic flowers on the table and drinks that were served in unbreakable, scratched tumblers. Just like when we were five, conversation between Ben and I was free and easy. We talked about my students, his kids, the economic crisis that's affecting church giving and school district funding, my mother, his mother, my sister, his brother, and summer plans which included a mission trip to Kentucky for him and a desperately needed temporary job for me.

"Would you dance with me?" Ben asked suddenly after we'd managed to pack in dessert and coffee. A comfortable lull had come about in the conversation. The truth was I'd been once again trying to figure out how I could get him to come home with me so we could ... get to know each other better, so to speak. Music had been playing in the background all night - an eclectic mix of everything from Madonna's *Borderline* to Alan Jackson's *She Likes It Too* to Roy Orbison's *Pretty Woman*.

I looked around the crowded dining room. "Here?"

"Through that door is a bar and dance floor. In about fifteen minutes there will be live music we could dance to."

"I didn't know ministers danced." When Ben didn't respond and just looked at me I said sheepishly, "That's getting kind of old isn't it."

"Am I that different?"

I sighed. I could always count on him to ask good questions. "What are you doing here with me, Ben Harayda?" It was the closest I could come to asking Aileen's question of him: *Do you think I'm lovable?*

Resting his chin in his hand Ben reached over and picked up a lock of my hair. It curled around his finger and he held onto it. I'd left my hair down tonight, just pulled off my face for control, and I suspect it was doing a happy dance everywhere. Just this evening getting ready I had wondered if I were getting too old to have it so long. Looking me right in the eye Ben said, "What are *you* doing here with *me*, Olivia Kelly?"

No fair. I asked first. "I'm not sure ..."

He gave my hair a tug. "Me either."

I said sadly, "I asked you one time what the perfect woman was like for Ben Harayda and you wouldn't tell me. Something tells me that she's absolutely nothing like me."

"You'd be surprised then." When I just looked at him he let go of my hair, sat back in his chair and crossed his arms. No matter what he wore he always looked good. I liked him dressed in suits just as much as I liked him as he was dressed now in a tee shirt and jeans. He even had a

little bit of beard stubble going on and it make him look ... well, just
yummy.

When I didn't say anything, Ben murmured, "Grannie Blue used to
tease me when I was little. Said I always was interested in 'dark-haired
lovelies'." He was looking at me intently; his green eyes watching my
reaction. "Marisa had long dark hair like yours. That's what first caught my
eye. One of the women at church teased me just recently when she heard I
was being fixed up again. 'Remember, he doesn't like blondes!' she
shouted. You want me to list physical attributes? I can't stand model thin
or tiny. I love it when a girl can look me right in the eye and has plenty of
curves when I hug her. Legs are a particular favorite, as well as lips. I can't
stand meek women. I want a woman who's not afraid to express her
opinion and doesn't have a deferential bone in her body. I can be a rather
... forceful ... presence in someone's life and I want someone who can
stand up to me." He leaned forward and picked up my hands, still looking
at me now ... like a starving man looks at a juicy burger. "I like a woman
who makes me work for it; nothing's more *unappealing* to me than being
given everything on a silver platter. A sense of humor that goes with a
quick, sharp wit is always guaranteed to keep my attention, too." He
paused for a moment and then murmured, "Even in the dark."

Suddenly, it was really hot in that restaurant. I realized that my
mouth was hanging open, and I shut it. To escape his intense expression I
looked down, but that had me focusing on both his hands holding both my
hands – his thumbs moving gently back and forth. "So you're ... looking
for love?" I couldn't help myself.

"Trust comes first. And respect. I couldn't love a woman I
couldn't trust or respect." He said that with a fierce intensity. "As a matter
of fact, I think love isn't really a person's choice. It just happens whether
... you want it to or not."

"Have you been in love before?"

He hesitated, looked down at our hands and sighed. "Yes, I have.
Right before I came here and took this job I was pretty serious with a
woman. We talked about a future and marriage and kids and all that."

"What happened?" But then I shook my head. "You don't have to answer that, Ben. It's too personal."

"All of this is personal, really. But it's important, so I'll tell you. We realized that even though we ... loved each other we were interested in different things. Wanted different things for our futures. And when it became obvious that neither one of us was willing to compromise, there wasn't much left to discuss."

"How mature. How neat and tidy, too." He blinked at me. "Do you still send each other Christmas cards? Maybe you're friends on Facebook?" Why was I suddenly so angry?

"No."

"Hmmm. Life isn't usually so neat and tidy. You're so fortunate it's been that way for you, Ben. But you know I sense that things were a little more complicated than you've painted it to be. But don't worry, I don't really want all the gory details. What I do want to know though was who walked away hurt?" When Ben didn't answer right away, I voiced my opinion. "I'm guessing maybe you did. You're an awfully nice guy, Ben, so if you had done the hurting you would have owned up to it. I bet you were willing to compromise more than she was, too. And maybe she taught you about love and trust going hand in hand, huh?"

Ben glared at me for a moment or two and then gritted out, "Grannie Blue used to always say, 'If you have nothing good to say then keep your big mouth shut.' That's what I'm trying to do right at this moment." Looking at Ben I realized something: I wasn't the only one at this table scared to death of getting hurt. Or capable of getting angry. "And you're wrong in your assumption, Olivia. You're awfully quick to always assume I'm the good guy in the equation and that's where your fault lies. Maybe you do need the gory details."

Whoa. It was getting way too heavy. "Want to know what my ideal guy is?" Ben just stared at me across the table. "He's tall, dark, and handsome. Decisive. In control. Capable. Confident. Dependable. He's not intimidated by me, in fact despite popular opinion he finds me quite intriguing." At Ben's continued silence I waggled my eyebrows and added, "So far, you qualify."

"Have *you* ever been in love, Olivia?"

Ah jeeze. A deep sigh escaped me. *If he only knew.* "Until a few weeks ago I didn't even acknowledge the existence of love," I said flippantly, "so the answer to that is a resounding 'no'."

Ben watched me intently for a moment or so. "So you've never loved anyone?"

"Well, I *was* planning on marrying you for quite a while," I joked.

"Actually, you told me you loved me when we were eight years old."

I flew back in time remembering the only moments of true happiness in my childhood which were with Dean and with Ben. Nowhere else. "You and Dean ... the two loves of my life!" I was still trying to be funny but suddenly things weren't so comical any more.

"Remember that time we rode our bikes up to the quarry? We were about thirteen years old. I think it was one of the last times you came to visit Dean that we got to spend time together."

I frowned in confusion. "No, I don't remember."

After staring at me for a bit, Ben finally said, "You're lying."

When I went to open my mouth in defense, I finally turned away unable to look him in the eye because he was right. I was lying.

Taking my hand, Ben spoke quietly, "I was always way too serious and intense about things and you were always way too angry and combative about things. But together, even when we were kids, we balanced each other out. Don't you think? There were times when I felt the only time I was ...," he shrugged as if lost for words, "normal ... was when I was with you." He leaned in and whispered, "I still feel that way."

"Too bad for you," I responded jokingly but it wasn't very funny. So much for Ben's opinion about me and my lovability. I certainly didn't need to ask him if he thought I was lovable or not as he'd all but spelled it out for me. I couldn't get past the realization that Ben didn't know my truth; and *when he finally did* (because it was as inevitable as death) he would most certainly be singing a different tune.

"What changed your mind?" Huh? I looked at him in confusion. "About love and its existence," he clarified.

I'm terrified it's you. "Two years of therapy."

Ben smiled. "I told you therapy was a good thing."

But talking about all this had made me more terrified than ever of me, him, and the concept of *relationship*. Specifically knowing exactly what was at risk of being lost was … gut wrenching. I struggled to swallow past the fear tightening my throat.

The music had started up next door; nothing big just maybe a guitar and a keyboard and I jumped at the deflection. "You still want to dance with me?" I asked, trying to redirect the mood. I reached my hand up to smooth back a lock of his brown hair that had fallen out of place.

"Yeah, I still want to dance with you." He said it almost like he was trying to pick a fight.

"Well, let's pay the bill then."

Therapy: The Truth About Me – Part IV

Setting: Aileen's office, May 10, 2010. I sit in my car for quite a long time
before I go inside to Aileen, which will make me
uncharacteristically late. My mind is a kaleidoscope of memories:
Ben's face as he asked me Friday evening, 'Have you ever been in
love, Olivia?' My mother's face as she said to me, "I don't know
what it's like to carry around the stigma that you are a child of rape,
Olivia." Alec singing, "I've got trouble all over me, I've got trouble
since the day I was born."

Aileen: Well?

Me: I didn't do my 'homework'. I haven't thought about anything and I
haven't asked anyone anything.

Aileen: Okay.

Me: Should I go?

Aileen: (Looking at me pointedly through her glasses.) That's what you
want me to tell you. It would be the easiest way out. You know I
don't do easy.

Me: And because you care *so much about me*. (She doesn't respond.) The
real truth is, Aileen, that you only care about me because *you're paid
to*. My mother only cares about me because *it's a rule mothers have to
follow*. Ben only cares about me because I'm one of those *spiritually
lost souls* that ministers are always on the prowl for. Erin only cares
for me because *it's the right thing for a good sister to do*. Alec and Dan
only care about me to keep on the good sides of their wives. Liam
and Janine care about me because their clueless children, but they'll
wise up eventually, I'm sure, because they're very smart kids.
Clotilde cares for me because I put on a good face when I'm
around her and she really has no idea what she's dealing with. I
could blow her out of the water (I snap my fingers) *like that*. All I
need to do is show my true colors and start flashing Max more
than friendly politeness and I'll see the back of her faster than you

213

can say, 'Stay the hell away from my husband.' (I'm actually breathing heavily when I'm finished, like I've run a mile.)

Aileen: I guess that sums up what you think about yourself and your ability to be lovable or not. So do you-

Me: (I hold up my hand to shut Aileen up.) You don't have to prompt me with any questions. I'll keep talking just like you want me to. I'll answer your damn question. *No, I'm not lovable.* I wasn't lovable as a child, as a teen, or as an adult and I never will be. The Real Olivia Kelly is the one who most of the world knows: angry, bitter, selfish, and caustic. What I've been struggling with my whole life isn't *how to fix it all* but just trying to understand *why?* Why the hell am I like this? Yet sitting here talking with you hasn't been a complete waste really because finally, *at long last*, I get it. *I understand* and it's all thanks to you and your insightful questions. I'm a product of a marginally sane woman and an anonymous, deranged sadist who my malicious grandmother brought home. There's my heritage! My biological make-up! *No wonder I'm such a mess!* I need to stop whining, and face the truth of what I am, how people see me, and what my influence is to those around me. HERE ARE THE TRUTHS I NEED TO EMBRACE: I am the number one reason why my mother is still so broken and so nuts. I am a constant, vibrant reminder of *the very worst experience of her life* walking, talking, fighting, and terrorizing her from the moment of my birth. I will always be the type of woman who nice girls avoid because I disparage and intimidate them with my attitude. *I don't like nice girls* anymore than I like nice men. They're foolish and gullible and insipid and insignificant. Why would I ever want to become one? I am the kind of woman that bad guys intrinsically recognize and are drawn to! Why I'm probably doing nice girls a favor now that I think of it. They should thank me. And I'm The Number One Potential for downfall for good 'ole Benjamin Harayda, #1 nice man and minister extraordinaire. Heaven will sigh in relief when I shift my sights back in the direction I've always been drawn.

Aileen: (Having sat and watched my show.) What has happened this weekend, Olivia? (I sit silent as a stone and fight back tears.) Something's really upset you. I've been with you long enough to know that this caustic personality you're throwing around right now is a result of something that's absolutely terrified you. (She taps her pen against her lower lip in thought.) Hmmm, what are you most frightened of? (She looks at me with a "Eureka I've got it!" expression.) Did Ben tell you he loved you this weekend, Olivia?

Me: (I shake my head but when I finally speak my throat is tight with emotion.) No, not in so many words. But it's coming. Like a freight train down a steep hill. It's coming.

Aileen: And why, Olivia, *why* must love be such a bad thing?

Honesty is the best policy, but insanity is a better defense.[30]

20: You Can't Go Home Again
Friday, May 7, 2010.

Ben made quick work of the check, grabbed my hand and the remains of his single beer (his dinner out allotment) while I scrambled to grab my purse and what was left of my wine spritzer. I couldn't tell if his haste was due to the idea of getting his idea of a dream woman out on the dance floor or due to the strong desire to get away from the heavy discussion at the table but his movements were quick and abrupt.

As he went to pull me up onto the dance floor I pulled back and he turned to me questioningly. Leaning in to be heard over the music I asked, "Are you mad at me?"

He stepped toward me putting one hand on my waist and the other to the back of my neck. "No," he said against my ear, "at myself. I haven't always been this wise, together, or good looking," he grinned. "There've been times in my life when I've been … an astronomical fool. And it still makes me mad sometimes over the choices I've made." He blinked at me. "Are you angry at me?"

Angry? *Hardly.* I shook my head unwilling to voice the growing terror over this relationship and where it was headed and what this man was going to want from me. "Aren't you concerned about the fact that I haven't been in love since I was … eight years old?"

Instead of answering, Ben kissed me on the cheek and then nuzzled my hair. Finally he whispered in my ear, "Dance with me, Olivia." That time I let him pull me out onto the floor.

Dancing with Ben Harayda on our date was almost better than sex. *Almost.* I'll put that right out there even though you'll probably feel it's TMI (too much information). The band that night was lousy (so lousy we laughed out loud a few times as we swayed to the beat) and the dance floor itself was smaller than the piece of linoleum on my kitchen floor. But we had the space to ourselves and the company was exquisite.

Dancing is very sexual and if you don't agree then you just don't do it right. Whether you're dancing up close and personal or wiggling your ... body ... in abandon to the beat, either leaves ample opportunity to express a myriad of messages. I was a good girl and Ben was (of course) a good boy. I let him lead and to keep me on the mental up and up pretended that the band consisted of parents of my students and that everything was being recorded for YouTube. But the fact remained: you might be able to hide a lit flame but you couldn't ignore the heat.

I'd never danced ... circumspectly ... I guess the word would be, and once again this novel experience was better than I had ever imagined possible. I can't tell you one song that was played; everything about the music was just slow and mellow.

Ben was a good dancer. Or maybe we just were a good fit. Or maybe I was just in a daze of unrequited passion ... His left arm was around my waist, and his right hand held mine between us as we swayed to the music. I got lost in the sensations of the feel of Ben so close, the delicious smell of him, the way his beard stubble scratched my cheek and the move of his muscles through his shirt. Neither of us said a word, and yet much was communicated. When the first song was over, we stopped where we were and looked at each other. I arched my eyebrows wondering if we were going to sit down, get a drink, say, "Hey, you having as good a time as me?", anything ... Ben just looked at me and tightened his arm around my waist as if to say, "Go ahead, try to get away." Where else did he think I wanted to go? I leaned in, kissed him and, as the music started again, rested my head on his shoulder.

We danced for almost an hour without saying a word. If I had only three wishes I know for a fact that I would have used one of them to be able to read Ben's mind during that hour of dancing. But no such luck.

For me, never had the differences between us been more blatant: he clearly intended on gaining a place in my heart and me clearly fixated on gaining a place in his bed. I reverted back to my old standby technique of being completely obsessed with the physical intimacy we were enjoying. At one point he tugged on my hair and I looked up at him in a daze. Again, before any words were spoken, he kissed me there on the dance floor … for a long time. It was glorious.

The lack of words continued on the drive home and even once he walked me up to my front door. I was out in the stratosphere of … I'll just say emotion. Standing there in the weak overhead porch light, we just looked at each. I found my voice first. "Want to come in?" I was going to say 'for coffee' but we both knew that would have been a lie, so I just stood there in front of Ben close enough to see his pulse beating at his throat.

"Yeah," he sighed, "I want to come in." I didn't move because I could tell more was coming. "But I'm not going to." He touched the side of my face and then my hair, tucking it behind my ears. "I'm trying to go slow, Jerry. Honest I am."

"I know. It seems to be getting harder and harder for us to 'stay on the right side' and all. It's not about a cup of coffee anymore."

Ben shook his head. "No, it's not about a cup of coffee anymore. And you're right. It probably never was." As if he couldn't help it, he kissed me, holding the back of my neck and pulling me as close as when we'd danced. "I'm going to that conference in Atlanta next week, remember?" I nodded. "I'll call and text, okay?" I nodded again. "I don't get back until late Sunday so …"

"Don't forget to bring me a souvenir." I teased.

"Yeah? What do you want?"

I tried to push him but he didn't budge. "I'm kidding. Don't you dare bring me anything." I hesitated looking at his serious expression, "Ben, I … I don't want to get hurt any more than you do -"

"No one's going to get hurt," he interrupted.

I wrestled the conversation back. "Let me finish okay?" At his reluctant nod I said, "The more we spend time together ... the more our differences are apparent to me. Take this time away to really think about us, okay? I keep hearing you say *neither one of us was willing to compromise for the other.*" When Ben went to say something, I put my hand against his mouth. "I'll *bet you* that girl was *a lot* more close to fitting into your life than I am now." He closed his eyes and I leaned into him. "I can see by your expression that I'm right," I whispered and I couldn't keep myself from putting both my arms around him and kissing the side of his face. "Just think, Ben, okay? *Just think.*"

Tightening his arms around me he said fiercely, "I'll think but I'll also pray, Jerry. You try it, too."

As I watched him drive away, I knew with absolute certainty that going out for a cup of coffee with Ben had been the biggest mistake of my life.

Thursday night, May 13, 2010, my phone rang and I knew it was Ben. Having had my big, bad blow-out session with Aileen it had to be A Sign that Ben had been away this whole week through Sunday night. *Why must love be such a bad thing?* and *Take the time to sort yourself out* were my mantras this week. *Think!* I'd written this in my journal a million times. Well, maybe twelve. Somewhere along the way I had decided that speaking with Ben (or texting) would only confuse my already muddled thoughts so I'd ignored every call and every text for the past five days.

Even though Ben and I had only a few dates under our belts this was a relationship that felt like a whole lot more. Already we'd fallen into a pattern of sorts. For him, work days and evenings were filled with ministerial duties that often included nighttime meetings and activities with the teens. Ben was a good guy, remember, so he did all the things you'd hope he'd do like staying in steady communication (texting) with most of the kids, attending their extracurricular activities as often as possible, and regularly hosting fun events that promoted "camaraderie and spiritual growth" (i.e. Christian rock concerts, etc.). We often talked about what was planned or what he was thinking of planning, and I'd already begun to feel his strong hope that I'd say something like, "Now that sounds fun, can I go?" or at least express enough interest that he'd feel comfortable trying to get me to come along. This gap between our two lives had gotten more and more obvious as we spent more time together and gotten more ... closer.

All week I'd been *thinking* about Olivia Kelly and what she is and what she was and what she's ... always going to be. Truth may have sucked but that didn't mean I was too cowardly to face it.

You know how in movies when the couple splits up because the one partner does something intentionally mean or cruel to force the other person away? Can you guess which part I'd decided to play? Prior to all my therapy those movies made me laugh cynically. I often couldn't understand what the appeal was between the two individuals, let alone the concept of loving someone so much you were willing to cause yourself pain to spare the other. What were they, nuts? But I understood now. About the caring and the sparing. Quite frankly, I knew that at some point I was headed for a world of hurt getting involved with Ben Harayda. No matter how much we liked each other the truth was he wasn't my type and I wasn't his. What was worse, I knew he was too much of a hopeful sap to acknowledge this. Based on glimpses he'd given me of his past, I suspected he might even have a history of this sort of behavior. Which was where I had to come in.

I let my machine pick up the call just like I'd been doing all week. Ben's messages had gotten progressively ... more ... concerned. I always knew he was a smart man which meant eventually he'd get the clue. If I had known Ben was in town I wouldn't have done this because he'd probably have driven over to make sure I was alive. For this call, however, Ben didn't leave a message and then immediately the phone rang again. Again I let the machine pick up and the person didn't leave a message, and again the phone immediately began to ring. Curiosity eventually got the better of me.

"Hello?"

"Livvie? It's me, Dean. You know, your father."

Holy cow. "Hey, Dad. Are you okay?" I pictured him calling me from a mangled car wreck or a hospital or … using his one call from the police station.

"Yeah, I'm okay. I'd almost decided you weren't home. Are you busy? Okay?"

"I'm … fine. To what do I owe this honor? I think the last time you called me when it wasn't a holiday or some other special occasion was like 2007. What's up?"

"It's possible that 2007 was the last time I had a cell phone ..." Dean said thoughtfully, and I pictured him frowning in concentration trying to remember. "You've, ah, been on my mind lately, Livvie. I was wondering if you'd … like to have dinner with me sometime."

Have dinner?! I stood there with my mouth hanging open in shock. "Are you dying?" I regretted it as soon as I said it given how my crack about Alec and prison went over just last week.

"Not immediately. As far as I know. Hey, have you had dinner *yet?*"

"Ah …."

"Because I'm out in your parking lot with a pizza. Extra cheese and mushroom."

I went over to the front window and there he was in his truck. Dean Kelly. My … father. I had a horrible thought then – *oh please let him be sober.* The interior light switched on and I saw him wave at me. "Come on in, Dad."

Journal: The Truth About Therapy
Monday, May 17, 2010

On Monday morning before I leave for school I call Aileen's answering
machine and cancel my appointment. The message I leave is, "Hey
Aileen, it's me, Olivia. As you might have guessed, I'm going to
cancel our session for today. Maybe I need to take some time off
from therapy. Sort some things out. I'll call you." You might
think it cowardice but I prefer to call it 'taking charge of my life.' I
know for a fact that Ben is back in town and having to deal with
him *and Aileen* in one day is more than my psyche can cope with.

On the way to work I develop a manifesto, a statement of self. I can almost
hear the crowds roaring as I speak into the microphone and shout
out to the masses the result of my therapy: *I am Olivia Kelly. Like it
or get out of my way.*

Last evening (Sunday) I wrote the following in my journal:
1. I will remember to have forward - thinking goals for myself, such
    as trying to be happier.
2. I am no longer angry enough to kill and I will continue to work
    towards the eradication of this emotion which definitely detracts
    from #1.
3. I will continue to spend time with my mother and count it a victory
    to walk away without having bitten my tongue. Mothers are
    important. You only get one. And maybe mine isn't as bad as I
    thought she was.
4. I will continue to work on my tentative friendship with my sister,
    who is not as perfect as I thought she was (which is a good thing).
    Perhaps I will discover additional imperfections which will make us
    closer and assist me with #1.

222

5. I now will date anyone who suits me (not exclusively married men) as long as he helps me work towards #1. *I will not change* just to please a man.

6. I understand that I need to accept who I am. I cannot please everyone and I will not try. I cannot change the facts of my life. The fact that everyone is influenced by their past must be accepted to achieve #1.

7. I will stop trying to change myself to fit someone else's standard of who I should be. I will be myself. The reality is that there are some people who I do not fit well with and vice versa. This includes both friends, family, and potential romantic partners. I will try to stay separate from these people to help me achieve #1.

That's as good as a therapy session, isn't it?

Hell is truth seen too late.[31]

21: Sometimes You Get What You Want
Monday, May 17, 2010

I was uptight all day Monday, May 17, 2010, and it had nothing to do with me canceling my session with Aileen. Ben's last communication was a phone message on Saturday night. He said he would be arriving late Sunday night and wouldn't call me since he knew I went to bed early on school nights. He said he hoped to talk with me on Monday, but his voice didn't hold out much hope since he'd been talking to just my answering machine this whole week. Aileen ruined that hard edge I used to have and made me aware of other people's feelings. Why couldn't Ben just take the hint and move on? Why was he going to make me spell it out in plain English when he had to have easily understood the message I'd been giving *all week.*

It was Clotilde who gave me an out when she mentioned the upcoming Board of Education meeting that all teachers were asked to attend to show solidarity. Dedicated union girl that I am, I decided to attend, which also kept me away from my house for a substantial period of time. (In the end, coward that I was, I didn't go home after school but stayed and graded papers, and then went with Clotilde and a number of other teachers to a local restaurant for dinner.)

Negotiations between the administration and the teacher's union had taken a serious turn for the worse, especially since state aid to the district had been drastically cut because of the national (and state) budget crisis. There had been a number of clashes between the administration and the union these past months and our new contract had not yet been settled.

Across all grade levels and subjects many teachers had gotten pink slips and all of us non-tenured teachers felt a distinct bull's eye on our backs. Seniority had become the only saving lifeline and I'd waited with resignation to be told I'll be out of work in September. The mantra "so far, so good" had became less comforting.

The board meeting was endless. I'd been to them before but usually only under duress. I sat in the back and filed my nails, annoyed Clotilde with obnoxious texts, and played Bejeweled and Solitaire on my phone. Periodically as people started to get hot under the collar I thought *oh now maybe things will get good* but nothing ever ramped up to make the *four hours* I'd spent worth it. Ten-thirty at night I wandered tiredly out to my car shouting obnoxious stuff to Clotilde who yelled back. As I opened my car door I heard my name called.

It was Phil. He'd been waiting in the dark for me. He made no move towards me and just said, "I've been trying to catch your attention all night."

"I didn't even know you were at the meeting," I told him honestly.

"The place was packed. What a nightmare. There's going to be a strike, mark my words."

"That wouldn't make me too happy. But I'm not going to worry yet. There's still time."

Phil shook his head. "Both sides are too stubborn. Plus there's a lot of anger and panic now, too." We stood there in the dark as all around us were people saying good bye, getting in their cars, and driving away. "I've been thinking about you, Liv," he said. "What's changed? When you first started working here you gave me all the signals. I tried hard to ignore them but you persisted. Then, as soon as we started ... connecting ... you changed your mind. You didn't impress me as the kind of woman who changes her course."

I let my mind wander for a bit standing there in the dark. I imagined inviting Phil back to my place and having him answer the phone when Ben called. Or, I imagined joining Phil in the fancy new Lexus he was leaning on. I even thought about waiting a few more minutes until we were the only ones around and spending some time with Phil under the stars. Did I start to glow or throw off 'I'm thinking about you' pheromones? Suddenly Phil was in front of me, pressing us both against the side of my car. "Come on, Liv, don't talk yourself out of it. There's no doubt in my mind that both of us would have more fun than we could even imagine."

He grinned when I didn't push him away immediately. I pointed out, "You're awfully brave propositioning one of your teachers out here in the Board of Education parking lot."

"Something tells me you're worth the risk." Phil kissed me, doing his very best to impress. It wasn't the first time we'd kissed – there was the night at O'Reilly's, but prior to that there were a number of hurried, passionate exchanges in … his office, a supply room, and the back of my classroom. Each had been hot, promising, and nowhere near satisfactory, building a level of expectation that at times was significantly distracting.

But tonight as Phil kissed me my mind wandered. How many teachers had he had affairs with so far? How would his wife feel if she could see us now? How many kids did he have? Did I leave my front porch light on? I wondered if I should take a shower when I got home as I'd probably be too tired to do it in the morning… I pushed against Phil's chest and we came up for air. "How about we make plans for Friday night? We could take the train into the city and catch a show, do a late dinner. I'll tell Ruth that I've -"

"Phil, I'm sorry. Yes, I acknowledge that I started this. I sent out signals. But that was almost two years ago, and I've been pretty specific the last few times you've approached me. I'm going to have to say definitively *no*, okay? Do you hear me? Is it sinking in? I … I just want more than you can offer, and I'm willing to wait until I can get it."

He rubbed his hand down his face and straightened his tie and jacket and trousers. I watched him silently. We stood staring at each other for a few moments and then he just turned and walked back towards his car.

"Phil." I called after him and he stopped and looked over his shoulder at me. "Don't approach me again. I mean it."

When I got home, I took note that I *had* left my porch light on and illuminated in the glow was a small, white plastic bag.

Sitting next to that bag was a very sad man looking very much like the first time I saw him sitting outside IHC.

We looked at each other through my windshield for a long time and finally I mustered up enough courage to get out of the car. Ben didn't say a word to me, just watched me walk towards him and finally sit down next to him.

"So what are you doing on my porch at ten forty-five at night? Sophie must be going nuts that one of her favorite people in the world is here and she can't get near him." I tried to smile … and I suppose I came close.

He looked tired, wary and not at all happy. He was dressed down in khaki slacks and a dark blue polo shirt. I approved of the loafers he was wearing and could see that he still wasn't wearing any socks.

Ben sighed. "It took me a while to clue in to what you were trying to communicate this past week but I finally think I've got it. Sorry if I was so slow and sorry that I've showed up here on your doorstep anyway." He gave me a sad smile. "Ever persistent and hopeful, I guess."

This was a Ben I'd never seen before and I didn't like the responsibility I bore in bringing it about. "It … it wasn't anything to do with you, Ben. It was all me."

In a low voice Ben said, "How do you know that for sure?! You didn't give us a chance to come to *any* conclusions about *anything*, Olivia. There wasn't any rush. I didn't have any agenda. I simply wanted to reconnect with someone who had meant more to me in my childhood than anyone else besides family."

"There was *a lot* more between us than just a simple catch up on old times and you knew it!" I answered fiercely.

He stared at me for a beat or two and then acknowledged bitterly, "Yes I did, Olivia. I knew it when I was thirteen and I know it now. Seems like you're admitting that you know it, too." He waited, looked at me, and finally said, "You asked me the other night what I was doing with you. Do you remember that?" I nodded. "I couldn't answer then but now I can."

I started to get up. "I'm sorry, Ben, but I don't want to hear it." Suddenly it was absolutely imperative that I *didn't* hear what he had to say.

As he gripped my hand, he said doggedly, "Too bad. It won't take long." He stood along with me and followed me to the door. "This is what I'm doing here with you, Olivia Kelly. I'm enjoying myself. I'm laughing and smiling and having fun. I'm looking into the future and suddenly I'm wondering just what interesting opportunities are there for me that I couldn't see and I hadn't thought of yet. I'm remembering good times and good memories that I had long forgotten. And I'm working hard to understand just what is important to me and what is not."

"All because of little ole me?" I asked through gritted teeth. Man, why couldn't I have recorded my Last Speech at Aileen's in which, among other things I stated categorically, 'I wasn't lovable as a child, as a teen, or as an adult and I never will be'? "Well let me help you with that, okay Ben? *Let me clue you in to something important.* You're enjoying yourself because I'm your physical dream woman and many guys ... have enjoyed that aspect of me. You're laughing and smiling and having fun because I'm a wise ass 90% of the time, but trust me no one has been able to live with me for very long. Look into the future and you'll see a mass of unresolved issues that I'm still carrying around like a bag of rocks. A bag of rocks that you'd quickly get tired of helping me carry ... that's again the voice of experience talking. And don't be lured by good memories. Sooner or later reality will seep in and you'll remember even more things you'd thought you'd forgotten. Like how I have a temper, how I carry a grudge, how I have a twisted sense of morals and am completely lacking in any real values. Trust me. Compromise is good, Ben, *but only when the other person's worth it.*"

Ben stepped in close, humming with anger, but he didn't touch me. I watched his face, fascinated with the raw emotion I saw. He hissed, "I agree with you about compromise, Olivia – one hundred percent. You think you're so astute about me but you are *so wrong.*" He faltered for a moment. "In the past I've been the one to … insist on certain things … not willing to offer any type of compromise. At the same time I had my priorities mixed up. I was dogmatic in some areas and completely weak and foolish in others. I relied too much on my own elevated opinion of myself and was willing to give up things that *I now know* were far too important to set aside for *anyone.*" He took a deep breath.

His little speech hasn't helped change my mind at all. "Okay, so you *have* dealt with women such as myself before. Even tried to "clean them up a bit" I assume." I gave him a sarcastic smile. *"Learn from your mistakes, Ben."*

Good ole Pastor Ben looked angry enough to scream. Or give me a good hard shake. I watched him struggle with his emotions and then finally close his eyes and take a deep, calming breath trying desperately to get on an even keel. "I fell in love with a woman who I discovered couldn't be faithful and didn't really know what trust and love were all about, Olivia. A lot of it was my fault. There were plenty of glaring warning signs that I should have acknowledged, but I believed that," his mouth twisted in disgust, "I could change her to fit my perfect plan." Looking at me pointedly he said, "I'm not the same man I used to be, Olivia. If you've been listening closely, I've not offered nor asked you to compromise *anything.* If you're really interested, I can give you a list of things that are deal breakers for me *no matter who you are.*" Wisely, I chose to stay silent.

"We haven't gotten far enough in our relationship for us to talk about those things – *let alone make a decision about the deal."* Ben shrugged. "At least in my opinion. So far, all I've done is invite you into my life, and I've been taking a look into yours. That's honestly all I want. Yes, it's more than a damn cup of coffee. Yes, things are going faster than I'd ever imagined. But so far, I've enjoyed every minute with you. I enjoy talking with you. You have a unique perspective that I've enjoyed discovering. You ask great questions that keep me on my toes. I was hoping to have more of the same."

Ben put his hand on his hips and I watched the anger work its way back front and center. "Give me one good reason why we can't take some time to get to know each other?! Why can't we have conversations about hopes and dreams and see if there's room for compromise ... or if there's not?! I wanted to try. In my opinion, you're worth the time and the effort. But it seems you've come to a different conclusion. It seems you don't think *I'm* worth *your* time or effort."

Ah, jeeze. Once again we'd had a deep discussion and I'd tried my best to be honest and he'd taken it completely wrong. The emotions on his face and in his eyes were so intense I had to look down. "You've misunderstood me, Ben," I began but he stopped me and put his hand under my chin, making me look up.

"Look me in the eye when you tell me hard truths about myself, Olivia. It might hurt me, but I can take it."

I shook my head. "I don't have hard truths to tell you about yourself, Ben. I'll say it again: *it's all about me*. I'm ... not right for you. I'm ... still a huge work in progress. There's so much I've done that I'm not proud of. I'm just ... a different kind of person than you are. You're all together and determined and confident and I'm still walking around in circles, blindfolded."

He frowned in puzzlement. "What are you saying, Olivia? Are you saying you're willing to sacrifice this relationship – before we're even sure what we've got – because you think I'm ...," he swallowed, "because you think ... I'm too good for you?" He whispered the last part like it was some horrible curse. Ben gripped my shoulders and almost shook me. "Do you hear how ridiculous that sounds?!"

The tears started then. Little trickles at first but I could feel an impending tsunami. "It doesn't sound ridiculous at all, Ben. It sounds exactly right." I tried to pull out of his arms. Tried to get my front door key. Tried to get away to be alone and miserable.

Instead, Ben wrapped his arms around me. "But that's *my choice* to make, Olivia! Not yours! You have no say in that. Now tell me you can't stand the sight me. Tell me you'll never be able to deal with the fact that

I'm a minister. Tell me you're in love with someone else. Tell me *you're just not that interested, or all this is just too intense for you to deal with.* Those are *your choices* to make and I've got to respect them. But don't stand there and attempt to make *my* decisions for me.

"You listen to me, Olivia Kelly," he said fiercely in my ear while I struggled half heartedly to get away from his words, "I like what I see! I'm scaring myself with how much I like what I see! And don't you dare trivialize what we have by implying that it's only a cheap, physical attraction or that I'm so shallow I'll soon grow tired of what I find so intriguing now." He took a step back, still holding tightly to my arms. "Look at me, Olivia. *Look at me.*"

I did but I could barely see him through my tears. "I'll leave you alone if that's what you want, but it's got to be because *you* don't want to be with *me.* Can you *honestly* tell me that?" I sniffled and just stared at him. If I was going to start lying, it for damn sure wasn't going to be about this.

Ben leaned in even closer, "Because if you decided to do that I'd ask you to remember this one important thing, Olivia." He paused and I thought, *Oh God, no one has ever said such wonderful things to me … ever.* Carefully, reverently, he gave me the gentlest of kisses and then whispered in my ear, *"I would miss you until the day I died."*

It wasn't until after Ben had left that I went and retrieved the small, white, plastic bag that had been left on my front step. He'd brought me a souvenir: a cute, little, stuffed swan.

Dean showed up Thursday, May 20th. Again. We were bonding, I thought, but still had some doubts. Last Thursday, over pizza, we spent about an hour sitting on the back deck eating and drinking soda. Conversation was very general. "How have you been?" and "How's work going?" and "What's new?" and "This is a nice place. How long have you been here?" I kept waiting for the shoe to drop … or the bomb. But nothing came up and as I said goodbye to him that first night and we shared an awkward hug he said, "Could I come again?"

What could I say?

He brought Chinese this time, a collection of familiar white containers, and we sat inside on the couch because it was raining torrentially. Dean became Sophie's best friend when he carefully selected pieces of pork from the fried rice and placed them at his feet on a napkin for her. Eventually, to my utter amazement, she curled up *in his lap* and went to sleep. *Maybe,* I thought, *it's just me she didn't like.* I brewed green tea which Dean politely tried to choke down, and I finally said to him, "We're not going to get anywhere, Dad, if you can't even tell me you don't like green tea."

Carefully he put his mug down and looked at me. "You still call me Dad. I appreciate that."

"You're the only Dad I knew," I pointed out.

"Which isn't saying much." Dean chewed on a dumpling and then said, "You've had a really raw deal, Livvie."

I had no desire to do this: rehash my lousy childhood and try to find some silver lining amidst all the clouds. I hated doing it with Aileen and I managed to avoid doing it with my mother, or even Erin. "Why are you here, Dad?"

"I've been sober for two years, two months and fourteen days. Did you know that's the longest I've ever been sober since I was twelve?" I shook my head and Dean nodded and smiled shyly. "I'm pretty damn proud of that. Thursdays were always my hardest days when I was drinking, which is funny 'cause you'd think it would be Friday – payday. But see, I used to start getting especially thirsty on Thursdays, anticipating Fridays. By the time Friday lunch time rolled around," he sighed and shook his head, "the thirst was just incredible. So I count my sobriety from Thursday to Thursday. Now I make it a point to have Thursdays be the best day of the week for me. Last Thursday I was standing at my favorite pizzeria waiting for my favorite pie and I remembered how you and I used to both like it. Then I thought, "I wonder what Livvie is doing?" He shrugged and looked at me. "So I called you."

It made perfect sense to this man and suddenly I thought, *who am I to question him?* This was the man who *knew for a fact* that I was not his biological daughter even when my mother looked him right in the eye and told him he was. This is the man who married my mother and took her home to his parents' house. He dropped out of school and started working construction full time at age seventeen to support us. This is the man who cared for me and supported me and behaved so that no one knew that he knew the reality of my paternity – not me, not my mother – until he acknowledged that he'd known a version of the truth almost right from the beginning. This is the man who never turned his back on me even after my mother left him, even after I refused to spend time with him, and supported me financially – as best as he could - all through college. Dean AKA Dad sat there looking at me with his big blue eyes, sun-bleached blonde hair, and still relatively buff bod, waiting for me to reconnect with him. He did take a bite of another dumpling though while I went through my thoughts.

"Why?" I just threw the single word out like you'd throw a dollar bill on the floor of a busy mall; it might make things interesting.

Dean rooted around in the container of kung pao shrimp with his chopsticks. "You mean why did I stay true to you?"

What a glorious expression in both its description and its accuracy. I actually mouthed it to myself silently and then looked at Dean and nodded.

"Life sucks, Livvie. For a lot of people. Before you, there was your mother. She lived with that witch of a mother and when we first met E was like a puppy that had been kicked so many times it thought that was the way life was supposed to be." He took a deep breath and then said with determination. "I won't speak ill of the dead … We hit it right off E and me." Dean grinned with a fond memory that I hoped he wouldn't share. "We were like a flashlight and a new set of batteries. We just clicked on bright and shiny.

"We both had our demons, E and me. For me it was alcohol and for E it was from being starved to death of love. Both of us weren't … whole as a result. When you came on the scene," Dean stopped talking and reached out to briefly touch my cheek with the back of his hand, "I didn't see any reason to cause you any more trouble than I knew you were already going to have. Elaine said you were mine and, even though I knew it wasn't true, even though I knew I was far from a good deal, I did love her. So I figured why not? Would you and Elaine be better off depending on Vera than on me? I sure as hell didn't think so. I hoped that maybe, between the two of us, we could at least do a better job with you than either one of us could on our own."

Dean put his chopsticks down and leaned back on my couch with one arm draped across his eyes. "I suppose you probably would have been better off adopted ... but who knows really? What I do know was that I loved you from the minute I held you and you looked at me with eyes and hair so different from mine. Even then I think I realized that maybe, just maybe, because you *weren't* really a part of me, you might have more of a fighting chance." He peered at me from under his arm briefly to say. "After all, look what I gave Erin to work with."

We're both quiet for a long time, lost in thought. Dean laid there for so long that I wondered if he'd fallen asleep until he murmured, "My demons ... they were always so big. Or maybe I was just ... so weak." He shrugged. "And they're still never far away. Some days I get so damn tired of fighting. But I've finally come to accept all of this and work hard each day to find ways to become stronger ..."

Dean sat up suddenly and looked at me. "Livvie, I'm sorry for all the hurt and disappointment I'm responsible for in your life. I'll take ownership of it all. Just slap it on me. Maybe, someday, you'll be able to forgive me. I'm not proud of much in my life, but I am proud of loving you and Erin. In fact, you and Erin are my two gold stars." He scratched his chin. "Teachers used to give you those in my day, and I hardly ever got any.

"One time, I conned my mom into buying me a package of them at the five and ten cent store." He gave me a grin that I'm certain had gotten him tons of attention from willing females. "I got in loads of trouble for selling them on the playground to kids like me who never got 'em." Dean laughed. "Was my mother furious!"

Getting up, Dean started picking up empty food cartons and dirty napkins. "This was fun Olivia. I appreciate you letting me come by and talk. I was on a high all last week after I left here and then got excited about coming here again tonight. You've probably got loads of better things to do with your evenings than entertain me ..." Whoever would have thought that the little girl who loved her daddy so much that she slept with one of his dirty tee shirts would recognize the same kind of longing in that daddy's voice?

"How about I cook dinner next Thursday? Don't expect gourmet, but I can make a mean chili."

Dean poked his head out of the kitchen doorway. "You sure?" When I smiled and nodded he said, "There's this pastry shop I know that makes the best cheesecake muffins I've ever eaten. I'll pick up a couple and bring them with me for dessert."

Journal: The Truth About The Person I Am
Thursday, May 20ᵗʰ.

I would miss you until I died.
Ben said that to me a few days ago and has called me every night since. He
   has told me the moment I stop answering his phone calls he's
   coming over. Furthermore, he's told me I can break up with him
   any time and he'll abide by my wishes. I just have to be *honest* and
   tell him that I can't stand the sight of him ... or something like
   that. Sigh. Like that's going to happen.
Meatloaf has a song in which a guy promises to love a girl until the end of
   time. The final chorus is *so now I'm praying for the end of time, so hurry
   up and arrive. Cause if I gotta spend another minute with you I don't think
   that I can really survive it ...*[32] In the dark hours of the night after Ben
   left Monday night (and after I agreed to keep seeing him) and every
   night since then, I've thought of that song and that final chorus.
   Flashes of me in various states of ... disaster ... paraded through
   my mind, and I wondered just how strong a person Ben Harayda
   really was.
*I loved you from the minute I held you and you looked at me with eyes and hair so
   different from mine.* My dad – yes, Dean Kelly is my dad - said that to
   me this evening. That's another stunning bit of information that
   I've learned. I never in my entire life ever thought that there was a
   love like that – let alone that it was directed towards me.
I probably should get back on the Aileen train. She'd be delighted to hear
   about what I've learned about my lovability without really asking
   anyone outright.

In my journal, I've decided to review the good and bad things at the end of
   each week. So, regarding this past week:

Good:

1. I continue to embrace the person that I am. This week I add to the list of: *brash, outspoken, opinionated, and independent* the additional quality of *decisive*.

2. I have *decisively*, once and for all, spoken plainly and clearly to Phil. He now should have no question in regard to the possibility of a relationship.

3. I had dinner with Dean for the second time in two weeks. He was sober. We ate Chinese. It would seem that we both enjoyed the evening and will continue to see each other.

4. Ben won't take no for an answer. Said he would *miss me until he died*. See below.

5. My being "unlovable" is now firmly questionable. I'm not saying I'm now part of Care Bear Nation or anything but it seems as if there are a few out there who are either extremely delusional or … have a different perception of me than I do.

Bad:

1. I continue to embrace the person that I am. I need to think on this a bit.

2. Ben won't take no for an answer. Said he would *miss me until he died*. See above.

3. Dealing with Phil took far too long. Two years? Perhaps 'decisive' is a bit over the top.

4. Ben still doesn't know the real truth about me.

5. The real truth about me.

I would never lie. I willfully participate in a campaign of misinformation.[33]

22: God, Me and Garbage: Perfect Together
Wednesday, May 26, 2010

By Wednesday, May 26, 2010, I felt increasingly tense over my job security as I was now one of only *four* non-tenured teachers who still *might* have a job come next September; all the rest had been told that they should look for employment elsewhere. This caused a whole different kind of stress: worry. There was still no finalized contract for any of us and things were getting edgier by the day. Self-centered as it sounds, it was one thing to hear about the economy on television but it was a whole other thing to have it staring you in the face. A hundred times a day I thought about what I would do if I lost my job. My district was just like every other school district in the state, so I couldn't just pick up my #2 pencils and go knocking on some other door and expect to get hired. How would I pay my rent? My car loan? My credit card bill? What would I do if I suddenly couldn't afford to live in my place anymore? Or afford the sporty little car that I enjoyed? Or buy that newest pair of excellent shoes I'd been eyeing at my favorite online store? What about health insurance? What if I got sick? I wasn't getting any younger … When I realized I was not even eligible for unemployment benefits since I was a ten-month contracted, non-tenured teacher, I almost started to hyperventilate. My anxiety just kept growing and growing with each passing day. I had a nightmare about living in Vera's house (still actually sitting empty, idle, and for sale with hardly a bite even though it was 'priced to sell'). In my nightmare, I was sharing the house with my mother and Alec who'd also lost their jobs. I lost count how many times I woke up in the middle of the night in a cold sweat with my heart pounding. I didn't remember worrying about things like this before Aileen supposedly helped me get so emotionally healthy. Being angry full time apparently had a few advantages.

After New Year, school had a way of feeling like a freight train coasting downhill. But after Spring Break, the engine burst into flame and flew off a cliff. There was a furious rush to get everything done in a span of time that seemed impossible. I was completely stressed over the need to make sure my performance was exceptional, my work was without error, and my dedication was beyond reproach. I spent many an evening late in my classroom grading papers, updating student records, filling out midterm reports, tutoring students before school, afterschool, during lunch, and during study halls for final exam prep, writing report cards, writing recommendations for outgoing seniors, and any one of nine million other things required to close a school year out. I worked through the weekend and Ben came over bringing dinner to me (because I refused to go out and leave my work).

We no longer discussed *if* we were going to get together; now it was just when and where and how. And it was no longer just on Fridays or Saturdays; sometimes it was a quick dinner, sometimes it was an hour before or after his church meetings. Somehow we had morphed into that comfortable understanding that showing up unexpectedly was not only okay; it was welcome. As I was in full hysteria with work, Ben was the one who did this more than I did. But you didn't hear me complaining. My growing anxiety over my job and the ever increasing work load didn't deter Ben from keeping company with me. Ben, like Sophie, seemed merely content to be in my presence. I grew accustomed to his size thirteen sloppy sneakers which regularly lay carelessly in the middle of my living room floor. I smiled at the sound of his laughter as he watched television (laughing through *World's Dumbest* and *Operation Repo* which I discovered he'd recorded on my DVR). I ate the Dunkin' Donut chocolate frosted donuts that regularly appeared at my elbow to fortify me. While I worked furiously at my dining room table with enough paperwork and numbers to sink a battleship Ben and Sophie calmly went on with their lives close by.

From all this came two clear and distinct things: I was absolutely certain that I loved my job and I was definitely in a romantic relationship … with a minister.

Ben was fast asleep on my couch when I finally finished up at midnight. I dragged myself over to the couch where he lay flat on his back looking cute and rumpled with sleep. Leaning down I gave him a gentle kiss on his forehead and with a deep sigh and a lazy smile I was hauled down next to him and wrapped tightly in a tangle of arms and legs.

"Hmmmmm, you finally done?" he mumbled in my ear and then kissed my neck.

"Yeah."

"You're just full of worry, Jerry." I got squeezed tightly. "You're not on your own you know."

"There's not much you can do, Ben. I don't think you're too skilled with lesson plans and I know for certain you can't write college referrals. Thanks anyway." I sighed with exhaustion and let my mind scroll out over all the stuff I still had to do. "I guess you could help me grade finals if you really wanted."

"I didn't mean *me*." He shifted and pushed himself up on an elbow and gazed down at me. Brushing my wild hair off to the side he tenderly stroked my face. "And I'm not talking so much about work. I'm talking about you worrying about your job."

Grinning up at him I murmured, "Are you putting in a good word for me with the Big Guy upstairs?" His hair had flopped down over his right eye and I reached up to give it a tug.

Ben stared at me for a moment and then nodded. "I usually pray for Big Black Arrows."

I smiled. "'Big Black Arrows?'"

"Yeah, no confusion, no grey areas. 'Paint a big, black arrow on the ground God and I'll follow it.' I pray for that for me and I'm praying for that for you, too."

"Did big black arrows get you to me?"

Leaning down, Ben clucked his head with mine and then kissed my nose. "I'd like to think so." He gave me a kiss on the nose, untangled himself and stood above me. "Thanks."

"What are you thanking me for?" I asked in surprise and I struggled to stand up, too.

"For listening to my God talk."

"Hey, you told me you and God go together, right?" Ben nodded. "So, I've come to expect it and have kind of gotten used to it."

What a wonderful kiss goodnight I got.

What if Ben's big black arrows involved me losing my job? *I really liked my job.* I fought waves of panic that regularly interrupted my train of thought and robbed me of sleep. The possibility terrified me.

I mentioned something to Clotilde about it after school, having wandered over to find her working diligently on her computer, like every other teacher probably. She had tenure, but just barely, and who knew about Max's job as a computer specialist at a small company. Surprisingly, when I voiced all my concerns, she just shrugged. "Max and I are praying about it, that's for sure. Four people have been let go at his company, but in different departments. But that doesn't mean that IT isn't going to be looked at soon."

"You're just praying about it?"

"Don't say 'just'." Clotilde stood up and walked over to me, her hands on her slim hips and glared at me. "You always run away when I talk about spiritual things, Olivia, but they're important to me. To Max, too."

My friendship with Clotilde was *in spite* of her spiritual life, not because of it. I get enough of the God stuff with my mother and Alec (Praise the Lord Jesus!) – and now Ben - and I for sure didn't need it at work. I had worked hard to have a deaf ear whenever Clotilde started doing her God song and dance. I wasn't trying to be rude, honest. If I didn't really listen then I wouldn't make fun or get sarcastic, so in ignoring her God talk (or running away) I was doing my best to preserve our friendship. But somehow, I didn't think Clotilde saw it that way. "Don't get bent, Clo. I know that kind of stuff works for you and Max but that's because you're into it. That's all." I suddenly had Aileen's annoying voice in my head saying, *If you're going to embrace someone's philosophy, then you need to get to the bottom of it. You can't just skim bits off the top just because they sound good. You need to go back and ask Clotilde some more specifics.*

"Praying isn't exclusive to just people who go to church, Olivia. You know that." She looked me right in the eye. "Or maybe you don't."

Now, you know very well that I caved on the whole love thing. Kicking and screaming, mind you, but cave I did. But there's only so much a person can take. At least *this person.* "Clo, God's ...," I swallowed and gathered my thoughts because suddenly Clotilde's looking at me very intently, "God's not for me." I held up my hands to ward off an attack. "God's been good for you and Max ... my mother and Alec ... Erin and Dan and the kids go to church on Sundays ... He's good for a lot of people. Heck, I'm dating a minister, aren't I? God's just not for me," I finished rather lamely.

"Why?" Clotilde demanded. "Give me one good reason why something can be good for a lot of people but 'just not you'." She was mad I suddenly realized. Ballistic even. Her hands, still on her hips, were now clenched in fists. Standing looking at me, Clotilde said through gritted teeth, "*Come on, Olivia. One. Good. Reason.* That's all I'm asking for."

She had the same intense look that Alec got that night on the deck when he'd played that song 'Trouble' for me on his guitar and we'd talked afterwards. My mother had the same passion when she'd said, *Nothing matters in the past, Olivia. It's all ashes.* And it's the same look that Ben gave me when he asked, *Is your heart just fine, Jerry?*

If I was going to be having this conversation about me and God, I'd rather have it with Ben than anyone else. I saw him looking at me and heard him saying *I'll miss you until the day I die* and I was stunned by the wave of longing I had for Ben. It hit me with a force strong enough to bring tears to my eyes, and I swallowed and walked over to one of Clotilde's classroom windows. Ben did a better job at talking about God to me, I realized at that moment. He seemed to truly be interested in my views; not just bound and determined to change me. Clotilde, on the other hand, looked ready to wrestle me to the floor and shove God down my throat.

But she was still my good friend and was waiting for an explanation. "You talked one time a while back about *everyone* being unlovable, Clo. I was stunned at how closely we agreed on that. You know some of my history, but not all of it, and I was just going to say that you have to take my word that it's bad because I am *never* going to tell it to you. I don't know what else to say, but that I don't really think God's much interested in me – and He shouldn't be. I'm not anything special, in fact I'm probably a lot more trouble than I'll ever be worth. There isn't a place in my life for God. I'm not complaining or being stubborn, I'm just stating the facts."

I stood there looking out the window waiting for a barrage of angry words as she tried to change my mind, but all I heard was silence. And then, finally, a sniffle. When I turned around, my good friend Clotilde was just standing there, staring at me, quietly crying. "You'd better think again," she finally said with absolute certainty. "Take a look at your life with an honest eye, Olivia, and then tell me again that God's 'not much interested' in you. I've never seen a person so focused in God's scope of attention in my whole life."

Clotilde's confident statement, *Take a look at your life with an honest eye, Olivia, and then tell me again that God's 'not much interested' in you* struck a louder chord than any other God - related comment from any other person. Watching her stand there so calm and self-assured in her understanding of me, my life, and God was incredibly unsettling. Think about it. Rarely do people really speak in definitive terms to other people about anything other than themselves or areas of knowledge where they had a confident expertise. In general, we make suggestions, offer insights, or drop polite innuendoes, but rarely do we look at someone and say flat out, "You are completely wrong." Clotilde didn't use those exact words but her meaning was the same.

And frighteningly, she made sense.

So I went home and thought about it. Sophie and I had a rather involved conversation regarding me and God, but we came to no clear understanding. I searched God on my computer and felt a little like Alice must have felt falling down the rabbit hole: curiouser and curiouser.

Did I ask Ben about God? My boyfriend the *minister?* No I didn't. Tuesday nights were youth group activities that kept Ben busy for most of the afternoon and night. Wednesdays were always meeting nights for him, so we only talked briefly on the phone. Thursday he knew Dean came for dinner. When we did see or talk to each other – in our brief hour here or there I had been crazy with work and who wanted to have some heavy duty God conversation? Okay, *yes,* I was avoiding having a discussion with him about subjects like God and church. And, nice guy that he was, he let me. Actually, I know what he was doing, he was being patient. It was an elephant we couldn't afford to ignore for too long, but for now I was determined to do just that.

However, when Dean showed up with Kentucky Fried Chicken (skinless version with coleslaw and corn on the cob sides for me, original recipe with mashed potatoes and macaroni and cheese on the side for him) I went so far as to ask him what he thought about God. Which was quite a trip but not necessarily in the direction I thought we were going to travel. And, of course, it *never* occurred to me that my father would make more sense than Clotilde.

Dean looked at me for so long I actually started to blush. "Well, He definitely exists," he said at last as he gnawed on a chicken bone. "I'm certain."

Now it was my turn to stare. I'd expected us to have a mutually disbelieving conversation. "How do you know?" I blurted out.

Dean spread his arms out wide, fingers and mouth glistening with chicken grease. "I'm here, aren't I?"

"So if you crash your truck and die on the way home then ..." Now, don't be shocked. You had to talk bluntly to Dean.

He shook his head. "No. I wasn't talking about me - although the fact that I'm still alive and kicking is pretty miraculous." He gave me a pointed look and didn't say anything until I finally looked away. "I mean, look at the world. Have you ever *really looked* at the night sky? I love taking the garbage out after dark when it's peaceful and quiet and there's nothing between me and God but the stars. It makes me feel really special but tiny, too. I don't know how anyone could look at the night sky and not believe there is a God." He looked down at his big, work-scarred hands lost in thought. His left ring finger had a Blues Clues bandage on the tip. "Or how about the magic of the way your hand heals after you smash it with a hammer?" He wiggled his injured hand. "Do you know how many times I've been hurt on the job? Or drinking? How about a baby? How incredible is that? You spend an evening with a woman ... you enjoy each other's company so to speak ... and then ... nine months later ... *a whole other life appears*." Dean looked at me. "Isn't that *unbelievable?!* I mean, really. Think about it, Olivia. *A whole new life.*" It was a surreal conversation and Dean was utterly sincere.

"I didn't realize you were so ... spiritual."

Dean helped himself to a corn on the cob and shrugged. "No? To be honest, once I thought about it, being 'spiritual' as you put it was a hell of a lot easier for me than being sober. Sobriety is a battle that I fight every day. *Spirituality* is was a nice, comfortable, *welcome* fit. You should try it."

"You trying to win me over to the God Club, Dad?"

"That's what your mother calls it, you know: The God Club." As Dean took a big sip of his soda he looked at me and laughed, "You wanna talk about miracles, Livvie? Bigger miracles than me and sobriety? Look at your mother. Who ever thought she'd live happily ever after, huh?"

Or that I'd end up being happier than I was angry.

Or that I'd end up believing in love.

Or that I'd end up eating dinner with Dean every Thursday night like clockwork.

Or that I'd end up dating a minister.

Or that I'd end up asking people about God.

245

Journal: The Truth About Me and God

Thursday, May 27, 2010

1. Taking the garbage out makes Dean feel closer to God.

2. Clotilde is positive God is interested in me. Enough that I made her cry when I told her I was sure He wasn't.

3. God has gotten to almost every single person in my life. Am I paranoid or is Clotilde right?

4. My mom + happiness = miracle of God or temporary illusion?

5. God is willing to take: alcoholics, ex-cons ... my mother ... does He have a limit?

6. Ben is willing to invest just about everything in God – even to his paycheck. Talk about putting all your eggs in one basket.

7. Grannie Blue vs. Vera – were they an example of life with and without God?

8. God's got lots of houses. Maybe it's time I visited one. Incognito. So that no one freaks out or jumps to conclusions. That way I'll have better ammunition to prove my point about why God + Me ≠ Perfect Together.

Beware: some liars tell the truth.[34]

23: Life Really Does Suck Sometimes
Friday, May 28, 2010

       Under no circumstances must *anyone* know that I have decided to attend a church service. It was perhaps the current biggest secret in my life.

       I was spared lying to Ben about my incognito church plans because Ben went camping with the youth and many of the church adults Memorial Day Weekend. They left Friday after school and planned to be back Sunday evening. Up until the very last second Ben tried desperately to get me to go. After his eleventh hour attempt (he was waiting for me on the front porch when I pulled up from work), I pondered just how clever and devious he could be and once again reminded myself not to underestimate him *ever*. Even though I got my way and he went camping on his own I somehow felt like I'd been had. Friday's conversation was like all the rest of our conversations regarding me not going camping except for the final clincher.

       "Ben, there is nothing you can do that will ever, *ever* induce me to go camping. With you or without you. *Nothing.* I did it once and hated it. Do you hear me? *I hated it.*"

       "There are cabins, you know, not just tents." I just stood there and stared at him. "Showers and flush toilets." I'm not sure I even blinked. "We have a great big bonfire each night and eat loads of good food and just hang out and commune with nature." My silence communicated it all. Aileen had taught me well. Finally he leaned in and nuzzled my neck and kissed me. "Please, Jerry? I'd really like your company. We could go for a walk in the woods and I'd have your company on the long drive both ways …"

I pictured dirt, bugs, communal showers, sleepless nights due to unfamiliar surroundings, continual contact with well-meaning church people and curious teens … the list went on and on. There was only one thing that could induce me to go: a pleading, handsome, persistent Ben Harayda. Almost. "It's not you, it's the camping, Ben. It's just as bad as skiing, except I didn't come home from camping in a leg cast the one time I tried it." I did come home with a wicked case of poison ivy and a cut on my leg that left a scar, but I'd already told him that a few times.

He looked so sad. "Are you ever going to do any of these things I've got to do, Olivia? Believe it or not, before we were dating I didn't miss always being on my own, but now that we're a couple I miss not having you with me." It was the first time he'd been so bold about me plus him plus church being united.

I sighed as though I were extremely put upon but deep down it was fun to know he wanted me with him so badly. I kissed him and then whispered in his ear, "The next church sponsored … thing … that you invite me to, I'll go, okay?" It was a major concession and he knew it.

Crowding me up against my living room wall he gave me a kiss that rocketed us both right out into the stratosphere and then looked me in the eye and said, "Will you come to church with me every Sunday for the rest of your life?"

My mother and Alec go to this rather … unique church. It was an old store front that had been converted to a meeting hall and attached to it was a pastry/coffee shop. The minister's name was … Crystal (I kid you not) and while there was no organ or piano there was an impressive band that looked like its members had been recruited straight out of Hell's Angels. During the week people used the pastry shop like a Starbucks or a Dunkin' Donuts but then on Friday, Saturday and Sunday nights (and other select evenings) the place converted into a Rockin' Rollin' House Of God. Actually, it was called Agape Shop. (I've been told a number of times what

"Agape" meant but I have had deaf ears and running feet with numerous other God talkin' people ... not just Clotilde.)

I'd been there only once. On my mother and Alec's wedding day in which (again) the groom appeared briefly in a batman mask, cape, and utility belt. But I had little memory of the day. That whole period of my life was clouded with innumerable issues all specifically linked to my own personal breakdown involving my paternity, my miserable existence, and my poor relationship with my mother. At the time of my mother and Alec's wedding I was only about six months into therapy with Aileen and had only been the recipient of Vera's brutal truth for about eight weeks. To say that I was in any way cognizant of anything other than the newly discovered reality of who I was ... and who I wasn't ... would have been a lie.

Now I am an intelligent woman, and I'd like to think that I wasn't ignorant. Yes, you could be both; ignorance was a *choice* to be uninformed as opposed to intelligence, which is an inherited mental ability. I could talk against my involvement with God and church, continue to maintain that God was not for me and maintain that I had no need to become a 'spiritual' (weird word, really – what did it actually mean?!) person ... But, I realized after Dean left that Thursday night that *that* attitude would, indeed, be ignorant.

You couldn't say you hated strawberries unless you finally tasted one and got all those gritty little seeds stuck in your teeth which then gave you a valid reason in the future to avoid them.

You couldn't say you were a klutz at skiing unless on your very first time down the bunny slope you fell and had to be taken away by ambulance and wore a full leg cast for six weeks and then eventually ended up having knee surgery.

You couldn't say that you're not interested in nice guys unless you met a handsome, tall, green-eyed minister that you couldn't stop thinking about even though you ... Sigh.

I couldn't, in good conscience, continue to say that God and church were not for me until I had the evidence to prove it. Aileen, I was absolutely certain, would nod her head in agreement.

So, in an effort to prove *my* point about me and God, and to disprove the growing list of God champions (which now included Dean Kelly) I followed through with my surprise visit to a Friday night service at Agape Shop. I told *no one*. I wanted to arrive incognito, collect my data, and depart with no one the wiser.

Aileen told me once that *life is what happens to you while you're busy making other plans,* [35] and that saying was vividly illustrated Friday evening. I showed up at Agape Shop. I picked Friday instead of Saturday or Sunday, because Alec regularly didn't invite me to that night and I assumed that he (and/or my mother) wouldn't be there. I was not sure what I expected having never been to a service there, but I assumed it would be a slightly less formal, dressed down version of church that I had pulled together from childhood memories, television, and movies. I still expected long prayers, endless hymns, and a boring sermon but …

Aileen also said one time that putting "but" in a sentence negated everything you said prior to that. Saying things like, "My sister is perfect but …" or "My mother tried really hard but …" or "Dean was a good dad but …" revealed my *honest* thoughts, involving a less than complimentary opinion of everyone.

Agape Shop was hopping when I walked in; the music was cranking, the people were grooving, and I relaxed immediately confident that my anonymity was secure. I found a seat in the back corner and I barely had time to sit and put my purse down when my phone signaled that I had a text. It was from Dean. Now a text from him wasn't necessarily surprising; as texting was regularly how we had been determining Thursday night's menu. But, the message he sent caused me to tense with shock and dismay: **saved seat 4 u**

I looked up with the heart pounding fear one would have in those dreams where you realized you were in front of your class getting ready to teach and suddenly remembered you had forgotten to put your pants on. I did a brief scan around the crowded room but could see no one familiar so I started to relax. Maybe Dean was confused. Not really a far stretch. Maybe he'd sent me this text thinking I was someone else. Until I got the next one: **look again back left row**

I turned slowly, desperately hoping that I was not going to see what I was afraid to see. No such luck. There, sitting casually in the back row (with one big arm draped across the back of the seat empty next to him) was Dean. He didn't wave or shout, *thank God*, but gave me a brilliant smile and a nod of acknowledgment. And then, just when I thought it couldn't get any worse, I heard Alec's voice from the front stage loudly and clearly shouting, "Let's get this party started!" and the place exploded in celebration.

As I made my way back to Dean and the place rocked and rolled I thought, *do regular churches know this stuff exists? Do regular ministers think this is okay? Are churches like this allowed? Is this a real church?!* People were singing and dancing and the music was blasting. Not one person could have possibly noticed that I got up and moved to the other side of the room.

Except one, I realized all too soon. As I sat down next to Dean and glanced up at the stage there was Alec singing and looking right at me with the most dazzling smile I'd ever seen on his face.

I was so screwed.

The music was infectious: enthusiastic, joyful, and compelling. Words to each and every song were flashed up behind the band, so whether you could understand the singing or not, whether you wanted to sing along or not, you couldn't escape the power of the lyrics. As I settled myself next to Dean and he gave me a surprising hug and a quick kiss on the cheek, the band roared into a rousing song and, while I didn't dance and I didn't sing, I couldn't help but read:

> *I come from a long line of leavers*
> *Out of the garden gate with an apple in their hands*
> *I expect and I believe*
> *You're gonna run out of love*

You're gonna give me the shove
'Cause that's the thing that lovers do
Then there's you ...
There is none both good and true
Then there's you [36]

I couldn't ignore the words my ears heard and that my eyes read ... and my heart jolted to.

"Not bad, huh?" Dean grinned at me as the band shifted and a young woman with long blonde hair, a pierced nose and a ... figure that rivaled mine stepped up to the mike in a tight tee shirt.

"Can you clap?" she shouted to the crowd and everyone yelled back, "Yes!" The band started the beat and the girl demonstrated the clapping rhythm. Slowly, reluctantly I got sucked into the tunes. It was impossible not to be, really. And I must admit that I enjoyed the wild ride of music; it made your blood pound and your ears ring. At one point the lights came down and there was Alec stepping up to the mike. I closed my eyes, suddenly scared of the whole emotional experience going on. But Alec's voice was hypnotic, and even though I couldn't see him or read the words with my eyes closed, I heard every word loudly and clearly:

I'm not trying to hide anything
I wear it on my sleeve, I wear it on my sleeve
I'm not trying to be something I'm not
This is all I've got, This is all I've got ...
Let me introduce myself to you
This is who I am
No more, no less
I am just a man who understands
Because of You I'm blessed
No more, no less ...
I hope you stare just long enough to see
The heart that's beating here inside of me

Embracing The Truth

Beyond all the things you may think you know
I'm just a kid trying to make it home, that's it
No more, no less
Lord, I want to go home
Nothing more, nothing less ...[37]

Gradually the songs worked down in volume and rhythm. When the last song was played, we were all standing. The words, sung by another one of the band members stunningly, were from a song I recognized. It was the rock version of Grannie Blue's favorite hymn. I heard Ben whispering in my ear, *It is well* ... I missed Ben. Maybe camping wouldn't have been *that bad*, I thought briefly.

When peace like a river attendeth my way
when sorrow like sea billows roll
Whatever my lot Thou has taught me to say
It is well, it is well with my soul ...[38]

Ha. Nothing was well with my soul. That was for darn sure.

I watched the people that night. Dean remained casual and relaxed throughout. While some people had Bibles to look at or even said, 'Amen!' out loud during some significant points that Crystal made, Dean just sat quiet and focused. Alec sat up front, I guess with the band, and I couldn't tell if my mother was there. It was surprising that the crowd wasn't all of one age or style or shape. It was a mish-mash of young and old and white collar professionals and biker gangs. Truly *anyone* walking in would have found someone like them.

Well, anyone except me.

Except, a thought came loud and clear in my head, *you've got Dean who's saved a seat for you and Alec smiling at you from the stage. I bet not everyone got that much of a greeting.* Surprisingly, that made me angry.

But maybe that's not so surprising.

Minister Crystal, or whatever you're supposed to call her, had that same intensity that Alec got when God came up. She wore a pair of white capris, yellow flip-flops, and a pink tee shirt that had some writing on it I couldn't read. She was tiny, I realized when she walked over to move one of the band's microphones out of her way and it towered over her. Her age was indeterminate; however; from a distance she appeared young and hip, but perhaps under closer scrutiny she might have been older than my first impression. I found it hard to believe that she was allowed to preach and teach and do 'minister things' (whatever they are) without a college education, so she had to *at least* be in her late twenties.

"A man named Horatio G. Spafford wrote *It Is Well With My Soul* back in the 1800's. *After*, he'd lost his home in a fire … his four-year-old son to scarlet fever …," she paused and let this all sink in, "and the boat that his wife and four daughters took to England … sank with no survivors. I would think that Horatio would have been a desperately unhappy man, don't you?

"There's a lot of sorrow in this life. Horatio's certainly not the first one to have it hard." Crystal looked pointedly at a number of people in the audience and then said quietly, "In fact, this life pretty much sucks.

"The Bible's filled with sad people, living sad lives, telling their sad stories. In fact, very, very few – if any - of the biblical characters had a life of joy and laughter. There was a lot of crying back then, just like there's a lot of crying today. Take a look." Behind Crystal, where the music lyrics had been appeared the following:

Genesis 23:2 – Abraham wept. *Love lost*
Genesis 33:4 – Esau and Jacob wept. *Regret*
Genesis 45:2 – Joseph wept. *Sadness*
Judges 2:4 – The People wept. *Guilt*
Ruth 1:9 – Ruth wept. *Helplessness*
I Samuel 30:3 – David wept. *Deep sorrow*
Esther 4:3 – The People wept. *Fear*
Mark 14:72 – Peter wept. *Shame*

John 20:11 – Mary wept. *Death*
John 11:35 – Jesus wept. *Grief*

"Ever cry for any of those reasons?" Crystal asked quietly after we'd all had time to read the list. She waited a bit and then said, "Do you suppose Horatio wept when his wife and children died?

"And yet, Horatio wrote this song about things being 'well with his soul'." Crystal scratched her head. "How could that be? How could anything ever be well again?"

She asked good questions. You could almost hear the cogs whirring as people sat and considered what she'd said.

"*But*," Crystal said, "Horatio didn't really talk about happiness, did he? He talked about *his soul* being *well*. How would you describe your soul? People all have different interpretations. I like to say that my soul is the stripped down, honest version of me. It's the only thing that God sees when He looks at me; the only thing He really cares about. As a result, it's *the only thing that really counts.*

"Horatio's soul, despite unimaginable sorrow and loss, despite endless days and nights of weeping, was *well*. That meant it was fine. Sound. Not broken. The hardships of this life had not separated Horatio's most important part from its most important source. Horatio believed in this verse." Crystal turned and behind her flashed:

> *I have told you all this so that you may have peace in me.*
> *Here on earth you will have many trials and sorrows.*
> *But take heart, because I have overcome the world.*
> *John 16:33*

"I'm certain Horatio believed this. How could he not? He had made a personal choice, and I would imagine he clung to this belief through his endless grief. How's your soul? How is that most important part of you? Is it well? Is it healthy and wise and strong? Is it focused on the Source of greatest strength and power? Do you believe that *God is greater*

255

than your greatest sorrow, your greatest problem? Or does that soul of yours waver with the wind? Fluctuate according to your personal happiness meter? It's a personal choice that no one can make for you."

Crystal had been wandering around up front all the while she'd been talking but finally she stepped back up onto the center of the stage and stared out at us. Hands on her hips she said, "Your life sucks. You can't seem to find joy in your life. Nothing goes the way you want it to. You're angry. Maybe, *just maybe*, you're looking in the wrong direction. Have you ever thought of that?"

There was more talking and more singing and some praying, too. At the end, everyone held hands and recited the Lord's Prayer (which I read off the screen in front because I didn't know it) and then everyone milled around shaking hands and talking.

"How long have you been coming here, Dad?"

"Two years, three months, nine days," he said instantly and then did his pointed stare again. Oh. Suddenly I got it. "There's a reason why this is the longest I've been sober, Livvie."

"How did you know to save me a seat?" I asked Dean and braced for the answer. He didn't disappoint.

Dean blinked at me with his big blue eyes and then shrugged. "I told God if He'd get you here, I'd save you a seat."

Journal: The Awful Truth About Horatio Spafford
Saturday, May 29, 2010

I did not sleep well last night. I tossed and turned, dreaming of Ben's
pleading eyes as he said, 'Will you go camping with me for the rest
of your life?', Dean's beautiful night sky illuminating a garbage
dump, and Horatio Spafford's little son continually asking me for a
Motrin to bring his fever down. And my dream has a sound track.
It is Alec and Dean singing *It Is Well* to the tune of *Paradise By The
Dashboard Lights*.

I lie awake and for the first time really, *really* miss … Aileen. With a start I
realize that part of her appeal now is that she really *doesn't* care
about me the way Ben or my mother or even Alec do. Because it's
her job she'd like to help me get healthy and strong but because
she has no emotional investment I now realize she's always going
to be brutally frank with me because she really doesn't care if I get
pissed off. *She's just doing her job.* I really need to talk to her:
Because I can be brutally frank with her, too, and I don't have to
worry about sad eyes or hurt feelings or even tears. Here are some
of the issues I need to vent about:

1. The shocking revelation that Dean goes to church and thinks he
   prayed me to attend on Friday.

2. Ben. (That could take another 3-4 years.) How he makes me feel
   (scared, guilty, angry are the top three). Why he makes me feel
   those ways. What he wants from me (more than I've got, I'm
   sure.) How do I handle telling him everything about me – *the whole
   sordid truth.* The terror that I feel regarding this is only exceeded by
   the all-consuming dread I feel regarding his reaction. Every day
   that I spend with him, the fear of losing him becomes greater.
   Every day that I spend with him, the guilt of not telling him the
   truth about me becomes greater. I'm still not sure that dumping
   him as I tried to do weeks ago isn't a better plan.

3. How confused and unsettled and … yes, angry … and melancholy and anxious I've been feeling. I now know that it's not all related to my job. I don't like this person … that I am … without Aileen's … guidance.

4. Horatio Spafford had a suckier life than I did and yet I think Horatio Spafford was more content than I am.

The man who fears no truth has nothing to fear from lies.[39]

24: Sometimes There's Nothing Left To Lose
Tuesday, June 1, 2010

I spend the whole weekend feeling like my skin is too small to contain all my worried thoughts. Concerns about my job, going to church with Ben for the rest of my life, honestly explaining to Ben my life history, Big Black Arrows that were or were not visible for me to follow, and money worries filled my waking and dreaming thoughts. Ben, sick with food poisoning from the camping weekend ("Please, don't say anything Olivia, I'm too sick to hear it!") failed to provide the necessary distraction for me on Memorial Day Monday. As a result, my journal was filled with endless lists of angst and observations.

Clotilde took one look at me Tuesday morning, June 1, 2010, and demanded to know what toxic illness I'd been battling all weekend. When I just stood there, mutely, she walked up to me and said, "Tell me," in a firm but worried teacher voice. But I shook my head, knowing full well if I started I'd never finish by the forty-five minutes I had until the first bell.

"Okay, Olivia. I'll mind my own business. Let me know if there's anything I can do."

I had hurt her feelings. She thought I just didn't trust her. "Take me out for a drink after work, Clo. I'll tell you my life story. But if I start talking now, I'll fall apart." She was standing in my doorway with her purse and her briefcase before the last kid had left my room.

So, I told her. Everything. Sitting in a dark, quiet booth at a local coffee shop (Clotilde didn't drink) I spilled my whole putrid story from start to present day. I covered my mother, Dean, my grandmother, my conception through rape, my childhood, my adolescence, my preferred preference in married men, Aileen, my sister's alcoholism, my most recent discoveries and improvements through therapy, Ben, Phil, my self-imposed celibacy, what Dean and I had for dinner last week, and how I believe that Horatio Spafford was more content than I. When I finished Clotilde sat and stared at me for a long, long time. So I went and got us fresh coffee.

"My father's a registered sex offender in the state of Virginia," Clotilde said to me in the same flat, monotone voice that I was fairly certain I'd used just moments before. "I haven't had contact with him in the past twelve years since social services removed me and my sister from our home and put us in foster care. He ended up serving only six years in prison despite what he did to both of us. My mother chose to believe what my father said rather than what Ingrid and I said, so I haven't seen or spoken to my mother since my father was convicted. She's still with him to the best of my knowledge." She took a sip of her coffee. "My father sends me birthday and Christmas cards; Max always tries to throw them out before I see them.

"I understand all you've told me, Liv, about why you can't escape your past because it's such an intrinsic part of you. I know what you're saying. It's in your DNA, right? I struggle with the same doubts now and then especially, when I'm faced with a memory or a situation that pulls me down. Max is a dream come true. He's my biggest champion and my staunchest supporter. He refuses to let my demons get the best of me." Clotilde reached out and took my hand. "That's what I want for you. That kind of love and support."

I heard her saying to me weeks ago *Max is my special gift*, and suddenly I remembered that what she actually said was *Max is my special gift from God*, only I originally ignored that last part.

"Nobody's life is perfect, Liv. But God never leaves us or forsakes us. He always gives us a lifeline to grab on to. It's just up to us to accept it."

"How can you say that, Clo?! How can you sit here, after what you've just told me, and imply that God cares about us?!"

"I told you one time, because you asked, that I thought we were all unlovable. I didn't have a chance to finish that day, and you've never been too receptive when I started talking God talk anyway. But being unlovable didn't so much have anything to do with me and my father's history, Olivia. It had everything to do with my belief that none of us is good enough or deserving enough for any favor. We are what we are and God is who God is. In the end I decided that I could look at my life as one nightmare after another *or* I could look at my life as points of light in the natural darkness. The first way offered despair. The second way offered hope." Clotilde shrugged. "I chose the latter. I couldn't see the sense in dwelling on the negative when I saw clearly that even when things were at their worst there was still something ... good. Something hopeful. Something that I could hold on to.

"I had my sister. And a teacher who listened and believed and cared. I had an outstanding social service worker who remained my sister's and my advocate even after we were too old for the system." Clotilde gave me a dazzling smile. "We have Easter Sunday dinner with her every year. And then I got the Martins, the family that at first fostered us and then eventually adopted both of us. They introduced me to a life - saving faith that sustains me to this day. And then I got my scholarship so I could go to college and become the teacher I'd always dreamed of being. And I got this job. And I got Max ..." She looked at me pointedly. "Can you see that in your own life Olivia? Or do you choose to dwell on the darkness? That's what I meant the other day when I talked about how God was certainly focused on you."

It's like when Aileen used to hit a hot point. I felt the tears coming; an impending tsunami. Clotilde reached out and grabbed both of my hands with a firm grip. "Olivia! Let me help you see what I see, okay? You've got me. You've got your sister. You've got your mother and your step-father. You've got Dean. Now you've got Ben. It sounds like you've had good, solid counseling from Aileen. You've got intelligence and common sense ..."

"No I don't."

"*Yes you do.* Intelligence means that you recognize good choices from bad choices – before, during or after you make them. Common sense means that you make the changes you need to make to turn your choices from good to bad – before, during or after. You are not a stupid woman, Olivia. Yes, you're stubborn, but don't fight it, let that work in your favor. Why does that have to be a negative? Fight for what you want and what you need! You say you want happiness. What is the key to you getting that happiness? Go out and find it! Look how far you've come already, Olivia. You've taken the fact of your conception – and instead of letting it destroy you, you've spent two long, painful years working to make yourself better than ever! You should be standing up straight and proud. Bravo! Well Done! Hip-Hip-Hooray! Keep up the good work!! But you need to finish the job. You need the full transformation. God promises you all that and more. Call it what you want: a clean slate, a fresh start, or a new life."

I sat there looking at my sweet, young friend through my tears. "This is what I'm going to do," Clotilde said with steely determination, "I'm going to commit to pray for you. Now, I do that anyway, but let me spell it out for you. I'm going to pray for you to have peace, strength, and wisdom in all you say and do. I'm going to pray that you will see clearly the direction that God wants you to go. And I'm praying that you will recognize *the only truth there is worth believing*: that God *loves* you and *wants* you to be His – no ifs, ands, or buts, Olivia."

Clotilde squeezed my hand. "Look at it this way, if you must: nothing else seems to have worked for you – what have you got to lose?" She blinked her big blue eyes at me and shrugged.

I hadn't turned a deaf ear or run away from the God talk this time, and Clotilde sat there silently for the longest time while I considered what she had said. I couldn't argue with anything, really. It was simply a matter of deciding to look at things from a different perspective.

The past is a different country.

It's all ashes.

It is well with my soul.

The only thing that really counts ...

All the barriers come from our end ...

I couldn't deny that each recent "visit with God" had been significant. Note that I didn't say "good" or "enjoyable" or even "welcomed". These visits had been a little like a bee sting that hurt when you got it and then itched like a son of a gun for weeks afterward.

And yet I *was* an intelligent woman. I *was* determined to be happy and stronger and wiser. I *was* determined not to be ignorant. And, since Clotilde is correct that I *was* stubborn, I might as well stop fighting the tide and try putting that quality to good use.

"What do I need to do first?" I finally asked Clotilde, who had sat there patiently watching me process everything.

"The hardest thing for me was giving up. Saying, 'Okay God, I'm all yours.' I'd spent so much of my life trying to 'manage' it all, you know? I'd been trying to steer my life into the direction that I'd wanted for so long that 'letting go and letting God' was," she sighed and looked at me, "and *still is* the hardest part for me. Other people have trouble with acknowledging that they're incapable of being good without God's help." Clotilde laughed bitterly and shook her head. "That wasn't a problem for me at all. I *knew* the truth of what I was! I'd been trying to escape it my whole life. Nor was it difficult for me to ask for forgiveness for everything I'd done wrong. The concept that I could *simply ask* for it all to be forgotten *and it would be* was something I couldn't do fast enough." My friend shrugged and held out her hand to tick off the steps, "It's that simple: *Ask* the Lord to take over, *Believe* that through the power of God and His son Jesus Christ all things are possible, and *Confess* those things that need to be forgiven. As simple as A-B-C."

"You really believe this."

Clotilde leaned towards me, "I really believe this, Olivia. It is the glue that holds me together and the only thing that keeps me sane."

Grannie Blue used to take Ben, Arthur, me and Erin every summer for a week of Vacation Bible School at her church. I was pretty sure I went four or five summers between the ages of four through 4th grade. Even after the divorce my mother made a point of driving me there those first few summers so I wouldn't miss the fun. Grannie Blue was in charge of the craft room and we used to make grand things over the course of the week under her skilled and patient direction. VBS week was filled with the smells of Elmer's Glue and shellac, the sounds of catchy tunes yelled at the top of our lungs and the taste of Welch's Grape Juice and animal crackers. It was fun-filled mornings with songs and stories. My favorite part was the missionary story that was told every morning over the course of the week. The lady used pictures and words and always stopped each day at the most exciting part, making her whole audience do exactly what she wanted them to do: cry out loudly, *"No! Don't stop yet!!!"* She'd grin at us from the front of the church and say, "I guess you'd better come back tomorrow to hear what happened next ..."

Every story – whether it was the missionary story or the daily Bible story we were taught was always filled with hardships, trials and triumphs. Clotilde's ABC's - asking, believing, and confessing - wasn't something new to me, but something I remembered singing about twenty-five years ago squished between Ben and hundreds of other sweaty kids. Driving home, trying to keep myself together, I suddenly had a vivid memory of asking Grannie Blue (from the back-back of her battered up Dodge Volare´ station wagon), "How come all the stories about these people are always so sad? So hard? Doesn't God want us to be happy?"

"Nah," Grannie Blue had said over her shoulder, and took the time to smack Arthur in the back of the head for sticking his tongue out at some stranger we were driving past, "God needs us to understand that we're at war. Life is *never* going to be easy for any of us because the world is naturally full of sorrow and hurt. We can't escape it. God needs us to get tough, be smart, and *fight* for what's right and good. "

I remembered thinking that through and deciding that I already had enough fighting and stuff going on in my life without getting involved with another battle. Even if it was God's business.

But of course, Grannie Blue was right about life. And even if I hadn't wanted to get on board with the battle for right and good, life had made me into a seasoned warrior when it came to fighting and scrapping. I don't think that anyone would doubt that if God needed fighters, I was sure tough enough to qualify. My conversation with Clotilde wiped me out. Tearful and confused, Sophie curled up with me on the couch when I got home. She sat at first and watched me cry and then, when it was obvious to her that this was going to go on for some time, she hopped up next to me and settled herself in. The only other time I remembered her doing that was when I had my breakdown after Vera told me about my real father. Sophie and I lived at a friend's beach house for almost two months, and whether she was terrified of the strange surroundings or my endless weeping and muttering, she curled up with me every night as I fell asleep.

I came through that time and Clotilde was right, I realized I was better for it.

As I lay on the couch clutching Ben's swan, I thought about these last few weeks and months all the way back to that first really bad visit with Aileen. I let myself go as far back as I could remember. I thought about the type of woman I was then and the type of woman I was now ... and acknowledged that while neither one was in very good shape, the one clutching a stuffed swan was light years better.

It was time to admit my recent mistakes; and there were, unfortunately, some significant ones. But at least I had Clotilde in my corner. And my mother and Alec and Dean and Erin. And Ben. Let's not forget Ben.

"Thanks," I finally said out loud, and then took some time to blow my nose, "for Clotilde." Yes, it was a prayer. Either that or I had finally gone off the deep end and was talking to myself. It suddenly made sense that if she was praying for me, I might as well let God know that I was on board, too. I sighed. "And Alec. He's a good guy. And Erin." I sighed

265

again. "And my mother. And Dean." The image appeared of Ben standing on the front step and saying earnestly, *will you come to church with me every Sunday for the rest of your life?* "Thanks for letting me experience that there are good guys out there ... I don't know about all this ABC stuff ... but I wanted You to know that I can see You've ... taken an interest in me. And, well, thanks and ... would You please keep it up?"

Ben kept a carefully neutral expression the following Friday night when I explained to him that I planned to go with Dean to another service at Agape Shop. Some weeks I'm now spending *two nights in a row* with him. When I invited him to tag along, he responded with as much subdued intensity as he could, "I wouldn't miss it for the world."

"Don't jump to any conclusions," I warned him with a stubborn glint in my eye. "I'm just on a fact - finding mission. I'm an intelligent woman who's determined to make an educated decision about the God business. I plan on checking out *all* the local God houses that all of you spend so much time in so that when I make my *informed, independent, final* decision about Olivia Kelly and God no one will be able to find fault with it."

Ben never reacted the way I expected him to, which was good because nothing was more boring than a predictable man (nice or not nice) as far as I was concerned. As usual, he didn't disappoint this time either. He looked me up and down (dressed down casual in shorts and a tee shirt) as he leaned in and kissed me on the neck. "I wouldn't have it any other way, Jerry," he whispered in my ear.

Minister Crystal's message that night triggered the Grannie Blue memory and then dragged me forward kicking and screaming even further. She was talking about something called The Beatitudes (which, if you're interested, comes from the Latin word *beatus* meaning "blessed") and about people who were blessed. But she gave a rather odd list of types of people: poor, those who were mourning, those who were humble, those who wanted justice, those who were merciful, those who wanted peace, those who were persecuted for doing good things … She gave a long list of different kinds of people and announced these people were blessed by God. *Present tense.*

And then she asked a question, "What does blessed mean?" and stood there looking out at all of us. For a minute I was afraid she was going to say, "Hey, you! Olivia! Hiding in the back row! What do you think blessed means? Tell the crowd!" and I slouched down in my chair. But she didn't.

"'Blessed' *is not* the same thing as 'happy.' You need to understand that first and foremost. Happy is immediate … and very temporary. You can be on the top of the world one moment and then something can happen and you crash in despair. Right? Happy is external and simple. Blessed is internal and very complicated. Blessed is something you work up to and you strive for, but once you achieve it it's hard to lose. Being blessed is being hopeful and joyful. It's not dependent on people or things, but rather completely internal and personal between you and God."

Crystal pointed to the list of odd people still on the screen behind her. "Does this promise you laughter, pleasure, or earthly riches?" I murmured 'no' even before I realized I was speaking out loud. "Nope, it doesn't. What Jesus *did* promise was that even in the darkest, hardest times you could be certain that there was always internal hope and joy *no matter what* external … garbage … was going on. It's a choice between temporary and permanent, fleeting and sustained, just now or forever. Tell me honestly, is that a hard choice?" It was Clotilde's earnest speech to me just sung to a slightly different tune I realized.

"No one can make this choice but you; however you need to know one very critical thing: *It's the only choice that counts.* And, here's a little extra push for you: making no decision is a decision. You're either hot or cold, in or out. If you haven't made a firm commitment to God, *you're out.* I don't care how nice you are or how generous or how smart or hard working. God only cares about one thing. If you're in or out."

Crystal stopped and put her hands on her hips. "What does God care about?"

267

Without even thinking, I joined the whole group in saying out loud, "If you're in or you're out."

I didn't like knowing that I was out. I turned and looked at Dean and he gave me a brief nod as if to say, "That's it, then." When I turned and looked at Ben, he gave me one slow, sexy wink.

Therapy: The Truth About Being Wrong

Setting: Okay, so after reading all this, what would *you* do and where
would *you* go? I'm spilling all this private stuff for you; I hope
you'll learn something. All I'll say is I *am* a smart woman and I'm
trying to use my stubbornness in a positive way. Clotilde was right
about a lot of things (and I'm still weeding through all the insights
she shared with me so I don't know how right she is). But I'm
determined to completely embrace her observation about my
stubbornness. I *will* let it work in my favor. Which means it's time
to forge ahead and admit a few things no matter how hard it may
be. It's Tuesday, June 8, 2010.

Me: Boy, you filled my Monday slot quickly. How lucky am I that you had
a cancellation? Otherwise I would have had to wait probably for
months.

Aileen: It's good to see you Olivia. I've been thinking about you. A lot.

Me: Miss me?

Aileen: Absolutely.

Me: (There's awkward silence on my part because I really do think she
missed me and I don't know how to handle that. And, I realize to
my horror that I'm quite happy to see Aileen, too. I've missed her
a bit, too. But I'll never admit it.) I'm ready to get back to work.
I've been journaling a lot and I've made lists. I'm embracing my
positive qualities. Being stubborn, brash, outspoken, opinionated,
independent, decisive, inquiring, smart and not as badly off as
some others so I can continue to forge ahead in a positive
direction. In addition, I'm determined to eradicate my negative
qualities of being cowardly, indecisive, anxious, melancholy and
angry." (I notice that Aileen's just sitting there.) Hey. Aren't you
going to write this all down?

Aileen: The list was always to help *me* help *you* to remember specific things,
Olivia. I don't think you need any help here.

269

Me: So I suppose you need to hear me admit that I was wrong. (Aileen
gives me an intrigued look.) So, I have a list about that, too. (I
take out my journal because I can't remember *everything*.) I wrote
this down yesterday. It's all the things I was wrong about and
what, if anything, I can do about them.

1. I was wrong about therapy. It's like medicine; not all medicine
    tastes good while you're taking it but it's worth it in the end. Even
    chemotherapy is so bad your hair falls out, makes you puke, and
    you usually feel like you're dying, right? As a result, I'm here,
    willing to go through whatever pain and humiliation you want me
    to go through in penance, all for the sake of getting better.
    Eventually.

2. I was wrong about my being unlovable. Maybe there are a few
    people who think I'm … bearable. I've actually had *two men* tell me
    some really wonderful things while I've been away, Aileen. They
    really blew my mind. One told me he'd *miss me until he died* and
    another one told me *he loved me from the first moment he looked at me.*
    How's that? (Aileen just watches me.) So, I've been forced to
    realize that it's not me, personally, who's unlovable but rather my
    behavior. Which is changeable. And which I want to do. I talked
    with my friend Clotilde, and if no one loves me then it's my own
    damn fault. Now, Clotilde didn't say that in so many words, but
    she talked about choices and attitude and making wise decisions,
    and I realized that if I'm not happy then I should stop whining and
    do something about it. So, I'm gonna. But since I'm still in need
    of therapy to get my head screwed on straight, I need to be careful
    that I don't jump to any incorrect conclusions.

3. I was wrong about people in general. I'm not any better or any
    worse off than the next person. Everyone's messed up in one way
    or another. Everyone's got past mistakes and disasters to run away
    from or at least wish they could make disappear. I need to get off
    my high horse and start looking at people and learning: using my
    intelligence to decide if something makes sense or if something is

ridiculous. I need to come up with a small list of people I can trust and start letting them teach me what I need to know. (I sigh and look at Aileen.) Like you. And Clotilde. And even Erin and Alec and – hold yourself up Aileen - Dean ... and my mother. And Ben.

4. I think I was wrong about staying with Ben. I tried to break up with him but he wouldn't let me. I'm confused about our relationship *and I don't want to be.* I'm scared to death of telling him all about me. And yet keeping my secret is killing me. He deserves to know. But I'm terrified how he'll react. He's a good guy. But ... everyone has a breaking point, right? (I swallow and look at Aileen. She blinks at me and stays silent. She knows I'm getting choked up and how much I hate being that way. After two years, she knows me pretty well. Which is a pretty good thing.) Sometimes, when Ben's looking at me or kissing me I want to scream, 'Do you know what I'm a product of?! Let me tell you about my *real* father!' And then I get physically sick thinking about how that's going to affect his opinion of me ... And then I get angry at Ben – I know, totally stupid – because then I feel so lousy about myself and who I am ... It's like a nightmare carousel that I can't get off. It's eating me up inside.

5. I think I need to reconsider my stand on God. (She arches her eyebrows in shock.) Now, I'm not going to start singing hymns and quoting scripture (even as I say that, though I think of Grannie Blue's verses ... *Love is patient. Love is kind. Love never gives up.*) but I think there might be something to all this God ... hype. I mean I look at my mother and Dean and I talk to Clotilde and think about Grannie Blue and ... (I sigh) ... even Ben, and I just can't stop thinking, *Now a smart person would see some sort of pattern here between people of ... quality ... and other people.* So, I'm going to check some of this God stuff out. I might go to church. I might talk some more with Clotilde or ... other people.

Aileen: I'm affiliated with a Christian therapist if you're interested in talking to him.

Me: What do you mean – "Christian Therapist"?

Aileen: A therapist who openly – some would say blatantly – makes reference to God, Jesus, etc. in his therapy sessions as a key ingredient to 'getting well'. Christian therapists ascribe to the belief that emotional as well as spiritual health must go hand in hand.

Me: You work together?

Aileen: No ... not exactly. Sometimes I refer patients to him and vice versa.

Me: Is he any good? (Aileen just looks at me. Ah, yes. This is one of those questions that I need to answer for myself.) Okay, I get it. You wouldn't refer him if he wasn't good. Hmmm, wait a minute, is he single? Forget about a minister!! He just might be the perfect man for me: a good guy therapist! A lifetime of counseling and action under the sheets for one low price! (I crack up laughing and then notice Aileen blushing furiously.) Hey, what's this guy's name?

Aileen: James Allen Burkhart.

Me: Your husband? (Aileen nods.) You're married to a *therapist?!* (Aileen looks at me and roll her eyes.) So you're a Christian? (Aileen just blinks at me.) Ah, not going to answer that one, huh? Because you're not a *Christian* therapist you don't want to use those words ... How about if I gave you permission? Kind of said, 'I, Olivia Kelly, do solemnly swear that it is perfectly okay for you to say God, Jesus, and any other holy stuff around me during our sessions and I promise not to freak out.'

Aileen: It's a whole different style of counseling, Olivia. An area that I'm not experienced or skilled at. Now one style is not exclusively good or exclusively bad. In fact you'll find good examples of therapists in each area ... as well as, unfortunately, bad.

Me: But how about if I just want to talk about God with you? Hear your opinions? Ask you questions that puzzle me?

Aileen: Then you should talk with a minister. Or James.

Me: Nah, I'm going to stay here with you, you lucky thing, and bug the hell out of you. Oops. Probably shouldn't have said that. This could be a lot of fun.

Aileen: We were talking about the things you felt you were wrong about. Which is quite impressive, I must add.

Me: That's it. The whole list. Five huge points. (I wave the journal at her.) There have been others, like things about my mother and perceptions of my past, etc., but you've heard all that before. But, hey Aileen, I bet you've got a list now, too. It's entitled, "Stuff I Should Never Have Admitted To Olivia" Number one is, "Admitting to Olivia that my husband James is a Christian therapist so now she has something new to give me a hard time about."

Aileen: (She just sighs deeply and closes her eyes.)

Me: Number two is …

The first reaction to truth is hatred.[40]

25: Sometimes Giving Up Is Victory
Wednesday, June 16, 2010

One week left of school and everyone was scrambling. Teachers were preparing final grades. Students were taking final exams. I'd been enlisted by a number of students for some "extra help" before, during (good-bye lunch), and after school. This morning was Wayne's day.

"Hey, Ms. Kelly, you doing summer tutoring again?" Wayne was 6'6" (no lie) and weighed about 62 pounds (okay, lie). Even though I came up only to his armpit I still believed I could probably snap him like a twig. He lived for, as you might guess, basketball. I tutored him last summer to get him through Algebra I (which he failed spectacularly during the school year and yet passed the summer course with a C+). As he was only finishing up his sophomore year (and failing Geometry just as impressively as Algebra I) I suspected he'd be a regular at math summer school for another few years.

"You're mother going to cook us lunch like she did last summer? I think I gained ten pounds on that fried chicken and homemade potato salad she sent in all the time."

Wayne gave me an ear-splitting grin. "She just loved how much you enjoyed her cooking, Ms. Kelly. You know, Momma wants to fix you up with my Uncle Frazier."

Hysterically, I had a flash of Walt Frazier the basketball legend or Smokin' Joe Frazier the boxer. "Now, Wayne. You tell your Momma I can't mix business with pleasure. I only eat the food she sends to keep up my energy level to teach."

274

Wayne patted the top of my head as you would a little child and walked backwards away from me down the hallway. "I told my counselor I'd only come to summer school if you were teaching," he shouted. "Do you know he said I was the sixth kid who had told him that same thing?"

Yeah, I did know, actually and I was still on Cloud Nine. Early this morning, Doris Docherty – my Department head - had come down to my room to ask me to teach summer school and participate in the optional summer tutoring program. Doris was a real dynamo. I had enjoyed working under her, had learned a lot from her, and she had always been willing to give advice or listen to concerns when I sought her out. I'd enjoyed doing the summer school last year but up until this morning still hadn't been asked to do it again this year. *After the fact* last summer, I learned that there was a lot of internal politics involved in getting those few, highly prized, paid summer teaching positions, and it was with some discomfort that I realized that perhaps *last year's* opportunity had been Phil's doing and not simply because I'd "lucked out" as I'd originally thought.

I was wiser and stronger now and when Doris offered me the opportunity this morning, I had given her a pointed look. "Why am I getting offered this at such a late date?"

"Because a number of other teachers decided to decline in protest of the budget cuts." Doris stared at me pointedly.

"I'm sorry, Doris. Could you help me out here? What am I supposed to get from that? Am I supposed to decline in solidarity as well?"

Doris shook her head. "No, Olivia. The three other math teachers declined so you could have it. They all are secure with solid positions for next year – as long as the new contract is ratified with the union and the district – and if you accept this summer position the district will have to offer you a position for September as well."

I stood up and walked slowly over to Doris. "Really?" All the worry and fear that had been with me these past weeks suddenly shifted. A little.

"That and the fact that more than six kids slated for summer school math had asked for you specifically. You've got quite a following it seems. The kids like you. Your colleagues like you. It's seems it's not *just* Phil after all."

We stood there and looked at each other for a moment or two letting her meaning solidify. "You were smarter than me," was all she finally acknowledged. *Oh,* I suddenly realized.

"Just by the hair of my chinny-chin-chin," I admitted with a grimace.

"Well, I wouldn't be standing here otherwise, Olivia. No one would have been willing to go to bat for you otherwise. Phil's got a ... reputation ... you see. As soon as you got a summer school job last year *everyone* knew."

"Everyone?"

Doris nodded and shrugged. "Sorry. Everyone knew at least who he'd set his sights on. The only question was how you would respond. For those of us who had been here for a while the pattern was rather predictable."

I looked down at my feet. "I considered it," I said honestly.

She put her hand on my shoulder. "I said, *you were smarter than me.* I was a twenty-one nothing coming out of college and fell for everything he told me. It took me months to figure out what a rat he was, and then years to recover my self-worth and my reputation. Thank God for therapy!" Doris laughed at my surprised expression. "I think everyone should get shrunk at least once in her life! You should try it."

Heading out the door she said, "So, I'll tell them you've accepted the offer, right? There are already at least nineteen students that I know of who have failed math in grades seven through twelve in the district. Quite a few are repeaters from last summer – and those are the ones who are requesting you. The complete work schedule will be determined by how many optional math tutoring sign-ups we finally receive, and I think the deadline for registering for that is Wednesday – the last day of school. Pay will be the contractual hourly rate like last summer. Did you have anything specific lined up for this summer?"

I shook my head, still in a daze of relief. "I've been too busy panicking about whether I had a job in September to do anything like that."

"I'll tell you Olivia, it's possible that you will be the only non-tenured high school teacher offered a contract for September. Good thing you're math. Your college credentials and your work experience in accounting and engineering have made you particularly exceptional. Then, factor in your initiative in trying new and different things." She took two steps back towards me. "Do you know that the administration has taken note of both your early morning math breakfast club and the independent tutoring sessions that you do during your study hall duty? At least eight parents have called with positive things to say about it." Doris chuckled. "The language arts supervisor is a little put out though because she's had some calls requesting similar offers from her department."

Doris paused and waited until I finally seemed coherent. *"Well done*, Olivia. Well done."

I was on cloud nine when I got home from work. For once Ben didn't have any evening meetings, and I'd texted him that I was cooking him a fabulous dinner and he should arrive hungry. *I had a job! I had a job!* That chorus kept dancing through my head over and over, and each time it did I smiled. At some point, between flipping the homemade sweet potato chips and basting the lemon fish in the oven I stopped and stood still and said, "Thanks." Dense as I was and as stubborn as I would no doubt continue to be, it wasn't lost on me that a string of good choices over the past months had led me to this point. Suddenly I felt certain that I didn't deserve full credit for this good place I found myself in.

The awful truth of my conception had pushed me to face the way I'd chosen to live my life. That had forced me to acknowledge the real truth about my family and recognize the truth that they'd continued to love me no matter what. As I stood barefoot in my kitchen with a spatula in my hand and Sophie sat on the refrigerator observing all the action I was forced to embrace the important truth. All these things could not be coincidence or luck, but rather a finely tuned and masterfully orchestrated plan of enduring love and purpose by Someone far greater, far wiser than me. Suddenly I understood what Clotilde had been trying to tell me: God wanted *me*, Olivia Kelly, even with my history and my baggage. My heart, as Ben had asked me, was *not fine*, and suddenly, I wanted it to be.

"Okay," I said out loud to God, "I give up. I'm going to buy in to the whole A-B-C thing. I'll let you be in charge from now on. I'll do my best to follow Your lead. But *please*, would you paint big black arrows for me to follow? I really don't want to screw up anymore, and You know better than anyone how messed up I can get. I'll follow, but You're going to have to make the path very clear."

I couldn't wait to tell Ben.

But I did wait. And wait and waited some more. Texts and calls got no response from Ben and by eight o'clock I was almost convinced it was time to start calling the local hospitals. It never occurred to me that he would stand me up; that just wasn't in Ben's makeup. And then I got a text: *sorry sick*

I stood there in my kitchen while Sophie enjoyed my fabulous lemon fish. "Is this a Big Black Arrow, God?" I muttered. There was no way I could slip into my Sponge Bob boxers and Gary The Snail tee shirt and just go to sleep. I tried to imagine what Clotilde, Erin and my mother would have done and every one of them would have needed more. So I got in my car and drove over to Ben's.

The reason we'd not spent more time at Ben's was primarily because having been to it once, my place was light years more homey. His place, on the top floor of one of those old homes, was a classic bachelor pad with no rugs, no curtains, no matching anything in the kitchen, and one old lumpy couch. I suspect, however, that the reason Ben hadn't pushed to have me come by his place more often was because the one and only time I was there we had ended up rolling around on said lumpy couch for a sizzling quarter of an hour and he didn't trust himself not to repeat that memorable experience.

Both his bike and his car were parked in the driveway, so even though I rang his bell and knocked on his door for at least five minutes with no success I knew he was home. Standing there on the porch, I vacillated back and forth about using the key I knew was hidden in the bottom of his mailbox. Or just go and leave the guy in peace. Then I remembered something Ben had said to me in jest, but also completely serious. "You try to break up with me again by not answering my phone calls, I'm driving over and breaking down your front door. You either tell me to my face to get lost or you're stuck with me." And while I was certain that wasn't what Ben was up to now, the emotion was the same. I dug out the key.

"Ben?" I stuck my head in through the doorway and peered around in the darkness. No lights, no television; just the dim glow of the digital time display on the cable box and the hum of the air-conditioning unit. "Ben? It's me, Olivia. I was worried about you so I came over to check." I stepped into the living room, shut the door and then listened.

The place was light years smaller than my mansion. The living room, dining area and attached kitchen made up the main area, through one door was the bedroom, and through another was the bathroom. Oddly, Ben had access to the attic through a third door but used it only for storage. And since he had driveway privileges he had explained that the downstairs apartment had back basement and yard privileges.

"Go away, Olivia," I heard from the bedroom. "I told you I was sick." His voice was rough, almost unrecognizable.

"Sick with what?" I took steps toward the center of the living room and waited.

There was a moment's pause. "Throw-ups. I think it's the flu."

"Do you have a fever?" I took two more steps towards his bedroom door, which was open just a crack. I could see Ben, his back to me, sitting on a straight backed chair looking out the dark bedroom window. That was weird. Whenever I had the throw-ups I was flat on my back when I didn't have my head in the toilet.

"Yeah."

"Do you have yellow spots on your throat? We learned about that strain of the flu at school. It's very contagious." I just made that up out of the blue to see what he'd say.

"Yeah. Yellow spots. *Go away, Olivia.* I don't want you to catch this."

My eyes had adjusted to the darkness now and I could see Ben clearly. Just sitting. In the dark. In his bedroom. Still with his work suit on. "What have you taken so far?"

He didn't answer me. I watch him reach up and rub his hands down his face. I recognized that motion. I'd seen it before. *Oh, God, he's crying.* I couldn't stop myself. I just walked into his bedroom. "What's wrong, Ben?"

He didn't turn around, just leaned forward and put his face in his hands. "For God's sake, Olivia, I need you to go. Will you please just leave me alone?"

I had a flash of him holding me while I struggled that night I tried to break up with him and him whispering to me, *I'd miss you until I died.* I had really wanted him to leave that night and yet he hadn't and I was so much better for it. I walked into the bedroom and sat against the wall under the dark window. "No. Sorry. I won't."

Ben looked at me then, and even in the dim light of the room I could see he was utterly and completely destroyed. *Someone's dead.* I knew it. "Who?" I asked. But as tears streaked down his cheeks, he remained silent and looked away from me to stare blindly out the window. So I scooted across the floor, leaned my head against his knee and waited for him to talk. And prayed desperately for help. God was probably already regretting our new alliance.

Therapy: The Truth About Me – Part V

Setting: It's Tuesday, June 15, 2010. I'm taking my 'medicine' with Aileen.

Aileen: Okay, so let's address you, Ben, and The Truth. You said last week that you were 'scared to death' about telling him the truth. You know what the best thing you can do when something scares you, Olivia? Think about the worst case scenario. If you can think about how you'd deal with that, then often the fear lessens significantly. So tell me, what are you afraid of?

Me: I'm afraid Ben won't be able to handle the truth.

Aileen: What is the truth?

Me: (I stare at her for a while and she stares right back.) That I'm a child of rape.

Aileen: Does that make you inherently evil?

Me: No.

Aileen: Bad to the bone?

Me: No.

Aileen: Criminal? (I shake my head.) A sexual deviant? (Another shake.) Inhuman? Worthless? Cruel? Hateful? Psychopathic? (I just keep shaking my head.) Okay, then what does it make you, Olivia?

Me: (I think. For a long time.) Sad. Regretful. Lonely. Different. (Aileen's waiting.) Stubborn. Strong. Independent. Outspoken. Brash.

Aileen: Would any of these qualities be a surprise to Ben? A problem?

Me: No.

Aileen: So *the fact* that you're a child of rape is only as big or as small in the make-up of who you are as you are willing to let it. Would you agree with that?

Me: Yeah.

Aileen: And you've spent a lot of time over the last two years determining that the fact that you are a child of rape is inescapable, but not a defining factor. That's *really* the truth, isn't it Olivia?

Me: Yeah.

Aileen: Okay. So *you know* the real truth. *You know* who you are and your
value as a person regardless of the moments of your conception.
But say Ben can't see that real truth. He not only can't understand
that real truth, he determines that your conception is a *huge* piece in
defining who you are to him. He looks at you and thinks (Aileen
leans forward and looks me right in the eye), 'Ruined, stained, dirty,
unclean, misfit, mistake, imperfect ...' That's all he thinks, Olivia,
and that's all he sees whenever he looks at you. And he tells you
that. To your face.

Me: (I look at Aileen. And swallow.)

Aileen: And let's say that even though he thinks all of this, you think he's
worth trying to convince otherwise. You try to explain and argue
and cajole. Maybe, you do like your mother did and you write a
whole big manifesto – hundreds of pages of personal, angst-ridden
thoughts and emotions for him to read in the hope that he'll come
to understand the real you; change his mind about you. (I think I
could just give him my journals. Drop them off at his apartment
and let him read about the horror of who I am.) Think about it,
Olivia: you are able to convince Ben that you're not ruined or
stained or imperfect ... and you stay together. *Or:* you're not able
to convince Ben of the truth of who you are and you break up.
(I'm looking at her with tear filled eyes. Aileen is still leaning
forward and she whispers her next question.) Which scenario
would you hope for? Changing Ben's attitude or breaking up with
him?

Me: (My tears are falling silently down my cheeks. I'm not raging. I'm not
angry. I'm just ... weeping.) I wouldn't want either scenario.

Aileen: Why not Olivia?

Me: (I sniffle. I blow my nose.) I want more than that. I don't want to
have to convince a man – *any man* – why he needs to love me.

Aileen: So ...

Me: So when I decide to tell Ben about my conception I want him to be able to see past that, like I've learned to do, and recognize the real truth about who and what I am.

Aileen: And that truth is ...

Me: I'm Olivia Kelly: strong, independent, stubborn, outspoken ... always growing, always changing ... determined to be happy and forward - thinking ... value that or get out of my way.

Aileen: You sure about that?

Me: Yes.

Aileen: Then you don't really have anything to be afraid of, do you?

A truth that's told with bad intent beats all the lies you can invent.[41]

26: I Am Different
Wednesday, June 16, 2010

I don't know how long Ben and I sat in the dark of his bedroom but finally he reached over and picked something up off the floor. "Here, Olivia. You want to know what's really wrong with me? Read this." Then he stood up and walked into the bathroom and locked the door.

I wandered into the living room, turned on a few lights, got myself a glass of water (in a chipped mug that said *Happy Bar Mitzvah Eitan)* and sat down to read whatever Ben had given me. It was a personal letter, handwritten on a piece of loose-leaf notebook paper. *Dear Ben Harayda,* the letter began in what I recognized as very familiar adolescent scrawl. *You don't know me because you gave me up for adoption when I was born.* I closed my eyes and put my head in my hand. I knew that there was sorrow and pain that had to be almost as bad as death, but Ben was only just discovering that.

I am sixteen and was born on March 19, 1992. I have known I was adopted since I was six. My parents wouldn't let me request information about you until I turned sixteen or you would have probably gotten this letter a lot sooner. Not because I want to meet you or anything. (Don't panic.) I was just always kind of curious about you and my birth mother.

I have the letter you left in my file. It made my mom cry. It made me mad though, which is finally why I decided to write. You say in your letter that you will always hope that I will contact you. Don't you get how screwed up being abandoned and given away as a baby makes you? Besides, sixteen years is a hell of a long time to hope

284

for something and I guess you've probably moved on about that anyway. You probably have a whole perfect family by now, and the last thing you need is this giant mistake from your past knocking on your door. But at least you had more courage than my birthmother. She didn't even want her name released.

I'm just letting you know that I don't want to have anything to do with you. Ever. You didn't want me when I was born and I don't want you now. So stop hoping if you haven't already.

Hope your life has been a lot better since I wasn't in it.
Daniel Fox

I got up, poured myself another glass of water, and heard Ben moving around in his bedroom. The distinct smell of his shampoo and soap wafted in to me and I leaned against the kitchen sink waiting for him to make an appearance.

He shuffled in barefoot wearing sweat pants and a tee shirt, went over to the refrigerator, grabbed a bottle of beer, and then went and threw himself down on the lumpy couch. I watched with interest, wondering what he'd say or do next. When he sat forward and reached for the remote I said quietly, "Should I go?"

He took the time to drink half the bottle of beer in noisy gulps and then looked at me and shrugged. "I didn't invite you in so I don't suppose I could ask you to leave ..." His attitude communicated clearly however, that it was exactly what he wanted me to do. He let the sentence dangle and then flopped back down on the couch and turned on the television. Loud.

Funny how I've never felt comfortable with single guys, or minister guys, or nice guys, or polite and thoughtful guys, but this angry, sullen, 'who gives a crap' guy I actually felt right at home with. Even downright cozy.

I went over and sat down on the couch next to him. "What did you honestly think was going to happen, Ben? At some point you were going to have some handsome young man show up at your front door with a big grin, you two were going to bond instantly, and live happily ever after?" Ben changed the channel and ignored me. "Hmmm," I said reaching over to touch his still damp hair that was making his shirt collar wet, "this must be the angry, sullen Ben when life doesn't go exactly as he planned."

He pulled away from my touch and looked at me then. *"Leave it alone, Olivia.* It would be best if you left now," he gritted out with barely controlled fury.

"What were you going to do about Daniel?" I said loud enough to be heard over the blasting television. Ben jumped like he'd been stunned at the sound of his son's name.

He turned off the television with a curse and threw the remote across the room. Resting his head against the back of the couch he crossed his arms and closed his eyes, doing his best to tune me out. I whispered into his ear, "Remember that teenage anger, Ben? Bright and hot enough to miss the truth of things, to make decisions that could forever alter your future, and to make you oblivious to all the hurt and sorrow you caused to those who cared most about you? *You remember it. I know you do.*

"Show me a teenager, Ben, *any* teenager, even those teenagers who have had a fairy tale life, and you'll find an angry child. What's important are the adults who take the time to wade through the anger, forge ahead despite seemingly insurmountable odds, and remain consistent from the first day to the last."

"Thanks for your advice, Olivia." I winced at his sarcasm. "However, you seem to have overlooked the fact that he doesn't want to have anything to do with me."

I couldn't prevent my laugh and matched Ben's sarcasm. "Yeah, he doesn't want anything to do with you, Ben. That's why *he wrote you a letter and established contact.* He doesn't want to see you even though *he practically begged you to do just that* if it wouldn't destroy your perfect family."

"It sounded like he hates me."

"Yeah, he probably does right now."

"He's never going to get over the fact that I 'abandoned him' when he was born. That horrible fact is going to be a part of his makeup until he dies."

Hello. Welcome to my world of horrible facts that are part of my makeup. I sighed. "Yup. That's true."

Ben turned and looked at me then, surprised it seemed that I didn't try to disagree with him. Or maybe soften the truth with kind words. I cocked an eyebrow at him. "What? You're talking to the woman who was mad at her mother for almost *sixteen years* for the lie she told about the man I thought was my father. Talk about something influencing you for your whole life." I laughed bitterly and then shrugged. "I've only just recently been able to not grind my teeth when I think about it." I let him digest that for a moment. "Of course, being the stubborn, relentless person that I am I made sure I found out the truth. I didn't let my mother's lie keep me in the dark. *Oh no.* And I had every intention of confronting her and giving her a piece of my mind once I knew the truth, too. Forget writing a letter. I was going to get right in her face and pound her into the ground with my discovery of the truth. I've told you a few times how anger has always been a force in my life Ben. For years it was probably the only thing that got me out of bed in the morning."

I'd intrigued him for a moment. He'd known part of the story but I'd never volunteered much and he'd not gotten up the courage to ask for more yet. "So do you know who your real father is?"

I looked him right in the eye. Ah well, here we go ... "In a manner of speaking."

"What's that supposed to mean?" He said it defensively as though I was purposely being evasive, not trusting him with the truth.

"It means that the name of *my mother's rapist* was never officially known." There. I'd said it. It was out. I sat and watched Ben process what I had just told him as though I was watching a made for TV drama.. "Try living with *that*, Ben. Truth doesn't always set you free." I sighed, stood up and walked to the door. "Look, you're the adult here, Ben. Be the *wise* adult. Who cares that an angry, hormonal, sixteen-year-old sent you an angst - written letter telling you to stay out of his life? When have you ever in your adult life taken the irrational, emotionally charged advice of a teenager? *When?* You work with teenagers all the time. How often do they make wise decisions about life?"

Ben had his head in his hands now. "Look at me!" I waited until he finally did just that. "I'm thirty-two years old and still dealing with mistakes my mother made as a teen, and still learning to live with all the fallout. Something tells me that if you play your cards right, Daniel adjusting to his good-guy minister birth daddy is going to be a hell of a lot easier to live with than what I've got to work with. But *that's not going to happen* if you just sit here hiding in your apartment feeling sorry for yourself."

I made my exit with head held high and eyes as dry as dirt.

"What did the acorn say when it was all grown up, Wayne?" The poor kid had gotten so tense over quadrilaterals that he'd begun to perspire. And it was only seven in the morning. Cramming for a final exam when you'd already failed almost every test given in geometry did that to some people. Even an unbelievable amount of Dunkin' Munchkins hadn't helped him much except to get white powder all over the front of his Lakers tee shirt.

"Ah ... I don't know Ms. Kelly." Even though we were both sitting he was looking down at me with an expression that communicated that he thought I was nuts.

"Gee, I'm a tree!" I grinned at him and waited until he finally got it.

"Ms. Kelly," Wayne said with a smile, "Will you be doing summer school math at least until I graduate?"

"I don't know, Wayne. I didn't get asked to do this summer's math school until just last week. How come?"

"Because I know I won't pass Algebra II next year, and I'll need your help again next summer."

"Do you know I do a morning math club some mornings during the school year? And I bring Dunkin' Donuts *every time*," I said cajolingly.

"Yeah, I know you do Ms. Kelly. But my Mom's a night nurse and doesn't get home from work until just before the school bus. I'm the only one whose around to get my little brother and sister fed and ready for school. We had to make all kinds of special arrangements so I could come in today for this."

I thought for a moment. "You should have asked, Wayne. I would have stayed after school and helped you out. Hey, what if I did an *afterschool* math club next year?"

Wayne shook his head. "I gotta work, Ms. Kelly. Every afternoon I work over at Hills Ice Cream. Then, I go home and do my homework. My mom won't let me do anything else but go to Pastor Ben's church youth group on Tuesday nights. He does a really fun youth group at Christ Church. But we don't attend there on Sundays." He sighed like it was a real hardship and rolled his eyes explaining, "My Mom likes to go to my Grandma's church where she grew up." He looked at me. "You're dating Pastor Ben, aren't you?"

I skillfully avoided that question. "We were childhood friends, actually."

"I told him one time that I see you all the time at school and that last summer you helped me with Algebra. He told me to count how many times I saw your dimple." Wayne blushed a bit and so did I. "All the girls love him."

I had a vision of Ben's tear - streaked face last night. There had been no calls or texts from him last night or this morning. I was addled enough with Ben thoughts and dimple comments that I said, "He's a great guy, that Pastor Ben. Seems like everyone who knows him, loves him."

Wayne studied me for a moment. "Pastor Ben's been talking about life influences ... good and bad. Thanks for agreeing to meet me before the final, Miss Kelly." He started. "Hey, are you coming to Pastor Ben's surprise birthday party?"

Birthday? "No, I-"

"Wait, let me call Kate and find out what time everyone's supposed to get there." He's already texting furiously.

Pistachio cake. That's what Grannie Blue always used to make Ben and I each and every birthday: his was in June and mine was in September. With vanilla ice cream.

"Kate says everyone has to be there at seven sharp because Pastor Ben is usually very punctual *and* she knows for a fact he's never really ever been surprised. We picked this date because it's not exactly *on* his birthday ..." Wayne frowned. "I forget what day it is ..." He launched into a new round of texting.

I had a vividly clear memory of Ben all tall and gawky and pre-teenagery singing Happy Birthday to me at the top of his lungs. We used to do that. He and I. The louder and the more off key the better.

"Tuesday. The 22nd. His real birthday is on the 20th and we're hoping he thinks that we've forgotten." Wayne looks at me. "You'll come right?"

"I-,"

His phone signaled a text which he looked down to read. "Kate wants to know if you know what his favorite cake is. He refuses to tell anyone."

"Pistachio," I heard myself saying as if from afar, "I'll bring it."

Driving home that afternoon I was lost in thought over Ben. There were big and small issues. Would he ever speak to me again? What should I get him as a birthday present? Was he completely repulsed by my paternity? Since when did he keep beer in his fridge? If I go Tuesday night, what should I wear? Did my talk help or hurt things between him and Daniel? Should I contact him or leave communication up to him? Would curtains make a difference in that dump?

Suddenly I was overwhelmed with reality. *I'd told Ben the truth.* The awful, unavoidable, inescapable truth and I felt ... okay. Relieved actually. I was surprisingly functional. Amazingly optimistic. Because clear as a bell I knew that *if Ben didn't want me because of that, then I didn't want him. I'd find someone better.*

"Wow. That's profound. And damn healthy, too," I said out loud to myself as I drove home. "Wait until Aileen hears about this," I mumbled.

My cell phone rang and it was my mother. "Hey, Mom, what's up?"

"If you were redoing your living room, do you think forest green would be too dark for the walls?"

"What are you doing? Redecorating the whole house?"

"Well, we had to redo the kitchen and the upstairs bathroom because of the broken pipe plus it turned out we had to do the ceiling in the living room too, so ..."

"You've got a lot of light in the living room. It might be nice. Plus you've got that glorious quilt you were working on when you and Alec got married."

"Hmmm, that's what Alec said. Okay, forest green it is."

"Now it's my turn to ask you a question."

I could feel my mother's delight roll over the phone connection. "Sure!"

"What would you buy for a birthday gift for a guy you ... liked a lot ... but were still newly dating."

"Oh. Well. Umm ... Let me think for a minute." We have a companionable silence for a few moments and in the background I hear the CD playing that I'd gotten her for Mother's Day: Sara Groves *Awakening*. "My favorite gifts from everyone – you, Alec, Liam, Janine ... are always things that *mean something*. It has nothing to do with money." I have a flash of the box of troll clothes she made me and my excellent Madonna rocker jacket of long ago. "Alec bought me a length of material one time that he saw at a store because he said it reminded him of me. He was able to talk about the feel of it and why he liked the color of it." My mother laughed. "He had no idea what he was talking about really, but he was just so sincere. It was ... very sweet.

"Your Mother's Day gift meant a lot to me: you got me a *Christian rock CD*, told me what songs you liked on it, and I know you even asked

291

Alec in advance if I already had it. Plus you wrote me that note." She was quiet for a moment. "I've got it in my purse right now. I guess what I'm trying to say is ... just go with your heart, Olivia. You can't go wrong if you do that."

The note I'd written her wasn't mushy. Just a "good things about the year in review" note. I thought she might enjoy having a list of positive things that she'd done as opposed to the endless list of things she's done wrong that I'd been reminding her about since I was old enough to speak.

"I really wanted you to say something like, 'Give him a blender. Guys love blenders, you know.'"

My mother laughed. "Sorry I got so deep."

Suddenly, I went with the moment. "One more question, Mom. This one's kind of serious."

"Okay ..."

"How did you and Alec ... come to the same ... place?"

My mother was quiet for a few moments choosing her words carefully, I suspect. "Well, I wasn't particularly encouraging. I did my best to drive him away. Had I gotten my way, I would still be alone." She laughed. "I was in-his-face obnoxious from the very first moment we started to ... converse. He's not let me forget how difficult I was."

"So ... why are you together? What happened?"

She hummed through the phone. "I have always had a tendency to sell myself short. Alec ... simply refused to let me do that. He was annoyingly capable of having a valid argument against every reason I came up with for why we shouldn't be together."

"And when you told him ..." I just let it hang out there unwilling to finish the sentence but knowing full well she'd know what I was alluding to.

She sighed. "That took me a long time. And I'll tell you something, Olivia. By the time I shared that secret with him I'd already reached a point where I wanted him in my life. I was absolutely terrified that he'd ... run away from me screaming, but I also was so tired of hiding that part of me." Quietly, my mother said, "When I did finally work up the courage to tell him he thanked me for trusting him enough to tell him the truth and," she laughed, "I got mad at him! Completely irrational, I know. But no one ever said I've spent my life making sense. You know that better than most."

"And the God stuff?"

"It's hard for me to explain, Olivia, but it just felt right. Good. It was a choice between random chaos – which I'd been living in my whole life – or purposeful joy. Once I realized the endless possibilities, there was no turning back." She hesitated. "God is knocking on your door pretty loudly, huh?"

"I'm hot for a minister, Mother."

She laughed. "I see your point."

"And my mother, her husband, my father, and my good friend at school are all singing the same song."

"And what song is that, Olivia?"

Now it's my turn to sigh. "That life's better, richer, fuller … when things are … well with your soul."

Her voice floated to me over the phone line. "So, how's your soul doing, honey?"

"Better than I ever could have imagined possible, Mom."

"Then just trust. Go with the flow. Stop fighting and *relax and enjoy the ride.*"

Journal: The Truth About Big Black Arrows
Thursday, June 17, 2010

Areas where I need God's Big Black Arrows to direct me. Big Black
Arrows being highly visible directional signals that I am willing to
follow.

1. <u>Ben</u>. Do I contact him? Do I leave him alone to think? It's ten
   thirty-eight (way past my bedtime) and I'm freaking out with his
   silence. What is he thinking about my complete revelation of the
   truth about me? Why doesn't he call? Will he at least call and say,
   'You disgust me, Olivia. Have a nice life. Good-bye.' or will I
   have endless days and nights of waiting. What a nightmare. My
   confidence and relief at spilling my deepest secret is ebbing as
   quickly as my optimism. Tomorrow I'll probably be barely
   functioning.

2. <u>Church</u>. I'm going to keep visiting churches because I really think
   I'm supposed to go. But will I ever find one I like? Right now, it's
   a bit like taking medicine or getting an injection. I'm doing it
   because I'm supposed to so I stay healthy, but I'm really not
   looking forward to it. What I'm concerned about is that I'll never
   really like one enough to settle. Has that ever happened to
   someone, God? And, if it hasn't, please could I *not* be your first
   case? I'll remind you, God, to look at how long it took me to
   accept my own family ...

3. <u>Me</u>. I had a really healthy thought today in the car about me and
   Ben. Aileen would be proud if she knew, since all her hard work to
   get me to this point. That doesn't mean I'm rock solid or
   completely self-confident though. In fact, I would like to formally
   let you know that I'd like to keep Ben. Yes, even if you think
   there's someone better out there for me, I still want Ben. Please.

P.S. God, even as I write this, I realize I still don't want Ben if he can't
   handle the truth about me. I don't want to go backwards. I want
   to go forwards. So, I guess I'll rephrase my formal request about

294

keeping Ben, even if there's someone better out there for me. Instead, I'd like to ask for a guy *just like Ben*, who won't let anything he knows about me interfere with seeing the Real Olivia Kelly and understanding what I'm all about.

And you will know the truth and the truth will set you free.[42]

27: Pansies Are My Favorite Flower
Friday, June 18; 2010

     I stepped out my front door on Friday morning and did a double take. In utter confusion I walked slowly down my front steps to the parking lot and then turned and looked back at my house. There were flowers. *Everywhere.* Pots of big beautiful mums in pinks and yellows stood like sentinels on each of my steps. Clusters of vibrant pansies in every imaginable color had been planted all along the walkway and in the front garden bed. Hanging from a hook (that the previous owner had installed) was the biggest fuchsia plant I had ever seen weighted down with bright pink blooms. And nestled in the corner was a bright orange watering can with a note taped to it that said "OLIVIA".

     I walked over to the envelope and recognized Ben's handwriting. I sat down on the front steps, put my purse, coffee mug, and briefcase down, and opened up the letter.

Friday morning, 4:00 a.m.

Olivia,

I hope you like the flowers. Feel their beauty and vibrancy? That's how it feels to have you in my life. Always has.

Always will.

I will be gone for a few days but will be back soon.

Then we need to talk.

<u>Because I love you, Olivia.</u> You can't stop me and I can't hold back saying it any longer.

Ben

In the end I had to go back inside to fix my makeup. As I looked into the bathroom mirror I said aloud to God, "Wow. When you decide to send Big Black Arrows, *You send Big Black Arrows.*" And I had to fix my makeup one more time.

I still hadn't heard anything from Ben by Sunday, June 20, 2010, which was when Clotilde had invited me to her church service. What could I do? Say no to the woman who'd sat with me for hours while I moaned and groaned about my life, and who then turned around and shared an even darker history? Say no to the woman who'd responded to my life's story by saying things like, Bravo! Well Done! Hip-Hip-Hooray! Keep up the good work!!? Say no to the woman who'd committed to pray for me, and had apparently been faithfully praying for me since she'd met me? Say no to the woman who despite my best efforts had become a treasured friend and confidant?

Not likely.

Which was why I found myself on Sunday morning at eleven o'clock sitting in a very traditional church listening to very traditional organ music surrounded by very traditional, churchy - looking people. I saw old men in suits and old ladies in hats (one even was wearing gloves). The minister wore a big, black robe and the choir was all dressed in maroon robes with shiny gold collars. No bikers. No tee shirts with sports logos. No bass guitars or smells of coffee and pastry. Not even a folding chair in sight.

But I didn't mind. I didn't feel any more or less comfortable than I did visiting Agape Shop. This church was actually more like my childhood church memories, when I went occasionally with Ben's family on Sunday mornings. Ben and I used to sit with Grannie Blue and Mrs. Harayda (and Mr. Harayda, of course, if his ship was in port). Arthur always got to sit with his friends up in the balcony, and Ben and I were positive they were causing all kinds of mischief but could never prove it. Grannie Blue kept peppermint Certs in her purse, and we were allowed one each. I remember my reading skill progressing until finally I could find the hymn page number, and then eventually I could follow along with the words. I don't remember much else except the time that someone got baptized. That was pretty cool. A big, tall red-headed man came out in a long white robe. Then I discovered that the place under the big cross up front was really a big pool that could be filled with water! That red-headed man got dunked completely under water that day by the minister, and I remember being completely blown away that *the church had an indoor pool.* Of course once I found out that you couldn't swim in it, and that it was filled only for special occasions – I was completely disgusted. What a waste.

I thought Clotilde's church probably had a pool up front, since the bulletin I was given mentioned "Baptism Classes" every Wednesday evening at eight, I suspected I was right. The minister was an enormous man and carried a Bible in one of his massive hands that looked like it weighed close to ten pounds. When he stepped out onto the center of the podium like an avenging angel I remembered thinking, *Oh man, this might be more than I'm ready for …*

But it was okay. He talked a lot and read the Bible a lot. But he did a simple thing right at the end of his sermon that stuck with me because it was so visible. He took out a small white candle and lit it. Looking up into the balcony he said, "Can't see that too well, can you?" There were a few murmured 'no's' from some people. "Turn out the chandeliers," he said, and suddenly all the fancy overhead lights went dark.

"How's that? Can you see it any better?" Some people mumbled 'yeah' but other braver souls said, 'no'. "Okay," the minister said, "close the drapes." Assistants had obviously been recruited, because with synchronized precision all the big windows were suddenly hidden behind dark draperies.

It was dim in the sanctuary now, and that little candle was much more visible. I noted that there were still recessed lights on the altar and strategically placed all around. "Why don't we go all the way?" the minister said and suddenly we were plunged into darkness as every electrical light was turned off.

The minister picked up the little candle which now glowed brightly in his hand. *"Now* can you all see it?"

"Yes!" everyone said.

"This is you," the minister said holding up the flickering flame which cast odd shadows across his face, "with Christ's light inside you. It burns brightly, faithfully, continually inside each one of us who has asked the Lord to come into our hearts. Sometimes when things are bright and good and happy you hardly seem to notice that ever present - flame. But during the darkest, hardest times of our lives, those of us with Christ beside us know with utter confidence that there is *no darkness so great that can extinguish the light of even one small flame.* We believers know that we are never alone – in the light or in the dark – because God never leaves us or forsakes us…"

There was more singing and more praying and then lots of hand shaking. Clotilde and Max gave me hopeful smiles. "Will you go out to lunch with us? We often go to a little sandwich shop on Sunday mornings."

"I think I'm just going to head home."

"He'll call, Olivia." I'd shared with Clotilde that Ben and I had had a pretty heavy discussion the other night, that I'd told him my *whole history,* and that we were taking some time to digest everything. She hadn't asked for a blow-by-blow description, and I'd appreciated being able to respect Ben's privacy. I'd also kept private his note on Friday morning, which I'd carried with me constantly since reading it.

"I know. I'd just like to go home, do some laundry and relax. There's nothing more to it than that." Except there was.

In the end it was a nice day. Even with my concerns over Ben, I was surprisingly content. I watered my flowers and made small vases of fresh ones for my living room and bedroom. (Did you know the more you pick pansies, the more they bloom? I liked the analogy between having something hard or painful happening causing them to grow in beautiful abundance.) With me squeaky clean from a shower and Sophie stretched out in a patch of late sunshine on the kitchen counter, I fried myself a grilled cheese for dinner and listened to tunes on my IPOD. You can laugh at me, but Alec's theme song, *Trouble*, was my new favorite song. Somehow, teaming up with God and all, singing about being *trouble since the day I was born* was ... okay now. I wiggled around my kitchen, flipped my cheese sandwich, poured myself a tall iced tea, and sang the chorus at the top of my lungs, *"I'm not above or beyond anything, so I know You must be good for me. As far as You can and as bad as I am, oh I know You must be good for me ...* [43]*"* ...

... only to turn around and see Ben lounging on my deck watching the show.

"Ben ... !" I gasped and almost dropped my sandwich. I pulled out my headphones and glared at him, totally embarrassed.

"You never told me you could sing." He was slouched in one of my deck chairs and his long legs were stretched out and crossed in front of him. He wore a Yankees baseball cap with dark sunglasses.

I stood there like a statue admiring the handsome eye candy on my deck. "I *can't* sing and you've just had embarrassing, vivid proof."

"You *can* sing, Olivia Kelly. How many other hidden talents do you have?"

The innuendo was clear, and suddenly singing was the last thing on my mind. I was dressed in loose, drawstring shorts and a bright pink tee shirt that my mother had given me which said, 'I'm confused. Wait. Maybe I'm not.' AKA my pajamas. I was also completely sans underwear. A very dangerous position to be in as far as I was concerned, so I continued to keep my distance. "What did you do, just climb up on my deck?"

"Yup. Don't worry, I rang the bell first, but I guess you couldn't hear me since you were too busy dancing and singing to your music. So, following your example, I just broke in."

I stomped my foot and I yelled, "I didn't break in to your apartment, Ben Harayda, and you know it! You showed me where the key was! I was worried about you. Is there anything wrong with that?"

He gave me a slow smile. "Come out here and kiss me."

He just seemed to ooze … trouble. "I, I'd better go upstairs and get dressed. These are … my pajamas."

"I know," he said, and he had the audacity to hum in appreciation. "I've been watching and enjoying the show for quite a while, remember?"

"Ben Harayda!" I was pretty sure I sounded like a shocked old lady. I walked closer but still didn't slide open the screen. He relaxed on my deck and watched me. I couldn't see his eyes behind the dark sunglasses. "Are you okay?"

Nodding he said, "Much, *much* better than when you last saw me. Can't you tell?"

I leaned against the door frame and said in a low voice, "Thanks for the flowers, Ben. It was the best present I've ever gotten in my whole life."

"Come out here and kiss me, Olivia."

Ever annoying I asked, "How come you don't come in *here* and kiss *me?"*

He looked at me for a moment or two and then sighed. "It's safer out here."

"Because it's outside? Public? Where anyone can see?" He just continued to watch me. I grinned at him and licked my lips. "Want me to start telling you about some of my other hidden talents?" When he stood up and started toward me, I squeaked and ran upstairs to get dressed.

He'd eaten my grilled cheese sandwich and was busy cooking two more when I finally came down. Sophie was winding around his legs, purring and kissing up to him big time. Once again I felt compelled to keep my distance. Probably because I didn't trust myself if he was close enough to touch. I was overwhelmed with how good it was to see him.

There were so many things for us to talk about, and the subjects crowded in my head like a frantic shopper trying to get in the only entrance of the world's best sale. I'd yet to tell him about my summer job and the contract I now had such confident hopes of getting for September. He still didn't know about how God and I were now on regular speaking terms. I was desperate to know where he'd been these last few days. Plus there was the dangerous aura floating around him as if suddenly *all rules were null* which needed to be addressed. And, of course, we'd yet to talk about the closing line in the letter he left me: <u>*Because I love you, Olivia.*</u>

"Where have you been?" I asked leaning against the door jam and enjoying the spectacular view.

"Around and about," Ben responded vaguely. He expertly flipped the two sandwiches onto one plate and held them out to me. "Here. I'll get the drinks." But when I stepped forward to take the plate he grabbed my hand and pulled me towards him. *"But first*, I'll have that kiss," he said.

Journal: The Truth About My Life

Saturday, June 19, 2010

I'm sitting here writing in my journal grinning like a fool. And why am I
grinning? Because I, Olivia Kelly, am happy. Amazingly. At long
last. (Any one of those fit.) Even better, for the first time I feel as
if I can probably keep all this going without too much blood,
sweat, and tears. Suddenly, the reality of my life is … quite nice …

The reality is that I have no more hidden truths. I kind of dumped them all
out in a haphazard pile on the floor of life and … shrugged. I
know, it took me a long time to finally be able to do that, but still
… all the people that matter in my life now know the Real Olivia
Kelly, and I'm going to have to trust that they will value what they
see or … walk away fast and spare me future pain.

The reality is that outside my front step are flowers planted by a man who is
crazy enough to claim that he loves me. Even more hysterical, he's
a minister. Even more unbelievable, I … believe him. Even more
astonishing, he told me he loved me *after* I told him my darkest
secret. And even more impossible than all that, I'm fairly certain
that I love him, too. And even more beyond belief than all of that,
I actually think this relationship … might work.

The reality is that I've accepted things that I cannot change such as the facts
regarding my birth father, and I've had courage to change the
things I could like my job, my attitude, my perception of the past
and my opinion about God. I'm fairly certain that I qualify as
being smart enough (although I won't be so bold as to say wise) to
know the difference. Maybe I should start my own recovery group.
What would I call it?

The reality is that finally, I feel that maybe, I'm a capable adult. Perhaps
that means it's time for me to look towards the future with an adult
attitude rather than an angry child attitude.

The reality is that at long last, I feel in control and have embraced all of the
truths that make up the person that I am: the good, the bad, and

the ugly. I am Olivia Kelly. I'm doing the best I can with who I am, and will continue to do so.

Truth is the only safe ground to stand on.[44]

28: I Will Not Be Ben's Stepford Girl

Sunday, June 20, 2010

Ben kissed me until I was dizzy, as he pressed me up against my kitchen counter. "You're different," I said when he finally gave me a chance to speak.

He took his hat and sunglasses off and tossed them on the kitchen counter. "Yes," he nodded decisively, "Yes I am. Come outside and sit with me and let's talk."

We ended up sitting on my deck munching on grilled cheese sandwiches and dipping carrot sticks into ranch dressing. When Ben had finished his (second) sandwich, he picked up my bare feet and held them in his warm hands. "Let's get one thing over with right off the bat. I *think* you might have doubted my … feelings for you. I *think* you might have worried that once I discovered certain facts about you and your … history … that I would pick up my marbles and go play somewhere else. *If that's the case*, shame on you. I'll tell you this once and for all: I don't care where you've come from, I only care where you're going. Okay?" When I looked at him silently he said, "I wrote that I love you in that note because I was afraid you would be thinking all those things. I've been wanting to tell you I love you for a long time, but didn't want to scare you away with my … intensity. But after you talked to me Wednesday night, and gave me a good," he grinned, "kick in the pants, I couldn't help but love you all the more. *I'm a better person when I'm with you*, Olivia and it was no longer an option for me to keep quiet about my feelings."

305

What a guy, huh? How did I find this pot of gold when I hadn't even been able to see the rainbow? *Thank You,* I thought with a rush of joy. *Thank You.*

Ben tugged on my feet. "You're just sitting there. I can see you're thinking a mile a minute. Do I need to say it plainer? Spell it out a different way?"

"So the fact that I'm a child of rape ... doesn't matter to you?" I purposely said the awful truth out loud because hearing it said plainly is so much more difficult to deal with than trying to sugar coat it.

"Absolutely it matters! It matters because of the sorrow it has caused you and, I suspect, will continue to cause you. It matters because it's made relationships harder to deal with than normal. It matters because I'm afraid you've agonized over telling me and were uncertain how I would react." Still holding my feet, he leaned in, kissed my cheek, and whispered in my ear, "It matters because I want all you've got to share with me – the good and the bad – so I can feel free to share the same with you. No secrets between us, Jerry. That's what will make us strong."

Okay, so I was crying by the end of his speech and had to put my feet down and blow my nose. Which only made Ben sit forward almost nose to (runny) nose with me. I shook my head. "You're too good to be true. I don't believe you're real, Benjamin Harayda."

He chuckled and nuzzled my neck for a moment and then whispered, "Right back at ya, babe."

He picked my feet up again and we sat in companionable silence for a long time. "I went and saw Daniel," he finally said, as though it was an everyday occurrence. When I sat and waited he sighed and said, "And he refused to see me."

"But he knows you cared enough to travel all the way to see him," I couldn't help pointing out. "Trust me. No matter how hard he tries – and he will try - he won't be able to ignore that. He now knows that you care."

Ben studied me for a minute. "I tried three times. Failed every time."

I shrugged. "No one said it was going to be easy. Or quick. I'm a walking example of that. But Daniel is going to discover that you're not going to give up easily. Because we both know you will go back. Again and again. That's something he won't be able to ignore."

"After the third time Daniel refused to see me I finally spoke with his mother. Her name's Kristen." He paused and looked away. "She's a nice lady. I didn't get to meet her husband, Keith, but I got a good feeling about him, too, from the way Kristen spoke about him."

"She was okay that you showed up unannounced at her door? Three times?"

Ben sighed and closed his eyes for a minute. "Daniel's been giving them a pretty hard time. They've apparently reached that kind of desperate level where anything that might help would be welcomed. Including having a perfect stranger show up at their door and claim to be their son's birth father. That's why they finally gave in and let him contact the agency and get my information."

"What kind of hard time?" I had a sudden flash of drugs and alcohol ... and all manner of other bad stuff kids could get into these days.

Ben squinted in thought. "She was vague. I mean I'm just this outsider who showed up at their front door, you know? But she mentioned school issues and constant fighting. They've got him seeing a counselor."

"I remember. Heck, Ben, I'm still dealing with it. Daniel is angry. Over all the stuff in his life he can't change no matter how much he wants to. He's beginning to discover that real life is hard and that Santa and the Easter Bunny aren't real. Sounds like he's got a lot going for him, though. You got a good impression about his parents, hopefully he's seeing a good therapist, and then, of course, there's you. It's always good to be in your sights. Look how good I'm turning out." I grinned at him and winked. As I pulled my feet away from the distracting warmth of his hands I leaned forward and touched his knee. "Those are things to be thankful for, right?"

Ben slouched down in the lounge chair and crossed his arms, studying me intently as though I were a virus under a microscope. "Never mind *me* being different, Olivia Kelly. *You're* different. Who is this woman talking about being thankful?" He narrowed his eyes at me. "And, here's a better question: *to whom* are you telling me to be thankful?"

Now it was my turn to break eye contact and study my next door neighbor's busy bird feeder. Sophie routinely spent hours with her mouth watering, watching the action over there from my bedroom window. Suddenly I felt extremely self-conscious. I shrugged my shoulders and said, "Grannie Blue told me one time that we're supposed to be thankful in all things. Sounded like good advice so I've been trying it out."

"Grannie Blue ... sang that song every day of her life." Ben smiled in fond memory. "Through the good times and the bad. My mother said the last thing Grannie said was, "Thank God I'm done with all this." He pulled his lounge chair close enough that our knees were touching and then put his big, warm hands on my thighs. "Who are you thankful to, Jerry?"

"You always call me 'Jerry' when you're getting intense," I said as I reached up and smoothed a lock of hair off his forehead and pointedly avoiding the question again. "I like it."

Ben sighed, resigned to let me play my avoidance games. He took a deep breath and said, "You said I'm different and I am. Most of what you see is the result of tremendous relief. I've been living in dread over the issue of Daniel all of my adult life. Kind of like knowing that there would be a devastating explosion in the future, but not knowing when or where or how it was going to happen. Getting that letter from him ... filled with all anger and bitterness ... was like my worst nightmare." He looked at me then. Really looked at me. "You did everything right that night, Olivia. After you left, I sat there and couldn't forget all the things you said. I'd have said the same thing to anyone who came to me in the same situation." He sat back and crossed his arms, still close enough to me that our knees touched. "I have a new appreciation for the parents I deal with now. I told Kristen that I would write to Daniel but send her copies of all the letters. And you're right, I also told her she could count on another visit from me very soon."

"Where do they live?"

"Ohio." When I started to say something he leaned forward, pulled me to him, and kissed me hard and fast. "I've got some more things to say, and it's difficult for me. Let me finish, okay? What I need to say is important."

"Okay ..."

Leaning forward he did that thing he does, tucking my wild hair behind my ears and touching a curl or two. I sure liked the attention. "But there's something else that's making me different, too. I've told you I love you, Jerry," he whispered and leaned in to kiss me again, sweetly and softly and slowly. "I think I've loved you my whole life. It may sound corny but I feel like I've been looking for you ... waiting for you almost. The relief of finally beginning to face the issue of Daniel is only one reason I'm different. This," he pointed to me and then himself, "is the other reason. But that's what I have to tell you. You see, I haven't always done a good job at love, and admitting that I'm in love with you ... well, you need to know a few things. You've shared with me your skepticism over love. I always had ... the opposite problem, I guess. I love ... too intensely – to my own detriment and everyone else's sometimes. I sort of get lost in it. I've always kind of lost my mind when I fell in love; lost perspective about right and wrong ..."

Ben sighed. "I want you to know my ugly history because I haven't gotten the love thing right yet ... I did it wrong with Marisa in my teens. Even knowing full well we were both young and immature and that she wasn't anywhere near as into me as I was into her, I was determined for us to be together. *I wanted her.* We were sixteen, for God's sake, what did I know?! Talk about adolescent stupidity." He shook his head. "I was willing to give up my dream of a baseball scholarship and college and ignore all the wise advice every caring adult took the time to throw my way just to hang onto that relationship. Hell, I *wanted* her to get pregnant so that she'd be ... compelled ... to stay with me. I had already had hints that we were drifting apart. I had been getting hints that she was losing interest. And when she *did* get pregnant, and then spent time considering an abortion, I was forced to look long and hard at the disaster I'd created. I'd held on so tightly that I almost destroyed both of us, and Daniel was the fallout.

"I spent a lot of time after Marisa on my own. Doing penance so to speak. Thinking I was getting my head on straight and gradually getting pretty full of myself and my exceptional personal recovery." His mouth twisted with disgust. "I pursed a college education and gave into the God route that I just couldn't turn my back on despite the number of times I tried. I met Jill while I was at seminary. She … wasn't a student but worked in town. But once again, I," Ben paused and dropped his head, "I just lost my head once I decided I was in love. I became this desperate, grasping individual.

"I drove that boat … again … right up onto the rocks. Jill … she loved me. I don't doubt that. And, I loved her … but it wasn't a good love." Ben had picked up my hands, and he held them, studying them instead of looking at me directly. "It was a love that totally made her transform herself to fit into my world. And it was clear that she wasn't welcome if she didn't get with the program. You guessed one time that I was the one who compromised too much in that relationship." He gave a bitter laugh. "But you were wrong. She wasn't given a choice, I just dragged her along. Looking back I can see how screwed up I was. When I finally found out that she'd been seeing someone else, I couldn't believe that once again I had painted myself into this impossible corner. Compromised what I knew was right to get what I'd decided I wanted above all else. I thought my way was better … right … and gave no thought to hers. I justified a lot of my choices to satisfy my own desires. I talked the God talk really well, but didn't walk it." He looked at me pointedly. "You want specific details?" His eyes looked sad but determined. I shook my head no.

"In retrospect, it was all so obvious that our relationship was doomed to failure. She tried to tell me, but was too … focused on what I wanted and what I was sure she needed … that I never heard a word she said."

Suddenly he looked so drawn and haggard. Absolutely miserable. "You don't have to tell me all this, Ben."

He looked me in the eye. "Of course I do. You have a right to know what kind of man I am. You've been honest and up front with me about your past, but I think you've got this impression that I'm a perfect spiritual do-gooder. You told me on the first date how I qualified as a good guy." Rolling his eyes he muttered, "That reputation comes with the profession, and some ministers let it go right to their heads. In some ways I have to admit that I've let you think that about me. It's worked to my advantage since I've had strong feelings for you … *forever.*" Suddenly he reached up and kissed me hard on the mouth. "This is what you have to understand, Olivia. I wanted Marisa. I wanted Jill. But the wanting is *nothing* compared to the wanting of you," he said fiercely. "I've been struggling with that … the wanting of you, almost since the moment I saw you at IHC. *I don't want to repeat old mistakes,* Olivia. The need to do things right this time is absolutely critical.

"But now I've gone and told you that I love you. It's only the third time in my life I've done that with a woman, and the last two times were flaming disasters. I want you to know my history in the way I've loved … Know what you're getting into. Especially since you're still so … so new with this concept of love. I want you, but I'm trying so hard for it to be on your terms and in your timeline."

Ben stared at me. I licked my lips. "So, let me get this straight. You love me, but you're worried that you're love is so powerful, that I'm going to turn into a mindless automaton and kind of follow you around drooling, doing whatever you say. Sort of like a Stepford Wife, but the Ben Harayda version. And you're concerned that all your badness in love will ruin my newly found acceptance of the wonders of love?" Ben gave me a pointed look, detecting my strong sarcasm. I laughed at him and rolled my eyes. "We're quite a pair, I guess. One of us loves to the extreme while the other claims to have never loved at all." He blinked his big green eyes at me. "What do you want from me, Ben?"

311

"I want you to tell me why you're different. I've tried *very* hard to not push my life style or my God agenda on you. But being who I am, doing what I do for a living ... that's just about impossible. I ... want to hear how things are with you in your own words."

He knew. About me and God and giving up and all. I must have been glowing or something. And I suppose singing God songs and dancing braless and free in the kitchen had clued him in a bit, too. "Well, if you want me to tell you that you haven't had anything to do with the choices I've made lately, I'm sorry I can't do that. In fact, as far as I'm concerned, if you don't have any impact on the person you're with, then you've got even more trouble as a couple. But that's another discussion.

"However, what you do need to know is that you're just part of one gigantic conspiracy that God's had in place in my life. I'll admit that you were the big in-your-face God component. Which was pretty hysterical given the fact that I'm also tremendously attracted to you, and boy, I never thought that would go together. But you're just the end of a long line really. A God parade so to speak. First there was Clotilde, who I suspect would do just about anything to get me onto the God side. I picture she and her husband Max holding hands in church and saying my name over and over, "Olivia .... Olivia ...," like a spell or something. And there's my mother who's literally been transformed before my eyes from an unhappy woman existing from day to day to a woman who ... shines with the joy of life." I stopped and rolled my eyes at how ridiculous I sounded, and I think Ben tried hard not to laugh. "Then of course there's Alec, husband number four, who seemed like a really decent guy. Do you know he's got a criminal record? Honestly, he has *served time in prison.* Yet, once again, his sincerity and diligence and blatant dedication to the whole God thing is hard to dismiss. Next is Dean. My ... father. Who has loved me with teeth-gritting determination despite his own personal demons and my contrary nature. Do you know that he thinks I'm attending church now because he *prayed me to do it?* How can I argue with that kind of logic?" I shook my head. "Even my therapist, Aileen, is in the God club, Ben. So if you're worrying that you've forced me into any of this spiritual stuff, then just get to the end of the line, buddy, because you're only one of many."

"Why are you different, Jerry?" He was sitting in front of me, leaning forward and hanging on every word I said. Even though I still hadn't said what he wanted to hear.

I sighed. "I'm different because I've given up. I've stopped fighting the tide and just decided to embrace The Most Important Truth Of My Life: God wants me. He's wanted me pretty badly, it seemed, because He's pulled out all the stops to get my attention. I figure I'd better buy into this before He decides to try something drastic and hit me with a bolt of lightning or something."

Therapy: The Truth About The Bible

Setting: Aileen's office. It's Tuesday, June 22, 2010. Today's our last
session before both of us take off for the summer. It is also my
last day at school. And Ben's 33rd birthday, and I've been invited
by Wayne to come to the surprise party the youth group is
throwing for him. It's a very pivotal day and I feel ... odd.

Aileen: So what did Ben do after you told him you'd 'given up' – which I
might point out also means that you've made what we Christians
call a *profession of faith.*

Me: After he kissed me some more? (Aileen gives me a look.) He's a great
kisser, you know. Have I told you that? I think he must be *fabulous*
under the sheets. (I hum with thoughtful consideration.) He asked
me what I was planning to do next. So I told him I supposed I'd
go to church with him on Sunday and check out his church.

Aileen: Did you follow through on that?

Me: Of course I did. But I didn't sit with Ben, because he sits up in the
front and I couldn't handle that. I tried out the balcony even
though all of the Haraydas invited me to sit with them. Do you
know that the senior pastor at Ben's church ... *is a woman?* My
mouth just dropped open when she stood up and started talking.
She's doing this series on couples of the Bible. Talked about
Abraham and Sarah. Boy, they had a screwed-up relationship. Did
you know Sarah got Abraham to get her slave pregnant because she
couldn't have a child of her own? How messed up was that?! Next
week, she's going to talk about Jacob and Leah, and Ben said that if
I had trouble with Abraham and Sarah I'm going to go nuts over
Jacob and Leah.

Aileen: (Laughing) Well, considering Jacob ended up married to Leah, her
sister Rachel, and his wives' two maids Bilhah and Zilpah ...

Me: You're kidding me.

Aileen: (Laughing still.) No, I'm not kidding. The Bible's full of ...
people in need of serious therapy! Very few of its characters are

314

happy, wise, and obedient. Absolutely none of them are perfect.
You'd be amazed at how many of them struggle with the exact
same issues we struggle with. You know how you love to journal?
Well, the Bible is one big journal of a whole collection of people –
some who got it right and many who didn't, and what happened to
them as a result. It's a very good read full of a lot of personal
insights into all kinds of people and situations. And, of course,
God's unfailing love and patience. You should check it out for
yourself. Don't you have Grannie Blue's Bible?

Me: Yeah …

Aileen: Well …?

Me: Maybe …

Aileen: So. What did you think of Ben's church?

Me: There's an awful lot of pressure to like it, you know. The joke is, I got
so engrossed in hearing about the wild and crazy relationship
between Abraham and Sarah that I forgot to … I don't know,
evaluate everything.

Aileen: So you'll have to go back again.

Me: Well, I'm not going to miss hearing about Jacob and Leah, especially
after what you've just told me. (Aileen's just smiling at me.)

Aileen: (Said with a really evil grin.) What did you *honestly* think of Ben's
church, Olivia?

Me: You know, this is getting very old. (I sit for a minute in silence, just to
make her wait.) It felt like home, okay? The people were nice.
The kids were thrilled to see me and gave me a really sweet
welcome. Mrs. Harayda gave me a *huge* hug and insisted that I
come to Sunday dinner. Arthur was there with his wife and their
new baby and they just looked … I don't know … so happy to
have me there.

Aileen: And what did Ben have to say about everything?

Me: Not much, actually. I told you how he's afraid he's going to become
some evil svengali, getting me to say and do things I don't really

315

want to do. In every direction I turn, I've got people talking God to me ... except for my minister boyfriend.

Aileen: Do you want to talk about God with him?

Me: Well ... eventually ... I think he's probably waiting for me to ask him questions or something.

Aileen: Remember what you said a long time ago? About *honest* communication and good relationships?

Me: (Finally, it's my turn to laugh.) I know. I know. Whoever would have thought that I'd be worried about honest communication in a good relationship, huh?

Aileen: Me. I never doubted you for a second.

Teach me thy ways, O Lord, that I might live according to your truth.[45]

29: Honest Communication Is Essential

Tuesday, June 22, 2010

I'd been working on Ben's birthday present since my phone conversation with my mother last Thursday. I wasn't sure when I'd give it to him. Certainly not at the surprise birthday party in front of eight million curious teenagers. There was even a possibility that I'd wimp out totally and not give it to him at all. So, I'd bought him a watch. A very nice watch. But it was just a watch.

I'd already told him he should show up for dinner Wednesday night (he actually cancelled a meeting so he could come) and I also told him that if he stood me up this time I *wouldn't* be coming over and breaking into his apartment. That was a onetime pass that he had already cashed in. He laughed a lot at me, I realized. At rather odd times. Never when I was purposely trying to be funny or clever. Always when I was trying to be serious, blunt, and firm. It was a very nice feeling to know that the hard side of me – that tough in-your-face side that usually pushed people away actually amused him.

The kids were thrilled that I had agreed to come to the party and the last few days of school I'd had an endless stream of co-conspirators popping into my classroom to ask or tell me things. The pistachio cake that Grannie Blue used to make us for our birthdays was a "secret" recipe, but I found one on the Internet that seemed close. Actually, the only thing secret about the recipe was Grannie's "mysterious ingredient" which Ben and I finally (after years of failed attempts) discovered to be 7-Up. I kid you not.

Rushing home from Aileen's I showered and changed. I decided on casual chic: no cleavage, big gold earrings, excellent new lime green sandals, and a cute summer top that brought my whole outfit together smashingly. Then I rushed to get to Christ Church early to help the kids set up.

It was a nice evening in the end. I don't think Ben was too surprised about the party, but he was certainly surprised to see me standing in the crowd. Oh my, the look he gave me across the room! I think I'll remember it ... forever. He just looked *so incredibly happy*. I realized as I stood there in the crush and confusion watching him that I'd never in my life been responsible for making someone as pleased as Ben seemed to be *just by my showing up*. He laughed and teased the kids, with good-natured, wise-ass humor as he worked his way towards me. They'd decorated the church lounge with black balloons and signs saying, "You're HOW old?!" *Ancient tunes* from Bachman-Turner Overdrive, The Eagles, The Bee-Gees, and Peter Frampton were blasting on someone's CD player and at least two kids were dressed like John Travolta in white suits.

"I was *a baby* when that movie came out," Ben pointed out when one of the John Travolta lookalikes asked Ben if he had a white disco suit somewhere in his closet. "Although, I might have one sparkly glove still in my underwear drawer." That made me laugh out loud and he turned and gave me *that look* again. When he finally got to me he said quickly under his breath, "You have two choices, so think fast. You can let me kiss you silly in front of everyone right here, or you can let me drag you someplace private where I will also kiss you silly." He winked at me. "Either way will cause some talk."

"I've learned," I said as I looked him in the eye, "that keeping secrets only causes more problems down the line." I held my arms out. "Go ahead. Do your worst." Immediately I was swept up in Ben's arms and kissed soundly and thoroughly to the delighted encouragement of the kids.

The kid's gifts to Ben were incredible. Each and every one of the kids (there were twenty-six) stood and told Ben something special he had done for that particular kid. I sat next to Ben with a lump in my throat as I listened to this incredible homage to who he was, and what he stood for. Some kids used humor: "I really appreciate you coming to watch me play basketball, Pastor Ben. But … don't come anymore, okay? Every time you show up I set a new record for lowest points scored." Some kids had obviously been coached by their parents: "You have been a significant source of encouragement to me and my family as we strive to walk closer to God." However, it was the awkwardly sincere ones that made me search for tissues in my purse.

"You … well, you told me I should start reading the Bible more if I had so many doubts and questions. And so I wanted to read a verse that I found that I liked. Actually, I've tried to memorize it," and the poor guy glanced around at the group listening attentively, "but I know I won't be able to remember it now." He looked down at the piece of paper clutched in his hand. "It's from the book of Psalms, chapter thirty, verse five. *For His anger lasts only a moment, but His favor lasts a lifetime! Weeping may last through the night, but joy comes with the morning.*" The young man looked up at Ben and gave a shy smile. "I liked that one a lot. It's kind of real, but also offers sunshine no matter how dark it gets."

That's the first time I had to wipe my eyes and blow my nose.

But not the last.

"Pastor Ben," a young woman said, "everyone keeps talking about all the good things you've done for them. You know, how you've helped them or counseled them or gone and watched their games or their performances. And you've done a lot of those things for me, but that's not what's affected me the most." She swallowed and looked quickly around at the group but then went right back to looking only at Ben. "You shared with all of us some of your … um, mistakes … and your sorrows and your regrets. You haven't made any effort to have us all think that you're perfect and that you've led a perfect life. In fact, you've told us how very, very badly you … uh, screwed up. My mom likes to say all the time, 'It takes a wise person to learn from his mistakes, and an ever wiser one to learn from someone else's.' You've really worked hard to help us … be wiser not only

by what you teach us but also by what you've shared with us. So, um ...
thanks. A lot." After *that* one even Ben had to wipe his eyes and blow his
nose.

My cake for Ben was a big hit, and if Aileen had been able to ask
what I thought about the evening I would have been compelled to answer
honestly that I had enjoyed myself immensely. I had fun hanging out with
the kids and once again thoroughly liked partnering up with Ben (I had
flashes of our rock concert date with the youth group). When everyone
starting cleaning up I was surprised at how quickly the time had flown by.

I couldn't miss the single beam of a motorcycle headlight following
behind me as I drove home through the dark streets. Had it really only
been two months since we reconnected? I thought back to that first
Saturday that I'd reluctantly gone to Integrated Health Center and the
crying man I'd noticed sitting on the bench that day. Then I thought about
him standing on my front porch saying intensely, "I'd miss you until the day
I died." Lastly I thought about me, Olivia Kelly and how very wonderful
this new country was that I had decided to live in with godly direction,
friends and family, and a handsome biker minister who said he loved me.

"Are you going to stay in there all night?"

I looked out my window at Ben, who was standing in the glow of
my porch light. I'd driven all the way home and parked completely on
autopilot, lost in thought. I grinned at him.

"You've been smiling an awful lot tonight, Jerry. You'd better be
careful or people will think that all this church stuff agrees with you."

"Nah," I said as I unfolded out of the car, "it's just you that makes
me smile."

Ben stood there and looked at me. "You don't usually say ...
mushy ... things."

He was right. I joked and provoked, shocked and put down, but I
rarely made an effort to be kind or tender. "What? Did I scare you or
something? It's your birthday. I'm trying to be the perfect girlfriend.
Enjoy it while it lasts."

Ben said with absolute sincerity, "I don't want you to be anything but yourself. *That's* what I enjoy."

I stepped into his personal space and kissed him. "I know," I breathed against his mouth, "that's why I'm here still grinning at you."

"*I love you, Olivia.* You have *no idea* how wonderful it was to have you there tonight. I couldn't have asked for a better surprise."

"I saw the way you looked at me. Repeatedly. I know how happy you were to have me there. So did everyone else."

"Was it okay that I kissed you in front of the kids? I didn't really give you much choice."

"Sure, it was okay. But you'd better be careful with those smoldering looks you give me. There is no mistaking what you're thinking when you do that."

He stared at me for long enough to blink his big, green eyes at me twice. "I can't help it."

I grinned at him again. "I know." I took his hand and dragged him towards my porch. "Come inside. I want to give you your birthday present."

Ben immediately dug his heels in. "Olivia ..." He swallowed.

I laughed out loud. "Trust me, Ben. It's nothing I couldn't give you in front of a crowd."

He murmured as he smiled, "You've been explicitly clear that being in public has never ... deterred you ... before." But he followed me into the house.

"I've got two presents for you," I said quickly before I could wimp out. Both presents sat wrapped carefully by the front door. "The first one is a standard present that would be a typical gift for a girlfriend to give a boyfriend." I handed him the wrapped watch. "It's what I got you if I didn't have enough nerve to give you the second gift." Which I clutched in my arms.

Ben studied the gift in his hands and the gift in my arms. "I want that one," he said pointing to the one I held.

"Of course you do. Open the one I gave you."

"Perhaps it's time for me to stop being so accommodating. That's really just an illusion anyway." Taking my arm he dragged me out to the deck and pulled me down to sit next to him. "I don't want a watch," he whispered in my ear giving me a shiver, *"I want you."*

"Well, I guess you'd better have this one then," I said handing him the other gift.

Erin had inspired me with her gift of long ago. For years I'd kept her beautifully carved wooden box with … nothing in it. But, I'd decided to give it to Ben. Filled. I sat and watched him unwrap the box and study its intricate details. When he looked up at me I said, "The important stuff is inside."

Using Erin's idea, I'd filled it with happy, positive things.

There was a framed picture of Ben and me at the concert. "One of the kids took that when we weren't looking. Apparently he wanted to text it to a bunch of people who couldn't come that night. I like the way you're looking at me." In the picture, I was staring intently at the stage, my face lit up in the glare of the spotlights and Ben is standing close beside me with his arm around me looking down at me. "You look at me a lot that way, you know."

Giving me the exact look he said, "Yes, I know."

Next was a folded piece of paper I'd printed from my computer. "I … I keep a journal. And I went back and looked for references to you. I was," I sighed and turned away for a minute, certain that I was blushing, "a little overwhelmed at how often you're referred to. These were just some of the funny tidbits that made me smile. I thought you'd get a kick out of them."

Unfolding the papers, Ben began to read out loud, "I knew a perfect man once. Nice guys never interested me. Rolos are my favorite candy. Some guys just won't take the hint," and he looked up at me when he said quietly, "Pansies are my favorite flower." He just stared at me.

I swallowed. "Yeah, well. I just thought you'd like to know that you've been a good influence seeing as how you're worried about being the evil seed in this relationship. If you need me to explain any, just let me

322

know." I shrugged. "I'll just read you the whole journal entry." But as he kept watching me, I began to squirm a bit. "Look," I pointed to the papers clutched in his hand. There are more pages. The next one is more informative. Sort of like full disclosure. It's a gift, although it might curl your hair, because I've never been willing to discuss these things with anyone else. Not even myself until very recently. But," I stopped for a minute and took a deep breath because suddenly I was feeling a bit teary. *Crap,* I think, *I probably should have just stuck with the watch. What was I thinking?* Taking a deep breath for bravery I muttered, "But I'd like to ... explore ... these topics more with you. I really like talking with you Ben. You ask good questions, give good answers, and you're a good listener. So, I figure if I've got to do more discovery, well, I'd like to do it with you. There's more. These are just the top ones."

So he finally looked down at the papers clutched in his hand and flipped to the second page. He read the list silently to himself but then blew out a breath and read them out loud. "The Truth About Happiness. The Truth About Me. The Truth About Love."

I touched his face so that he would look up at me. "So, that's my way of saying that there are no more taboo topics or questions, okay? Openness and honesty all the way now. Sometimes I feel like your head is *just full* of stuff you'd like to ask or say, and you're forever holding yourself back. Stressing that something is too much or too little or too touchy or too private. This here," I tap the paper, "is your license to let it all hang out, so to speak. Okay? Except there's one more. On the next page, because I had a truckload of questions that I already wanted to ask you and I figured ..." But I stopped talking because he'd already flipped the paper and I knew I'd lost him when he read the top line: The Truth About Me & God. "I've been looking at Grannie Blue's Bible and ... well ... I feel *really* uncomfortable that she gave it to me. I think it should stay in the family, don't you? So, I want you to know that I plan on giving it back and I *will not* debate this with you, Benjamin Harayda. Anyway, while I have it, though, I've been reading it and to be honest, it's created a lot more questions than it's answered. So ... ," Ben was now looking at me again, except now he had tears in his eyes, so I shut up.

"Go on, Jerry," Ben said with an encouraging smile despite his tears, "Keep talking. I want to hear every single thing you've got to say to me."

I whispered self-consciously, "I just wanted you to know that I'd like you to tell me some cool stories about God. And what you believe about God and what you don't. But be prepared for questions. Probably a million of them. Such as: If God knows everything, then He had to know that Adam and Eve were going to screw up in the garden. Why did He even bother? And Grannie Blue has a lot of verses underlined in her Bible so I know what her favorites were. But what are yours?"

I began to warm up to my topic. "You know, Ben, I've got all these people talking God stuff to me, and the only one who isn't is my minister boyfriend. I *really don't think* that's the way it should be and it's time you stepped up to the plate -" I stopped talking because suddenly I was being kissed. As though the world was about to end ... or perhaps as if the future had just begun.

Finally, I pushed Ben back. "Hey! There's one more thing in your box, and it's pretty important."

Ben clunks his forehead against mine. "I don't know if I can handle anymore."

"Tough. This is Olivia Kelly. This is what you signed up for." But I kissed him right after I said that.

Reaching down, Ben picked up the last item in the box. It was a small box almost exactly like the size and shape of a box that would have a ring in it. Looking at me questioningly, I watched as he opened it and took out ... a Rolo candy.

"Do I love you enough to give you my last Rolo?" I whispered as Ben looked at me intently. I nodded and smiled through my tears. "Yes. Yes, I do. I love you, Ben Harayda. I hope you're ready for everything that means."

Journal: The Truth About My Summer

Sunday, June 27, 2010

Good grief, Jacob and Rachel!! Bible couples would have been a real hit on the Jerry Springer Show.

Tuesday, June 29, 2010

On only my second time to Senior High Youth Group (it was the last meeting as they break for the summer) and I was presented with a pair of overalls and my very own hammer, both decorated with my name. *Then* I was told that they wanted me to go on the youth mission trip to Kentucky. I was compelled to explain to them The Truth About Me and Physical Labor.

Friday, July 2, 2010

I *think* my father is dating a woman named Tonya. She's *maybe* thirty, has a pierced nose, long blonde hair, and a shape that leaves you speechless. Oh yes, and she's in the band at Agape Shop. Who says God doesn't have a sense of humor?

Sunday, July 4, 2010

Picnic at Ben's church. Lots of laughter. Tons of food. And the fireworks were excellent. (And that was *before* it got dark.) Ministers light my fire.

Monday, July 5, 2010

First day of summer school. Summer was not meant for school. Wayne's mother sent in fried chicken and Uncle Frazier's phone number. Rather awkward.

Thursday, July 8, 2010

Met by a handsome biker dude when I got home from work. With a picnic dinner. I could definitely get used to this in-love thing.

Saturday, July 10, 2010

Today, after a causal dinner and fun smooching and watching TV, Ben got down on one knee and proposed. Actually begged and pleaded: that I'd go with him on the Kentucky mission trip in August. Unfortunately for him, you don't always get what you want.

Sunday, July 11, 2010

Last Biblical couple to be preached about: Priscilla and Aquila. A power couple in many ways. Good with God. Good with each other. Good with others. Always good to end on a high note. Glad my name isn't Priscilla. Or that Ben's isn't Aquila.

Wednesday, July 14, 2010

Dinner at Erin and Dan's with Ben in tow. Liam and Janine have a new favorite person and it ain't me. Vividly remember the black eye I gave Ben so many years ago. Not because I was mad at him. No - more terrifying than that – it was because, stunningly, I am glad I could have babies.

Friday, July 16, 2010

Ben and I double date with Dad and Tonya after Agape Shop. Too weird indeed. Tonya younger than me by *four years*. Dad seems happy though. Tried not to wonder if there are other piercings that I can't see. Counted nine in ears … Broke it to Dad that I would probably only be attending church with Ben from now on. Excellent shock value all around, as I had not discussed this with Ben either. Don't want to miss the next sermon series entitled "Personal House Cleaning: Garbage, Recycling, and Compost."

Sunday, July 18, 2010

Sunday dinner at Erin and Dan's with Ben in tow. We are indeed a couple; I sit next to Ben in church *in the front row*. Mom and Alec in high alert for their upcoming mission trip to Haiti. I have agreed to board Harry. Wait until Sophie hears. Every time the phrase "mission trip" is said (and it was said many times) Ben gives me sad, puppy dog pleading eyes. Sometimes love is painful.

Thursday, July 22, 2010

Hot, hot, HOT day. And just when I cool down in the air conditioning, Ben arrives! Whew! This straight and narrow path we're on … very difficult and not too much fun sometimes. We end up going for a walk just to keep ourselves upright. If we don't see each other, we talk for hours by phone each day. Have covered all kinds of topics. We rarely fight but occasionally disagree. Tonight we debate the validity of a worldwide flood versus a 'known world flood' regarding Noah and the Ark. He laughingly agrees with my perception: When God wants to get your attention He knows how to do it.

Sunday, July 25, 2010

After a sermon that confirmed, as I already know, that I have extensive garbage in my life, Ben and I go to the Round Valley to sunbathe and swim. My boyfriend has a six-pack. And I'm not talking alcohol.

Monday, July 26, 2010

Harry here while Alec and Mom on their mission trip. Very unhappy. Sophie snotty as can be. Threaten to take her to Aileen in September if she doesn't rethink her attitude. Unfortunately, some nuts just can't be cracked. Ben coming to dinner on Wednesday. Says he has a surprise for me. I suspect it's another attempt to get me to go to Kentucky. That boy will not quit. I guess it's time I bite the bullet and decide to go.

Wednesday, July 28 2010

Okay. So I'm ... evil. But sometimes it's fun. I've decided to go to Kentucky with the youth group but why not have a bit of fun with the whole thing? Knowing how much Ben was desperate for me to go and knowing how consistently I'd refused to go along and knowing he was on his way over to ask (beg?) me once again to reconsider and go ... Next to my favorite chair, lying open prominently on the arm, I have the book *Weird Kentucky: Your Travel Guide to Kentucky's Local Legends and Best Kept Secrets*[46]. And on the coffee table I had a magazine called *Family Handyman*[47] that I'd also picked up at Barnes & Noble. Plus, sitting by my kitchen garbage is a big, empty bag from *Eastern Mountain Sports*. And for dinner I serve ... Kentucky Fried Chicken, of course. Poor Ben he is so distracted about asking me to go on the mission trip for the millionth time *he doesn't even seem to notice*. Until I looked him right in the eye and informed him that the only person I'd share a bedroom with in Kentucky was him. You should have seen his face!! He just stares at me speechless with shock. I have to finally spell it out for him clearly: Surprise! I am going with him on the mission trip! So he better make sure that I have *my own room* when I go on the blasted mission trip to Kentucky with him because there is no way I am going to room with a teenager! Sometimes love is shocking!

Love is the only reality and it is not a mere sentiment.
It is the ultimate truth that lies at the heart of creation.[48]

30: Sometimes Love Takes You By Surprise
Tuesday, August 10, 2010

It was T minus twelve days and counting until The Blasted Mission Trip To Kentucky, which was what I insisted on calling it. Everyone laughed when they heard me call it that, so don't think I was offending anyone. Ben was a nervous wreck about all that needed to get done before we left. I'd never seen him in such a state: preoccupied and short tempered – even with me! He had dark circles under his eyes from not sleeping and even appeared to have lost weight. The other day I told him he looked like a gang-banger with his shorts riding so low on his hips.

We still rarely saw each other on Tuesdays even though youth group ended for the summer. I was crazy busy with my required morning summer school attendees (Wayne's doing high C work again!) and on Tuesday afternoon I've got four private tutorial sessions. I was usually completely exhausted by the time I got home which was never a good thing. However, this Tuesday, in the midst of walking Evelyn through quadratic equations, I thought as clearly as a bell, *Ben doesn't really want you to go on the mission trip. That's why he's been so uptight about everything.*

Tracing back, I realized that Ben hadn't been the same since I'd told him I'd go along on the trip. What if he was regretting his invitation and my acceptance? And as soon as the thought entered my mind I couldn't make it leave. Suddenly, it made perfect sense to me. Which was why I decided to take the bull by the horns and go over and ask him flat out which was why I was in the car on the way to his place the moment he texted me that he was heading home.

329

We pulled up at the same time and got out of our cars like we'd choreographed it. Being *me*, I wasted no time getting right to the point, not even giving Ben a chance to say hello. "I know why you've been so stressed, Ben."

His tired green eyes widened in surprise. "You do?"

"Yup. It took me a while to figure it out, but I did."

"How did you figure it out?"

The poor man. He had no idea how transparent he'd been. "Ben, we're practically inseparable. We talk all the time. I think we're past the ability to hide important stuff like this from each other. Why didn't you just tell me?"

"*Tell you?*" He looked at me like I was nuts. "You just wanted me to flat out *tell you?*"

I rolled my eyes and put my hands on my hips. "HELLO. You know the license I gave you for openness and honesty a few weeks back? When I told you *I loved you?* When I said that I didn't want there to be any more worries about taboo topics or questions? I told you to stop holding yourself back, Ben. HONESTY AND OPENNESS!" I'm pretty sure I stomped my foot. "I demand that! That's what I want this relationship to be all about." I looked him up and down as I shook my head in disgust. "It's just *ridiculous* that you've been afraid to tell me *the truth*."

He looked like a guilty child. "I was going to ... tell you. I'd decided that the only thing that was important was *our* timing. That I needed to stop stressing about whether I should say something or not. Remember? I told you I had a surprise? It was that Wednesday night when *you* surprised *me* and told me you'd decided to go on the mission trip. I'd been stressing about when to say something all night trying to figure out the perfect time and the perfect way to ... tell you. But you threw me when you announced you were going to go on the trip and ... well ..." He looked at me. "Remember? You said, 'I won't sleep with anyone but you on that mission trip, Ben Harayda.' Even after you explained what you'd really meant, I'd pretty much completely lost my train of thought."

Suddenly a wave of tremendous relief washed through me. *I didn't have to go on The Blasted Mission Trip To Kentucky!!* So what that he hadn't spoken right up that night? The important thing was that he was being honest now. Relief made me magnanimous. "And you lost your nerve. Oh, Ben. Was all this misery worth it? If you'd just come right out and told me then and there that night that you didn't want me to go, it would have spared you all these weeks of stress." I reached up and kissed him. "It's *okay.* You know I didn't want to go on the mission trip. I was only going because you'd been asking me – no begging me - for weeks. You'd guilted me into going. Honest. I'm actually relieved. You look completely shell-shocked. You can relax now. I know and I'm not upset at all, okay? Why don't you go inside, take a shower and relax? We'll talk tomorrow."

But Ben was frowning down at me in obvious confusion. Twice he started to say something but didn't. Finally, he said haltingly, "Ahhh ... don't you want to know why I ... didn't ... want ... you ... to ... go ... on ... the ... mission ... trip?" He spoke slowly and carefully as he watched me intently. Obviously he thought there was some deep - seated anger I was hiding.

I shrugged. "I'm pretty high maintenance, Ben. I know that. There's my complete absence of the ability to enjoy anything that qualifies as 'roughing it'. I need my daily showers, electrical appliances, morning Frapuccino, private bathroom and a bed with real sheets. Then there's my fear of bugs and spiders. And I'm about as skilled with a hammer and screwdriver as," I smirked at him, "you are at telling me how you *really feel* about certain things."

He stared at me for a long time. And then threw his head back and laughed out loud. When I glared at him with my hands fisted at my hips he worked really hard to compose himself going so far as to take a number of deep breaths and then rubbing both hands over his face. Of course he knew I didn't like to be laughed at. Tough topics were never areas I did well with and we both knew that *at this particular moment* I was being astronomically patient, understanding and mature. Narrowing his eyes, he stepped in closer and gripped my upper arms. "I've always been honest about how I feel about you."

"Yes," I sighed dismissively, "I know all about how much you love me." I wasn't trying to be flip and funny because *I did know*.

"It's more than that," he said low, "and you know it."

Yes, I knew that, too. We'd long past acknowledged that what we had, this connection between us was quite inexplicable. It made no sense how drawn and connected we felt to each other in such a short amount of time. Unfortunately, whether he told me verbally he loved me or showed me in numerous other ways, it still didn't mean that I could buy into it all. He *knew that*, too. We'd spoken endlessly over my penchant to perceive myself as the evil seed. This whole godly concept of forgiveness and new life and stuff was still something I wasn't sure I qualified for – no matter how much I wanted to. He knew I still struggled with its ... all-encompassing scope.

Out of the corner of my eye I saw Old Mrs. Frueh from across the street come out and sit on her front porch. She'd probably decided to come outside because she hadn't been able to hear well enough from inside. I grinned and waved at her which she ignored. "Are we talking about how you're warm for my form?" I teased and stepped in so that we were now completely touching front to front. Sex has always been such a wonderful distraction for me, and it still was an excellent tool with Ben. It totally dismissed any conversation or argument we were having and effectively proved my point about me and my worthiness and ... stuff. "And how I'm hot for yours?" The sexual attraction that was ever present between us had morphed into a little game we had learned to play with each other. When one of us seemed to be losing the desire to stay on the straight and narrow path, the other one always pulled back and became the voice of sanity and reason. And yes, despite my history, sometimes it really was me who made the circumspect choice.

But that day Ben shocked me. "Yeah," he breathed, "that is what I'm talking about. You're right about me not being honest. I'll tell you this: I'm tired of waiting, Olivia. We both know how we feel about each other.

I don't want you to leave. Not now. Not ever. Come inside with me and let me show you *exactly* what I mean," and he kissed me right there on the sidewalk with old Mrs. Frueh sitting on her porch across the street enjoying the show.

My mouth opened in shock. Or, it would have if I wasn't being kissed and hugged and physically dragged up the steps into Ben's apartment. I battled with my body as it did the Rocky victory dance and screamed, *"At last!!!"* while my head was thinking, "Surely he can't mean this …"

Faster than a speeding bullet we were in his apartment, the door was slammed shut and Ben was holding my face between his two big hands as he kissed me. Pulling back, he looked at me. "So okay. Here's full on honesty, Olivia Kelly. I don't want to wait any longer to be with you. I don't want to sleep alone anymore. I don't want to wonder what it's like to *be* with you. I want you to be the first thing I see in the morning and the last thing I see at night."

My head was reeling. "Uhhh …" How far had I destroyed this good man? Wasn't this living proof of everything I'd been afraid of all along? How far reaching was my bad influence? Here he was, having just come home from work from the *church* where he'd been making preparations for the youth *missionary retreat,* and he was proposing that I move in with him to *live in sin.* "Ben," I heard myself pleading, "this isn't really what you want."

Ben looked at me like *I* was nuts and nodded his head emphatically. "Oh yes it is. I've wanted you almost from the first moment I saw you back in March. You called me on it then; you saw the truth. You told me I wasn't being honest when I told you it was just a cup of coffee and *you were so right.*" He gripped my hand and dragged me over to his sorry old couch. I sat there stiffly, knowing that this couch had seen significant passionate action between us.

"This is the deal, Olivia. You're everything I want: you're smart, independent, opinionated, strong, reliable, loyal, clever, funny …," he sighed, "besides being absolutely gorgeous and sexy." He said, as he closed

333

his eyes, "Sometimes I just look at you and think, How could anyone be so lovely?"

"Ben, I-"

He leaned forward and kissed me to shut me up. "Now, Olivia Kelly," he whispered into my ear, "you challenged me to be honest with you and tell you what I've been holding back from saying, and you're going to hear it now. Every last word." Moving back so he could look me in the eye he waited to see if I was going to cooperate. I felt like Pandora must have felt once she opened that box ...

Satisfied, that I was going to sit still and be silent to hear everything he had to say, Ben stood and began to pace. He fiddled with stuff on his book shelves and things on his desk. Finally he turned and said, "I treasure the time I spend with you. Everything I do with you by my side is better. *Everything.* I love talking to you and hearing your thoughts.

"But now that I've been honest with you about how I feel, I also have to tell you that you were completely wrong about me not wanting you to go on the mission trip." He watched me process what he said and grinned at my horrified expression. "Yes, that means that I'd still really enjoy having you along with me on the trip. You suddenly agreeing to go simply complicated things for me that night. Especially the way you presented it to me." When I frowned in confusion he said, "You do remember telling me that the only person you were going to share a bedroom with in Kentucky was me?"

"Oh. That." Jeeze. Me and my big mouth.

"Yes, *that*. Even after I understood what you were *really* saying – that you were merely refusing to room with a teenager - I couldn't get my thoughts back on track. The moment was lost ... the mood was broken. Since then everything's been so crazy with the trip and stuff there has never been a good time. But I've regretted every day since then that I didn't," he started to laugh and then caught himself, "tell you what I wanted to tell you."

Now I was really confused. "So ... what were you going to tell me... "

Suddenly, Ben was right next to me. "Olivia Kelly, I have loved you most of my life. But lately, over these past months I've discovered a truth that is just as wonderful: I *like* you. There's no one else in the world I'd rather spend the rest of my life with." Suddenly, from out of thin air it seemed, he was holding a beautiful sapphire ring out to me. "As per your own specific advice only moments ago, rather than asking you, I'd like to *tell you* that as soon as possible I've decided to make you my wife."

I looked at Ben, then down at the ring he was holding, then back up at Ben, and then down at the ring …

"If you'd rather," he whispered as he leaned in and kissed my cheek and nibbled my neck, "I'll ask politely and properly like I was going to do the other night. But you're only allowed to give me one answer. *Tell me yes, Jerry. Tell me now.*"

"How soon is soon?" Always difficult, I know.

Ben picked up my hand and slid the ring on. "We've still got time to go to a justice of the peace so that we can share a bedroom in Kentucky if you want. But I suspect that will annoy probably every person who knows and cares about us."

He was right. I blinked at him. "They'll all say we're going too fast."

Ben looked at me and then narrowed his eyes. "I don't care about everyone. I only care about you and me."

"Do you want a big wedding or a small wedding?"

"I just want you. Nothing else matters."

"Will you want -"

"*Jerry, tell me yes.*" Ben and those big green eyes of his just stared at me.

I felt a smile start in my heart and flow through my body and up to my face. I'm pretty sure I started glowing. My future, my hopes, my dreams were all so much brighter with this good guy standing with me. "You know I've been trouble since the day I was born …" I said and felt happy tears begin to trickle down my face.

"Oh yes," he said with a long suffering sigh as he used his fingers to gently wipe the tears from my face, "I embraced *that* truth long ago. It's one of my favorite qualities about you."

I leaned in and kissed him and then breathed the one word he wanted to hear against his lips, "Yes."

Therapy: The Truth About Me And My Skin

Setting: Aileen's office. It's Tuesday, September 14, 2010, my first time back after our summer hiatus. There have been major changes since Aileen saw me at the end of June. Good changes. I made a list last night in my journal, and it's quite extensive:

1. I'm more comfortable in my new skin. What I mean is this new existence which embraces a positive attitude, thoughtful decision-making, and daily godly influence. Mature behavior isn't so hard anymore. In fact, when I start to slip back into my old style, *that* feels awkward and wrong.

2. I'm more comfortable with my history. Nobody's perfect. I didn't necessarily believe that, but now I do. That's not a license to go crazy, but it is a reason to continue to strive to improve no matter how spectacularly you may have failed. Ben showed me this cool Bible verse that's my new favorite (they change almost weekly). *My grace is all you need. My power works best in weakness.*[49] Isn't that a cool concept? Who would have believed that where you are the most inept and have the greatest potential for disaster, is the exact area that God can do His biggest work? When I heard that verse I said, "Oh man, if I buy into this whole God thing, I could probably rule the world." That made Ben laugh.

3. I now realize I have a calling. I survived the Kentucky mission trip (okay, I'll admit it: it was fun and I can't wait to go next summer). But more than that, I'm now a regular senior high youth group leader. You'd think I'd get more than enough of adolescents with my job, but apparently not. One of the kids gave me a wonderful back door compliment the other day. He said, "You're great, Miz Kelly. You tell it straight, just like it is, and don't take anything less than that." Which was immediately after I'd

337

said to him, "Okay. That's what you think I want to hear. Now tell me the truth." It would appear that all this angst and upset and anger I've been carrying around with me for most of my life has made me *absolutely perfect* for understanding and dealing with teenagers. Go figure.

4. I have a church home. That I would have picked even if it hadn't been Ben's church. The preaching is great, the way it's run suits me fine, and the people are … becoming my family. The other day a visitor, who happened to be one of last year's more difficult parents, started asking me school questions as we were visiting and talking during coffee time. I stood there unsure how I should handle a situation that was rapidly becoming very awkward. Then one of the elderly ladies (who's barely five feet tall and who was wearing a bright red hat) walked over and said, "Leave that child alone!! She's relaxing in God's house today!" and then winked at me. Who would have thought little old ladies would be sticking up for me, huh?

5. I'm in love. Head over heels, gloriously and completely in love. You can make all the fun you want about how I've changed my whole attitude on love. I don't care. I have a partner and a friend. He looks at me all the time with this big, goofy grin and says, "I like you." Whoever would have thought that expression would be the epitome of happiness for me?

Aileen: What have you got for me, Olivia? You've come bearing gifts?

Me: I've got stuff to show you. Kind of like a visual diary of my summer.

Aileen: Is it a tragedy or a comedy? Will I need tissues?

Me: You need tissues sometimes for love stories, too.

Aileen: (Giving me a look.) So do you …

Me: I've got a lot to tell you so we're going to have to move quickly since we've only got … 46 minutes. We need to pack away all our sarcasm and banter. I've got a lot to tell you and can't waste a second. First, take a look at this.

Aileen: A newspaper article ... *Local Church Group Barnstorms Kentucky.* (I give her time to skim the article. Then, when she starts, I know she's noticed what I wanted her to notice.) Is that you *standing on the barn roof?*

Me: Yup. Helped shingle it.

Aileen: So you went on the trip after all. Despite all your insistence to the contrary. (She looks at me rather smugly.)

Me: Don't you dare look smug. You never in a million years thought I'd go on that trip.

Aileen: Maybe not. But I did know that you were in love.

Me: I never admitted that to you.

Aileen: (She laughs.) What point does *that* prove?

Me: (Deciding to change the subject because I know I won't win this battle ...) Okay so here's the next thing I want to show you.

Aileen: My, it's quite a show and tell day isn't it? (Looking down at what I've given her this time. There are three papers.)

Me: The first page contains the final grades of the fourteen kids I taught during summer school. Those kids all failed out of whatever math class they had taken the past school year. Being a numbers geek, I averaged their final summer school grades.

Aileen: An 84.6 average. (She's impressed.)

Me: My supervisor, Doris, said that was one of the highest math averages of *any math course* over this past year. The other two pages are letters that were put in my permanent file. One's from a parent and one's from my supervisor, Doris.

Aileen: (Flipping through the pages, Aileen looks up and gives me a smile.) Good for you, Olivia. It seems that not only are you happy where you are working, but more than that, you're fulfilled. That's a gift you know. Not everyone experiences fulfillment in his or her profession. In fact, I'd say very few do.

Me: Do you get fulfillment from your job?

Aileen: Sometimes. Not always. But I've always enjoyed challenges. (The look she gives me tells me I've qualified as A Challenge.)

Me: I've got one more thing for you.

Aileen: A letter?

Me: No, an invitation. (I wait a beat.) To my wedding.

Aileen: (Looks intently at me and I just sit and let her see what she's 'created'. Finally, she opens up the envelope and reads through it. Then she throws her head back and laughs out loud.) *This Saturday?!*

Me: (I shrug.) It was as long as we were willing to wait. Everyone's been scrambling on both sides to put something together.

Aileen: Big crowd?

Me: Well, the wedding itself will probably be standing room only between the church people and all the kids and stuff. Afterwards we're just going to do a nice private dinner with family and friends. Would you come Aileen? You don't have any policy against that kind of thing do you? It would give you an opportunity to find a bit of fulfillment. And I need to see the guy who keeps sending you tulips. Bring him, too.

Aileen: People don't typically invite their therapists to their weddings you know, Olivia.

Me: Has that happened so much with you and your clients that you've had to set a policy about it, Aileen? Do you have a lot of clients getting married and going off into the future happily ever after because of your excellent therapeutic skills?

Aileen: I thought you said we were going to pack away sarcasm and banter.

Me: I did. I have. It's my way of saying thank you, Aileen. I can't put a value on what you've done. How you've helped me. We've both worked hard, and you can't deny that.

Aileen: (Sighing as if she's tremendously put out.) I suppose I'll have to buy you a wedding gift.

Me: Absolutely. A Big One. I've got to recoup some of my deductible
  costs, don't I?

Footnotes

---

[1] Caedmon's Call, "Manner and Means", from the album *Back Home*

[2] Michael Levy http://thinkexist.com/quotation/you-can-bend-it-and-twist-it-you-can-misuse-and/386405.html

[3] Clarissa Pinkola Estes, Women Who Run with the Wolves, http://www.dailycelebrations.com/questions.htm

[4] Galileo Galilei http://thinkexist.com/quotation/all_truths_are_easy_to_understand_once_they_a re/10831.html

[5] Oscar Wilde http://thinkexist.com/quotation/the_truth_is_rarely_pure_and_never_simple/153 927.html

[6] Pearl Bailey http://thinkexist.com/quotation/you_never_find_yourself_until_you_face_the/18 8430.html

[7] Leslie Poles Hartley, http://thinkexist.com/quotation/the_past_is_a_foreign_country-they_do_things/14056.html

[8] Winston Churchill http://thinkexist.com/quotation/a_lie_gets_halfway_around_the_world_before_t he/15786.html

[9] John Lennon, http://thinkexist.com/quotation/life_is_what_happens_to_you_while_you-re_busy/171775.html

[10] William Safire http://thinkexist.com/quotation/never_assume_the_obvious_is_true/226861.htm l

[11] Ayn Rand, http://thinkexist.com/quotation/-the_truth_is_not_for_all_men-but_only_for_those/346292.html

[12] Walter Cronkite http://thinkexist.com/quotation/in_seeking_truth_you_have_to_get_both_sides_of_a/226449.html

[13] Friedrich Nietzsche http://thinkexist.com/quotation/all_truth_is_simple-is_that_not_doubly_a_lie/205981.html

[14] Billy Wilder http://thinkexist.com/quotation/if_you-re_going_to_tell_people_the_truth-be_funny/152962.html

[15] Maya Angelou http://thinkexist.com/quotation/there-s_a_world_of_difference_between_truth_and/152823.html

[16] Martin Luther http://thinkexist.com/quotation/peace_if_possible-truth_at_all_costs/150788.html

[17] I Corinthians 13:1-7, select pieces, from *The Message* by Eugene Peterson

[18] Robert Gary Lee, http://en.thinkexist.com/quotes/robert_gary_lee/

[19] Mark Twain http://thinkexist.com/quotation/truth_is_mighty_and_will_prevail-there_is_nothing/216707.html

[20] http://thinkexist.com/quotation/to_change_is_difficult-not_to_change_is_fatal/13210.html
[21] Harry S. Truman http://thinkexist.com/quotation/i_never_give_them_hell-i_just_tell_the_truth_and/7781.html
[22] Napoleon Bonaparte http://thinkexist.com/quotation/truth_alone_wounds/148812.html
[23] William Randolph http://thinkexist.com/quotation/truth_is_not_only_stranger_than_fiction-it_is/185741.html
[24] Friedrich Nietzsche http://thinkexist.com/quotation/how_much_truth_can_a_spirit_bear-how_much_truth/13420.html
[25] Spencer Johnson http://thinkexist.com/quotation/integrity_is_telling_myself_the_truth-and_honesty/14800.html
[26] "Awakening" by Sara Groves, from the album *Past The Wishing*
[27] "Manner and Means" by Caedmon's Call, from the album *Back Home*
[28] "Walk With Me" by Caedmon's Call, from the album *Back Home*
[29] "Trouble" by Caedmon's Call, from the album *Overdressed*
[30] Steve Landesberg http://thinkexist.com/quotation/honesty_is_the_best_policy-but_insanity_is_a/164066.html
[31] Tryon Edwards http://thinkexist.com/quotation/hell_is_truth_seen_too_late-duty_neglected_in_its/176785.html
[32] "Paradise By The Dashboard Lights," by Meatloaf, from the album *Bat Out Of Hell*
[33] Fox Mulder http://thinkexist.com/quotation/i_would_never_lie-i_willfully_participate_in_a/206014.html
[34] Arab Proverb http://thinkexist.com/quotation/beware-some-liers-tell-the/347279.html
[35] John Lennon, http://thinkexist.com/quotation/life_is_what_happens_to_you_while_you-re_busy/171775.html
[36] "The Only One", by Caedmon's Call, from the album *Long Line of Leavers*
[37] "No More No Less", by MercyMe, from the album *Coming Up To Breathe*
[38] "It Is Well", by Audio Adrenaline, from the album *Underdog*
[39] Thomas Jefferson http://thinkexist.com/quotation/the_man_who_fears_no_truth_has_nothing_to_fear/144564.html
[40] Tertullian http://thinkexist.com/quotation/the_first_reaction_to_truth_is/175392.html
[41] William Blake, http://thinkexist.com/quotation/a_truth_thats_told_with_bad_intent_beats_all_the/150004.html
[42] John 8:32, *New Living Translation* of the Bible (Tyndale House Publishers)
[43] "Trouble" by Caedmon's Call, from the album *Overdressed*
[44] Elizabeth Cady Stanton, http://www.quotationspage.com/quote/1676.html
[45] Psalm 85:11a, *New Living Translation* Bible, Tyndale House Publishers

[46] *Weird Kentucky: Your Travel Guide to Kentucky's Local Legends and Best Kept Secrets* by Jeffrey Scott Holland, Mark Moran, and Mark Sceurman, Sterling Publishers, 2008

[47] *Family Handyman,* RD Publications

[48] Rabindranath Tagore, http://thinkexist.com/search/searchquotation.asp?search=love%20and%20truth&page=2

[49] 2 Corinthians 12:9a, New Living Translation Bible, Tyndale House Publishers

www.ingramcontent.com/pod-product-compliance
Lightning Source LLC
Chambersburg PA
CBHW030249270626
47156CB00021B/297